# PRAISE FOR CHARLES MARTIN

"Very few contemporary novelists have found acclaim within mainstream and evangelical markets, but Charles Martin is among them. His latest novel is both a stand-alone story and a sequel to his highly-praised *The Water Keeper*. It hinges on the Scriptural message of forsaking the found in order to seek the lost, a theme Martin brings to poetic and brilliant life. A man broken by events beyond his control accepts the challenge to walk dark ways in order to bring the lost and helpless home, but he comes close to losing himself in the process. Despite the hardship and heartache, Martin's story shines with the light of eternal hope."

—Davis Bunn, writing for *Christianity Today*

"Martin excels at writing characters who exist in the margins of life. Readers who enjoy flawed yet likable characters created by authors such as John Grisham and Nicholas Sparks will want to start reading Martin's fiction."

—*Library Journal*, starred review, for *The Water Keeper*

"*The Water Keeper* is a wonderfully satisfying book with a plot driven by both action and love, and characters who will stay in readers' heads long after the last page."

—*Southern Literary Review*

"*The Water Keeper* is a multilayered story woven together with grace and redemption, and packed tight with tension and achingly real characters. This one will keep you turning pages to see what else—and who else—Murph will encounter as he travels down the coastline of Florida."

—Lauren Denton, *USA TODAY* bestselling author of *The Hideaway*

"In *The Water Keeper* Charles Martin crafts a compelling story with skill and sensitivity. Current fans won't be disappointed; new readers will understand why Charles Martin is on the short list of contemporary authors I recommend above all others."

—Robert Whitlow, bestselling author

"Martin explores themes of grace, mercy, and forgiveness in this sweeping love story . . ."

—*Publishers Weekly*, starred review, for *Send Down the Rain*

"Martin crafts a playful, enticing tale of a modern prodigal son."

—*Publishers Weekly* for *Long Way Gone*

"Charles Martin never fails to ask and answer the questions that linger deep within all of us. In this beautifully told story of a prodigal coming home, readers will find the broken and mended pieces of their own hearts."

—LISA WINGATE, NATIONAL BESTSELLING AUTHOR OF
*BEFORE WE WERE YOURS*, ON *LONG WAY GONE*

"Martin weaves all the pieces of this story together with a beautiful musical thread, and as the final pieces fall into place, we close this story feeling as if we have witnessed something surreal, a multisensory narrative for anyone who enjoys a redemptive story."

—JULIE CANTRELL, *NEW YORK TIMES* AND *USA TODAY*
BESTSELLING AUTHOR OF *PERENNIALS*, ON *LONG WAY GONE*

"A beautiful story of redemption and love once lost but found again, *Long Way Gone* proves two things: music washes us from the inside out and Charles Martin's words do the same."

—BILLY COFFEY, AUTHOR OF *STEAL AWAY HOME*

"Martin's story charges headlong into the sentimental territory and bestseller terrain of *The Notebook*, which doubtless will mean major studio screen treatment."

—*KIRKUS*, STARRED REVIEW, FOR *UNWRITTEN*

"Charles Martin understands the power of story, and he uses it to alter the souls and lives of both his characters and his readers."

—PATTI CALLAHAN HENRY, *NEW YORK TIMES* BESTSELLING AUTHOR

"Martin is the new king of the romantic novel . . . *A Life Intercepted* is a book that will swallow you up and keep you spellbound."

—JACKIE K. COOPER, BOOK CRITIC, *HUFFINGTON POST*

"Martin's strength is in his memorable characters . . ."

—*PUBLISHERS WEEKLY* FOR *CHASING FIREFLIES*

"Charles Martin is changing the face of inspirational fiction one book at a time. *Wrapped in Rain* is a sentimental tale that is not to be missed."

—MICHAEL MORRIS, AUTHOR OF *LIVE LIKE YOU WERE*
*DYING* AND *A PLACE CALLED WIREGRASS*

"Martin spins an engaging story about healing and the triumph of love . . . Filled with delightful local color."

—*PUBLISHERS WEEKLY* FOR *WRAPPED IN RAIN*

# THE

# LETTER

# KEEPER

# ALSO BY CHARLES MARTIN

## THE MURPHY SHEPHERD NOVELS

*The Water Keeper*

*The Letter Keeper*


*Send Down the Rain*

*Long Way Gone*

*Water from My Heart*

*A Life Intercepted*

*Unwritten*

*Thunder and Rain*

*The Mountain Between Us*

*Where the River Ends*

*Chasing Fireflies*

*Maggie*

*When Crickets Cry*

*Wrapped in Rain*

*The Dead Don't Dance*


## NONFICTION

*What If It's True?*

*They Turned the World Upside Down*

# THE
# LETTER
# KEEPER

A Murphy Shepherd Novel

# CHARLES
# MARTIN

THOMAS NELSON
*Since 1798*

*The Letter Keeper*

Published in Nashville, Tennessee, by Thomas Nelson. Thomas Nelson is a registered trademark of HarperCollins Christian Publishing, Inc.

Published in association with The Christopher Ferebee Agency, www.christopherferebee.com.

Interior design by Mallory Collins

Thomas Nelson titles may be purchased in bulk for educational, business, fundraising, or sales promotional use. For information, please email SpecialMarkets@ThomasNelson.com.

Publisher's Note: This novel is a work of fiction. Names, characters, places, and incidents are either products of the author's imagination or used fictitiously. All characters are fictional, and any similarity to people living or dead is purely coincidental.

**Library of Congress Cataloging-in-Publication Data**

Names: Martin, Charles, 1969- author.
Title: The letter keeper / Charles Martin.
Description: Nashville, Tennessee : Thomas Nelson, [2021] | Series: A Murphy Shepherd novel | Summary: "New York Times bestselling author Charles Martin returns to his beloved characters from The Water Keeper and continues to ask poignant questions about the memories that haunt us all"-- Provided by publisher.
Identifiers: LCCN 2020056023 (print) | LCCN 2020056024 (ebook) | ISBN 9780785230953 (hardcover) | ISBN 9780785230960 (epub) | ISBN 9780785230977
Subjects: GSAFD: Christian fiction.
Classification: LCC PR9199.4.M3725 L48 2021 (print) | LCC PR9199.4.M3725 (ebook) | DDC 813/.6--dc23
LC record available at https://lccn.loc.gov/2020056023
LC ebook record available at https://lccn.loc.gov/2020056024

*Printed in the United States of America*
21 22 23 24 25 LSC 5 4 3 2 1

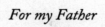

*For my Father*

# CHAPTER 1

---

FLORENCE, ITALY

S he didn't move when I opened the door. She lay stretched across the bed, her skin cold. Eyes half closed. Pupils rolled back. Her carotid pulse was slow but strong, which suggested medicated sleep and probably total loss of memory. I compared her face to the picture, and while she was skinnier, hair shorter and darker, and eyes painted in darker circles, I'd found her. I pressed her thumb to my phone, scanned the print, and sent it to Bones. Seconds later, the match returned. After twenty-seven days, four countries, twenty-some thousand miles of travel, and little sleep, I'd found Christine Samson.

Chris was a high school junior. Cheerleader. National Honor Society member. Beginner violinist. Restaurant hostess. Weekend babysitter. Boy-crazy Snapchatter. And she was the daughter of an absent dad and divorced parents. Her mom worked a couple of jobs but made less than forty thousand a year, which meant Chris attended the seventy-five-thousand-dollars-a-year West Florida boarding school on a merit scholarship. She was currently ranked third in her class and had already received offers from most Ivy League schools. She could take her pick.

The scumbags who brought her here had vetted her through her Instagram account. She looked great in a bikini. Never met a stranger. Didn't drink. Not one to party. Innocence wearing skin. Through a direct

1

message from an up-and-coming amateur soccer player, she agreed to a milkshake. And a cheeseburger. Jean Pierre, who was twenty-one and preferred the name JP, drove a Porsche. But he was no gangster. No gold chains. He wore button-downs and chinos. Somewhere in a greasy burger joint, they laughed through the burger and then the milkshake, but he couldn't stay out late because his team was playing a doubleheader the next day and the pro teams would be watching.

Chris remembered laughing and singing along to the radio as he drove her home at two miles over the speed limit. *Mom would approve.* Finally, a good guy.

She woke the next morning in a hotel room across town. Her muscles ached. Her head thumped, and when she opened her eyes, he was next to her. One eye swollen shut. Busted lip. Blood caked to his face. And just as naked as she. She sat up as the shock set in, but no matter how hard she tried, she could not remember how they got here or what precipitated it. Neither could he.

She grabbed her phone to call the cops and only then saw the photos. Who were these people and why were these pictures in her inbox? Then she looked closely. Her face. His face. Their bodies. She tried to focus. How did this happen?

*If these get out . . .*

She started to cry, but JP took charge. Gently. "We've got to get out of here." They dressed, slipped out the back, and spent the morning looking over their shoulders and trying to piece it all together. Little developed. But he was calm and assuring. When he dropped her off, he asked to come inside and suggested they tell her mom everything. She made him swear. Not a word. To anyone. Ever.

A week ticked by. They talked every day. Their emotions intertwined. Most conversations centered on the photos, but she had one question she couldn't verbalize.

*What if they took video? If so, my life is over . . .*

Late in the week, as they greenlit through worst-case and end-of-the-world scenarios, he described how his coach had been understanding about his no-show at the game and how professional soccer teams were beating down his door. Some were even Northeast clubs. Driving distance to Ivy League schools. Maybe he could get picked by a club near her. He could keep an apartment. He just needed somebody who understood him.

After a week, she was no longer holding her breath. Maybe the worst had passed. One and done. When not working, they were inseparable. He was a gentleman. Held the door. Paid for dinner. Didn't put a hand on her—although she needed him to.

But then the attachments showed up in her email. His too. She threw up in the bathroom. When his Porsche arrived, she signed herself out of school.

Exhibiting the strength she needed, JP sent the videos to his dad. An international lawyer with offices in Germany and France. His father immediately canceled meetings and got on the phone, demanding answers from the authorities. He was flying in tonight to meet with a special crimes unit that handled this sort of thing, hire an investigator, and spend some much-needed time with his son. They were headed to the islands for the weekend. A short trip to the family home. She was welcome to come along. They had a sailboat. *They could just get out of here.*

He'd set the hooks deep.

Her mom dropped her off, exchanged phone numbers with the dad, and Chris promised to call when they landed.

That was twenty-seven days ago.

JP, whose real name was not Jean Pierre and who had never been a semipro soccer player, had one thing going for him. A boyish face. While I don't know the particular facts, I know his type. On their first date, he had slipped something in her drink, driven her to a hotel, and staged the photos— which, when they awoke, made him look like just as much a victim as she. Completing the act that knit them together.

The last bread crumb led me to a small villa outside Florence. One more stop on the underground railroad, although this one did not lead to freedom. More like a train to Auschwitz. I tore a strip off the bedsheet and tied a tourniquet around my arm. JP was no high schooler but he was a knife guy, and the puncture was deep and the blade serrated. I hate knives. Maybe worse than guns.

I press-checked my Sig. One in the chamber. One in the magazine. Not much to work with so getting out should be interesting. Footsteps and angry shouting thundered above us. Multiple languages. Evidence that the fire I'd set was spreading toward the tank. We didn't have long.

I pulled her cheerleading sweats onto her sweat-soaked body and felt a profound sense of sadness. Why hadn't I gotten here sooner? What evil had been inflicted while they transported her and other girls in a drug-induced haze by bus and boat and plane? I stared at JP lying limp on the floor beneath me. *Why do the evil prosper?*

Bones had taught me that. I pushed him out of my mind. He pushed back.

It had been three months since I learned the truth about Marie, and I still hadn't come to grips with the reality. For fourteen years, Bones had known she was alive and yet not told me. Fourteen years while I circled the globe looking for her. Logically, I understood why he said nothing as a priest. Emotionally, I could not wrap my head around how he kept silent as my friend.

I would have walked through hell if I'd known she was alive. He knew that. The chasm between knowing why and how was a lonely, painful place. I tried to shake the memory. Dwelling on matters of the heart in moments like this would get me killed.

I glanced at Chris. Tender, young, and now wounded. One more casualty in a twisted world where sick and wealthy men with no conscience buy what they want because they can. No matter the damage. Trafficking in people is an evil without comparison. And the motivations of those responsible are beyond comprehension.

If I got her home, I'd offer to find her and her mom a place at Freetown and nurse them both back to life. I'd suggest a gap year because while some of this would wash off quickly, some would not. She needed time. Her tendency—like all of them—would be to "just put it behind her." Bury herself in the present. Focus on next steps. College. But in my experience, she could either deal with the trauma now or wait until it festered and the residue spilled out her chest. Neither would be fun. Bones and the team would surround her with girls who had the same experience. Let her know she wasn't alone. Rebuild her one tear at a time. Undoing what had been done.

I often marveled at the resiliency of the wounded. Who would walk out the other side?

I glanced at JP's leg unnaturally canted across the doorway. If there was any consolation, and there wasn't, it was knowing Jean Pierre and his "father" would cause no more damage. Prison is not kind to those who traffic in flesh.

No matter how many times I'd done this, I could not get used to how attached the girls grew to their captors. It was the deepest form of emotional warfare. JP had played the part to the end, as evidenced by the fact that as I lifted Chris off the bed, she reached for him.

*Don't leave him* . . .

In truth, JP was an emotional terrorist. They all are. He'd done this to dozens, maybe even a hundred girls. For Chris, it would be a while before the light clicked on. But when it did, how deep would be the well of her hate? Would she hate men? Could she ever trust another?

I wouldn't blame her if the answer was no.

They had stolen something she had wanted to offer. Her hope. Which is a crime against the soul.

And betrayal of the soul is . . .

I carried her out of the house where flames rose from second- and third-story windows. Frantic shouting sounded from inside. I had cleared a half mile before the gas line lit. When it did, Chris again reached back for JP, crying.

I lifted her into the jet where the pilot closed the door and the nurse inserted an IV into Chris's arm. To flush the toxins and the drugs. Broad-spectrum antibiotics. Something stronger would be needed to flush the memories.

Eight hours later, we landed at a private airport outside of West Palm. Chris's mother was inconsolable. We loaded them into an ambulance as the rain began to fall. I was stepping into my truck when the text came in. I leaned my head back and closed my eyes. Another beep. All I wanted to do was go home and pull the covers over my head.

*Send somebody else.*

In my mind, I could hear Bones's response. *There is no one else.* A pause before the next text. "This one matters."

I thought, *They all matter.*

Then I did the one thing that makes going home all but impossible. I looked at the picture.

# CHAPTER 2

Montana

When Bones had sent the picture, he'd included the words, "Tight window. Now or never. And . . ."

"What?"

"He might not be the only one."

At the time, I had sat in my truck wanting to tune Bones out. Completely. But I could not mute this kid. Not his blue eyes or the dreams behind them.

I pulled gear from a West Palm storage unit and returned to the plane. When the copilot shut the door, my phone rang. It was Bones. "One more thing."

I waited while the nurse inserted an IV needle into one arm and started stitching the hole in the other. I planned to use the flight time to replenish the fluids my adrenaline had spent.

"The owner of this ranch is not your average cattleman with a Stetson. Instead of chaps and boots, he wears a collar, a robe, a big silver cross, and a you-can-trust-me smile."

"He's a priest?"

"At one time."

"I thought you said, 'Once a priest, always a priest.'"

"For him I'd make an exception." He continued, "Just don't take anything at face value. Nothing is as it seems."

Four hours later, the jet touched down an hour outside of Whitefish in the shadow of Glacier National Park, where the landscape had become popular with A-list actors, rock stars, and hedge fund moguls who stood in streams casting shiny new equipment trying to look like Brad Pitt.

All the world was white. My GPS routed me forty minutes down a two-lane asphalt to a spiderweb of dirt roads. I parked the rental at a vacant house where I found a three-seater snowmobile and, judging by the throttle response, enough horsepower to slingshot to the moon. I wound through the trees for an hour to the boundary of a sixty-thousand-acre ranch. Complete with its own bison, elk, and cattle herds, the spread was larger than many cities. I stashed the snowmobile, donned snowshoes, and tried to ignore the pain in my arm. Every step reminded me.

Bones would call me the moment the satellite showed them fueling the jet. If they wrangled the kid onto the plane, it became extremely unlikely we'd ever see him again this side of eternity.

As the sun set, I crested a hilltop and looked down over the compound. Multiple buildings. Cabins tucked into the trees. All of which had been constructed out of giant timbers. Many of the logs were too large for two people to wrap their arms around. In the surrounding areas stood several hundred horses, cows, and llamas. Across the river that serpentined out of the mountains and through the property sat a private airport complete with seven Gulfstream G5s. Several barns were filled with hay bales and multiple tractors, snowmobiles, Jeeps, and ATVs of every shape and size.

The main house looked to be twenty thousand square feet and was lit up like Christmas. Smoke spiraled out of six chimneys, filling the air with a festive scent. As I stared down on wonderland, I saw fifty to seventy-five people milling about the porches. Slender girls in bikinis swam in the heated pool or frolicked in the sauna with a dozen cigar-smoking men, most of whom were visibly rotund or grossly overweight. Somewhere music played. From my perch beneath the arms of an evergreen, I counted seven patrolling and armed guards. And those were just the ones I could see.

Bones had no idea where they were keeping the kid, but every man has a basement.

It's where we hide the skeletons.

I waited for cover of darkness because I wanted them as medicated and heavy-lidded as possible. Under clouds and a quarter moon, I crept the last mile to the barn, where I let myself in and checked the snowmobiles for keys and gas. Both of which they had. If they were expecting me, or someone like me, they didn't show it.

The trick to getting inside a house in which a party is under way with some hundred or more partygoers is to look like you belong. The porch sprawled across the mountainside and wound around two pools and three hot tubs. Spaced throughout, three bartenders and multiple servers kept the partygoers topped off with liquid courage. Supporting the flow of alcohol were three young guys whose sole job it was to keep the bars stocked, bus glassware, and light cigars. They were hopping. When one young bar stocker made his way to my side of the barn to refill an ice chest, I shoved him in the cab of a tractor and borrowed his sheepskin jacket.

I press-checked the Sig 220, screwed on the suppressor, counted six magazines inside my belt, and set my AR inside the ice chest. Then I dialed Bones on the sat phone. The earpiece allowed us to talk while also amplifying noise around me—which was helpful if people tried to sneak up behind me. I spoke briefly. "Radio check."

Bones responded, "Check." I entered the house carrying the chest, wandered through the kitchen, and descended into the basement. Three minutes later, I changed my mind. It wasn't a basement.

It was a dungeon.

At the base of three levels of stairs, a bunker door led to a long, dimly lit hallway that reeked of cigar smoke and incense. A dozen rooms had been designed for sadistic people to live out their fantasies. From a massage parlor to a bathhouse, locker room, theater, circus, no expense had been spared to meet whatever level of otherworldly depravity descended the stairs. Judging from the construction, each room had been lined with foam insulation and sound panels guaranteeing that a rock concert could not be heard in the house above. Mood lighting, soft music, and spinning ceiling fans—not to mention the smell of human sweat and various essential oils—suggested all the rooms had been inhabited just moments prior to my arrival. Some of the sheets were still warm, drops of sweat were on the floor, and one of the bathroom showers was still running, pouring steam through the opening above the glass door—suggesting someone had been standing in there when I appeared. Mounted on every ceiling and in every corner were cameras. Each room had at least six, and those were just the ones I could count.

I worked quickly, clearing each room. If the kid had been here, he was gone now. Along with everyone else. I spoke to Bones. "No boy."

His response was quick. "Check."

The hallway ended at an elevator shaft, which I supposed lifted the trolls who visited here back to the surface, where I was rather certain cars waited to whisk them to waiting jets. I returned to the stairs, climbed back to the ground floor, and felt my anger growing. Something in me told me I was caught in a game of cat and mouse while the puppeteer used young lives as bait.

That many cameras had to lead somewhere, and I wanted to find that room. More than that, I very much wanted to find the guy who sat in the chair staring into the monitors—and more than that, I wanted to find the guy who paid him to do it.

While the underground had been emptied, the surface party continued unfazed. As if the two were oblivious of each other. I turned left from the kitchen and scurried down a hallway that led to what looked like an office. Mahogany walls, stylistically lit artwork, ivory tusks—the room was a museum, but two things surprised me. First, the far wall was covered in swords of varying type, size, and purpose. Many looked quite old. Second, the room was void of photographs. Not one.

I had a feeling the entrance to the media room could be found there, but I didn't have time to search for secret doors and hidden stairs. I circled the desk, which looked unused and ornamental. I doubted anyone had ever sat at it. On top sat a Wi-Fi picture frame. Every few seconds, a new picture flashed onto the screen and rotated through. I walked to the back of the desk, studied the viewer, and was surprised to see a picture of me, taken moments ago, as I crossed the field to the barn. The following fifteen pictures traced my progression into the house, down into the dungeon, through the kitchen, and down the hallway into the office—some thirty-five seconds ago.

Someone was watching me.

When I lifted the frame, the picture changed again to one of me holding the picture frame. Judging from the angle of the camera, I studied the wall and found a dime-sized camera lens posing as one of the eyes in the artwork hanging above the fireplace. The picture flashed again, this time to a picture of me holding the frame and staring into the camera. Present tense.

When the frame changed again, it showed the towheaded boy I'd been sent to find. The photographer had taken the picture close up. The boy's pupils were dilated and eyelids droopy. I doubted he was conscious. I studied the picture, trying to make sense of the blurred images in the background. Finally, my mind put the pieces together. They were bodies. Intertwined like driftwood.

I was in the process of setting the frame on the desk when it flashed one last time. To a picture of Ellie. My daughter. The photographer had been standing behind her and the picture was taken over her shoulder. She was studying at a coffee shop on Main Street in Freetown. Head tilted, shoulders relaxed, the fingers of her right hand unconsciously twirling her hair. Something she did when she was thinking.

I placed my fingers on the screen, expanded the picture, and read the date and time off the top of her laptop screen. The picture had been taken ten minutes ago. As I stared in disbelief, it changed again. This time to Angel. Playing Ping-Pong. The white ball hung suspended in midair, hit by an opponent with her back to me. The expression on Angel's face was one of elation. I expanded my fingers over the news report on the TV screen in the background. Date and time showed twelve minutes ago. When the frame flashed a final time, I was staring at a black-and-white picture of

Casey as she typed at a laptop in her room, Gunner asleep at her feet. This picture had been taken from a distance through her bedroom window.

"Bones?"

"Check."

"Lock down Sally."

Bones and I had worked together long enough to develop a language that meant much more than the words themselves. *Lock down* meant, "I have reason to believe someone we love is in imminent danger. So secure everyone at Freetown. Right now. DEFCON 1." *Sally* added specificity to the threat and told him who to find: the girls.

Bones responded without comment. "Check."

My experience thus far told me there were two parties going on here. One party in the underworld and one on the surface. Which was smart on somebody's part. It allowed for plausible deniability—if you had a really good lawyer.

The numbers around the pool were thinning, suggesting those who knew the real purpose of the party were departing while those who did not remained.

I needed a diversion, and fire had always been my friend. The sight of an in-house sprinkler system suggested that unless I blew up the house, the fire wouldn't last long. And while I'd enjoy the fireworks, I ran the risk of hurting some people who, in all honesty, thought they were simply attending a party and had no idea what was going on in the tombs below.

I quickly descended the stairs and held my lit Zippo beneath a fire sprinkler, causing multiple alarms to sound. Accompanying the earsplitting racket were umpteen streams of high-pressured water soaking every square inch of the basement and stairwell. While I preferred fire damage because it just felt better, water damage can be worse. It can also make life uncomfortable in subfreezing temperatures, but I'd worry about that then.

I headed back up to the kitchen and glanced out the window. Scuttled either by sound or water, additional armed guards appeared from a cabin behind the house and began filing across the pool deck with purpose.

I held my Zippo to the kitchen sprinkler, which sent signals to one half of the house, and watched as partygoers began scurrying like scared cats. Standing in the kitchen while the water rained down, I studied my options.

As I thought, Bones rang into my earpiece. "Sally locked down. Gunner standing guard. All good."

"Check that."

Through the kitchen window, I counted seven private jets sitting along the runway. Given the glow of their engines glistening through a light snowfall, all of them were warming up. Bones chimed in my ear again: "Engines hot." That's about when I heard the report of the rifle and felt the fire scorch my left leg.

The massive kitchen island was constructed mostly of stone, so I tucked myself behind it, made a makeshift bandage out of a kitchen towel and a curtain pull cord, secured it around my leg, then belly-crawled to the porch. I grabbed the spare propane tank beneath a portable fryer and set it on a grill set to high. I then returned to the kitchen and used a butcher knife to hack off the feed line to the gas stove, pouring propane into the open air. I exited the kitchen about the time one hundred thousand BTUs heated the tank beyond its holding ability. The first explosion blew out all the glass in the kitchen, which ignited the propane-laden air in the kitchen, which blew out the sides of the house, which then lit the gas line leading to the much larger tank that heated the pool and secondary houses.

The three explosions must have registered on Bones's satellite feed because the next words sounding in my ear were, "You good?"

"Check."

The explosion shook the second half of the house and disintegrated any glass that remained, allowing me to hear the jet noise on the runway half a mile away as one jet after another lined up to disappear into a gray Montana sky.

Bones again. "Wheels up."

"I see 'em."

Whoever sent me the pictures of the boy, the bodies, and the girls was trying to keep me busy while everyone boarded their planes and disappeared into the night sky. A head fake. I knew this. I also knew I couldn't very well leave the captives to fend for themselves. And I knew men hide bodies in basements.

I returned down the stairs through a shower of cold water into the basement, asking myself where I'd hide people I didn't want found. I searched every room. Looking for seams in walls, secret doors, secret crawlspaces. Anything that offered space enough to hold several people. My search brought me back to the elevator, but this time one thing stood out that had not before: a trail of liquid smeared along the floor. Urine. I punched the button and the elevator door opened, revealing a completely normal elevator. Save one thing. The trail of liquid continued across the floor of the elevator and beneath the far door—as if whoever'd left it had been rolled through the opposite door when it opened at the floor above. My problem was simple: whoever had left that trail would have sat there while they rode the elevator up. Making a puddle. But no puddle existed. They hadn't sat at all. They'd been dragged. Straight through.

I studied the buttons. "1." "2." "3." "In Case of Emergency." And "Light." Oddly, the two most worn buttons were the last two, causing me to wonder just how many emergencies one residential elevator could have. Judging by the wear on the buttons, they had been pushed simultaneously. And often. I pushed both and the back door of the elevator rolled open. Revealing another hallway.

In the back of my mind, I heard Bones. *Nothing is as it seems.*

I stepped into the hallway, triggering the motion lights. If I thought the first hallway was a den of iniquity, I had another thing coming. My room search took me to a locked door behind which I heard scuffling, which was either a really big rat or a person trying to get out. Fortunately, the lock and light switch were on my side. Just like in a prison.

I flipped both and tried to slide the door open, but something prevented me. I pushed harder and slid the obstruction out of the way enough to squeeze my body through the opening, where I found a sleeping teenage girl at my feet. A quick scan and I counted nine more. All unconscious and poorly clothed, if at all. Scanning the room, I found two eyes staring back at me.

The eyes of a boy.

He was shaking more from shock than cold, but what does it matter. He was leaning against the concrete with his arms wrapped around his knees, leaving me to question whether he was hugging himself or bracing himself. When I squatted across from him, he flinched. "You cold?"

Chattering teeth. Puffy eye. Bloody nose. He was a fighter. I liked him.

I draped a comforter over his shoulders. Blond hair stuck to his face. He never took his eyes off me. Or the Sig.

He wiped his nose on his sleeve. I looked a second time at the finger-shaped bruises on his neck.

"Can you walk?"

He stood. Unsteady. Working hard to focus his eyes. If he was aware that he'd wet his pants, he didn't show it.

When Bones had sent the picture, he'd included the words, "Tight window. Now or never. And . . ." I stared at the bodies strewn about me and remembered his last words: "He might not be the only one."

I needed to get these kids out of here, so I rode the elevator to the surface and took a look around. My shadow in tow. The kid never let me get beyond arm's reach. The elevator opened into an empty garage large enough to hold a couple of tractor trailers. Two bay doors suggested vehicles drove in one way and exited another. I returned downstairs, grabbed every blanket, sheet, or jacket I could find, and then loaded the elevator to capacity. Getting everyone topside required two trips. When finished, the floor of the garage looked more morgue than triage. The kid and I wrapped each of the girls in the bedding. We put two in each cocoon, hoping they'd unknowingly share body warmth. I didn't know what they'd been given, but each pulse was strong, suggesting the concoction produced sleep and not death.

When we'd finished, I waved my hand across them. "You know any of them?"

He shook his head.

I glanced out the bay door. The main house sat down a slight hill some two hundred yards through the trees. The party had long since ended, but

I wanted to look around. I had a strong sense the puppeteer was hanging around. I turned to my shadow. I knew what he was going to say but asked anyway. "Can you wait here?"

He stepped closer and shook his head.

Another glance out the bay door. I squatted in front of him. "I'm going to burn their playhouse down. Can you do what I tell you?"

He nodded without hesitation.

# CHAPTER 3

We rode the elevator down, returned through the catacombs, and climbed the stairs. This time as we neared the top, I chose the smaller stairwell and found myself staring into the service entrance that fed the kitchen. The house was empty.

Clearing the room, I spoke out loud. "Bones?"

"Check."

"Turned one into eleven. All require medical attention. Stat."

"Roger. En route. Check."

The exterior propane tank explosion had set the pool house ablaze. Black smoke and flames climbed above the trees. Staring across what used to be the back porch, I saw a tall, fit man wearing sunglasses and a black suit exit a cabin beyond the far end of the house and begin strolling casually across the scorched earth to a golf cart waiting to ferry him to the airport. He walked as if he hadn't a care in the world. Just another stroll in the park. I leveled my AR and studied him through my optics. He was handsome, tall, broad-shouldered, and walked purposefully while the firelight danced upon his face. For one brief second, he turned and looked. Directly at me—which was strange given that I'd attempted to hide myself. The look lasted two or three seconds. Something he intended. Through the smoke and reflection of the flames, I saw chiseled, familiar features, long salt-and-pepper hair, and a white trimmed beard. I could not place the face, but his expression told me this was his world. Everything I could see or touch for miles belonged to him. Further, the smug look in his eyes said that even what I thought belonged to me belonged to him. I checked for my shadow.

The man stepped into a cart driven by an armed gorilla, casually crossed one leg over the other, and turned down the hill for the runway. Driving into the darkness, he pulled off his sunglasses and glanced once more over his shoulder. Right at me. A slight smile. A slightly upturned eyebrow. I turned the dial on my scope, increasing the magnification, and placed the crosshairs on the bridge of his nose, equally spaced between amber-colored pupils that matched the fire around him.

I'd met a lot of bad men in my life. Most wear masks to conceal their dark hearts, but regardless of makeup, costume, or plastic surgery, their eyes betray them. Bones told me early in my training that the eyes are the lamp of the body. They magnify the soul, reflecting the truth of the person housed below.

This man's eyes were black holes.

Reminding me that the best way to kill a snake is to cut off the head.

I exited the kitchen door and began running down the hill to the barn, the boy on my heels. I threw open the barn door where the Ferrari-red engine cover of the snowmobile caught my eye. I cranked the engine and catapulted out of the barn while the boy latched a death grip around my waist. Seldom had I reached eighty miles an hour so quickly. I carved an S-curve through the back pasture en route to the airfield where two jets, engines glowing red, remained on the tarmac.

The cart carrying the man drove through the gates of the airport, circled, and dropped him at the stairway of the first jet. While I redlined the engine, shooting a rooster tail of snow some sixty feet behind me, he casually climbed the stairway, only to stand atop it and light a cigar. Not a care in the world. I leveled my AR to disable his engines with .223 rounds when he lifted a phone from his pocket and dialed a number. No sooner had he finished dialing than the empty garage exploded and an angry ball of flames climbed into the night sky.

With an expression of satisfaction, he held out both hands. The suggestion was clear: *Me or them?*

I turned the snowmobile ninety degrees, and the boy and I climbed the hill toward the garage as the man's plane taxied away.

We reached the garage where the explosion had blown off everything to the left of the elevator, which was fortunate given that I'd stacked the girls in their cocoons along the far right wall. Sometimes you get lucky. While the girls smelled like smoke and soot covered their faces, not a one had woken. They'd never remember it, which, given the hell they'd endured, was good.

Overhead, his jet roared through the night sky. I stood in the trees and watched the vapor trail dissolve into two snake eyes. I did not like losing.

Bones landed, medical personnel tended to the ten girls along with my new friend, and Bones found me standing in the woods staring at the house. He spoke as soon as he saw me. "Girls are all good. Gunner too."

"How'd he get those pics?"

Bones shook his head. "He planted a guy in Freetown. We've got him on video. And he did more than just take pictures of the girls. He took video."

"Of them?"

"No. The grounds."

It took a second for this to sink in. "He's scoping us out?"

"Looks that way."

"How?"

"Walked into the hospital as one guy, then out as another. We didn't catch the disguise until he'd exited the perimeter."

"I thought our security couldn't be beat."

"It can't."

"Except for this guy."

"Don't beat yourself up. He's good."

"What about that facial recognition software we spent so much money on?"

"He knew how to avoid it."

He pulled a double cheeseburger out of a bag and handed it to me. "Sorry. It was all I could do on short notice." I ate it, followed quickly by a second. He offered me a beer but I declined, choosing to eat the fries instead. All I really wanted was a shower and a bed.

While the pool house had been entirely consumed, the main house and most of the other buildings remained standing. Structurally sound, they could be brought back to life. "Bones, who is this guy?"

"He sells himself as a philanthropist. Said to have made his money in tech, but it's a cover. He keeps friends in high places. And not just the church. He owns dozens of homes around the world, and a couple times a year he flies in 'friends' from around the world. Priests. CEOs. Politicians. Powerful people who either have, or have access to, money. Calls them 'Soul Restoration Summits.' It's a shell game. Most of the partygoers have no idea what's going on behind closed doors."

"He have a name?"

"Several."

Bones took a breath. "Peel away the layers and you'll find he's the owner of the second largest pornography company in the world. He employs several thousand people who canvas the planet for young, fresh 'talent,' and he has single-handedly bought and sold more flesh than possibly anyone in modern human history."

"How do you know so much about him?"

"More on that later."

"How come we've never bumped into him?"

"You have."

"What do you mean?"

"Forty-seven names on your back once belonged to him. And those are just the ones we know of. Could be twice that."

"That would explain the expression on his face."

"Which was?"

"Looked like he knew me. Like we'd met before."

A pause followed by a slight change in his voice. "Chances are good you've cost him more than any person alive."

"How long have you known about him?"

He looked into the memory. "A long while."

I stared at the house, and something inside me wanted to send a signal. I climbed the hill, walked into the house, disabled the sprinkler system, and then doused the great room with fifteen gallons of gasoline meant for the snowmobiles. I lit my Zippo, threw it into the room, and returned to Bones while the flames grew. By tomorrow morning, only the foundation would remain.

We turned toward the plane, but when I tried to take a step, I stumbled and Bones caught me. My energy reserves had almost played out. He locked his arm in mine, saying, "Weebles wobble."

"Yeah, and all the king's horses . . ." By the time we reached the stairs of the plane, he was almost carrying me. "That guy played me tonight . . . a pawn on the chessboard. He used those kids as decoys." I was losing the ability to think clearly. I spoke through the fog. "Why're you just now telling me about him?"

He shrugged. "Some things are better left unsaid."

Maybe I spoke because I'd been shot. Maybe I spoke out of exhaustion. Maybe I was tired of losing to evil. Maybe I spoke because I needed to hear the truth. Whatever the case, the words left my mouth before I had a chance to filter them or call them back. And when I spoke, my tone changed and I made eye contact for the first time. "Like Marie?"

He exhaled. "That's different."

I knew my words had caught him off guard and stung him. I wanted to take them back, but silver bullets never return once fired down the barrel. So I faced him. "You may have convinced yourself of that, but not me. Remember that."

We leveled off at forty thousand feet and I slipped into an uneasy sleep, drifting in and out of conscious thought. Bones helped the nurse change the bandages on both my arm and leg, then sat back and sipped his wine. When he spoke, I could feel his whisper on my face. "I do." He took another sip as he stared out across Montana blanketed in moonlight white. "Every day."

# CHAPTER 4

NEW YORK CITY

I pulled my collar up, my beanie down, tucked the roses beneath my arm, and buried my hands deep in my pockets. My exterior wounds were healing, leaving only scars and sandpaper skin in their wake. Those on the inside might need more time.

Central Park was cold. I missed Gunner, Clay's laughter, and the quiet of the water. Weaving among greedy pigeons, I found myself looking down. At gum. At feet. Cracks in the sidewalk. Anywhere but at people. I didn't want to read their eyes or their hurts or the emotions painted across their faces.

My back was stiff so I stretched, but it did little good. Tender from the needle and fresh ink. When Peacock finished the last two names, he told me, "Grow taller or start a new list. Not much room left back here." He smiled. "No pun intended." During a pause, I heard him counting, touching my skin every ten with his finger. When finished, he whispered, "Two-fifty." He slid his stool around to face me. "Can you still remember them?"

The slideshow returned and I nodded.

Summer had called me six weeks ago. A producer in New York had contacted her, having seen her instructional videos on YouTube and read through her résumé, and asked if she'd help train young dancers for an off-Broadway production. She was calling to ask what I thought.

I thought the idea stunk, but I kept that to myself. "You should go."

"You think?"

A nod. "Definitely."

"You'll come see me."

"Just as soon as you're settled."

A pause. "They're putting me up in my own apartment. One room. Not much space but . . ."

I knew what she was asking. I cleared my throat. "New York isn't my favorite place. I have this thing in my head that starts beeping whenever I land. An internal clock. I have about forty-eight hours to leave the city or my head explodes."

She knew this. "But you'll come see me?"

I smiled. "Yes."

"When?"

Our conversation ended when I promised I'd come up for the first show.

Walking across Central Park, the clock in my head was ticking. Forty-four minutes and counting. I had come a day early to surprise her. Our phone calls had been sporadic since rehearsals had kept her busy—sometimes twenty hours a day.

She'd become "Momma Dancer" to the younger dancers. And after she told them the story of us and the Intracoastal, she said they couldn't wait to meet me. No telling what lies she'd told them.

As a credit to her own abilities, plus a lifetime of training and teaching others how to dance, the producers had given her a bit part in one of the last acts, which included eight other dancers onstage. Because Summer was old school, one of her talents was tap dancing. And since time was short and she'd known the routine for twenty years, they let her audition. They also discovered Summer's innate ability to read people by how they danced, which was invaluable to the production team and the three dozen girls now under her care. She could write her own ticket.

Unexpected and "late in life," as dancers go, this was her shot. "Maybe my last," she'd said with a laugh.

"You should take it." And I meant it. I just wasn't ready for what it meant.

At least that was what I was telling myself as the pigeons strutted across the asphalt in front of me. Every phone call she was excited. Out of breath. "I can't wait to show you . . ." But she was also tired. Burning both ends. Life in the city.

I bought my ticket. Balcony. Couple rows back. The place was packed. When the curtain lifted, I looked around and felt sort of foolish since I was the only one holding two dozen roses. But I had quit caring what other people thought long ago.

Sitting for long periods of time had grown more difficult over the years. And in the last three months, while my wounds sustained in the Keys had mostly healed, the more recent batch from Italy and Montana had not.

But the flesh wounds I'd sustained in recent days were grammar school compared to the piercing one in my heart. Most hours of every day, my mind returned to Marie. The thought of her wasting away alone in that bed in that convent and why Bones had not told me about her. The wound in me was festering, and I simply could not wrap my head around the fact that for fourteen years he'd known, even been to see her, and yet he never told me she was alive.

How did he keep that a secret?

I pushed the thought out of my head as the curtain fell, marking an intermission and a chance to stretch my legs. I left the roses in my seat and walked to the bathroom. Showgoers milled about the red-carpet hallways, a throwback to the theater's illustrious past. Pictures on the walls showcased the greats who'd performed there. Fred Astaire. Pavarotti. Judy Garland. When I saw the picture of Ginger Rogers, I could hear Summer's voice. "Ginger did everything Fred did except backward and in high heels."

In one of our last phone calls, Summer had told me there were nights when rehearsals ended and she'd stand on that stage and close her eyes and listen for the echo of Ginger's feet following Fred's.

"Have you heard it?" I asked.

She laughed, embarrassed by her own childish reminiscence. "I can't believe this is happening. It's like I'm living somebody else's dream."

The guy in the hallway was muscled. Shaved head. Tight suit. Scanning eyes. The bulge in his jacket told me he was not in compliance with New York City firearms regulations. The girl was drug-skinny. Attractive. Or had been. Coming down off something. Clinging to him. Looked like someone else had dressed her. Maybe him. Her eyes looked down. Hair covering her face. His hand was walking up and down her back and bottom, suggesting ownership.

I turned left, shook off the image, and found the bathroom. When finished, I returned to my seat by another hallway. I did not have the mental bandwidth to enter another story. Which, if I'd been paying attention, should have told me something.

The third act started and I sat up straighter. Summer, in what she'd told me was her first of two solos, appeared stage left and put on a dizzying display of foot speed and rhythm, which captivated the audience. Including me. She was thinner. But fit. Looked twenty years younger. In fact, she looked better than many of the girls in the show. I watched dumbstruck. I knew she was good, but I had no idea she was this good. She was next-level.

In three dance routines, Summer stole the third act. And when the curtain fell and then rose, and the cast appeared for a bow, the producer introduced all the stars and finally Summer—who, he added, was making her return debut to Broadway after a twenty-year absence.

Watching the show had been fun. Watching the standing ovation spread delight across Summer's face was like a balm on my insides. She, of all people, had earned this, and she deserved every accolade.

I waited across the street outside the "Cast Only" door. Roses spread in front of me, behind me, and then across my arms. Eventually, I just held them off to one side. One cast member, her face still painted with too much makeup, scurried past me and quipped, "Those for me?"

I smiled. Wouldn't be long now. I had waited weeks to see her. Waited until I was healthier. Till my head was clear. Or at least, clearer.

When I'd returned from Montana, Clay had flown down on the jet and joined me at my island. Said he needed an escape from the Colorado snow. In truth, I had the feeling that after sixty years in prison, he disliked being cooped up and enjoyed—probably more than most all of us—the freedom to come and go as he liked. He'd grown fond of private jet travel. Plus, I think he just missed me. I didn't mind. I'd missed him. I loved that old man and the slow, measured way he spun his stories.

Clay helped me clean up. Heal. And he didn't talk too much. But then, he'd never felt the need to fill the air with needless chatter, which was one of the reasons we got along so well. He knew when to be quiet and I did, too, which was most of the time. When I told him I was coming up here, he paused, sipped his coffee, and said, "Think that's a good idea?"

I shrugged. "You don't think so?"

He tilted his head to one side without looking at me and didn't say anything, which was his way of saying a lot. After a minute, he asked, "How much longer you gonna keep doing this?"

"Which *this* are you talking about?"

"The *this* where Bones sends you a pic any hour day or night and you drop everything and take off. Always with the possibility of never returning."

Hearing him say it reminded me that my life of abnormality had become the status quo. Upside down and backward. I wasn't exactly boyfriend material. I shrugged.

He leaned forward. Care in his eyes. "Mr. Murphy, you're numb and you don't know it."

The temperature had dropped so I zipped up, pulled my beanie down over my ears, and wrapped my scarf tighter about my face. Summer exited the door. A sunflower reflecting the sky. While she'd always had muscled calves, the last two months had shaped them further. This was no longer the mom I'd met in the Intracoastal carrying an extra fifteen. Her dress flowed and draped across her legs as she wiggled her arms into a full-length down coat popular among true city goers. She was laughing. A concert of beauty and movement. Younger girls floated about her in a circle. High-pitched voices. Rapid-fire questions. They pulled on her, stuck to her like magnets, and invited her for drinks, but she refused, saying—unlike them—she needed her beauty rest. She reminded them about early morning rehearsals.

When they had cleared and she stood alone, I stepped from the shadows. As I did, a handsome, slightly older gentleman stepped out the back door. Confident. Fit. He was immaculately dressed. Suit. Overcoat. Polished shoes. Impressive watch. I had no idea how much all that cost, but it didn't look cheap. He waved a hand and a Bentley appeared from my left, cutting off my approach.

He pulled on the door latch, gestured to Summer, and held the door while she stepped inside.

Smiling. Like she'd done it before.

I retreated to the shadows, and I heard him tell the driver, "Tom's. And take us around the back." Watching them leave, I can honestly say I did not dislike him.

I had no idea what or where Tom's was, but that was not my primary concern as I watched the taillights fade and heard the clock tick louder inside my mind. Obviously, he was somebody. Had money. Could take care of her. And judging by the way he had brushed her waist with his hand as she'd stepped into his car, he wanted to. Maybe he already was.

I walked the twelve blocks to my hotel beneath the buzz of streetlights and the hum and honk of taxis, not cognizant of the fact that the night air had frozen the roses. Unbeknownst to me, my route brought me in front of Tom's Brasserie—a popular late-night restaurant with a ninety-minute wait, even after midnight. Only in New York City. Snow started to fall as I leaned against a lamppost and stared up through the two-story window that faced the street.

Summer and Mr. Bentley sat at a corner table. His back to the glass. Her left shoulder to me. The tables did not have tablecloths, which made it a popular destination for street gawkers to stare up beneath the tables. A weird voyeurism. I wasn't the only one.

I tried to shake myself away and could not. Summer never looked better. She laughed. He held her hand. At one point, his hand slipped beneath the table and touched her thigh. First, her knee. Then higher, toward her hip. Even sliding a finger along the seam of the slit in her dress. A gentle yet intimate gesture. One that brought a smile from Summer.

Two older ladies walked toward me, arm in arm. Guarding against the cold. I separated the roses. Gave them each a dozen, and they thanked me in Russian.

The conversation in my head as I walked to my hotel was a machine-gun volley of two competing voices.

Why should I be mad? She doesn't belong to me. She owes me nothing. She made no promises.

*But what's she doing with him?*

She's been here two months. Without you. What'd you expect her to do? Sit alone in her apartment and stare at the phone?

*There's something between us. She's got to feel that.*

She's healthy. Living her dream. You promised her nothing. She's not getting any younger. You're never home and you never call. What'd you expect?

*But I told her I was coming!*

Right. Tomorrow. She doesn't owe you anything.

*I know that.*

You don't act like it.

I had no answers for me. All I knew was that she looked as healthy as I'd ever seen her and like she was having fun. Why would I interrupt that? I should be happy for her. Problem was, I wasn't. By the time I got to the hotel, I was engaged in a full-on pity party, tripping over my bottom lip.

When my phone rang, I didn't answer it and I didn't need to check the caller ID. Right now I did not want to talk to him. Usually when I decline a call, he gets the message and leaves me a voicemail. But not tonight. I was standing on the balcony overlooking Central Park, the noise of the city a few floors below me. After the third decline, I clicked Accept but said nothing.

He said, "Looks cold in New York City."

I'd not told him I was coming. "It is."

"How was the show?"

I'd also said nothing about a show. "Summer's . . . in her element. She was . . . unreal."

28

"She happy to see you?"

"Seems happy."

"That didn't really answer my question."

"She was busy."

"She talk you into staying a few weeks?"

"Headed back tonight."

In the last few months, despite his persistent calls, the quiet between us had grown. He tried to bridge the gap, tried to engage me in the conversation that swam beneath the surface. But when I didn't move out from behind the emotional bunker I'd constructed to protect the few remaining pieces of my shattered heart, he didn't push. When I got home and my bullet and knife wounds began to heal, I found that my heart had not escaped the shrapnel. The first casualty at the altar of betrayal was trust. Which meant I was questioning everything. Including him.

By now, I knew he knew I felt this way. And he knew I knew that he knew.

"You got plans when you get back?"

"Thought I'd take *Gone Fiction* north. Maybe skirt the East Coast. See some different country."

He'd done what he wanted. He'd let me know he was thinking about me. "I'll check in on you in a few days."

One of the hazards of my job was complacency. This meant Bones sent me a new phone every couple of weeks. The frequency depended on use and travel. I hung up and dropped my phone in the trash can.

# CHAPTER 5

## MY ISLAND, NORTHEAST FLORIDA

I found Clay as I'd left him. Standing beneath the shade of a tattered straw hat, a pole in one hand, iced tea in the other, content look on his face. He'd taken to island life and, to his credit, had a stringer full of fish. Which he held in display. A wide smile told the story. Clay had a thing for cornmeal and hot oil, so we'd eat well tonight. The events of South Florida had knit us together. So, even in Colorado, he was never far. Gunner sat beside me, attached to my hip. Smartest animal I'd ever known. One quarter human. I don't know how he knew what he knew, he just did.

I sat on the stern of *Gone Fiction*, a pen in my hand. I'd not written a single word since Marie died and I rewrote the ending to the last book. And I really didn't intend to now. But a pen was a comfort, and I thought best with one in my hand. I often didn't know what I thought until I'd written it out and could see it. Only then could I know if I knew it.

I was tapping my teeth with the pen when Gunner started pulling on my flip-flop. Snarling in a playful way. I told him to go away but he wouldn't listen. I sat on the captain's bench, propping my feet on the steering wheel, and he started tugging on my shorts. Under normal circumstances, this meant he was lonely and wanted to play, but unfortunately, I was about to learn these were not normal circumstances. I threw his training buoy in the water, and I should have asked myself what was going on when he didn't follow it—but my mind was elsewhere. Finally, Gunner tugged on my shorts so hard they tore, snarling in a way that was not playful. When I told him to get lost, he ran down the dock, jumped in the water, and beckoned me to follow.

I tilted my hat back and tapped my teeth, "Go on. I'm not in the—"

I don't remember the blast that launched me from the boat. I don't remember my flight through the air. And I don't remember landing face-down. Nor do I remember the sensation of my skin being set on fire. The only thing I do remember is the sound of Clay's garbled voice, but I was too far inside myself to hear what he was saying.

In hindsight, landing in the water was a good thing. It put the fire out.

Clay later told me that the helicopter ride to Savannah General was both a lot of fun and one of the more fearful things he'd ever done. When the pilot told him he was not legally able to ride in the helicopter, Clay had answered, "Scooter, either you fly this thing or I will. But one way or the other, I am taking this man to the hospital."

To my knowledge, Clay has no idea how to fly a helicopter.

I woke three days later with a furry warm body breathing next to me, his muzzle resting on my chest. Tail wagging across my legs. Clay told me the nurses objected at first, but then Gunner did that thing with his ears and made that little noise he makes, and they relented.

When my eyes cracked open, all the world had gathered at my feet. Dressed in white, each face a story of concern. Bones, Clay, Angel, Ellie.

And Summer.

Somewhere inside me, I heard the echo of a James Taylor song. *Frozen man.*

At my stirring, Summer sucked in a breath and knelt next to the bed, sliding her hand beneath mine. Her tearstained face wore torment. I tried to speak, but given the tube down my throat, I motioned for a pen and paper. The words were smeared and slow in coming. I could barely read my own writing. "Did somebody die?"

The laughter did them some good.

Apparently someone had set a bomb beneath the gas tank of my Whaler. It was set to a pressurized timer triggered by my weight in the captain's seat. I don't know how Gunner knew about the bomb—I don't know whether he smelled it or heard it—but I do know he tried really hard to get me off that boat. When the bomb ignited, it did so beneath ninety-two gallons of fuel. Clay said he heard the explosion and saw rocket man arcing through the sky like Halley's Comet. When he got to me I'd been facedown in the water nearly a minute.

My injuries included a concussion, burns across my backside and arms, one collapsed lung, and various cuts and contusions. The technical diagnosis suggested that I'd live but recovery might be slow. It took a week to get me walking on my own, my biggest hurdle being the concussion. During that time, Summer never left my side. Which I found strange, given Mr. Bentley. Ordinarily I would've said nothing, but hospitals have good drugs, which lessened my defenses.

"Don't you need to check in with your boyfriend?" That was probably a bit blunt, but again my filter was not working.

She looked surprised.

I tried to let her off easy. "The one with the Bentley and the nice suits?"

She looked more surprised. "You mean George?"

My head was spinning and I sounded drunk. "Don't know his name. But he drives a Bentley and he wears really nice suits."

She moved closer and nodded. "George." She held my hand with both of hers. "He's the producer of the show. And he thinks we're better friends than we are."

Again, the drugs. "But I saw you at dinner. You held his hand. He stroked your leg."

"You were in New York?"

"Came early to surprise you."

"When you didn't show, I just figured Bones had you someplace else. I tried to call . . ."

I leaned my head back on the pillow and moved my feet clumsily beneath the sheets. "Ginger's got nothing on you."

"You really thought so?"

"You were amazing. And then all those people stood . . ." My eyes focused on her. I shook my head. "I was standing outside the stage door when his car appeared."

"Why didn't you say something?"

"A future with me looks different than a future with him."

Tears dripped onto my cheek as she kissed me. Once. Then twice. She tasted salty. "George is a friend. That's all. He'd like to be more. He's not." She placed her hand on my chest. "Won't ever be."

The drugs kicked in and I faded off. When I woke, she was in bed next to me. Her head on my shoulder. I lay there several minutes, just breathing. The mixture of her smell and the strong rhythmic pulse of her heart was intoxicating.

George could wait his turn.

# CHAPTER 6

---

## FREETOWN

B ones secured my release a few days later and transferred my care to our Colorado team housed on-site at Freetown. The paramedics helped transfer me from hospital to runway, where the seven of us, including Gunner, boarded the plane. Three hours later, we touched down and reversed the process. That much activity tired me out, so I slept throughout the trip.

When Bones and I opened Freetown, we knew we needed a secluded fortress. Some place high, protected, and tough to get to. Drug-addicted women who have been emotionally, physically, and repeatedly raped for profit need a safe space to unwind all the knots the evil has tied. Getting free is tough enough without looking over your shoulder.

What had once flourished in the late 1800s with schools and churches and shops and kids playing in the streets became a ghost town when the silver ran out. Situated in a high alpine valley, it's one of the more beautiful places I've ever been. And given newer technology and better roads, it's now accessible while also hidden. The altitude takes some getting used to when you're two miles above sea level, but acclimation doesn't take long. Especially for the young. Most folks who live around there have no idea we exist. We like it that way.

For security, Bones brought in some ex-Delta guys and SEALs and retired Los Angeles SWAT officers. We give them each a cabin. Educate their kids. Free healthcare. And then pay them to put all their training to good use. Which they do. Rather zealously. Not only that, but most are still on some sort of active duty, which requires them to stay current in their training. And because the mountains around us are some of the toughest anywhere, they bring in their military friends and conduct mountain and cold-weather urban training all around us. Sometimes they even let me play along. We share stories at twelve thousand feet.

While Bones plays the happy-go-lucky grandpa everyone loves to love, he walks these mountains morning and night, and there isn't a footprint or broken twig that gets past him.

These are his sheep. Freetown his pasture.

For lack of anything more creative, we used to just call it the Town. But somewhere in our first year of operation, one of the girls said something to change all that. She'd had a rough go. Through no fault of her own, she was taken from her home and sold as a slave. For two years, she was traded around. Suffered horrors untold. To medicate her reality, she took anything she could get her hands on, numbing the pain of the present and past and future. Took us a while to find her. When we did, we airlifted her to the Town. She stayed in ICU for two months.

Bones took her under his wing, which I thought was amazing when we learned what she'd endured. The fact that she would ever get within arm's length of another man surprised me. But Bones is like that. Everybody's grandfather. Or the grandfather they never had. Four years into her stay here, she'd graduated college—with a nursing degree, no less—and taken a job in our hospital. Working with the girls. Nursing them back to life. She met a guy. One of ours. Bones liked him. They set a date. She asked Bones to walk her down the aisle.

During the early years of the Town, many of the girls wanted to climb to the top of the mountain, which leveled out just above fourteen thousand feet. Problem was, most of them were in such bad shape or they'd been beaten so badly that they were months from being physically able to make the trek. So Bones and I bought a chairlift from a defunct ski slope and had it installed. All the way to the top. It sits four across. We also built a cabin. Roaring fireplace. Espresso machine.

We called it the Eagle's Nest.

A few weeks before her wedding, this girl and her fiancé and Bones and I had ridden to the top and were sitting on the porch, sipping coffee, looking out across a view that spanned seventy to a hundred miles in most every direction. And as we sat up there, she started shaking her head. She said, "There was a moment in my life when I was lying in the darkness, a different man every hour, on the hour, day after day after week after month, and I felt my soul leave. Just checked out of me. Because to live inside me was too painful. I let it go because I couldn't understand how anyone, much less me, would ever want to live inside me. Too filthy. Too . . ." She trailed off, just shaking her head.

Finally, she turned and looked at us. "Then you kicked down the door. Lifted me up and carried me. Here. And slowly, I learned to breathe again. To wake up and see daylight. And what I found with every day was that something in me stirred. Something I'd not known in a long time. Something I thought was long since dead. And that was my hope. Hope that somebody, someday, would see me. Just a girl. Wanting love and willing to give it—to give all of me. I had this hope that somebody would accept me without holding my past against me. Without seeing me as stained. As the horror. As something you just throw away. But somehow . . ."

She sank her hand into the snow resting on the railing. "Like this." For several minutes she just cried in the arms of her fiancé. But it was what she said last that changed the name. Looking from Bones to me, she said, "I never thought I'd walk down an aisle in white. How could I ever deserve that? Not when . . . And yet, I am." She shook her head. "I don't really understand it, but somehow, in some impossible way, love reached down inside me, took out all the old and dirty—the scars and the stains that no soap anywhere would ever wash out. And love didn't just clean me but made me new. And maybe the craziest part of that is how I see me."

She held her fiancé's hand. "It's one thing for him to see me as I want to be seen. It's another thing entirely for me to see me, and I want to see me." She laughed. "When I look in the mirror, I don't see the freak. The maggot. The refuse. I see the new. Sparkling. Radiant. And I like her. I have hope for her. I think she's going to make it. She is now what she once was . . . beautiful. A daughter. Soon, a wife. Maybe one day, a mom. If you only knew how impossible that seemed not so long ago."

She waved her hand across the Town nestled in the valley below. "I cannot begin—"

We sat in silence several more minutes. The temperature was dropping. I stoked the fire. She reached into the air in front of her, made a fist and returned it to her chest. Pounding. "I was there. Now I am here. Love did that." She spoke through gritted teeth. "I am free."

And in that moment, the Town became Freetown. It worked in West Africa; why can't it work in western Colorado?

Years ago, I signed over the royalties of my books to fund Freetown. Then Bones and I chose a board out of a select lineup of executives from New York to California—all of whom either have or had children here. While the success of my books was the seed and continues to fund a large portion, these corporate partners write large checks. And because they understand the need to operate under the radar, they don't seek the marketing glory that would ordinarily come with sponsorship. As a result, people here pay for nothing. If it sounds like utopia, it's not. The barrier to entry is slavery. And having been enslaved, everyone, to the person, chooses freedom.

Returning here is a bit of a homecoming for me. It's here and really only here that I possess some sort of celebrity status. Interestingly, these girls know nothing of my artistic career. Know nothing of my books. In fact, not even the corporate partners know. They simply know we have an invested benefactor. Of course they read my books. They're scattered across the shelves here and there, but they have no idea I wrote them. They simply know me as the guy who kicked down the door. Some don't even know that. Most think I'm just one of the guards.

Which is fine with me.

Every time I come back, I like to remind myself what we do here. It reconnects the disconnected parts of me. I pull on a hoodie and a hat, shove my hands deep in my pockets, and try to hide as I meander Main Street. I find a bench near the pet store where we give away free puppies, rabbits, and all kinds of birds. There, I close my eyes and just listen for one sound.

The universal sound of freedom.

Laughter.

# CHAPTER 7

I woke after midnight in a darkened room. Gunner at my feet. Staring at me. Wagging his tail. Ever faithful. Across from me, Angel slept in a chair beneath a reading light. One of my books lay open in her lap. Lately, she'd taken to acting like a crazed fan since she knew a secret millions would love to know. She had also seen what it cost me to protect that secret, so I knew it was safe with her.

During the months of her stay, Bones had kept me updated as to her progress. Given all the stuff that had been pumped into her system, Angel's detox was difficult and not without challenge. Which meant she'd sweated most of it out. A gut thing. And difficult to watch. But here on the other side, she'd gained some needed weight and was talking about college. She'd make it. She looked good. No, scratch that. She looked awesome. More than that, she was free.

As I studied her, I found myself asking a familiar question: *What is freedom worth?*

She stirred, her eyes popped open, and she stretched. "Hey, Padre." A sneaky smile. "I'm a goooood kisser."

I tried not to laugh.

"How you feeling?"

I studied me. "Not too crazy about this gown."

She lifted her eyebrows once. Ever playful. "The view from the back is fun."

I chuckled, which intensified the soreness in my ribs.

She slid a stainless stool next to the bed and rested her head on her forearms. "Mom and I were giving you a bath last night and I noticed something."

I stared at the ceiling. "I know you well enough now to know that the next words out of your mouth will make me uncomfortable."

"It's no big deal. I closed my eyes for . . . some of it."

"I have no memory of that."

Another playful smile. "Shame. It was epic."

I decided to play along. "What'd you find?"

"Despite our history, which I'd like to think links us together in some cosmic way, my name is not etched into your back. I thought I, of all people"—she tapped her chest—"had earned a place on the wall of fame."

"I have a feeling you're going to make a point."

Her head tilted sideways. "Was I just having a bad dream, or didn't you rescue me?" She raised a finger. "And if I remember correctly, although things do get a little fuzzy when it comes to the details, I think I had my own page on the black web. An auction even. With bidders. Lots of them."

"Let's just say I snatched you back. But truth be told, it's tough to rescue someone who doesn't want to be, but you did."

"When did you first know?"

"Know what?"

"That I needed and wanted rescue?"

"The chapel. First time we met."

"You're all right, Padre." She paused. "But you still haven't answered my question."

"Your name is not the only one missing."

She nodded but said nothing.

"Your mom's, Ellie's, Marie's."

"Why?"

"Tattoos can be burned off and shot through, so I wrote your name where no one could erase it."

"Where's that?"

I laid her hand flat across my heart.

"You've gone sappy on me. I don't even know who I'm talking to any-more. Are you taking estrogen pills?" She wiped her eyes on my sheet and raised a finger. "You should be a writer. You'd have people wrapped around your finger."

"Working on it."

She laid a hand on my leg. "Your secret's safe with me." She stood, smearing mascara. "Mama said to wake her when you woke up."

She turned to go but I stopped her. "What about the show? New York?"

She shook her head. "Seriously?"

I nodded.

She shrugged as if I'd lost my mind. "Mom quit."

I tried to sit up but thought better of it. "What?"

Angel disappeared. Two minutes later, Summer arrived. Sleep in her eyes. Looked like she'd worked a double, which meant she'd been by my side twenty-four-seven. During the last decade or so of my life, I'd buried my love. With no hope of a life with Marie, I figured I had no use for it so I didn't give it much bandwidth. Buried it deep and closed the cellar door, focusing on the job in front of me and letting what remained of my heart wither.

But summer always follows winter. A fitting name.

And while part of me felt guilty because Marie still held my heart, I felt twinges of something I'd not felt in a long time. Part of me inside was coming to life, and that part had not lived for many years. Yet every time Summer walked into the room, I took a deeper breath than the one I'd taken seconds before.

She kissed me on the cheek, checked my forehead for temperature, and then began doing that thing girls do with their hair where they twist it and twirl it into a bun while wrapping a rubber band around it at close to warp speed. "Hungry?"

Her movements were graceful. Purposeful. Nothing wasted. A dancer by profession. A dancer in life. "Yes . . ." I swallowed. "But not for food."

Angel smiled. "Aaaaand I'll be leaving now."

Summer tugged on her sweatshirt. "Help me turn him."

The two of them rolled me on my side and began changing my bandages. From what I could gather, the Whaler saved my life. The bomb had been placed below the deck, directly beneath the captain's bench. When it ignited, the blast shot me out of the helm much like an eject seat on a fighter jet. Under ordinary circumstances, the bottom section of the bench also served as a cooler, and given the advancements in construction and proprietary materials and patents held by the Boston Whaler company, the bench held together, allowing the blast to propel me forward and protect my backside and chest cavity.

I keep promising to write the good folks at Whaler a letter in appreciation but just haven't gotten around to it yet.

Summer and Angel fussed over my bandages and then made comments about my butt, which were good-natured and helped mask the severity of what almost happened. Gunner watched with an entertained, tail-wagging grin. He was no dummy. He knew if he hung around long enough, he'd get some food out of this.

Given that small movements exhausted me, I dozed while Summer cooked breakfast. In my haze of sleep, the slideshow of my life returned on repeat behind my eyelids. A seamless mixture of both dream and memory. Faces of the lost and found. The living and the dead. Joy and pain. I wasn't sure how to understand what my body was telling me other than it was tired. It was true the explosion had forced my convalescence, but I'd been in need of triage for much longer. After months and years on the road, my soul and body were spent. Empty.

Every dreamy slideshow ended with a strange picture of me. One I'd never seen. Dream and memory were difficult to differentiate.

I lay faceup in the snow, which was soaked crimson given the hole in my side. My breathing had slowed and my muscles were no longer tense, which meant the fight was over. Won or lost, I did not know. My breath exited my lungs and turned to smoke in the air above me. My right hand clutched an old single-shot buffalo gun. Smoke spiraled out of the long, octagonal barrel. Gunner lay across my legs. Unharmed. For which I was glad.

Around my neck was a scarf that smelled like Summer and in my heart was a longing. The dream always ended the same: Me staring down on me. Watching me. Unaffected by whatever had just happened. I was peaceful. As my breath turned to smoke, I faded upward like a hot air balloon until I could no longer see me. My body down there. Me up here. Where the air was quiet and the sun was warm on my face.

I did not mind at all.

Bones's voice woke me. "Freetown policy prohibits fraternization with the nursing staff."

"Make new policy."

"Have to take that up with the governing board."

"I intend to just as soon as I peel myself off these sheets."

He laughed, sat on the stool, and tapped the bag being filled by my catheter. "At least you don't have to get out of bed to pee. It's the little things."

I spoke through heavy lids. "Who blew up my boat?"

He shook his head. "No trace. Which means they know what they're doing." He busied his hands by flattening a sheet beneath my arm. "Given your history, it could be anyone."

"How'd they find me?"

Another shake before he crossed his legs. "Good question. I'm working on it. But *Gone Fiction* is not all they blew up."

My eyes moved but not my head.

"They razed your island to the ground."

We sat in the silence. He knew I wanted more, so he patted my leg. "Another time." He stood when Summer walked in carrying a steaming plate. Before he left, he set a pen and a pad of paper on the bed next to me. "Rest up."

# CHAPTER 8

Casey had come a long way from the steam-filled shower in which her captors had left her to die in Miami, little more than discarded refuse. Casey's recovery had been rough. She'd walked out of hell only to reenter by another door. Detox nearly killed her, as did the memories and the PTSD.

Of all the girls, her story hurt the most. Abandoned from birth, abused by almost everyone, forgotten, told she was nothing and always would be, she was sold into trafficking by foster parents before puberty. While she still believed the tooth fairy was real. In the years that followed, she routinely checked her mind out of her body for months on end so she didn't have to live in it while so many did what they wanted to her.

Her recovery had been slow, but she had taken to Freetown, and especially Angel. And me. By her own admission, I was the first man in her life who did not want something from her. Who told her she was of great value. And worth rescue. Words that were, to her, unbelievable. Given that, I said them often.

Recovering in my room, I woke one morning to find her staring at me. She was rubbing her hands together. Saying nothing.

I sat up, which hurt. "You okay?"

Her lip trembled. She waved her hand across me. Her style of communicating was terse because all the small talk had been beaten out of her. "Am I responsible for this?"

I shook my head. "No."

"How do you know?"

"Bad men did this. Not you. You've got nothing to do with it."

She didn't look convinced. A minute passed. When she tapped her chest, I didn't know she was changing the subject. She didn't look at me when she asked, "What do I do with the pain?"

I rubbed my eyes and tried to focus. Waiting. We were now several feet beneath the surface. Down where our ears were starting to pop.

Unable to speak, she extended her index finger and pointed at her heart.

Finally, I understood. I pointed at my books on the shelf. Books that, by now, she'd read several times. "I wrote mine down."

She stared at them. "You teach me how?"

The next morning we met for coffee. "I have a few simple rules. Maybe they'll work for you. First, books don't write themselves. Every day we show up to a white page. Which means you've got to put in the time. If your butt is not in the seat, then you're probably more enamored with being called a writer than actually being one. There's a difference. Second, I sweat my books more than write them, and I'm a better rewriter than writer. So just get it on paper. Sounds gross but just vomit it out. You can edit later. But you can't edit what's not there. Third, honesty trumps intelligence. So tell the truth and don't use words you don't understand. Readers can spot a fake a mile away."

She laughed. "Don't worry."

"Last, you are the only you on planet earth. Out of seven billion people, you're the only one who sounds like Casey. No one else has your voice. So find it and use it."

"What if no one likes that voice?"

"We as people can't stand a counterfeit. But we're pretty willing to sit up and listen when someone speaks the truth no matter the cost. So just do that."

She squinted one eye. "No matter?"

"John Milton wrote an essay called *Areopagitica*. Our founding fathers used it to argue the basis for our First Amendment rights. In there, he says something like: 'Let truth and falsehood grapple. On a field of open encounter, who ever knew truth put to the worse?'"

She considered this and nodded.

I slid a Mac laptop across the table. "And save everything. All the time. Save it everywhere. On the cloud. Hard drive. Create several email addresses and email your work to yourself every time you get up and walk away. Don't ever have just one copy of anything. This will save you some aggravation, time, and hair."

"Hair?"

"Yeah. You won't be—" I made a tugging gesture toward the top of my head.

She laughed. "Got it."

# CHAPTER 9

T he next few weeks were difficult for me. The pain I could overcome, but having someone do everything for me was not something I adjusted to easily. When Angel called Summer after the explosion, she'd left on the next flight. Never looked back. She exchanged standing in the shower of the pixie dust residue of her dreams for a dirty washcloth, bloody linens, second-degree burns, and a man with limited ability to get what he thought out his mouth.

An unfair trade.

But every time I drifted off, she was there. And every time I woke, she had not moved.

Gunner, too, was never far. And often it was his sniffing muzzle that woke me, checking to see if I was still alive. *Come on, old man, let's get out of here.* To entertain him, we began playing a game. I'd hold an article of clothing that belonged to someone—say Ellie, Angel, Summer, Bones, or Casey—and then say, "Find Angel," or "Find Ellie." He caught on pretty quick. He'd exit the room and scour Freetown until he found them. When he did, he'd bark, or tug gently on their clothing, or run around them in circles until he got their attention and proved he wanted something. Often he would herd them to my room like a sheepdog, where they would laugh and ask, "What do you want now?" Or "May I help you, Your Highness?" They thought it was just me being lazy, which I was, but it was also strategic— and they knew that too. So they played along.

Bones, in his wisdom, had convinced Ellie to return to boarding school with the caveat that he'd fly her home to Freetown every Thursday evening after class and return her every Monday morning in time for the first bell. Given this, we spent the weekends walking the trails around Freetown, trying to get my strength back. She had ten thousand questions, and given that she was growing into the spitting image of her mother, I did my best to answer them as slowly as possible.

While my physical body was healing, I still had one problem, and both Bones and Clay could read it on my face. If they, whoever they were, could get to me at my island, they could get to me at Freetown. Despite being tucked high in the Colorado mountains and guarded by a perimeter of well-trained men, my presence here was a danger to everyone. They knew it, and they knew I knew it, and they knew that I knew that they knew. Which didn't make things any easier, but at least there were no secrets. At least not about that.

Late one night, Ellie walked in. She sat on the end of my bed and crossed her legs. "Dad?"

I smiled. "Yes."

"Will you teach me how to be tough like you?"

"You're assuming I'm tough."

She laughed but fumbled with her hands, which suggested she was serious. "I've seen what you can do. You're . . . different from other dads."

I sat up, which required more energy than I had. "What's bothering you?"

She looked away. "I was just wondering . . ."

Despite the wounds, the pain, and the drugs, I had a moment of surprising clarity. Fourteen-year-old Ellie was sitting on the end of my bed because she was staring at a big world and afraid of what she saw. I tried to stand, wobbled, and she caught me.

"Whoa." She laughed.

"Told you I wasn't too tough."

She put my arm over her shoulder and wrapped one arm around my waist. She had grown taller. I smelled her hair.

I smelled Marie.

I said, "You feel like going for a walk?"

We walked down the stairs to the basement. I punched in my security code to the vault door, which swung open. She looked curious so I shut it and brought her closer. "When your mom and I were young, she got lost one night in a boat. Washed out into the ocean. I found her, pulled her back to shore. When she asked me why, I said the three words that came to mind. So if you ever need to get into someplace that I locked and there's a keypad, chances are good the code is 'Love shows up.'" She smiled and let out the breath she'd been holding since she walked into my room. I motioned to the keypad, she punched in the letters, and the door swung open to the basement where I hid my secrets.

I pointed at the keypad. "Just between us?"

She nodded and made a motion with her hand in front of her mouth like she was turning a lock held in her teeth and then throwing away a key.

The lights clicked on and she walked in while Gunner and I followed. Weaponry covered three walls. *Armory* might be a better word than basement.

Her eyes were wide as Oreos. "You know how to use all this?"

"They're just tools."

"This looks like something out of a movie. What is all this?"

I waved my hand across one wall. "Those are pistols. Glocks. Sig Sauer. CZ. Wilson. Les Baer. STI. A few others."

She looked at me suspiciously. "Does Uncle Bones know about this place?"

I laughed, walked to another door, pushed it open, and clicked on the light, revealing several thousand bottles of wine.

"How's he get down here?"

"That tunnel connects to his house." Another wave of my hand. "Those are rifles. Carbines. Shotguns."

"Why are they different?"

"Some are for long range. Some are for close quarters." I pointed to another door. "That room is just for ammunition."

She walked to a wall of pistols and pointed. "Can I touch one?"

We were about to step into some deeper water. I limped to the wall, pulled down the Glock 19, dropped the magazine, cycled the slide, and locked it back, exposing the visual fact that the chamber was empty and the pistol unloaded. I held it between us. "There's a thing happening in this second that I really need you to understand. I am putting something in your hand that, left alone, is harmless. But the moment you put your hand on it, it becomes something that breathes fire and deals both life and death. We're not playing with crayons, and this is not a video game."

She nodded. "I know."

I placed it in her hand where she held it like a seashell. After a minute, she gave it back. Another point. "What's that one?"

"Uncle Bones's favorite." I lifted it off the wall and handed it to her. "A Sig 220."

"It's heavier."

"Yes. It is."

Another seashell flat across her palm. She handed it back. "What's all that?"

"I call this my piddle table. It's the stuff I use to clean all this. Tools mostly."

"Why?"

"Why what?"

"Why do you call it that?"

A chuckle. "'Cause I come down here and piddle."

"Can I piddle with you sometime?"

This was not the question on her mind. I walked down the hallway to a door, pushed it open, and clicked on another light. She squinted down the tunnel. "What is that?"

"It's where I shoot all that stuff."

"Where do the bullets go?"

I laughed. "Into the mountain." I made a shape with my hands. "At the end is something like a mailbox. Stuff goes in but doesn't come out."

"How long is it?"

"One hundred meters from that bench."

"Is it loud?"

I pointed at the walls. "They're designed to bounce the sound away from you. Plus"—I held up a set of earmuffs—"these help."

She put them on, looking like an airport worker directing planes. "How do you breathe?"

A perceptive question. "This tunnel was once part of a silver mine, meaning it's ventilated." I pointed to a large air handler above us. "That cleans the air."

She turned in a circle. Taking it all in. The unconscious turn showed the influence of Summer rubbing off on Ellie. "You come down here often?"

I considered this. Truth was, I did more than I cared to admit. I nodded.

Her eyes suggested I'd not answered her first question. "Probably best if we don't start today." I raised my arm, exposing the IV port taped to my skin. "Too many drugs still swirling around in my blood, making me foggy. Let me sweat some out first. Okay?"

She had what she wanted. She smiled and helped me climb the stairs. "Dad?"

"Yes," I said, starting to sweat as I reached the fourth stair.

"I'd say you're pretty tough."

I sat on the stair. Catching my breath. I waved my hand across the basement below us. "Those things don't make somebody tough. They're just tools. If you have them, use them. If you have a spoon, use the spoon." I pointed at her heart. "Tough or not tough comes out of here."

Her next question spoke of a lifetime of not being told. "How do you know if you have it?"

"Time."

"Do I have it?"

I nodded. "You're one of the toughest kids I've ever met. Don't ever let anyone tell you otherwise."

"How long have you known?"

"The moment I first opened the door on the Whaler and found you hiding below." I pulled myself up on her arm. "And for the record, you get that from your mother."

She smiled wider and placed her shoulder beneath mine. "Dad?"

"Yes."

"Tell me about Mom."

# CHAPTER 10

Ellie propped me up in bed and made me some oolong tea—something she'd learned from Summer. I didn't mind the taste. Add enough honey and it's tolerable.

Then she climbed up in bed and sat cross-legged in front of me. Waiting. A rose on the verge of bloom. Absent the thorns.

"You mean you want me to tell you about her right now?"

"Dad—" She was using a tone of voice that told me I was about to get worked, but I'd like it anyway. "You tell stories read by millions around the world. I want the unedited story of how you met Mom."

It was a beautiful ask. And I hoped I could live up to her expectation.

"Are you comfortable?"

She nodded enthusiastically.

So I told her the beginning of the story of us.

I grew up around the water. Fishing. Swimming. Paddling my skiff. I might have been born on land, but water was home. I lived fifteen miles north of Jacksonville, Florida, on Fort George Island. Only four or five miles around, Fort George was once home to the Timucuan Indians, and it's covered in live oak and magnolia trees that create a natural canopy and always made me think of Medusa's hair. With the Intracoastal to the east and a world of creeks and tributaries to the west, I was surrounded by water and adventure. Not to mention shell mounds. From what I could tell, a large portion of the Indians' diet consisted of oysters, which meant the island was covered in shell mounds—a gold mine to a curious kid. Due to the distance from Jacksonville, and the fact that it wasn't all that easy to access, the island was sparsely populated. Mostly by retirees. Meaning I had the island to myself and more pretend friends than real.

Which made meeting your mom such a surprise.

We met at the curious age of nine. I was digging for whatever I could find in a mound on the northwest side of the island when I heard, "What'cha doing?" echo from above my head. I'd been digging this particular hole for the better part of two days, so my head was a foot or two below the surface of the mound. When I looked up, I saw a girl. Freckled nose peeling from the sun, cutoff jeans, bathing suit top, flip-flops, and neither one of us anywhere near puberty. Just two kids.

I looked around, wondering if she'd brought anyone else to my gold mine. "Just digging."

She wrinkled her nose. "Why?"

I reached in my pocket and pulled out an intact arrowhead, which I handed to her.

She turned it over in her hand and handed it back. "You found that in there?"

I nodded.

"You think there are more?"

I pointed to the pile of broken heads at her feet.

She said, "Can I dig with you?"

I was the solitary sort and didn't like giving up the location of my best find, but two diggers might be better than one, and she'd already found me. Plus, I'd have somebody to talk to. "You got a shovel?"

She shook her head.

"Well . . ." I stepped aside, making room in the hole, and handed her mine. "You can use mine."

We dug till dark, and she was a good digger. Strong. Didn't mind sweating. And unlike a lot of other girls I'd met, she didn't talk incessantly about nothing. She was curious like me and talked about stuff I liked. Like shells. Arrowheads. And what life must have been like for the Indians. She said her mom was a nun who had moved to the island to escape the shame of sin, which her birth had brought upon her.

I asked, "What do you mean?"

She shrugged. "Nuns don't marry. They're not supposed to have kids."

"Oh." That didn't make sense. "So how'd you get here?"

She shook her head. "She won't tell me."

"Are you a mistake?"

Another shrug. "Maybe. I don't know."

"My mom tells me I was a mistake caused by strawberries and champagne—whatever that means."

She considered this. "My mom doesn't like champagne. Says it itches her nose."

"Oh. How'd you end up here?"

"I walked."

"No. I mean, how'd you two end up on the island?"

"Not quite sure."

"Where do you live?"

"Parson's house. Mom helps plan the events at the retreat center. She's the director."

"Where were you born?"

"Italy."

"Italy?"

She nodded. "But I don't really remember it. We left when I was a baby."

I was no geography whiz and I couldn't quite place Italy on a map, but I knew she had to cross the Atlantic to get here. "That's a long way from Florida. What're you doing here?"

"Not sure."

While she loosened the dirt using the long-handled shovel, I lifted it out of the hole with the hand shovel. We made a pretty good team. "You got many friends?"

She shook her head.

"You want one?"

A nod. "Sure."

"Okay."

We dug all summer.

The rumor among the old-timers at the bait shop was that you could find huge shark and whale teeth if you looked hard enough. Especially after storms. Bordered by a river, the Intracoastal, and a spiderweb of tributaries, the island's location made it prime for teeth. They could wash up anywhere. And if they could wash up anywhere, that meant they had to be in the ground to begin with. Which meant we might stumble upon one at any time.

I routinely found teeth. That was nothing new. Had several jars full at home. But anything bigger than two inches was out of the norm, and I'd never found an intact megalodon tooth—a really big one about the size of your hand. I'd found pieces, but never a whole.

A couple weeks into our dig, Marie had learned how to handle the shovel so as not to crack or crush whatever she was digging into. It was a feel thing, and she'd developed the feel. One morning she sank the shovel into the base of our ever-enlarging hole and struck something that didn't want to move. The sound caught my ear so we knelt, began digging gently, and next thing I knew she pulled out this intact tooth some five inches across. It was perfect. And it was ginormous.

We stared in dumbstruck disbelief as she held it in her hand like a fine crystal bowl. Afraid to move. Afraid to touch it for fear of breaking it. Then we started dancing around the hole like Peter Pan pretending to be an Indian and singing, "What Makes the Red Man Red?"

We couldn't believe our luck.

Out of breath, and delirious from our good fortune, we climbed out of the hole and sat on the riverbank. Just smiling. Talking about how much we thought it was worth. She asked me, "You really think it's worth something?"

"Oh yeah, the ads in the back of my comic books advertise those things at ten thousand dollars each." I nodded, trying to act like I knew what I was talking about. "I'll bet that one'll go for twenty or twenty-five.

Easy. We could take out an ad in *Thor* or *Superman* and probably get more than that."

She stared at it a long time, holding it in both hands. Finally, she held it in the space between us. An offering. "Sell it for us and let's take the money and run away. Together."

It was the first time I had any idea of the size of the hole inside Marie. And when I heard her say it, the depth of the pain in her voice convinced my nine-year-old mind that I'd spend the rest of my life and all my money trying to make it go away.

Before summer's end, we found six more. Together. And each time we danced and sang like a couple of idiots. But we didn't care. We were just a couple of kids, digging into possibility and out of pain.

If that summer taught me anything, it was this: girls need their father. Period. And I couldn't really tell you why other than it's the father who tells them who they are. Until he does, they're just floating in the earth like that tooth. Buried in some trash mound. Waiting to be discovered by somebody with a shovel who won't crack it or crush it.

Last day of summer, the sun falling over our shoulders, we leaned on our shovels and stood in silence. Neither wanting to talk. Finally, I broke the silence. "We can dig on weekends and maybe after school some."

"Yeah."

More silence. "You been to the store yet?"

"Went last night. Pencils and notebooks and stuff."

I shrugged. "We're going tonight. Maybe."

She stared at her shovel a long time. And at the bottom of our hole. "Where do you think this goes?"

I shook my head. "Don't know."

She talked without looking at me. "I have this globe in my room. Opposite us is China." She pointed matter-of-factly. "We'd end up in China."

I'd never given it much thought. "Never been there."

She tilted her head. "Maybe Australia."

I considered this possibility. "I'd like that."

A tear broke loose from the corner of her eye and trailed down the side of her nose. "Me too."

I held out my hand. "Can I show you something?"

She took it. "Sure."

A couple of weeks ago, I'd found something that I'd been keeping a secret. I didn't know who owned it, which meant the minute we stepped foot on it we were trespassing. And because I didn't want to get shot, I'd been snooping around by myself. But I really wanted to show it to Marie.

We rode our bikes to the north end of the island and ditched them in the palmettos where the trees grew thick and tall and the Spanish moss draped six feet down. To me, the northern end was a no-man's land. I'd always thought of it as the "dark" end of the island, and I didn't venture up here much. Virgin timber, thick undergrowth, never developed, it had been left as Florida had been created and much like the Indians last left it. Or so I thought.

We wound our way through the undergrowth and vines and then popped out onto the bank that overlooked a small creek connecting the Fort George River with one of its tributaries. The creek was maybe thirty feet across, the bottom was hard-pack sand, and at low tide you could cross in ankle-deep water.

One of the amazing things about this area is that the land melts into the marsh and vice versa. It's often difficult to determine where the land ends and the marsh begins. The two bleed together. Seamlessly. This means it's tough to tell one piece of land apart from another, unless you've been there. It can all look the same.

Marie's eyes widened. "I didn't know this was up here."

I took her hand. "Me either." And led her across the creek.

We climbed the bank on the other side into a world unlike any I'd ever seen. Marie's reaction suggested the same. The island was smaller than Fort George. Some of the oaks were as big around as the hood of a car, and the magnolia trees climbed fifty feet or better. Spanish moss hung from spidery oak limbs and fell like hair some six feet to the earth. There was little undergrowth because the canopy was so high. This meant you could see a long way through the trees and there was little to trip over. Few to no weeds. It was also cooler and slightly darker. But not eerie. The light was softer.

We had walked maybe a hundred yards into the heart of the island when Marie tugged on my shirt. "Have you ever been here?"

"Couple weeks ago."

She stared upward. "It's like a . . . sanctuary."

*Sanctuary* was a good word. I tugged on her hand again. "Just wait."

We wound through shell mounds, muscadine vines, acres of ferns, and what can only be described as a grove of unkempt citrus trees—overgrown, sagging with fruit, and planted in neat rows. We exited the grove into neatly planted rows of live oaks that formed a road of sorts. The tops of the oaks had overgrown the road and the limbs on the right had intertwined with those on the left, like fingers of opposite hands. The road wound through the island a quarter mile and emptied onto the highest section, where we found the Tabby remains of several old buildings. *Tabby* means small crushed shells and lime used to produce a concrete-like building material a couple hundred years ago. And as a testimony to its durability to withstand hurricanes, the walls were still standing—though the roofs had long since rotted or blown away.

Marie was silent. She let go of my hand and tiptoed through the remains, afraid of disturbing the memories. The Tabby had been bleached by the sun and worn smooth by both human touch and weather. The ten buildings had been built in a cluster, which suggested they were living quarters for someone maybe two hundred years ago. Set across a small yard and situated beneath ginormous oaks were the remains of a larger rectangular building. The walls were thicker, taller, and inside lay the remains of what looked like old hand-hewn benches made from cypress or cedar—both of which don't rot and are impervious to bugs.

Marie turned in a circle. "What is this?"

"I think it's a church."

"Who built it?"

I pointed to the remains just across the yard. "I guess whoever lived there."

"How old is it?"

I led her to one of the remaining exterior walls and allowed her eyes to adjust. When they did, her jaw dropped. Carved into the wall were names and dates. The dates started in the 1700s and continued until the mid-1900s.

For a long time, we stood silently. Staring. Unwilling or afraid to disturb the peace we found there. When the sun went down, leaving us in the dusk of the afternoon, and the cool and breeze replaced the heat, I sat on one of the benches and ran my hand along the smooth wood, darkened from generations of hand oil and sweat. And maybe tears.

When Marie spoke, she was staring where the ceiling once hung, now replaced by cloud and star and Spanish moss. "I've never been anywhere like this."

"Me either."

She sat alongside me, shoulder to shoulder and thigh to thigh, and whispered, "What do you feel?"

I spoke the word that came closest to the feeling. "Safe."

She nodded, staring at the walls around us. Rising up like whitewashed tombstones standing in defiance against the years and waves that threatened to wipe them off the face of the planet. Somehow, despite Septembers in Florida and the hurricanes that raked the shoreline, this place was still standing.

As the shadows fell and a mourning dove cooed somewhere above us, answered by an old owl farther off, we walked to the walls and stood in unmoving silence. Marie ran her finger through the grooves of the names, retracing the letters. A single phrase had been etched above the names: "Even the rocks cry out." Finally, she placed her palm flat against the Tabby, as if she were listening to the story it would tell her.

Looking back, I felt a sacred holiness I'd never known. A quiet, unspoken reverence. This wasn't just an island, not some unforgotten map dot. It was a stake driven into the surface of the earth. A declaration. It was one voice that became two that became ten thousand, and they were shouting at the top of their lungs. To this world. And every other. A one-word chorus.

As the last whisper of daylight crept down the wall, Marie asked me, "If these walls could talk, what do you think they'd say?"

I stared at the names. The benches. The worn floor. Just before I spoke, the breeze filtered through the moss above me, which waved like a hundred banners in unison. I whispered, "Freedom."

We walked off the island in silence. Like two people leaving a grave-yard. Standing in the creek, the tide having raised the water level to mid-shin, I turned and spoke boldly for a nine-year-old kid. I don't know how I knew it then, but I did. Something in me knew. "I'm going to buy this island one day."

Marie stood next to me. Staring up. Stars had poked through a silver heaven and shone down on us.

I continued, "That way if one of us ever feels unsafe, we can come here."

She stood alongside me. Two kids washed clean by the river in which they stood. She hung her arm on my shoulder. Steadying as much as con-necting. "I'd like that."

We never told anyone about our island. Because that's what it was. It was ours.

By the time I finished, Ellie was curled up next to me, her right arm across my chest. "You should write that story."

I shook my head. "No. I think maybe I'll just keep that one between us."

She liked that. "Dad?" She also liked using that word. Like she was trying to make up for all the time she hadn't said it. Which was perfectly fine with me.

"Yes?"

"Thanks."

# CHAPTER 11

Later that week I gave Ellie her first lesson. We started with the safety talk. "One, we always treat these things as if they're loaded, even when they aren't. Two, we never point it at anything we aren't willing to destroy. Three, we never touch the trigger until we're on target and ready to fire. And four, make sure of your target and backstop."

She had followed me until then. "What's that mean?"

I held up a .45 ACP cartridge and placed my fingertip on the bullet protruding from the casing. "When this comes out that barrel, it's going to hit something. Hopefully, your target. It's then going to travel through that and into something else. And possibly something else. Think about those something elses. Life isn't a video game, and you have to consider collateral damage if you touch this thing off."

She nodded knowingly.

Earmuffs on, I taught her how to hold, load, and—equally important—unload a handgun. Then we moved on to aiming, sight picture, trigger control, and trigger reset. She learned quickly, and once she realized the fire-breathing part went away from her, she settled a bit.

After an hour, we turned out the lights and began walking out of the basement. Noticing a light at the end of a long tunnel, she said, "What's that?"

"Bones's darkroom."

"His what?"

From the first day I met him, Bones had carried a camera. But don't think "sideline photographer at the football game with the latest and greatest." In the age of the iPhone when everyone was an instant photographer, Bones was a dinosaur. Luddite. Ansel Adams in a Luke Skywalker world. Bones had a penchant for black-and-white, color slides, and medium format, which meant he couldn't care less about digital photography. More importantly, he developed his own pictures. Always had. A tedious and time-intensive hobby. When I asked him why he didn't transition into the modern era and shoot digital, telling him it was much easier and much less work, he looked at me like I'd lost my mind.

Over the years, I'd learned he was actually quite an artist, and film was just the canvas on which he painted. I also learned that whatever he did in his darkroom was really just therapy. If I wrote my way out of my own pain, then Bones developed his way out. The pictures he captured with his old-school, clunky cameras replaced some of the painful pictures that life had imprinted on the backs of his eyelids. The ones he had a tough time forgetting. And even though I'd known him half my life, I was pretty sure he'd never shared with me the deepest and most painful. Whatever the case, his art produced some of the more beautiful pictures I'd ever seen.

I'm no judge of the value of a picture, but if Bones had a talent in taking pictures, maybe even an eye, it was in his ability to capture moments that housed emotion. His knack for doing so was uncanny.

I knocked on the door. Bones swung it open, and Ellie's jaw dropped slightly. Dean Martin sang quietly in the background and the smell of chemicals hung in the air. The room was actually several rooms. A smaller one off to the right served as Bones's actual darkroom where he developed his pictures. Evidently, he'd just exited there, as several black-and-white prints hung drying from a line strung across the room.

The room in which we stood could best be described as a gallery. Thousands of pictures of all sizes and colors covered almost every square inch of every wall. Looking at every one would take hours. Maybe days. In the middle of the room stood a long, thin wall made of two sheets of glass, maybe an inch apart, that ran floor-to-ceiling and divided the room. Between the sheets, suspended in straight, vertical rows, hung thousands of slides. Hand-picked by Bones. A robotic arm, attached to a projector, moved at random up and down the rows, shining a light through each slide and projecting the image on a white wall at the far end, creating a continual slideshow.

Isolated in the center of the room stood one worn leather chair and ottoman. When Bones wasn't developing, he'd select something from his wine cellar, sit in his chair, and sip while the memories returned.

Bones beckoned and Ellie walked into the room. Eyes wide. "Uncle B, what is this?"

Bones eyed a lifetime's worth of pictures and shrugged. His honesty was disarming. "I'm never quite sure how to answer that."

Ellie studied the walls and put the pieces together. She pointed up, toward Freetown above us. "You mean, all those pictures running up and down Main Street. Hanging in the hospital. Displayed on every wall. Not to mention the show at the Planetarium. You took all those?"

Bones considered this and nodded. Ellie continued studying the wall. After a few minutes, she jumped back and pointed as if she'd found a golden nugget. "Hey, there's me!" Another second produced another laugh and more excited pointing. "And here I am with you!"

I'd always thought Bones's slides showcased his best work. I can't qualify this for you or tell you why other than Bones had always told me that slides were very difficult to "hit." When I asked him what this meant, he said, "They're finicky." Over time, I learned that in order for a slide to produce a really great image, the focus had to be crystal and the exposure had to be perfect or the image would be either fuzzy or overexposed. Meaning, out of several hundred slides, he might get only one wall-worthy image. A good slide was a needle-in-the-haystack thing.

After a few minutes, Ellie's attention turned to the slideshow being cast on the wall. Mesmerized, she moved to the chair, sat on the edge of the ottoman, and stared for several minutes as the robotic arm silently moved the light source through dozens of slides. Bones watched Ellie staring at the wall and a smile spread across his face. Finally, she stood up and sank her hands in her jeans. "It's . . . amazing. Unlike anything I've ever . . ."

Bones bowed slightly.

She turned in a circle. "And here I was the whole time thinking you were just a crotchety old priest."

He laughed and studied his life's work. Then he glanced at me. "I also priest."

I loved it when he used the word as a verb.

# CHAPTER 12

E llie had become comfortable walking into my room, sitting on my bed, and waiting for me to resume my story. Being around her was like standing next to a river. So much life held within its banks.

These times had become precious to me, and I found myself listening and waiting for the creak of the door. And when I heard it, and she sprang into my room and catapulted herself onto my bed, eyes and ears expectant and heart longing, I stretched out the story.

When I turned eleven, I found myself caught in that weird no-man's-land of innocence mixed with the beginnings of hormones. Which meant I was both stupid and invincible. Not a good combination. House rules during the summer allowed that I could fish all night provided no boats were involved. Period. Feet on the bank at all times. That wasn't open for discussion.

One night a full moon appeared through my window so I slipped out and started walking the bank. A mile from my house strange lights shone through the trees accompanied by a strange commotion. Loud talking. Stuff breaking. Somebody wasn't happy. All were noises not often heard around there.

I crept toward the sound and found a dilapidated river boat tied up to a forgotten dock attached to a deserted house. Or it had been deserted. The boat, *Black-Jack,* was an old troller. Forty-plus feet. And while she'd seen better days, she was very much in service.

Because black-hearted Jack and his strange boat were invading my home turf, I felt emboldened. Which again supports my stupid theory. I hopped onto the bow and spied through the galley glass where a fat, shirtless, bearded man the size of a bear was roughing up two girls who, judging by the looks on their faces, did not want to be on his boat. The brunette had a black eye mostly swollen shut, and the sandy blonde had blood dripping out the corner of her mouth and nose. They were tied back-to-back, dressed only in their underwear, and I recognized them—they waited tables at a place called the Seagull Saloon. A local burger joint along the docks in town.

The old man had run out of booze and was turning the place inside out looking for a bottle. Not finding one, he was blaming them. He'd slap one, cuss the other, then smack the second and cuss the first.

Stumbling, he backhanded the blonde, demanding to know where she hid it. Her voice shook, and while I couldn't hear what she said, I could tell she didn't have it.

Not convinced, he moved to the brunette, who responded no better.

Enraged, Jack put his fist through the window and split several of his knuckles. Wrapping his hand in what was once his T-shirt, Jack began tearing up the rest of the boat. While he rummaged below, the girls fought their ropes. But that was useless because evidently Jack knew a thing or two about knots, which made me wonder if he worked on a boat other than this one. With Jack occupied in the engine room, and without really thinking about my next move, I climbed down into the galley and—to their wide-eyed surprise—cut the ropes with my two-bladed Barlow. Once free, they grabbed their clothes and we bolted down the dock followed by Jack's spit-filled tirade. When our feet hit dry land, those two girls took off as if shot out of a cannon. They never looked back.

That's when I heard the third girl scream.

On the boat.

It had never occurred to me that he might have someone else tied up in there. The next scream convinced me he did.

Returning through the darkness toward the water's edge, I found Jack in a bad way. And from the sound of the screaming, he was taking it out on the girl I'd not seen. I crept back onto the boat, climbed down into the galley, and peered below, where I found not one but two more girls—whom I did not recognize—less dressed and in a worse situation than the first two. Descending the stairs with my Barlow, I was about to cut their ropes when Jack wrapped his bear paw around my esophagus and stopped all airflow to both my lungs and brain.

Jack lifted me off my feet and stared into my eyes. His breath made me nauseous and would gag a maggot. I nearly threw up. He breathed on me, laughed, shook me hard enough to sprain every muscle attaching my head to my shoulders, and then decided to turn my face into a punching bag—it only took one blow to turn out my lights.

For which I was thankful.

I woke the next morning in my bed. My face was swollen and almost every muscle and joint in my body felt as if it had been hit by a truck. I limped to the kitchen, where my suspicious mom asked what happened. Having all falsehood forever beat out of me by Giant Jack, I told her the truth, to which she responded with pancakes, excusal from my chores for a day, and a rather excited phone call to the sheriff, who appeared thirty minutes later with a yellow pad of questions.

My head was splitting, but I did my best to answer his questions. I ran into trouble trying to answer his last two. For these, I had no response: How did I get away from Jack, and how did I get home?

"I have no idea."

I also had no idea what had happened to my Barlow, and given that it was my only pocketknife, I was in a bad way.

Two days later, I rode out our driveway on my bike and pedaled to town, where I found the Seagull Saloon in the post-afternoon rush. A couple of the dishwashers were sharing smokes out the back door, but the brunette and sandy blonde were nowhere to be found. I walked around front, took a seat at a booth, and kept staring over my shoulder for Jack when a handsome, chiseled man wearing a hat, sunglasses, and long-sleeve shirt appeared on the bench across from me. Given the shadow and stubble, it was difficult to make out the face. But unlike Jack, he did not scare me. For a few seconds, he sat with his hands folded, studying me.

When he spoke his voice was calm. Kind even. "How's the face?"

I rubbed my chin and something told me less was more until I figured out just whose side this dude was on. "Okay."

"Your head ache?"

"A bit."

"Jack's a big man. I can't decide if you're brave or stupid."

My voice cracked when I spoke. "I felt brave until he started choking me, and then I felt stupid."

The man laughed and then, without explanation, he slid my two-bladed Barlow across the table and set it in front of me.

I wasn't sure if I should touch it.

He leaned against the seat behind him. "You dropped that."

My eyes lit as that mystery had been solved. "Guess so."

"Why'd you go back?"

I wasn't sure I wanted to engage this joker in any more conversation than necessary. I didn't know what he knew, and I didn't want to let on to what I knew. "Sir?"

"Onto the boat. A second time."

"You saw that?"

A single nod.

I stared at my knife. "Um . . ."

He gestured. "Go ahead. It's yours."

As I picked it up, he whispered, almost to himself, "So just why did you venture back into a hole that dark when you'd only just escaped?"

"But," I stammered, "they were screaming."

He nodded. "Yes, they were."

I tried to turn the focus off of me. "What were you doing there?"

He considered my question and his answer. "Watching Jack." He pointed at me. "You like to run?"

"I'm sorry?"

"All the medals hanging in your room . . . you must be fast."

I guess that solved the next mystery but surfaced another one: How did he know where I lived? My head bobbed on a swivel, but I gathered control of it long enough to nod. "Faster than some."

"You like to run?"

I nodded.

"How about the training? You like all that running in circles?"

"Don't mind it." I squirmed in my seat. "Sir, can I ask you something?"

"Sure."

I looked over one shoulder and then whispered, "Where is Jack?"

"Jail."

"What will happen to him?"

"Prison."

"For how long?"

He considered this and pursed his lips. "Long time."

I let out the breath I'd been holding since Jack grabbed my throat.

"Sir, can I ask you something else?"

A nod.

"Am I in trouble?"

He chuckled and shook his head once. "No."

"Are you a police officer or something?"

"Or something."

"Well . . . can I ask you something else?"

"You already did that."

He was right, I had. "Well, can I ask you another something else?"

His laughter exited his stomach in an easy exhale. Like a man who had earned it. He gestured with his hand, suggesting I continue.

"Why were you there?"

Without speaking, he reached in his pocket, set what looked like a coin down on the table, and slid it in front of me. Then, with the movements of a cat, he stood, put his hand on my shoulder, and said, "Keep running, kid. It probably saved your life." After a pause, he said, "And maybe the lives of those girls."

As he walked away, my voice stopped him. "Sir, are they okay?"

As the question left my mouth, a beautiful waitress with sandy-blond hair walked out of the kitchen carrying a glass of ice water. She wove through the tables, set the water on mine, and asked, "Ready to order?" Her bottom lip was slightly puffy and she'd attempted to cover a single scratch beneath her eye, but the sweat from working had washed off the makeup.

And to my surprise, she did not recognize me.

I didn't see the man again until the following spring. Track season. He appeared at three of my meets. He'd stand off to the side, watch me run, and then disappear just as quietly. And while he never said a word, he stood there long enough and allowed me to see him—to know he'd been there—which said plenty.

As for the coin, it was either platinum or pewter. Something silvery. But not fancy. Worn from what I could only guess were years in his pocket. Engraved. Six words on one side. Five on the other. Looked like he had it made a long time ago to remind him of something he didn't want to forget. That day at lunch I had placed it in my palm and read it. Again that night. And every day for months and years thereafter. It was a puzzle. A riddle even. It became as constant in my pocket as my Barlow. Many a night I sat awake staring at the engraving, wondering what on earth it meant. And why he gave it to me. A couple of times I even tossed it in my trash can only to dig it out hours later. Eleven simple, universe-shattering, paradigm-wrecking words that, when strung together, made about as much sense to me as the man who gave it to me.

Who was he? Where'd he come from? Why was he there? And what was his interest in me? I had no answers for any of these questions.

Ellie didn't like ending on a cliffhanger. She raised an eyebrow. "You still have it?"

I slid it from my pocket and laid it in her palm.

She ran her fingers across the worn edges. "This is it?" Then, looking up at me, she said with disbelief, "Really?"

A nod.

"You've carried this with you?"

"Everywhere."

"Even while you were looking for Mom?"

"Especially while."

# CHAPTER 13

Weeks passed. As I busied myself in telling my story, or better yet our story, to Ellie, Casey buried herself in the telling of her own story. The unpacking. She cried. She screamed. She vomited her life both in the toilet and on the page. Days with no sleep. Weeks without rest that bled one into another. Throughout her life of inconsistency, one thing had remained consistent. Casey had kept an electronic journal. A cloud record of her life. Wherever she went, it went. Its presence known only to her. Because of this, the telling of her story was quick, honest, and raw.

And true.

Finally, she brought it to me. Afraid at first. "I was wondering . . ." I waited. "If you wouldn't mind . . ." She handed me a hundred pages. "It's pretty rough. I just . . ."

A beautiful offering.

From page one, she had me. Seldom, if ever, have I read a heart so open. So inside out. I wept, I laughed, I wanted to kill several people, and I wanted to lift her out of that sick world and place her anywhere but. I'd never read anything like it. The next morning I knocked on her door. The sound of clicking keys stopped. The hummingbird resting on the edge of the desk. I set the pages next to her and she bit her lip.

"You can be honest. Really. I can handle it." She faked a smile. "I've probably heard worse."

"I'd like your permission to send it to my publisher."

She sucked in a breath and pulled her knees to her chest. Tears immediately appeared in the corners of her eyes.

"What do you mean?"

"You should publish this."

"Nobody would ever buy this—"

I interrupted her. "We don't write books because they sell."

"Why then?"

I pointed at the printed pages of her electronic journal. "Because we can't not." This she understood.

"You think a publisher would actually . . ."

I nodded.

"But . . ."

I waited.

She stared at the pages and shook her head.

"What?" I asked.

She bit her lip again. "What if . . ."

"Casey, we're all afraid." I sat opposite her. "And fear is a liar."

"Even you?"

"Even me."

"What about terrified?"

"Terror is a liar too."

She was still hesitant. "There are people who do not want this story told."

"I know."

"What if they come for me?"

"It's a risk."

"Can you protect me?"

"I can."

"Will you?"

"I will."

Tears leaked from the corners of her eyes. Her lip was trembling again. "You promise?"

"With all that I have."

She slid the papers back across the desk to me while the hummingbird returned to the edge of the feeder—and gorged.

A contract quickly followed. Accompanied by a small advance.

My publisher sent galley copies to media outlets around the country. As Casey was unknown and her rescue not covered by the nightly news, most tossed it, thinking, *People don't want to hear this right now. It's . . . too painful. Too . . . real. She's just one girl.* The few who made inquiries never followed through. The book died before it had a chance to breathe.

While my publisher truly liked Casey and wished the environment were different, she gave me all the really good business reasons why this book would never sell and why they were now slating it for a limited release. "People just aren't ready to hear this. People read for entertainment, and this . . . is not all that entertaining. So we're pulling back the reins and going out with a little more discretion. Just enough to make Casey feel as though she's had a book released to the world. You and I both know I'm doing you a favor, and . . ."

I told her that if she ever wanted another book from me she'd put everything in her arsenal behind this book. And I meant everything. She thought I was kidding. I convinced her otherwise.

After a few weeks, she relented, they put their publicity engine behind the book, and then they released the first video interview with Casey. Casey had been trafficked for a lot of reasons, but one of those was that she was quite possibly one of the most beautiful people any of us had ever seen. And despite the horror she'd lived, she still was. Scars and all. What's more, her eyes did not speak anger or bitterness. They spoke something else. Something intangible that you can't buy or fake.

It was close to kindness but deeper than that.

Word of mouth picked up, the video went viral, and so did the momentum. A few weeks later, given the presale numbers, my publisher called to thank me. Casey's book was promising to be a big seller. She was elated. And while that excited her, it scared Casey.

# CHAPTER 14

Ellie and I climbed to the Eagle's Nest before daylight. Something she'd taken to doing lately. And something I loved doing with her. Her athleticism reminded me of Marie, and while I couldn't explain it, every step we took toward the clouds healed something in me.

At the top, I built a fire in the fireplace while she boiled water for hot chocolate. With fire and steam, we met on the couch. She sat alongside me, threw a blanket across our feet, lifted my arm up and over her shoulder, and then gently pressed her index finger into my chest like she was pressing Play on a cassette player. That was all she needed to say.

My senior year rolled around. My friendship with Marie had blossomed from kids searching for sharks' teeth, to dragging her out of the ocean miles from shore, to two kids in love and worried about what next year might bring. For the first time in either of our lives, we were staring down the uncertainty of life and unable to answer the questions that swirled beneath the surface. Given Marie's love of everything other than school, her college options were few and none overlapped with mine. Given track, mine were many. For three days, I kept the letter hidden. Colorado was a long way from Florida. And I wasn't sure how it had come to be because I'd not sought it out or applied. It simply appeared.

When she found it, she feigned a smile and shook her head. "An appointment."

I waved it off. Acting as if I'd dismissed it outright.

She waved the letter. "They don't hand these things out to everybody. You've got to be somebody to get one of these."

While I could run fast, my test scores revealed something I did not know—I possessed a particular problem-solving skill set that the U.S. government valued. Through some analytical engine, they surmised that I was able to make quick decisions based on limited information and not second-guess the decision. Based on this, I had been "invited" to join next year's cadets at the United States Air Force Academy in Colorado Springs.

Marie looked at me with admiration. I was looking at a map, counting the states between us.

She ran her fingers through my hair. "I'll come see you. You can take me flying."

"I don't . . ."

Marie didn't like being alone. I'd known this since we were kids. And she knew that I knew this, but she also didn't want to be the reason I declined the appointment. So she put on a show. "Bish—" Marie called me by my middle name. She was the only person to do so, and most often she used an abbreviated version. She said it again. "Bish, it's free. You don't pay a dime. Actually, they pay you while you're in school."

That was the loneliest bus ride of my life.

By Thanksgiving I was cold, tired, and ready to quit. Every minute of every day was filled from before sunup to after sundown. Every decision was dictated. What we ate. How we dressed. How we spoke, walked, and marched.

For cadets, calisthenics were a daily requirement. Whether we liked it or not. We marched, we ran, and we did push-ups, pull-ups, and sit-ups until most of the class either threw up or quit. Once a month, we ran this three-mile obstacle course. For time. Through the woods, over a mountain, up ropes, down ladders, through the mud or snow or ice, and every member of the company was required to cross the line under a certain time. If not, the entire company ran it again. And again. Until the requirement was met. To make matters worse, they started us at two-minute staggers and we were given orders not to assist one another. This was more time trial than group race. It was our job to get ourselves over that line, and they were measuring our individual ability to push ourselves, not our corporate ability to come together.

I understand the need for a fit and strong army. It's common sense. But some people's bodies just weren't made for speed. And even less for power. Few produced both. The first time we ran it, they had started me about fifth—and because it can take over an hour to complete, I passed everyone in front of me. So, having finished a few minutes before everyone else, and staring at a line of cadets strung out across the mountain, I could easily see some would never make it. Much less on time. I understand now that this was part of the weeding-out process and, in hindsight, maybe I should have let them weed out a few. It might have made life easier, but something in me just could not do that.

So, against orders, I turned around. Ran back. Which did not go unnoticed. I didn't make a very good cadet anyway, so if they wanted to get rid of me, I thought I'd help them out. Some of my fellow cadets appreciated it since they didn't want to run it again. Some were jealous and thought I was just brownnosing for notoriety and advancement.

Neither was the case.

Regardless, while my fellow cadets were granted a twelve-hour leave, I marched or cleaned or stood at attention in the freezing rain.

The week prior to Thanksgiving everyone in our company crossed the line with seven seconds to spare. The only company to do so. Even my critics were thankful. It meant a weekend pass—even for me. But while I excelled in the physical and mental aspects of being a cadet, I didn't really fit in and wasn't good at making friends. I wanted to, but more often than not, I found myself alone and left out. While friendships and packs naturally formed, I remained a group of one. One day two of my company commanders were talking and didn't know I was listening. One described me to the other as "Does not play well with others."

I never understood this. And I never understood the constant disconnect between what I experienced and what I intended. It was as if I was living in one world, and everyone else lived in another. Plexiglass in between.

Meanwhile, letters from home dwindled. What had started out as three or four a week became one a week and then one every three or four weeks. Four pages became half a page. For most of our lives, my presence—time with me—had filled the hole in her heart. Marie had grown up with no father. Had never known him. No name. No picture. No nothing. So she grew up with an insatiable need to be needed. To be reminded that she was beautiful and of value. When we met as kids, and throughout high school, I filled that. At least for a time. But during our freshman year at college, word trickled back that she was a regular at most every party. I knew her well enough to know she was hurting, and being around people having fun numbed her ache and medicated the loneliness. Because she'd never known it, physical presence and touch affirmed her at a deeper and louder level than letters from Colorado. So while I wrote every day, the infrequency of her responses told me that either she wasn't listening or she'd begun listening to someone else.

The only place I found solace, and the only place I knew freedom, was on the track. So when they cut me loose to train, I did. A lot. And because winters in Colorado Springs are both cold and white, I spent hours in our indoor track facility.

Most days, as I ran in circles, a fit, G.I. Joe–looking individual would sit up high in the cheap seats, eat a sandwich, and watch me run. What made the sight strange was his clothing. He wore white robes and a collar. An odd sight amid the uniformed world around me. And what was odder was that my training schedule was determined by other people, so my times on the track changed daily. There was nothing consistent about them, which they did on purpose to keep me from finding comfort in routine. And yet, every day, this robed man appeared high in the seats and watched me.

The first week in December I'd made up my mind that I was finished. The U.S. government could shove their appointment. I was beyond miserable. Over the last month, I'd secretly put in applications to run for schools closer to home. Closer to Marie. In her few letters of the last month, she'd even started talking about dating other people. *Just for a while. But nothing serious. Till things get back to normal.*

Two weeks before Christmas I was a fuming ticking bomb venting my anger through a workout we called "Flying 200s." Run two hundred meters, walk two hundred, run two hundred, and so on. And like every other day on the track, White Robes stared down on me while digging his hand into a bag of potato chips, a camera slung around his neck.

After the workout, I was lying on the turf, trying to breathe, when he appeared alongside me, his shadow stretching across me. It was the first time he'd ever walked out onto the track. Mind you, he had not said a word to me in over four months. By now, I had learned not to speak unless spoken to.

He dropped a potato chip in his mouth. "You like Nashville, Tennessee?"

"Sir?"

"Simple question."

I sat up. "Sir, I don't—"

He licked his fingers. "How about Montreat, North Carolina?"

"I've never—"

"Statesboro, Georgia?"

All three cities contained colleges with track programs where I'd applied in the last month. And I was the only person on planet earth who knew that. Or so I thought. "Sir, I—"

He stepped closer. Within two feet. Emptying the bag of chips into his mouth. "Tell me something"—he spoke around the crunch—"why'd you turn around? Go back?"

I shook my head. "Sir, I'm confu—"

"The obstacle course." He thumbed over his shoulder. "You went back. Why?"

"They weren't going to make it."

"Why do you care? Did you know them?"

"No, sir."

"Do you now?"

An awkward silence. "I've tried, but . . ."

"And?"

I shook my head. "Not really."

"Not really or no?"

I pulled on a sweatshirt. "No, sir."

"Why?"

"Well . . . we're busy during the day and there's not much time for social—"

"No, why'd you go back?"

I shrugged. For the first time I answered his questions with a question. "Does it matter, sir?"

His eyes studied the track where I'd been running and ended at the puddle of sweat next to me. "You disobeyed an order not to. The obstacle course is, by design, a singular achievement. It's why they stagger the start."

"And yet we suffer as a group if one person doesn't make the time."

"Orders are orders."

"It's a bad order."

"That attitude'll get you thrown out of here."

"Sir." I glanced around to make sure no one else was listening. I figured any conversation with a priest was protected. "Do I look like I care?"

He raised his eyebrows. "You know you're only the second one on record to do that."

"What? Disobey an order?"

"No." He laughed. "Go back. Return to help the stragglers cross the line."

"Maybe I was the only one who could, sir."

He nodded, "Maybe." Then he wiped the corners of his mouth with a napkin. "All three of those colleges are going to deny your application."

"But, sir—"

"Along with the other seven to which you applied."

In truth, I had applied to ten schools. I didn't know how he knew, but I did know he knew what I'd been doing in my spare time. I said nothing.

He waved his hand across the world of the academy in front of me. "You don't like our fine institution?"

"It's not that, sir."

He knelt. I could feel his breath on my face. "What is it then?"

"Don't really fit in, sir."

He nodded. "I'd agree with you."

Then his expression changed. More curious. Less interrogating. "But that raises the larger question."

Now I was confused. "Sir?"

"Have you ever?"

"Ever what?"

"Fit in?"

I was about ready to punch this joker in the teeth. I sized him up. My size. Maybe thicker, but I was younger and faster. "Not really."

"Least you're honest about it."

"Never been much of a liar."

He was about to leave when he turned back. "You haven't answered my question."

"Which one?"

His expression softened and his eyes focused on me. "Why'd you do it?"

"You mean turn back?"

He nodded.

"I don't think you'd understand."

"Try me."

It was no use. What would a priest know about that anyway? He was just some passive has-been with nothing better to do than hassle me. A pansy, passivist has-been who, because he couldn't hack his time here, spent his days now trying to redeem his pathetic life by convincing the disheartened to lay down their arms, choose the pathway to peace, and turn the other cheek. I shook my head. "Just something somebody told me a long time ago."

He chuckled. "You mean after you climbed back onto Jack's boat a second time?"

"Sir?" How would he know about that? I didn't put that in my application, and I'd never told anyone else—save Marie. I stood there with my mouth open.

He leaned closer. "David, maybe we're not trying to get rid of you." He patted my shoulder. "Maybe I'm just trying to figure out why you're really here . . . and who you want to be when you grow up."

"You said I was the second. Who was the first?"

He considered my question, then without another word, he walked off. Laughing.

Given that all ten schools denied my application just like he said they would, I returned for the spring semester having seen very little of Marie over Christmas break. She'd been aloof, tight-lipped, emotionally distant, and surprisingly fragile. I wouldn't say unkind because there were moments when she let down her wall and I saw glimpses of the old Marie, which bolstered my hope. But the person to whom I'd returned was guarded. Despite my every attempt, I could not reach her. Where we'd once talked about anything at any level, she'd spent two weeks keeping me at arm's length, making excuses as to why she couldn't see me. Even when we did see each other, she never dove beneath the surface. And yet for most of our lives that's where we lived. I knew something was wrong when I invited her to our island and she turned me down.

Nothing made sense.

If I'd left Colorado in a bad mood, I returned in one slightly worse only to find that my entire academic schedule had been changed. The classes I'd selected were nowhere to be found. I also discovered I had a new advisor. Some guy I'd never heard of in some building I'd never entered in a far corner of the campus to which I'd never ventured. The office was a dungeon of sorts—off by itself and connected to nothing. When I walked in, I found the white-robed eater of potato chips. Pieces of Nikon cameras were spread about the room. Black-and-white pictures on the wall. This time he was dressed in BDUs, his black boots were polished, and the look on his face a little less passive. More chiseled.

"You're late," he said without looking at me.

As I studied him, I realized his BDUs were not standard issue for the academy. The color and pattern were different. The one thing that did stick out were the markings on his collar, which said he was a colonel. Of that I was certain. And given the depth to which I'd disrespected him in our last conversation, I was also certain I was headed to either a military prison or a level of discipline I would not enjoy. I had a feeling my weeding out was about to start.

I had just run a mile and a half through the falling snow, which now produced a puddle on his office floor. "Sir, I want to apolo—"

He tossed me a key and pointed to a room next to his office. "Three minutes."

I held up the key and glanced at the room.

He continued. "Two fifty."

I thought I'd try a different tactic. I held up my class schedule. "Sir, I think I'm in the wrong . . . Um, I didn't—"

"Two forty-five."

While I was not an extraordinary cadet, I had learned when to shut up, and now was one of those moments. So I opened the door and found a locker with my name on it. Inside, I found several sets of clothes, fleece sweats, shoes, boots, and BDUs that matched his—all my size. Having not been told what to wear, I pulled on something similar to what he was wearing and returned to his office. He threw a small backpack at me and said, "Follow me."

"Sir, I'm going to be late for my next class."

He spoke over his shoulder. "I am your next class."

We ran out of his office, through the campus, and immediately up one of the mountains that served as the rather picturesque backdrop for the academy. He took the lead, picking his way up a narrow track with the agility of a cat and strength of a bear. I followed, amazed at his conditioning and his fitness. Never once did he stumble or misstep. When we reached the peak some forty-five minutes later, he wasn't breathing much harder than I.

Finding a suitable lookout, he sat and motioned for me to do likewise. More than a thousand feet above the academy, all of Colorado stretched out before us. Had I not been so confused, the view would have taken my breath away. He pointed to the trail we'd just run up. "You like my trail?"

"Yes, sir."

He glanced at me. "But you could have run it faster."

I could have. "Yes, sir."

"Why?"

"Why what, sir?"

"Why didn't you?"

I shrugged.

For the first time I got the impression that he was about to speak *with* me and not *at* me or *to* me. "Lesson number two: no shrugging. Indifference is the twin sister to resignation, and both will kill you or get you killed."

Evidently I'd missed lesson number one, but I kept that to myself.

He took my pack from my shoulders, emptied the contents onto the ground beneath a rock shelter, and told me to make a fire. Given the sub-freezing temperatures, I acted quickly. He pointed at the spread before us. "Thanks for hauling our lunch up here."

"Glad I could help."

He took a bite of his sandwich. "Tell me about Marie."

I swallowed hard. "Sir, can I ask you a question first?"

Before he answered, he pulled out a small bottle of wine and poured himself a few ounces. Then he sipped and nodded. "Sure."

"I'm pretty confused right now."

Another sip. "That's a statement. Not a question."

"Who are you?"

"My name is Ezekiel Walker. My friends call me Bones."

I was surprised that he had friends, but that, too, I kept to myself. As he spoke, I noticed that his cross dangled beneath his shirt. "How do you know so much about me?"

He weighed his head side to side and pointed at the fire. "Might need more wood for that conversation."

I scratched my head. "Sir, I—"

He held up a hand, and we watched in silence as a bald eagle floated effortlessly on the updrafts below us. A minute later, it disappeared over our heads. He continued, "I come up here sometimes. To make sense of what I can't make sense of."

"What doesn't make sense?"

He sipped, and when he spoke, he stared through me. "Love in an evil world." He poked the fire and added wood. He chewed on his words before he spoke them. "If you want to transfer, I'll help you get into any school of your choice. You're free to go."

"How can you do that?"

He smiled without looking at me. "I know people."

I pressed him. "You've got to do better than that."

"I was once a lot like you." He waved his hand across the academy spread below us. "Didn't fit in too well. But I was good at a few things so they kept me around. One summer break I was camping my way across the west. Just me, my truck, and a skinny dog I picked up on a beach in Louisiana. One night, about 1 a.m. at a truck stop in Montana, I was putting gas in the tank when a greasy fat man backhanded a scared kid, sent him rolling head over butt, and then threw him into the cab of an eighteen-wheeler. Something in me didn't like it. So I started listening. And with nothing better to do, I followed that truck. To a hotel in Idaho. When the driver disappeared into a back door of the hotel, I climbed into his cab, where I found the kid had been tied up and gagged. I carried him to my truck. He had his share of bruises, but it was the fear in his eyes I couldn't shake. I fed that kid a burger and watched from across the parking lot as the driver returned. Finding his cab empty, he raged and screamed—but he couldn't go anywhere because of the flashing blue lights surrounding him.

"A few hours later, that kid's mother hugged her son while the father cried so hard his shoulders shook. Eight days they'd been looking for him—from California to New York and Miami. Eight days of torment that had split their souls down the middle." He paused and sipped again. "That father is now one of the heads of our government. You've seen him on TV. And . . ." This time he turned, and when he looked at me, there was a tear in his eye. "That boy is a cadet in your class. You know him."

"I do?"

"You helped him cross the line. Something he could not have done without you. So when I tell you I know people," he said, chuckling, "I know people."

I swallowed. Even more confused now than before. "But how'd you get from here to—" I pointed at his clothing—"the robes."

He poured more wine and stared across Colorado and maybe into Canada. When he spoke, his voice was a whisper. "I also priest."

It was the first time I ever heard him use that word as a verb.

We sat in silence several minutes. The fire warming our backs. "Sir?"

"Yes."

"Who was the other one?"

"Other one?"

I pointed at the obstacle course winding through the hills below us. "To turn back."

"You're not going to let that go, are you?"

"In case you haven't noticed, I'm alone here."

"So what good is the answer to that question?"

I shrugged. "Might help me feel not so alone."

He sipped without looking at me. "You just shrugged again."

"You dragged me up this mountain and made me carry our lunch without much explanation, so until you start answering my questions and stop speaking in riddles, you can get used to my shrugging."

A long smile, and then he stared into what I could only guess was memory. "Me."

"I had a feeling you were going to say that."

"That surprise you?"

"Can I ask you another question?"

"You do that a lot."

"What? Ask questions?"

"Well, that too, but you normally start by asking if you can ask another question first."

"Well, can I?"

"Sure."

"Why'd you do it?"

"I've already answered that."

"When?"

"That was lesson number one."

"Must have missed that one."

"Nope, you didn't."

We were perched at about ten thousand feet where the air was a bit thin. "You mind telling me again?"

"No need to."

"Why's that?"

"You carry the answer in your pocket."

When he said that, a giant unseen hand lifted the veil that hung between us. The veil of mystery he had used to disguise himself. As it lifted, I saw the mysterious, riddle-speaking man who sat across from me at the Seagull Saloon. Then, to remove any doubt, he turned around and pointed to the granite wall behind us where someone—no doubt him years ago—had scratched into the stone the same eleven words that had echoed in my mind since he'd slid that coin across the table:

**Because the needs of the one outweigh those of the many.**

The sound in my mind as this realization settled in was akin to driving eighty on the interstate and throwing the gear shift into park. Stuff was exploding beneath the surface. The connection that Bones had been the man to rescue eleven-year-old me out of Jack's death grip, and then sit across from me at the Seagull Saloon, sparked more questions than it answered. Why? How? I had no answers for any of this.

I reached in my pocket and pulled out the hand-polished and well-worn coin. "You're him?"

He eyed it affectionately and nodded. Then he reached in my pack, pulled out his Nikon, and snapped a picture of me with that realization plastered across my face and all of Colorado behind me.

"But—" I protested.

He held up a hand. "In time." He eyed his watch and the airport in the distance. "Right now I've got to catch a plane." He threw snow on the fire and looked at me with a smile I would later come to love. "Race you down."

Following that run up the mountain, my experience at the academy changed. A lot. In almost every way. On the surface, I lived the life of a cadet. Responsible for everything my class did and studied. Beneath the surface, I was anything but a cadet. Like Bones, I learned to live a double life. When my class earned a forty-eight-hour pass, Bones would blind-fold me, drive me hours into the mountains, drop me with what I carried in my pockets, and say, "Find your way home. Without asking for help." Sometimes he'd wake me at 2:00 a.m., drive me to a truck stop, order eggs and coffee, and then ask me the color of the waitress's eyes and what the tattoo on her ankle said. Then there were afternoons when he'd take me far into the dungeon that comprised his world, and he'd teach me weapons systems. Loading. Unloading. Aiming. Trigger reset. Malfunctions and how to fix them. If it breathed fire and went *boom*, he made me learn what allowed it to do that. Every piece. And how to make it work to my benefit.

One afternoon he handed me a fifty-year-old rifle with ammunition that didn't come close to fitting it and shut me in a supply closet, telling me, "You can come out when you fire that thing." The lesson taught me to look outside the box and use what was available. Somewhere toward midnight, I shot a segment of copper tubing through the two-way glass through which he watched me.

Late in my sophomore year I broke the course obstacle record, which had stood since he'd set it ten years earlier.

And then in what was possibly the strangest turn of events, Bones walked into the weapons closet of the dungeon where I was cleaning a rifle and handed me a stack of strange-looking books. "Congratulations. You've been accepted. Class starts Monday. Tests every Friday. First two years are online. Get the requirements out of the way. Last two you attend on campus, which shouldn't be a problem."

I glanced at the titles. "What are you talking about?"

"Seminary."

"You must be joking."

Bones considered this. "I seldom joke and I never kid." Both of which were lies.

"But I don't want to—"

"And," he cut me off, "you can't be enrolled there and here simultane-ously, so I changed your name."

"What?"

"To God, you'll be known as Murphy Shepherd."

"Stupid name."

"Maybe, but it's yours, so get used to it."

"It's still stupid."

He didn't let me finish, which was his way of saying I had no say in this matter. "One day soon, you're going to encounter people in prison. And often the bars that hold them will be of their own making. It's one thing to unlock someone's prison door—it's another thing entirely to loose the chains that bind their heart." He tapped the barrel of the rifle. "To do that, you're going to need to know how to do more than just poke holes in them."

Thus began my first day of seminary.

Bones's seminary was as much a mystery as he. Called by an obscure Greek name, Google produced a website and pictures of a campus in Spain with satellites in Italy, Austria, France, South Africa, and, you guessed it, Colorado. Having been founded or chartered by the Catholic Church nearly a millennium ago, the college—if you can call it that—didn't follow standard academic protocol whatsoever. They had no desire at all to allow for accreditation of any kind. They couldn't care less. Also unique to the school was the one-to-one professor-to-student ratio. Throughout the course of his study, each student worked with one professor. A priest. Don't like your professor? Tough. Don't like your course of study? Too bad. And while administrative offices with a physical address did exist in Italy, Spain, and France, the institution had no formal classrooms. Class location was determined by the priest.

About three months in, having not slept for much of that time, I asked him, "Just when am I supposed to sleep?"

He shrugged. "Beats me."

"You do realize that the human body needs sleep."

He shook his head. "Overrated."

More often than not, our "classroom" was our lookout atop the mountain, which became a welcome break from the sterile instruction of the academy. Strangely, and despite my initial protests, I enjoyed the seminary assignments and found myself engrossed in the writers, thinkers, and philosophers we read. What I noticed throughout my course of study was that, while the academy taught me to calculate, and to do so effectively, efficiently, and with relative speed, Bones was teaching me how to think outside that well-defined box. Both were needed, but each was made stronger by the other. While my fellow cadets accepted deployments throughout their summers, I was attached at the hip to a white-robed, riddle-speaking, wine-sipping priest who was not-so-quietly disdained by his colleagues, more often rogue than team player, and—while older than me—the strongest human being I'd ever met.

The contradictions were glaring.

As was my continued lack of sleep. While my fellow classmates snored in their bunks up and down the hall, I slept—at best—one or two hours a night. Several nights a week I slept not at all. Meaning I constantly bordered on sleep deprivation. Weeks felt like one long day. Much of my waking hours felt like an out-of-body experience, leaving me a little edgy.

A few months later, when the reality of my workload hit me, I threw one of the books at his head and asked him, "Why on earth do I need to know any of this?"

He looked at me as if the answer were self-explanatory. "Because you can't fake it."

"Fake what?"

"Priesting."

All told, ninety-nine percent of my time and experience at the academy was dictated by Bones. When I asked him how he got away with such a singular existence amid such a military mindset, he just smiled. "I know people."

What I discovered was that Bones was something of a genius. Given his experience saving the son of the then vice president and former head of intelligence for all U.S. government operations, he had been given broad latitude to develop a program with hand-picked people who were a lot like him. Bones was in the elite business of finding people. Specifically, lost people. He didn't bother with a large organization and lots of people. His singular aim was finding one person at a time. He kept staff to a minimum, and most worked intelligence behind computers.

When Bones explained this to me, I said, "So you work for the CIA."

He shook his head. "No, but they often work for me."

When he wasn't dropping me off in the middle of nowhere or dragging me through the mud and snow, he sometimes disappeared for a few days. And sometimes when he returned, he'd be nursing an injury. Protecting some part of his body. Later that year he returned from a week's absence with an obvious problem in his shoulder.

I said, "Cut yourself shaving?"

He didn't respond.

"You want to talk about it?"

He reached into his pocket and held out a bullet. Not the cartridge that contained the shell casing plus the bullet. Just the bullet. The spent projectile, with emphasis on spent. When he dropped it in the palm of my hand, I picked up on the fact that Bones was playing for keeps and this whole clandestine training thing ended somewhere other than a grammar school playground.

He stared at it. "Life is not a video game, and there is no do-over."

Around the academy, Bones was known as Father B, and as a general rule of thumb, he was looked down upon by most everyone else. People thought of him as a token spiritual advisor who'd been given some plush, no-responsibility assignment because he knew somebody somewhere—although no one could say just who. Seldom seen without a Nikon camera around his neck, he wore nerdy-looking glasses and occasionally taught a class when it didn't interfere with his schedule of torturing me.

Given the mystery, rumors swirled about his backstory. The most popular suggested that twenty-five years earlier he'd been a cadet who dropped out after his first love shunned him for another. Adding insult to injury, she accepted a career on the Vegas strip, which now explained his self-imposed life of celibacy. The second theory bubbled up from the "Coexist" bumper sticker on his Prius and centered on the idea that an undisclosed experience in the summer of his junior year caused him to dig into his soul. When he did, finally getting in touch with his real self, he dis-covered—to no one's surprise save his own—that he didn't believe in war and violence. Of any kind. True to his conviction, he quit wearing leather, refused to fire a weapon, and went completely vegan. The academy didn't know what to do with him, so they politely showed him the door.

Whatever the case, and however it had happened, he was dishonor-ably excused from the academy whereupon he backpacked to Italy or Spain or some such place to study something other than war. Following his foreign education in all things pertaining to God, he responded to a "calling" and returned here by invitation to sway other misguided souls like his own from a wayward life of war-mongering because someone somewhere thought it a good idea that the cadets have a well-rounded academic education free from bias and bigotry. If nothing else, he would serve as the voice of the opposition.

In other words, general consensus agreed that Bones was completely useless.

Which was exactly what he wanted.

Yet during my time in the academy, I knew of twenty-seven high-profile abductions and subsequent rescues that took place in sixteen countries—about which Bones never spoke a word and yet for which I knew he was singularly responsible. Somehow he did all that with astound-ing secrecy. Everyone around me thought him the court jester while I knew him to be viceroy for the king.

Thanksgiving break of my senior year I'd been granted a ninety-six-hour pass, and my only desire was to get home to Marie. Waiting at the gate for my plane to board, Bones sat down next to me and handed me a picture of a little girl. Ponytails. Not yet ten. "We have forty-eight hours before they transfer her across the border and she disappears."

I tried not to look at the picture. "Bones, not now . . ."

He waved the picture in front of me.

"What do you want me to do?"

"Bring her back."

"I'm . . . ," I stammered, "not you. I'm not qualified. I don't know anything about how to—"

"Experience is not transferrable."

Another riddle. The flight attendants were calling my seat. "What's that mean?"

"Some things I can't teach you in a classroom. Some things you have to learn on your own." He pointed through the huge glass windows of the terminal. "Out there."

"Why don't you go?"

He showed me a second picture. "Can't be in two places at once."

I held her picture in my hand.

Three days later, as I sat exhausted in the driver's seat of a cattle truck departing from a Mexico border town in Texas, having never seen Florida or Marie, I found I had learned a good deal. First, this line of work—if you could call it that—required not only the ability but the willingness to pivot on a dime without thought. To change plans at the drop of a hat. No matter the emotional connection or damage. Second, this line of work cost far more than it paid.

But when I pulled into Dallas, and the mother of that little girl who slept on the bench beside me clutching a dirty doll lifted her off the seat and sobbed as she held her to her chest, I knew I'd pay it.

Ten thousand times over.

Bones was right. Experience is not transferrable.

A week before my academy graduation I submitted the final thesis required for my divinity degree. Forty pages on one verse in Scripture:

Matthew 18:12. When Bones handed it back, he'd written one word on the last page. "Pass."

"That's all I get? Pass?"

He shrugged, wrote "Nice Job" next to it, and handed it back.

"Oh, thanks. That's so much better." I held up the pages. "I put a lot of work into this."

"I can tell. And"—he raised a finger—"truth be told, you're not a bad writer."

I would remember this in the years to come. And he is quite fond of reminding me how he recognized first what so many have since come to know.

In obtaining my seminary degree, Bones had served as my only advisor and professor. When he handed me the diploma, true to his word, it had been made out to Murphy Shepherd. The fake me.

"What good is this if I can't take credit for it?"

He responded, "You didn't get that so you could hang it on the wall. You got it because you can't fake it."

I raised a finger. "Correction. I got it because you made me."

"You could have quit at any time."

"You picked a fine time to tell me."

He smiled.

That same day he handed me a box and said, "Inside are three things you might need. The first is something to help you arrive on time. Hopefully you'll use it, because you're always late." Which was a lie. I'd never been late. But he knew this. "Second, there is a memento of our time together. Something to remember me by. On the other hand, you might need it. And third, a letter."

With that, Bones turned and walked away. No goodbye. No "Nice job the last four years." No "Have a nice life." No "Thanks for the memories." Just his backside walking away. To be honest, I had expected as much.

I opened the box and did in fact find three things. The first was a Rolex Submariner. The time had been set five minutes fast. A note attached to it read:

There are two reasons for this. You didn't quit when I gave you every reason. Your life would have been easier, but easy is overrated. You should get something for tolerating the hell you endured. Two, if you ever find yourself in a bad way and need to barter out of it, this will get you partway.

The second item was a Sig 220. Another note:

Do this long enough and you will find that the two worst sounds in the human ear are *boom* when you're expecting *click* and *click* when you're expecting *boom*. This one has always gone *boom* when I needed it, which has been a comfort on more than one occasion.

The last was a key taped to a letter. The letter read:

This fits two doors, both of which lead to the rest of your life. Unlock door number one and I'll give you a recommendation for any job any- where or grant you any military assignment you desire. You pick. Walk through this door and I can guarantee you a fast track to advancement and compensation on Easy Street. The world at your feet. You've earned it, and I owe you this much. In the years I've been scouring talent for someone like you, you're the first not to quit. Congratulations. The pre- vious thirteen bailed and told me where I could stick certain things. That makes you either crazy or just simply better. I'm still trying to decide which.

Door number two is a little different, and before you unlock it you need to know that once you walk through, there's no turning back. No "Can I get off now?" No "This isn't what I signed up for." No "Oops, I changed my mind." You make up your mind here and now and you live with it. No matter the cost. For the rest of forever. That's the price you pay. If you don't like it or if this somehow offends your sensibilities or if it is hurtful to the child housed within you, then don't insert that key into this lock. Because wrong motives, mal intent, or a half-baked, half-cocked,

"Why not?" naivete only lead to a lifetime of regret. And probably you dead in some ditch or quarry or mine shaft on the back end of the earth with no one to hear your last breath.

Given that you're still reading, I gather I've piqued your interest. What then, you might ask, is the value of door number two? If door number one is cash, prizes, and life laid out on a silver platter, why would anyone in their right mind choose anything else? Why not just ride the gravy train into the sunset? Unfortunately, there's only one way to know. I will tell you this, and I'm qualified to speak because I walked through the door before you: there is something more valuable than money. Although you will have to dig deep to find it. I cannot promise you that door number two will lead to all your dreams coming true. In fact, a few will be shattered. But walk through it and I can promise you this: one day you'll look inside and amid the scars and the carnage and even the heartbreak, you'll find something only a few ever come to know.

While my class celebrated and threw their hats in the air, I stared at the locker in the dungeon. My life encased in a sweaty metal box. I turned the key in my hand and reread the letter several times. While I was not certain that door number two offered the answer, I was certain door number one did not. When I inserted the key, lifted the latch, and opened that locker door for the last time, I found a white robe, vestments, and a collar. Pinned to the robe was a note containing an address for a church in South Carolina and the words, "See you in a week."

Ellie sat up. "So you walked through door number two?"

The fireplace had melted to coals and Gunner snored before the hearth. "I did."

"Any regrets?"

"Just one."

She looked surprised. "What?"

"Not being there when you were born. Watching you grow up."

She lay down against my chest and threw her legs over mine and then one arm. If I tried to stand up, I'd have to take her with me. Vines were less intertwined than the two of us at that moment.

"Dad? We've got time."

# CHAPTER 15

The weekend rolled around and the seven of us—including Clay and Gunner—walked down Main Street en route to Bones's latest show. A pajama-clad and slipper-footed crowd carrying sleeping bags and pillows had formed at the door of what we affectionately referred to as the Planetarium, where every month Bones revealed his latest pictures. The Planetarium had nothing to do with planets, but it was the closest word we could find that described what happened there. In the center of the room stood a robot-looking thing, constructed by the tech guys, that was actually a projector, or a bunch of projectors, which, like a spinning disco ball, simultaneously projected Bones's slides onto the bare walls. The result was a constant and rotating chronological timeline that simultaneously broadcast more than a dozen pictures at once, all of which magically appeared like popcorn hanging or scrolling along the walls.

The reveal occurred on the first Friday of every month as Bones added more pictures. The photos focused on the moments the girls shared with one another. Most everyone at Freetown came from broken homes or broken relationships. As a result, most had never had their picture taken. Most had never sat for a family picture and certainly not a portrait. The pictures they "sat" for were images taken by men who weren't really interested in their faces. As a result, most of the girls were queasy around a camera when they first arrived. Bones knew this, so he was careful. But when they walked into the Planetarium and saw what he did with it, their comfort level grew.

Bones made a point to leave no one out. He'd sit at a volleyball or Ping-Pong game, wait while they chopped carrots, or just sit idly on a bench on Main Street until he got the one pic of the one girl. And these weren't staged or cheesy photos. They were organic moments of expressed emotion. Given Bones's multiple and rather large lenses, he could sit at a distance and not be intrusive. Most often he was invisible. They never knew he was there. Which made the reveal that much more amazing and fun.

Because the slideshow played twenty-four-seven, Bones could walk into the Planetarium and find several girls, often groups, huddled together, laughing, watching wide-eyed. Giggling. Pointing. Oohing and aahing.

Years ago, when he first showed me the architectural plans for Freetown, I had asked, "What's this huge space?"

"Every one of these girls comes out of a place where men who probably look a lot like us told them, in both verbal and nonverbal ways, 'You're nothing. Just property that can be bought and sold at a negotiated price. Here solely for my pleasure, so shut up and do what I tell you.' I want to undo that. Write over it. I want to tell each of them they are Mona Lisa. Priceless. Beautiful and worth celebrating.

"And," he said, nodding, "the right kind of picture can do that. Most of what they see in their mind's eye comes through a cracked rearview. They don't like it and they never want to look at it again. So while I can't erase their memories, I can give them something new to look at. Moments worth remembering. Memories that drown out the painful noise from before."

He smoothed the plans with his hand. "The walls of Freetown need to be covered with poster-sized pictures of every one of them. Every hallway needs to be one visual celebration leading to another. Every time they turn a corner, they need to be met with another moment that brings a smile to their face. Hope to their heart. We need to run out of wall space be-cause"—he waved his hand across the plans—"we've covered it with them."

He tapped the architectural plans. "And this ginormous circular room, which in any other setting would be a total waste of space, is going to be our centerpiece. The epicenter. Everything revolves around this. We want to route as much of the foot traffic as possible through this very room. Got to get to the dorm? You walk through here. Visit the hospital? Walk through here. Going to eat? Work out? Hike? Catch a movie? All roads lead through here. And when they do, they'll be met with a running, silent slideshow, which is just us screaming at the top of our lungs the truth about them. And to make it interesting, we're accessing facial-recognition software so that when they walk in, the computer recognizes them and automatically shuffles the pictures so that an inordinate amount of them flash and scroll across the wall. Where random isn't so random. Where every image tells them they are . . . beyond measure."

"Did you come up with this idea all by yourself?"

He shook his head but offered little. "No."

It worked too. Day and night, girls curled up in sleeping bags, just staring as more than a hundred pictures scrolled across the walls and ceiling—a new one popping up every few seconds and then scrolling along like a shooting star.

When the doors opened that Friday, we filed in. Piles of people soon developed, stretched out and staring at the walls and ceiling. We opened the theater concession stand, and everyone loaded up from the eight main food groups: popcorn, Skittles, Twizzlers, Swedish Fish, Milk Duds, Sour Patch Kids, Mountain Dew, and Dr Pepper. The coming sugar crash would be epic.

Most residents of Freetown gravitated to Clay like magnets. Something about gray-haired, low-voiced, slow-talking, deep-laughing, paternal ex-convicts resonated, so Clay had become the grandfather everybody never had. When Bones started the show and the first few slides depicted Clay walking down Main Street in his tux and penguin wing tips, which he wore every Friday night to dinner, the girls went nuts and simultaneously jumped to their feet singing "Staying Alive."

A great way to start the show.

The following few pics showed Gunner, who was currently making his rounds through the piles of people and letting his nose tell him what candy had fallen to the carpet. Gunner was even more popular than Clay. I called him the mayor of Freetown. Every picture showed several arms wrapped around or hanging on him and ear-to-ear smiles. His tongue was usually hanging out. In truth, Gunner had become one of the best and most significant therapies we employed at Freetown. Despite the fact that we'd rescued these girls from horrific circumstances, they were slow to trust men. Including me. Trust took time. But Gunner was different. They trusted him instantly. And he knew it and, to his credit, he milked it for all it was worth. Once we witnessed his effect on the residents, we got much more serious about our full-service pet shop on Main Street. Pets, specifically dogs, were able to crack open places in these girls that no therapy on earth could budge. This meant most everybody had a dog, and girls were knocking down the door to offer to work there. It also meant the landscape crew picked up a lot of poop.

Bones let the slideshow play, and over the next hour we watched in wonder as the girls' faces lit, as smiles and laughter spread like wildfire, and as tears welled and fell. I watched from the shadows, remembering where I was when I found each of them. Where they were. What hell they were living in and then lifted out of. Watching their faces, both live and in picture, I found myself shaking my head. I'll never understand what happens in a man, or sometimes a woman—although it's mostly men—to cause them to think they have the right to own another human. To force another member of the human race, made in the image of God, to do what they don't want to and wouldn't in ten million years. All for money.

Staring at the sea of girls walking the road from broken to not, I whispered the question I'd never been able to answer: "What makes one man think he can enslave another?"

Bones, standing next to me, shook his head and whispered back, "Where does that evil come from? How dark is that darkness?"

Bones offered his slideshow to encourage and celebrate these girls, to etch new identities into the scars of their souls. But it did something else: it reminded me why we do what we do. And what's at stake.

I was pretty sure Bones knew this too.

He was holding a bag of popcorn. While everyone else craned their necks and watched the show scroll along the white walls, he watched them watching. He was beaming. Feeding off the euphoria. He stood quietly several seconds, finally whispering, "It never ceases to amaze me . . ."

I turned to him.

He continued, "When light walks into a room, the darkness rolls back like a scroll." He paused, his eyes narrowing. "It has to. Darkness can't stand light. And it has no counter for it."

Despite the wonder in their eyes, one face in the room was not watching the show. Her head was tucked into a pillow, arms wrapped around herself, eyes darting.

Casey.

Summer noticed Casey's discomfort, sat alongside her, and wrapped both a blanket and an arm around her. The unofficial mom of Freetown.

The story of Summer's attempted rescue of Angel, how she stole the boat and headed off into the night in deep water while unable to swim, put her on a pretty high pedestal with many of the girls. And the fact that she'd voluntarily put on a dental floss bikini in Key West and baited herself to get Angel back, *then* took a ride on the Daemon boat, elevated her to mythical proportions. For most everyone sitting here, Summer rivaled Wonder Woman. All of them were now coming to Summer with questions they'd always wanted to ask their moms. From questions about boys, to questions about their own bodies, to what it's like to go on a date with a man who doesn't own you, Summer had become their confidante. The one they trusted with the stuff that, until then, they'd only told Gunner. It was a beautiful transformation. While Summer might have had a life and a successful career on Broadway, she'd found purpose on the streets of Freetown. I doubted I could drag her away.

Summer leaned in and tried to draw Casey's attention to the show. To her credit, Casey tried, even lifting her head, smiling, and offering a laugh.

But there was no joy in it.

I'd purged my own pain, or most of it, in the process of writing. But right there I began to wonder if my remedy would work for Casey. Was some pain deeper than the words could dig out?

# CHAPTER 16

Ellie knew we were approaching the end of the story. One final install-ment. A conclusion she both wanted and didn't want to reach. Along the way, she had retold the story to both Casey and Angel with—I would later learn—considerable embellishment. Which made it all the more fun and made me look far more capable than I really am.

That last night she walked in with Casey locked on her right arm and Angel on her left. Her partners in crime. Ellie assumed her cross-legged position in bed, while Angel and Casey pulled up chairs. Summer appeared moments later carrying bowls of popcorn, mugs of hot choco-late, and a glass of wine. "I wouldn't miss this for the world." She kissed my forehead and then did the index-finger-in-the-chest thing. "Hit it, Shakespeare."

After Bones found the vice president's son, he was invited to join, and eventually run, an elite and unnamed government agency created by executive order decades earlier. An agency with a singular task: to seek out and return the loved ones of high-profile abductions. Meaning the children of powerful people.

Bound by no geographical lines, the only rule was secrecy, which explains why Bones spent years vetting me. He had to know if he could trust me. That meant only a handful of people knew about the agency's existence, which was both good and bad. It meant we could operate undetected without a lot of red tape and make situational decisions on the fly. It also meant we didn't get a lot of help.

Bones had taken the reins from the previous leader, who'd served several presidencies and begun his own impressive record of rescue and recovery. By the time Bones tapped me at the academy, he held a storied position among the Washington elite, where the rumors surrounding his abilities and successes had reached mythical status. As time passed and those forever grateful children grew into powerful people in their own right—men and women who owned powerful companies and took powerful jobs around the world—the extent and influence of Bones's own reach exceeded the extent and influence of many of those who employed him.

In short, Bones could do whatever he wanted, whenever he wanted, however he wanted, wherever he wanted, and he asked no one's permission. A pedestal that even Bones admitted tested the limits of absolute power and its effect on those who wielded it. But his challengers were few, and no one opposed him to his face. Why? Because of the long line of people behind him who owed him their life. It's simply difficult to argue with a saved life. Especially if you put your own at risk in saving another. The problem Bones's success created was that of a successor. Who would take up the mantle?

I was oblivious to all this.

For me, the question that nagged at me was what Bones had been doing on the banks of my island when he rescued me out of Jack's bear-paw death grip. Why was he there? When I asked Bones, he simply shook his head and shrugged. As if the memory were painful. The issue unsolved.

The address in the locker led me to a church in South Carolina. Bones had taken up lodging in the attached pastoral retreat that served priests from around the country, allowing them to rest, pray, walk in the woods, and restore their weary souls. In the year prior, Bones had recovered the governor's niece, but the question of who had taken her remained a mystery. Someone was hiding at the top. A single clue surfaced in her retelling of the story. The clue was a name. Had it been Mark or Jim or Bill or Bob, it would have mattered not at all, but it wasn't.

The name was Genefrino.

Bones brought me in to peel back the layers. Once I started digging, I learned quickly that power is not shared; there is always one person in charge, and he who has the money has the power. Most nights Bones and I would debrief either in his pastoral retreat or some prearranged diner. For my education on the sick and detestable world of human trafficking, it was immersion by fire. I soon found out Bones had forgotten more than I'd learn in a lifetime. St. Bernard of Clairvaux had once championed the doctrine of Christian humility, in which he stated we are all but dwarfs perched atop the shoulders of giants.

Bones was my giant.

Six months in and I'd followed the bread crumbs. Whispers from people afraid to talk. Mysteries from confidential conversations. All led me to the church's largest single donor. He gave all the time. For everything. The orphanage. Boarding school. Homeless shelter. Building campaign. If there was a need, his wallet was open. Further, he was a hugger. An affable, touchy-feely teddy bear who filled his vast estate with a thousand eggs at Easter and loved nothing more than to button on the red suit at Christmas and bounce the kids on his knee. Make all their dreams come true. One "ho-ho-ho" at a time.

But every time I got around this man, I had an uneasy feeling that his gift wasn't so much an offering as a purchase. A down payment. The closer I got, and the more I played the naïve young priest unwise in the ways of business but eager to earn his trust, the more certain I became that he was trying to buy not only the absolution of his guilt but permission in the future.

If there's anything worse than sin in the past, it's premeditated sin in the future. I left every interaction needing a shower.

I guess you don't need me to tell you that his name was Genefrino. "But my friends all call me Gene," he said, smiling. "'Cept the kids. They call me 'Uncle G.'" When he first introduced himself, he apologized for his name and said the only reason he didn't change it was because his mother asked him not to before she died. It was her father's name. And so on.

How do you argue with a man who funds orphanages and schools and hospitals around the world? How do you argue with a man who spends his life's talents and resources to place unfortunate and hand-picked children with wealthy families around the world? Many in Europe. Or how do you argue with a man who takes a green-eyed girl from a trash heap in Africa to a boarding school in Carolina where he pays for her tutors and medical bills? "Whatever she needs."

You can't.

Unless, of course, one of those little girls escapes from the hell into which he "placed" her only to spend her last few breaths telling her story to a nurse in a third-world country where the bodies of children are stacked up like cordwood en route to the furnace and the memory of them disappears though the chimney. It was Bones who found the nurse, though he never found the girl. Later that year, a teenager from Central America, a ninth grader in the boarding school, killed himself on the steps of the church. Followed weeks later by a second younger boy. No explanation was given.

Something unspeakable was happening to these children. And Uncle G was inconsolable.

Santa's problem was that he had a thing for little girls. And more so for little boys. But the jolly old man was also smart. He owned an import-export company and traveled internationally in a fleet of personal jets. Given the bighearted teddy bear that he was, he would bring children in from other countries. Kids rescued from squalor, rejection, and abandonment who didn't speak English. As the church's ambassador, he'd give them a home in our orphanage—or, if they were able, a slot in our boarding school. He'd buy them clothes and toys, celebrate their birthday as the day they were "rescued," and take them for spontaneous rides in his jet, where he'd set them in his lap and let them steer a few knots shy of the speed of sound. Then, when he'd sufficiently endeared himself, he would lead them by the hand into his basement theater, pop some popcorn, and tell them, "You're so beautiful. You can do anything you dream."

You see where this is going, right?

When he was finished with them, or when they grew strong enough and threatened to reveal his secrets, he "found" them homes around the world, whisking them off in the middle of the night and "placing" them via personal jet.

Erasing the evidence.

But while he could make kids disappear into thin air, there was one thing his billions could not erase: his own shame and guilt. So as his sin multiplied, so did his extraordinary benevolence. They were intrinsically connected. The devil with no soul was trying to buy his way out of hell.

A couple months in, Bones asked me how I was doing and I shook my head. Afraid to be heard. "Evil has a face." But Evil also had an Achilles' heel. He liked to binge-watch reruns.

Early in my employment, Gene had sought me out—as Bones had thought he would—and endeared himself to me in a gentle, uncle-in-law sort of way. At first, he just wanted to know how he could help. "If there's ever anything I can do." Soon, as he toiled alongside me serving food to the homeless in our shelter, he confided that he needed a man like me in his life, and that he much admired my devotion. My singular focus. Soon he was a weekly regular on my calendar, doling out more personal insight. Life lessons. Offering to introduce me to Senator So-and-So or some Fortune 500 executive. Asking me to accompany him on day excursions to Vail and Aspen to meet with investors, where he needed my spiritual wisdom.

Soon, expensive dinners teetered on confession. Tears were frequent. He would put a hand on my shoulder or my arm and pledge transparency via false piety. "Ask me anything."

Three months later, he pulled me aside and asked through a quivering bottom lip and cracking voice if I would hear his confession. That the unspoken weight of it was crushing. That he finally felt he had found a man in his life with whom he could trust the details of his story without fear of judgment. "Would you please?"

I didn't want to hear it. Any of it. Ever. I knew the moment he opened his mouth, I'd want to hurt him. To push him in front of a moving truck. To exact revenge for those he'd abused and silenced. I also knew I could not lay a finger on him. Nor could my facial expressions betray my disgust. I had to listen, nod empathetically, and bury it.

No matter what he said, I could not come across as overly eager to know what he hid in his basement. I needed to exhibit priestly under-standing and pastoral empathy. To show I was not his judge. Nor his jury. His telling me was not a soul-wrenching purge. It was predatory. Could he trust me with the evil that he spawned?

Feigning piety, I waffled, telling him he didn't need me. "We're Anglican. Not Catholic." I put my hand on his shoulder and glanced at the stained-glass image of Jesus carrying His cross outside of town. One of twelve such depictions Gene had so selflessly commissioned. "Take it to Him yourself." The touch was purposeful. Endearing. A page out of his play-book. Truth was, I needed not only to hear it but to record it. To post it on the internet and watch his world come crumbling down as he rotted in some prison for the rest of his natural life. My bigger problem, which Gene also knew, was that the confessional falls under protected speech. While there are exceptions, I had a feeling his words would flirt with the edge of that protection yet never cross it. Was he evil? Absolutely. Was he stu-pid? Not in the least bit. As evidenced by the fact that asking me to hear his confession had placed our relationship into the realm of protected speech. Of priest and confessor. Of absolver and penitent.

A condition he was counting on.

Given that I didn't "play well with others," I didn't make or keep many friends. This character flaw made me ideal for Bones's purposes—he needed an unflinching lone ranger—but it brought with it a chronic and endemic loneliness. Something I'd not yet learned to medicate. It also made me a poor judge of people who said they wanted to be my friend, which was interesting. I could spot evil in other people's lives from a mile away. No question. But when it came to me, I was blind as a bat. Upon my arrival in South Carolina, I met a parishioner and business executive named Roger working out in the church gym.

Roger was in his midtwenties and he traveled the world for a venture capital firm researching possible investments. He described himself as the boots-on-the-ground assessor. The one who got his hands dirty when his Ivy League bosses wouldn't. He was connected twenty-four-seven to two cell phones and a satellite phone, and he reported to Wall Street at all hours of the day and night. But when home, he was quick to disconnect and turn with intention to his friendships—something he admitted he'd not done well most of his life.

We were cut from the same cloth.

When Marie visited on the weekends, Roger fit right in. From pizza to Ping-Pong, the three of us became inseparable. As my suspicions of Billionaire Santa grew, I revealed them to Roger. Roger listened, asked insightful questions, and even helped me guard against possibilities. One of his gifts was seeing what might be, and given his worldly experience, he knew human nature to an extent I did not. At least not yet.

Although I'd learn a good bit about it soon enough.

Those were difficult months. I could trust no one, I seldom saw Bones, and Marie worked all week and had taken a second job waiting tables on weekends, leaving me even further isolated. In this complicated and lonely soup, Roger became a welcome and trusted friend.

The night Marie and I got engaged, Roger was working out of the country. When we called him, he immediately caught the next flight back and took us out for beer and wings. A true celebration.

In a blink, what had been difficult became good. I was engaged to the love of my life, had formed and was developing my first real friendship in a long time, and had a job that I knew was making a difference, even if I could tell no one about it.

I had found my place in this world. My *raison d'être*.

Unfortunately, I was not the only one pretending to be someone I was not. And as I was soon to learn in the most painful lesson of my life, others were far better at it than I.

In December, I attended Gene's annual Christmas Eve party where, as his guests sang "Auld Lang Syne" and sipped eggnog by the fire, and the kids opened gifts with glee, he led me into his basement under the guise of a soulful admission of sin. The time had come. The truth of himself laid bare. Something he could carry no longer. Leaning heavily on a cane, which he'd begun using, giving the further impression that the weight was in fact too much to bear, he spoke with bowed head about how I was the first person he'd ever known with whom he felt able to share his dark secrets. The skeletons in his closet. Locking the soundproof door of his theater, he clicked Play. Too ashamed to look at his own in-home movies, he hid his face in the shadows. The video had been purposefully edited, keeping him well within the confines of what was legal. But what it suggested and what it left out said far more than the video itself.

It was bait.

This was the moment to which the last six months had led. Consummation. He clicked off the power, ashamed at the video's contents, palmed away the tears, knelt alongside me, placed a heavy hand on my knee, and began babbling a tearful, hasty, and well-rehearsed confession.

His performance was Broadway-worthy.

As he vomited his penance into the air around me, I wondered how much innocence had been lost in that dungeon. How many souls had been severed in two by this preying man? Crushed by this evil sleight of hand? Why place a massage table in a theater when the house was ten thousand square feet? Contrary to the words coming out of his mouth, this predator didn't want forgiveness. He wanted to turn me. An accomplice. He wanted the power he perceived in my collar. God's approval. Interestingly, it was about here that he pledged his enormous wealth to God. "Every penny. And I have hundreds of millions, just waiting for . . ." He trailed off.

The message was clear.

Not only was he playing me, he was trying to buy me.

I could take it no more. I was young, cocky, angry, and acted on emotion. Rough edges that later years would attempt to smooth. Unable to listen to one more word coming out of his mouth, I splintered his cane across his face, breaking many of the structural bones and forever relieving him of many of his teeth. With the assistance of substantial pain, I persuaded him to tell me the combination to his media vault, where I stuffed several hard drives into a backpack.

Feeling good about myself and wanting to be rid of this sick maggot at my feet, I stepped over him en route to leaving the basement with enough evidence to put him away for a dozen lifetimes—which was when I heard smug laughter followed by the sensation of fire entering and exiting my body.

Not my best day.

Another tough lesson—evil people do not lack motivation when it comes to hiding their sins. In fact, there's nothing they won't do.

I lay on the floor and stared at the ceiling as the carpet turned warm and red beneath me. I remember shaking my head and cussing my own stupidity as I wondered when he'd fire the next shot and turn out my lights. I also sensed a strange emotion I had not expected—that my death would not only hurt Bones but would let him down. Mission not accomplished. Waiting on the next lightning bolt, I heard a high-pitched squeal followed by what sounded like tearing ligaments, breaking bones, and the thud of a limp body falling onto the carpet. A second later, Bones appeared out of the corner of my eye, threw me over his shoulder, and carried me up and out of the house and into a hospital with a trauma unit. I have no idea where he came from, as I had no idea he was there. I was fading in and out when I heard him call Marie and tell her our wedding might get delayed.

When she asked, "Why?" he responded with, "Bodies don't react well to bullets."

Through twelve hours of surgery and ten units of blood, I flatlined twice and finally a third time before I stabilized. Once out of surgery, I was moved to the ICU, where I spent a month breathing through a tube, much of which I don't remember. After three months in the hospital, they transferred me to a rehab wing, where I spent six months starting with the impossible assignment of lifting a two-pound dumbbell. In that time, Marie bathed me, cut my hair, maintained my meds schedule, massaged my muscles to fend off atrophy, and changed my bandages. She never left my side.

Our wedding was delayed a year and a half.

While I fought to live, Marie fought to understand. Who would shoot a priest? And more importantly, why? Which led to a bigger question: What was I actually doing? Bones had allowed me to tell Marie that my job as priest was actually cover, and that my true employer was an unnamed agency in the United States government. And while all of that was true, it was the half-truths to follow that did the most damage. Raised more suspicion than explained.

I told Marie I'd been employed as an "investigator." That's all. My job was simply gathering intel. I was never to have anything to do with physically catching bad guys. That had been left to the professionals. When she pried as to specifics, I was little help. Given Bones's warning, I knew better than to tell her the specifics of my work. Too dangerous. When she asked, I deflected. Unbeknownst to me, this avoidance produced in her a mistrust. And out of that grew a desire to talk to someone. Someone else.

Fundamentally, Marie stared at my bullet-riddled body and asked herself, *Can he be telling the truth?*

The evidence proved I was not. These were long months. I was little consolation, and Marie carried the lion's share of the work.

Eighteen months passed. The chapel was small, but that's the way they made them back then. I stood at the altar, and the room was full of friends and family. Bones stood to my right, groomsmen and bridesmaids lined up in either direction, and Roger was just over my shoulder. My best man.

When the music started, I blinked and she appeared. An angel flying too close to the ground. I remember seeing white and sunshine, and my knees nearly buckled. Roger caught me, bringing a laugh out of Bones and all the attendees. Then she took a step and I watched in slow motion. It was as if whatever world had been there before just faded, leaving only her. I'd never seen anyone so beautiful. She made it halfway down the aisle, and her maid of honor handed me a handkerchief. Evidently, I was crying. More laughter. She climbed the steps, and when she took my hand, hers was trembling. As was her lip.

Marie was afraid. But for the life of me, I couldn't track the source of the fear. Was it me? I didn't think so. The thought of marriage and lifelong commitment? Not likely. Fear of the unknown? I didn't think so.

In the years ahead I would learn to pay attention to that hair standing up on the back of my neck and that piercing pain in my heart—but in that moment I did not. While I was afraid to tell Marie the truth of me, she was more afraid I'd learn the truth of her. An idea that had never crossed my mind.

She took my hand, and as we stood waiting on Bones, she whispered through the veil, "You sure you want me?"

"With all of me."

Sometimes, when I walk back through this memory, I force myself to stop here. Where the dream of us still projects into one frame. Where I am still standing . . . and in one piece.

When I finished, the bowls of popcorn were empty. Angel, Casey, and Ellie were all sitting cross-legged on my bed, eating chocolate and clutching some part of Gunner, who was milking the attention. Summer sat in a chair opposite me, an empty wineglass at her side, her feet resting alongside mine. She used a tissue to dab the corners of her eyes.

# CHAPTER 17

My daily walks lengthened. A block turned to a quarter mile, to a half mile, to two. Finally, with Summer's help, I managed to climb to the Eagle's Nest at fourteen thousand feet where I could once again overlook the world. When I collapsed on the couch, she built a fire and then sat with me as I dozed. While I was enjoying the attention, I also knew I was softening—and a man in my line of work can't afford to soften. It's an occupational hazard. If I thought like my enemy for a second, I'd want me soft. And distracted.

Summer prompted me, "What're you thinking about?"

I spoke into the fire. "If they can blow up my island, they can attack me here. And while I'm enjoying being with you, I'm vulnerable. And that's bad."

She nodded and smiled. "Time to up my A-game."

I wasn't quite sure what that meant, but when she walked in the next morning at five, set my boots next to the bed, and clicked on the light, I knew there'd been a change in my level of care. She kissed me and spoke with a smile. "Soft and tender is on the bench. Rough and tumble, suit up."

I leaned on one elbow. "Maybe we should ease into this."

She slid my boots toward me and pointed out the window toward the cabin sitting three thousand feet above me. "When you get back." She pointed at the gondola, which would lift me on eagle's wings and drop me on my porch with zero effort. "No cheating."

I was sweating when the sun broke the skyline. Gunner trotted and hopped in front of me. Below me in the valley, Freetown was moving. People waking to new lives. To freedom. The thin air tasted sweet as I gorged on it.

My inability to breathe was evidence that I was in bad shape. As much as I didn't want to admit it, Summer was right to kick me out. We lose fitness much faster than we gain it. When it's lost, there's only one way to get it back, and there's usually a fight—with the enemy being yourself.

The first day it took me four hours to get to the cabin and two to get back down. Twice my normal. Clay was waiting on me at the top with a warm cup of coffee and a PB&J. On my descent, he waved at me from the gondola. When I returned after lunch, I slept four hours and woke as the sun fell behind the peaks.

Days bled into weeks, and the time of ascent and descent—plus my subsequent nap—reduced gradually and not without a good deal of pain. After a month, I stared down from the porch. My trip up had taken ninety minutes. It wasn't so much a jog as a fast hike with the occasional bound thrown in. Still, whatever it was and however ugly it looked, somewhere in there I knew I was returning to me.

Summer had everything to do with it. Without her, I doubt I'd have climbed out of bed. Which was strange because I never needed a reason before. I had one: Marie. Or rather, the thought of Marie. One morning it struck me that a subtle change had overtaken my thinking. I'd substituted Summer for Marie, and as I searched around inside myself, I felt no guilt. Which caused me to feel guilty. Beneath all that lay something else.

A thousand feet later, as I stood on the porch of the Eagle's Nest, I realized the root and voiced it out across the expanse before me. "It's hope."

Behind me, I heard a soft voice. "What is?"

I didn't know she was there, which I credit to oxygen deprivation caused by climbing at two miles above sea level.

"Huh?"

"You said, 'It's hope.' Like you were answering a question." Summer's voice was curious and a little playful. "So . . . what's the question?"

"I've been trying to name the thing that keeps me climbing up this impossible mountain day after day."

"And?"

"I think it's hope."

"What makes you say that?"

"You can mute it, wound it, stab it, shoot it, and shove it in the corner, but no matter what you do or how hard you try, you can't kill it. Sooner or later, some part of you is going to look at that mysterious shape in the corner and compare it to the wound oozing in your chest, and you'll think to yourself, *I wonder if that'll fill the hole.* And when it clicks perfectly into place, you wonder how it knew. How did that one thing fit the hole nothing could ever fill? Too jagged. And yet it did. Custom fit. That thing is hope."

She stepped closer. "So what are you hoping for?"

"I don't have words for that yet. I'm still trying to wrap my head around the thing." I smiled. "Gimme a few weeks . . ."

She locked her arm inside mine, and we stood staring east across Colorado. We could see nearly a hundred miles. After five or six minutes of silence, she leaned in and kissed me. Something she had grown fond of. After a second kiss, she placed her index finger on my chin and smiled. "I've loved our little chat, but don't think for one second that this sweet little Hallmark moment means I'm going to let you step one foot in that gondola." She pointed at her condo some five miles away. "You want dinner?" She pointed at the foot trail. "Get stepping."

"That obvious?"

She nodded.

"I thought I played that pretty well."

"This ain't my first rodeo."

I sucked between my teeth and headed for the trail. "I gotta up my Hallmark game."

Sometimes in the evenings when we sat on the porch or before the fire, I'd find her foot tapping or her finger tracing the lines of a dance choreography along her leg. She didn't even know she was doing it. To me they were unconscious signals, reminders even, of what she'd given up to nurse me back to health, and in one word, it was everything.

Six months ago, we'd been thrust together on the Intracoastal Waterway, where I got to do what I do best—rush in, shoot the bad guys, and rescue people in need. And all of that usually occurred, to some weird extent, on my terms. That doesn't mean I was in charge of what happened or the circumstances we faced, but I did dictate our response to what we encountered because I was the only one who'd ever been there. For all the right reasons, she'd looked to me. My leadership in our shared dance had been mandated by one simple fact: I'd danced that dance before. She had not. Hence, I led. A no-brainer.

But as I stared back over the weeks since somebody blew up my boat, the dance had changed. While I'd been stabbed and shot and beat up in the past, I'd never been incapable of caring for myself—not since Marie nursed me back to health. But in the last few weeks, I had been. Completely. I could not prepare my food. Could not change my bandages. Could not bathe myself without passing out. Contrast that with Summer, who, given her occupation as a dance instructor, had been taking care of people like me for decades. People who couldn't put one foot in front of the other. That care had produced a patience and perspective I did not possess.

The explosion had reversed our roles. And as much as I didn't want to admit it, Summer led this dance far better than I.

Something else had happened while Summer bathed me, fed me, and washed my sheets. We'd become friends. And friends, like softness, were occupational hazards in my line of work. It'd been a long time since I'd had any, and far longer since any of them could be called close.

One day as I napped on the couch, she hurried through the room, her arms full of my laundry. My stinky, sweaty, dirty clothes. I had no memory of anyone doing that. Ever.

I wanted to thank her, so I spent about half a second thinking about how I might. That's when I realized I had something else to do first.

# CHAPTER 18

H ome life in Freetown depended on need. If medical care, recovery, triage, or a more intense detox was required, then we offered either the hospital, which was more like a four-star hotel with medical staff, or townhomes that provided more independence and freedom. For more permanent residents, such as myself, we'd built over forty cabins and tucked them up into the trees with space between each. Most were two and three bedrooms. A few were larger. A couple smaller. Because my cabin was only one bedroom, Ellie had moved in with Summer and Angel.

Over the last six months, Ellie had been making her way through her mom's copies of my books. Savoring Marie's handwritten notes in the margins as much as my words printed on the page. I climbed to the second floor and found Ellie propped up in bed, wrapped in a blanket. A fire in the fireplace. "How many does that make?"

She held up my last novel. "Third time."

I nodded. "A true fan."

She smiled and tried to hide a tear that had been hanging in the corner of her eye. "Tell me about Mom."

Gunner hopped up on the bed and lay on the other side. Tail wagging. The slideshow clicked on in my mind's eye. "She liked old straw hats. Scarves. Wouldn't let me bait her hook. Could throw a cast net with accuracy. Wasn't afraid to sweat. Loved to get her hands dirty. Tender while not needy. Fiercely independent yet hated to be without me." I sat next to her on the bed. "Pretty stubborn." Ellie laughed, which spilled the tear down her face, allowing me to thumb it away. "Wore cowboy boots in summer. Self-protective to a fault."

"Did you ever forgive her?"

I nodded. "The moment it happened." A pause. "And every moment after."

"You miss her?"

I nodded.

"You love Summer?"

"I think so, although . . . it's weird."

"How so?"

"When I fell in love with your mom, I gave her all of me. Nothing held back. When she died, that didn't just return. So now I'm walking around trying to patch together the pieces of me, and I find I don't have as much to give. I'm only part of me. But whatever part remains is drawn to Summer. I like her a lot."

"Love or like?"

"Both, I think."

She fell quiet a minute, running her palm across the cover of my book. "Mom read this more than a dozen times."

Inside the front cover, Marie had recorded by date each time she finished and started over. I nodded.

"Does that comfort you?"

"It does."

Ellie looked up. More tears. "You've been hanging out with Summer a lot lately."

A question posed as a statement. "I have."

"You going to marry her?"

I put my arm around her. "Not without your permission."

My answer surprised her. "You mean that?"

"I do."

"Why?

"Because I don't want your heart to hurt any more than it already does."

She clutched the book to her chest. "What about your heart?"

"It'll be just fine."

Gunner licked Ellie's face, then lay back down and licked the faceplate of Ellie's phone. Ellie shook her head. "I'm not so sure." A pause, and another glance at the book. "So if I say no, you won't marry her?"

I nodded.

"Even if that's what you wanted?"

"Even if."

"What do you think Mom would want?"

"I think your mom would want me to spend my life being your dad. Watching over you. Hanging out with you. Asking your boyfriends a couple hundred questions before I ever let you out the door."

Ellie laughed. "Yeah, I kinda feel sorry for them." Then her tone changed as more tears fell. I was watching a woman bloom before my eyes. She placed her head against my chest. "Dad?"

Part of me melted. "Yes?"

"Who's gonna watch over you?"

I ran my fingers through her hair. Such a big question for so young a person. I pushed her hair out of her eyes. "When'd you get so big?"

"You're dodging my question."

"Bones does a pretty good job."

"Bones is a man."

I laughed. "I'm aware of that."

"You should marry Summer."

I knelt alongside the bed, my eyes level with Ellie's. She nodded, which spilled more tears down her face. "Mom would want you to."

"What do you want?"

"I want you to be happy."

"I am. I have you."

"I'm your daughter." She held my hand in hers. "I'm serious."

I asked a second time. "What do you want?"

"Mom's never coming back. And Summer really loves you . . ."

"How do you know?"

"Dad. I'm a woman. I know these things."

I shook my head and marveled. Ellie had something she wanted to say. It was the reason she'd started this conversation in the first place, but she wasn't sure how I'd receive it. I prompted, "You can say it."

"Summer shouldn't have to pay for what she didn't do."

"What do you mean?"

"She didn't take Mom from us. If you don't marry her, then, in a weird way, you're making her pay for that."

I studied her and thought, *Out of the mouths of babes . . .*

Gunner sat up, tilted his head, and pushed his ears forward. Staring at me.

I wrapped an arm around Ellie. "You get this from your mother, you know."

"What's that?"

"A spirit that stands in a hurricane, shakes her fist, and says, 'Bring it.'"

She sat up, chin up. "One more thing."

"What's that?"

She held up her left hand and pointed at the ring finger. "You need to get with the program. Stop being so thickheaded. The clock is ticking."

I sat on the bed again. "About that . . . I've been out of the dating game for a little over two decades and things have changed a lot. You think you could help me?"

She smiled and raised her eyebrows, looking just like her mother. I kissed her, walked out, and began descending the stairwell to the basement. I needed to have one more conversation.

# CHAPTER 19

Angel sat on the floor. A dozen books spread across the space in front of her. Windows open. White coals in the fireplace. Gunner walked in, licked her face, and lay down within arm's reach.

"Homework?" I asked.

She held up her hand. Palm out. And didn't look at me. "Yes."

"Yes, what?"

"Yes, you should."

"Should what?"

She turned to me, raised one eyebrow, and said, "Padre." She did not look impressed. "Don't pretend like you're just wandering by and thought you'd check in on me."

Busted.

She smiled. "I know what you want."

"You do?"

"Of course."

"How?"

She held up her phone.

"I don't follow you."

She raised her phone, allowing me to see the screen where Ellie waved at me. "Hey, Dad."

I pointed at the phone, calculating the fact that I'd left Ellie's room less than twenty seconds ago. "You heard all that?"

Angel nodded matter-of-factly. "Of course."

"How?"

She shrugged as if it made total sense to her. "We were talking when you walked in."

I pointed up. "But . . . she's upstairs."

"And your point is?"

I shook my head. "I thought that was private."

Angel nodded. "It was. Just the three of us."

"But I didn't know that."

"You didn't need to know it."

I stared out the window. "What is wrong with the educational system in this country?" I turned to Gunner. "Are you in on this too?"

Ellie laughed. I could hear her both through the phone and echoing down the stairwell. Angel returned to the papers in front of her. I picked up her phone and spoke to both of them. "Both of you, kitchen. Now."

They appeared in the kitchen and sat hip to hip at the breakfast bar while I poured a cup of coffee, leaned against the counter, and hovered over the steam lifting from the mug. When I tried to open my mouth, Ellie interrupted me. "Dad, we're like sisters. We share everything."

Angel nodded.

"And you do this often?"

Angel responded, "What's that?"

"Talk on the phone when you're ten feet apart."

They both shrugged and nodded.

That struck me as strange, but whatever. "What if I want to have a conversation with one of you?"

Angel spoke first. "You can."

"I thought that's what I was doing."

They both shook their heads. "We were talking when you walked in."

I wasn't quite following this line of logic. "Therefore?"

They looked at me like I had six eyes.

I angled my head toward Ellie. "It didn't cross your mind to tell me that when I walked in? Like—" I pretended to be her and mimicked talking on the phone. "Hey, Dad just walked in. I'll call you right back."

She shook her head.

I turned to Angel. "And you didn't think it just common courtesy, even respectful, to speak up and say, 'Hey, I think I'll let you two have this conversation without me'?"

Angel shrugged and shook her head.

I spoke as much to myself as them. "I feel like I'm standing on Mars."

Gunner stared up at me with that goofy grin he does. I shook my head. "Don't look at me like that." He lay down and grunted.

Ellie raised a finger. Her tone serious. "Dad, this does raise the larger question of why you'd want to."

Angel nodded in agreement.

"Why I'd want to what?"

"Have a conversation with one of us versus both."

I looked at one, then the other. "Wouldn't you like to be able to have a conversation with me sometimes without the other one there?"

They shrugged. "No. Not really."

"Why?"

They looked at each other. Then me. The answer obvious. "We're sisters."

Gunner grunted again.

I scratched my head. "Oh." I felt like I was swimming in an estrogen lap pool.

They stood and turned to walk out. Angel again, "We done? I'm way behind."

I leaned against the counter and sipped my coffee. This had not gone as I'd intended. I'd never been more confused in my life. "I guess so."

They walked out and then down into Angel's room in the basement, where I heard the door shut—followed by raucous laughter.

About then it occurred to me that I'd been had.

When I pushed open the door, they were sitting on the bed. Covering their mouths. Angel was holding her stomach.

As I leaned against the doorframe, reality started to sink in. "So you two are yanking my chain. Right?"

Ellie laughed the most beautiful, high-pitched giggle. Angel gave me another stop-sign hand. "I'm about to pee myself."

"So do you want me to talk with you one at a time or both together?"

Angel crossed her legs like an accident was imminent. The two looked at each other, then smiled innocently at me.

I turned to leave. "I need a manual."

Angel got the words out before the laughter. "For what?"

"You two."

Nothing was making sense. I pointed up. "She upstairs?"

Angel nodded and mimicked someone typing. Having a conversation with Casey meant climbing into the attic, which, at this point, was easier said than done.

I climbed out of the basement to more raucous laughter. When I reached the ground floor, I was shaking my head. And staring at two more flights. Laughter was all I heard.

They'd make it. They'd be okay. I, on the other hand . . .

I grabbed the package from my publisher and climbed to the second floor, caught my breath, and then made the final push up into the attic, where I heard her fingers tapping the keys at the speed of hummingbird wings. Winded, I landed on the balcony and leaned on the railing. She spoke through a smile. "Want me to call someone? Or should I just start chest compressions? I can't remember . . . is it ten and one or five and two?"

# CHAPTER 20

I stepped inside her room and handed her the package from New York. She stared at it but didn't touch it.

"It won't bite you."

Slowly, she peeled open the padded envelope and held up the promotional copy. In the business, we call it a galley. The cover picture was a close-up of half her face taken as she stood atop the mountain peak behind the Eagle's Nest. The photographer had focused on a single scar on the left side of her beautiful face as well as the jagged, wind-carved, snowcapped peaks that stretched out behind her. On one side, pain, hardness, and torment untold. On the other, wonder, majesty, rare beauty, and all possibility. It was there, atop that mountain, that she'd first heard the title whispered inside her: *The Resurrection of Casey Girl.*

She brushed her fingertips across the cover, sucked in a quick breath, which had been taken away, and finally whispered the last cry of her heart. "I'm so scared . . ." She shook her head and said no more.

"Of?"

"Being known."

"For?"

"What I truly am."

"Which is?"

I waited.

"Used up. Disposable." She held up the book. "Who could love me after reading this?"

"If they don't"—I brushed her hair out of her face—"you don't want them."

My words bounced off her. She spoke while studying the cover. "Is this a mistake?"

I sat next to her. "There's a thing that happens when we start to believe the lies about ourselves, and when we think other people believe them too. Those lies become our prison. The bars we see through. They hold us captive. It's like some giant hand holding our head beneath the surface of the water. Every few minutes it'll let us up, only to sink us farther the next go-round. A vicious cycle. In my experience, only one thing on planet earth breaks the power of that hand and flings open wide the prison doors."

She nodded, whispering, "The truth?"

"And until you speak it with your mouth, out loud, you're bound." I eyed the book. "Casey, you're one of the bravest people I've ever met. To endure what you did and not only live to tell about it but actually tell it. Your story will set not only you free but countless girls like you who believe the same lies. Every tearstained, horrific, and blood-bought page will save lives. Literally rip prison doors off their hinges." I hefted the book and brushed the cover with my hand. "This isn't just a book. It's a rescue mission. You and your beautiful and unconquered words will personally walk down into hell, loose the shackles, and walk others out into the sun."

She shook her head and looked away. As if the thought were too good to be true.

I continued, "Think like your enemy a second."

"What?"

"If you were your enemy, would you want this to be published?"

Her face revealed she'd never had this thought. I continued, "If I were your enemy, I wouldn't want the world to know this. I'd want to keep it hidden. Want you to keep your mouth shut. Want to make you afraid that no one ever will or could love you after they'd read it. But truth is, I could never make you as afraid of me as I would be of your words. So I vote we hack off your enemy and publish this thing in as many countries as we can."

Her response was quick and unrehearsed, which meant honest. "You promise to watch over me?"

This was the second time she'd asked.

"Yes."

When she looked up, the tears were real. As was the tremble in her lip. "I don't ever want to go back to—"

I stopped her. "You're not. Ever."

She leaned into me, laying her head on my shoulder. "You think there's really a guy out there who, after reading all this, would ever want what's left of me?"

"I think the entire male race would be crazy not to."

She palmed away the tears and tried to smile. "I'm not sure who's more crazy, you or me, for hoping you're right."

"If I were your enemy, there is one thing I'd want more than anything else."

"What's that?"

Casey's walk out of hell would take longer than most. And while I could rescue her body, her heart might take a while. "If I could render you hopeless, kill your desires, and destroy your dreams, I could crush you— which would allow me to continue doing what I want to do, when I want, to whomever I wanted."

She bit her lip and the anger flashed. Which was a good sign.

Footsteps sounded as Angel and Ellie climbed the steps, hopped on the bed, and wrapped their collective arms around her.

Casey looked at me. "What if they laugh?" She laid her hand flat across the pages. "At me?"

I nodded. "It's a risk we take."

Her head tilted sideways. "We?"

"Us writers."

The revelation surprised her. "Is that what I am?"

"Truth is, you're a better writer than me." I knelt, eye level, and waited until she made eye contact. Then I told them a story I'd never told anyone. When I finished, she held the book in her hand, afraid to open it.

After a moment, she lifted the cover and peeked inside, afraid to look but wanting to.

She asked, "Did you?"

Halfway through writing her manuscript, as the weight of telling her story became real to her, Casey had asked me, "Will you write the foreword?"

"Me or David Bishop?"

She'd smiled. "What's the difference?"

Writers, many of whom spend a lot of time alone behind screens, just need to know they're not alone. So I agreed.

Angel and Ellie had not known I'd agreed to do so. They leaned closer, eyes wide as Casey flipped to the page, saw my words in print for the first time, and held back a sob. Maybe then she knew I was in it with her. "Read it to me?"

# CHAPTER 21

## *The Resurrection of Casey Girl*

### Foreword

Years ago, I was working in Italy. I'd heard of Michelangelo's *David* but never seen him. So I bought a ticket and walked down a long hallway lined with what look like half-finished sculptures. Huge square chunks of veined marble with forms of people being released. Works he never finished. I thought, *What a shame. A waste.* Then I turned a corner, and there he was. Towering. Perfection. It's the first and only time I've ever looked at a piece of stone that took my breath away. No matter how long I sat and stared, I could not understand how human hands did that. How did Michelangelo know David was in there? Hidden in the rock. Spotless. No blemish. Just waiting for the sculptor's hands to fling wide the prison doors.

Only one other time in my life have I felt this way. And the source of that awe you now hold in your hands.

From the moment we're born, life chips away at us. With every hammer stroke, we watch in horror as the pieces that once made us fall to the ground. Soon we stand amid the rubble. The fragments. The shards and slivers. And we think to ourselves,

*I need that. I can't leave that here. It was once a part of me. I'm no longer whole. I'll never make it without it.* So we spend much of our time chasing or collecting the pieces that break off, those that are stolen, or the ones we leave behind. Pretty soon, the pieces we carry are more than our hands can hold, so we throw a bag over our shoulder and stuff it full. Eventually a backpack. Before long, we're reduced to vagabonds scouring the earth. Tormented by the fear that we're incomplete, never whole until we find every single piece. Soon our pack is bigger than us and we're bent over, inching along. A beast of burden walking under the crushing. Focused on what's missing rather than what's revealed.

But every now and then, one brave soul comes along and risks what the fearful won't and never will. Despite the possibility of open rejection, abandonment, criticism, mockery, laughter, and shame, she lifts her pack off her shoulder, empties it before the world, and lets strangers sift through the pieces. Holding each by hand. Gemologists studying her imperfections under a magnifier. Every piece a word spoken.

When Michelangelo freed David from the cold marble cell that held him, the ground below the scaffolding was littered with pieces. Pieces that once made up the rock but not David. We know this because when finished, Michelangelo didn't sweep all those discards into a pile only to hang them in a pack on David's back. Why would he free him only to curse him through all eternity with carrying the marble walls of his own prison?

For reasons none of us understand, Casey has suffered the pain of the hammer and chisel, which makes her uniquely and singularly qualified to show the rest of us that we're better off without all that deadweight. That despite the scars on the surface, there's something beautiful, perfect, and without blemish just inches below.

Her majestic, powerful, soul-cleansing, pain-riddled, and

triumphant words woven through a tapestry of sweat-soaked and tearstained pages are a masterful mosaic made up of all the broken pieces that mirror the whole. Stand too close and see only jagged rocks. But back up . . . and a giant killer emerges.

Casey Girl.

Writers are not like other people. We are the piece-keepers. We gather and guard. Holding fast throughout all eternity the discarded pieces that whisper the majesty and wonder of what is. What was. And the ever-elusive and exceedingly dangerous truth: what could be. We alone carry and share them. Carving pieces into letters that make up the words that heal us. And once they are carved, whether by hammer, chisel, or damp velvet cloth, we spill them selflessly across the earth's table, where they walk the hurting from broken to not. From unable to breathe to laughing. From sickness of the soul to tears dripping off the corners of a smile. From lost to known and accepted in the knowing. This is the matchless and immeasurable power of our words. That's what we do. We wander the earth. We unearth David. We slay giants. For we alone are the keepers of the letters that set us free.

—David Bishop

I closed the book.

Casey tucked her knees into her chest and laid her head on Angel's lap, rocking back and forth, her eyes staring ten thousand miles behind us. In the entirety of my life, I'd never heard anyone cry like that. I'd like to think what I heard was a cleansing. Niagara washing her from the inside out. And while I wanted to reach in and hold her, I knew better. I could not ease her pain. So I stood and watched her shake and heard an almost inhuman sound emit from the pit of her stomach. Something was loosed. Something I couldn't see. A shackle she'd been carrying but wasn't any longer.

# CHAPTER 22

I made it to the Eagle's Nest in good time. My body was healing and most of my strength had returned. I was starting to feel more like me. That did not mean I wasn't breathing hard. I was. But my lungs were letting me push my body, and I was starting to put on muscle and take off fat. Gunner stood next to me. Not breathing hard. He looked at me like we'd just taken a walk in the park. Evidence that he, too, had healed.

I was standing at the railing, Colorado stretched out before me, rehearsing my lines when Bones appeared over my shoulder. I'd not heard him coming. He said, "Trying to get your nerve up?"

"Something like that."

"You afraid she'll say no?"

"No. I just . . . Summer's had a hard go. She deserves the fairy tale—to be asked rightly. By a knight who can speak in complete sentences and not bungle the words or drool down his chin."

He stood staring, finally acknowledging what stared back at us. "Peaceful."

"Like the pain and the hurt can't climb this high."

He reached in his jacket pocket and retrieved an envelope. Then studied me a minute. "I know you have questions. Doubts even. Why I didn't tell you about Marie." He weighed his head side to side. "Were I you, I'd doubt me too." He handed me the letter. "I don't have your gift with words, but now that you're healthy, I've attempted to explain. Give you the backstory." A shrug. "I'm not sure anything justifies my reasons . . . but there they are."

We stood a moment, breathing the cool air. Then he turned, walked to the stairs that descended to the trail, and turned. "It's been killing me for fourteen years. I'd rather it not kill me any longer." He paused, choosing his words. "I don't want to go through the rest of our lives with this standing between us." He pointed to the letter. "I'm asking you to forgive me. And to do so . . . you'll need that."

He descended the stairs and began picking his way down the rocks like a cat. Ten years my senior and stronger than any thirty-year-old I'd ever met.

I turned the letter in my hands, the piercing in my chest returning. When I looked down again, Bones had become a speck in the distance. The letter felt heavy. I knew he meant well and part of me wanted to read it, but the pain in my chest would not let me. Not now. Too soon. I needed space. Time. While my body was healing, portions of my heart felt raw. So I slipped it in my pocket and stared out across the world and back into memory.

The next morning Summer clicked on my light at 5 a.m. for my ascent up the mountain of pain—and found me dressed. But not in running shoes. She rubbed her eyes. "You okay?"

I was wearing dress jeans, a black leather jacket, and a fitted light blue shirt with a collar, which Angel had told me was "in my color wheel." Whatever that is. I stood. "We leave in forty minutes."

"We?"

A nod.

She smiled. Evidently liking the mystery. "Where are 'we' going?"

"Telling you that will ruin the surprise."

She pressed a finger to her lips and considered me. A look of confusion. "Who dressed you?"

"Me."

A laugh. "Not in this lifetime."

I relented. "Angel."

"Figures."

She ran her fingers through my hair. "Did you actually put product in your hair?"

"Well, Angel said . . ."

She sniffed my neck where I'd sprayed the cologne Angel and Ellie had bought me and walked out laughing.

My voice followed her. "You don't like it?"

Ninety minutes later, we stepped into the plane where our chef had prepared her favorite: eggs Benedict. She put one hand on her hip and raised the opposite eyebrow. "What do you want?"

I laughed.

We landed in New York City two and a half hours later, where a car drove us to her apartment to pick up what few items she'd left behind. Some memorabilia, show prints, and her tap shoes. She wanted those most of all. Under a brisk fall day, we walked Central Park, ate lunch at a café, and sipped a cappuccino while watching the polar bears frolic through the glass of the park pool. Every few minutes I'd notice her studying me out of the corner of her eye. She did not like not being in control of our schedule. Around one o'clock, the driver returned us to the airport. Thinking our adventure over, she let down her guard and said, "Thank you for this. It was very thoughtful."

"You're welcome."

Two hours later, we landed again, and when she exited the plane into a balmy seventy-eight-degree afternoon, she turned with suspicion. "This doesn't feel like Colorado."

"That's because it's not."

She looked like she'd bitten into a lemon. "Where are we?"

"Florida."

"But I hate this place."

I laughed.

The car drove us to the south side of the St. Johns River, within eyesight of where I'd first found Gunner, and parked in front of a high-rise. I held the door while she looked at me with quiet suspicion. She said nothing on the elevator, simply tapped her teeth with her finger, and then stepped off when the doors opened at the thirty-seventh floor, where I led her down one hallway, into a second, and finally rang the bell at suite 3714.

She stood tapping her foot, but I don't think she was aware of it. The suspense was killing her.

Old man Harby had changed since I last saw him. Blond hair had given way to white. He shook my hand. "What's it been, twenty years?"

"Twenty-two."

He opened the door and led us into a foyer sparsely decorated with sofas, chairs, and bulletproof glass that looked into the showroom where he kept the jewelry. His secretary buzzed us in, and he led Summer into his candy store where everything glistened. Per my request, Mr. Harby had laid out several dozen items across his display cases. Pendants, bracelets, crosses, necklaces, every type of jewelry you can imagine save one—there were no rings. This wasn't that type of trip. I was trying to thank her, not marry her. At least, not now.

She looked at me. Not breathing. Not asking the question on the tip of her tongue. I stepped aside and said, "Pick one."

She sucked in a deep breath.

"Okay . . . two."

She covered her mouth, tears bubbling into the corners of her eyes. "Why?"

I waved my hand across the countertops. "I wanted to thank you."

"For?"

"Giving me a reason."

"To . . ."

I stared down at the river. Directly below us lay the body of water where I'd first lifted Gunner into the boat. From here it flowed east where it bled into the Intracoastal. And finally south where it ended at the edge of the world. I turned to her. "Breathe."

She let out a short cry, nodded, and dabbed her nose with a handkerchief that the assistant, appearing out of nowhere, gave her. Summer looked impressed that I'd actually thought this whole thing up. The trip to NYC, picking up her stuff, lunch in Central Park, and then diverting on a flight she thought was coming home. She nodded. "Good answer." Walking to the counter, she turned and pointed at me. "There's no way you thought this up all on your own. You had help."

"Lots."

"Like?"

"Bones and the girls were helpful with New York, but this . . . is all Clay."

She spoke through a smirk, though without looking at me. "Knew I loved that old man."

Over the next thirty minutes, she oohed and aahed and touched every single thing on the counter. Even picked up a couple. Eventually she waved her hand across the top of her chest and said, "Is it hot in here or is it just me?"

Mr. Harby looked at her over his jeweler's glasses, tugging down his Mr. Rogers sweater. "Temp is set year-round at sixty-five just for this purpose."

You could have hung meat in that place.

Pretty soon, I noticed a theme. Whenever she'd pick up something, she'd set it on her wrist or lay it across her neck or pin it to her blouse and then stare in the mirror, saying, "Doesn't this look just like Angel?" Or "That looks like Ellie." Or "Angel would love this . . ."

All of this was evidence of the life she'd lived—always caring for others. Which had produced the beautiful and selfless inability to think of herself.

I had a feeling things would end this way.

In my career, I had made it a habit never to give gifts to anyone at Freetown. I knew the tactics of those who'd kidnapped them in the first place, and gifts were often used to manipulate hearts. Jewelry was commonly used in the psychological warfare in which the girls found themselves. In their minds, glitter equaled deception. A down payment for the evil that was about to be inflicted on them and the revolving door their bodies were to become.

I never wanted to be associated with that. But Casey was somehow different. While I'd rescued her body, her heart had yet to follow.

For Casey, I made an exception. Doing so meant I ran the risk of further attaching her to me, but she was fragile and still badly broken. There were pieces of her soul that had yet to return to her. And, if I'm honest, most every time I looked at her, I remembered lifting her off the floor of that shower, feeling her limp legs in my arms, and thinking to myself, *What kind of world am I living in now? What evil has been done to this child?* And I remember being very angry.

So we left with three diamond necklaces and a sterling Hamilton pocket watch from the twenties.

Descending the elevator, Summer stood alongside me, her arm locked in mine, smiling at me in the door's reflection. She looked giddy. She kept saying, "They're gonna love them."

The driver drove north up Heckscher Drive and stopped when I told him. I led her through the woods to the water's edge where I'd stashed a small skiff. I cranked the engine, and we routed up the Fort George River against the tide toward my island.

It was the first time I'd been back since someone had tried to kill me, and the sight did not welcome me. The island had been burned. Everything. To the ground. Barn. Dock house. Outbuildings. Even the chapel. The only things still standing were the ballast stone walls that were more than two feet thick. It'd take more than fire to bring them down. I wandered the island, picking through the wreckage that was once my life.

Turning up stones.

It was not easy and it hurt more than I'd thought. I was glad Gunner was not here.

I found myself staring at the charred walls of the chapel, tracing the grooves of the names and touching the jagged remains of the hooks where I'd displayed the archery pieces I'd brought back from my journeys to parts unknown. All of the oily, hand-worn pews were gone, as was every shiny fragment of stained glass. Adding insult to injury, some kids had spray-painted "Frank was here" and "For a good time, call . . ." across the stone that once supported the altar.

The place was a good picture of me.

Summer appeared next to me. Once again feeling more for someone other than herself. "I'm so . . . so sorry."

We walked to the water's edge, where I'd played as a kid, and waded in. Shin deep. A gentle current pulled across our feet and tugged at us. Washed us. I had wanted her to see this. To remember where I came from. That despite what our idyllic life in Colorado might allow us to forget, this was the womb that birthed me.

My contingency plan had two parts. Both from Mr. Harby.

I held her hands in mine. "I want to give you something."

"Haven't you given me enough today?"

"No." I laughed. "We are giving Angel, Ellie, Casey, and Clay something. And despite lunch in Central Park and eggs Benedict on a private plane, you have yet to let me give you anything."

"Well . . ."

I opened the blue box revealing a Jerusalem cross.

She covered her mouth. Then touched it gently.

I lifted it from the box and clasped it around her neck.

A breeze filtered through the palm trees. Cooling our skin. She tried to talk but bumbled her words. Finally, she laughed at herself, which was one of her best traits. "Is it hot in here or is it just me?"

I breathed in. Then out.

She stared at it. Then me. "What's it mean?"

"Unconquered."

The word on my tongue was somehow tied to a floodgate inside Summer's head, and when I spoke it, the gate opened. She pressed her head to my chest and stood listening to my heart pound. After several minutes, she stood back and stared at the glistening thing. Letting it rest gently in her palm. "My history with men is not . . ." She shook her head. "Ever since I met you, I've been afraid somebody was going to tap me on the shoulder and tell me, 'Move along. My turn.' Every morning I wake up in that dreamlike world called Freetown and I watch my daughter bloom into this woman who amazes me, yet I keep waiting for a knock on the door that doesn't come where that same person tells me, 'Time's up, honey. Clear out.'"

She laughed at herself. "Now, every time I see this thing in the mirror,

I'll wonder if that same jealous lover is going to snap their fingers and hold out a hand."

"Nobody's going to take this from you. And nobody's going to kick you out of your room."

She let out a cry. "You sure?"

I laughed. "Pretty sure." I turned it over. "There is one thing . . ."

Her complexion changed.

"Mr. Harby inserted a chip. It allows me to—"

"Don't tell me you're—"

I continued, "Track you for seven days from the moment I turn it on."

"I was afraid you were going to say that."

"Only if I need to find you."

Her reaction wasn't much better.

I pointed. "It looks like a diamond."

Her suspicion spread. "You do this to the girls' gifts too?"

I shrugged.

"Some might accuse you of being paranoid."

"One man's paranoia is another man's preparation."

"Cute. Who taught you that?"

"Bones."

"Figures." Her eyes narrowed. "How do you turn it on?"

"Satellite."

"Seriously?" She pointed up. "From forty miles in space?"

I calculated. "Something like that."

"So . . . you click a few keys and X marks the spot?"

"I think it's more of a red flashing thing."

She frowned. "And here I am thinking you're being all romantic."

I tried to explain. "There are evil people out there who would love to hurt you because you mean something to me."

"Something?"

As the sun fell westward of the Intracoastal, bathing us in soft light, I spoke over the memory of me. Something I'd been in the habit of doing lately—looking backward. "When I was a kid, nothing but cutoffs and sun-bleached hair, I fell in love in these waters. Somewhere within a few feet of us, I gave Marie me. Not some portion, but the piece that holds all of me." I paused as the daylight fell to dusk.

"Over the years, after Marie left . . . I would look inside me and stare into the hole and wonder how to live. What would fill it? I tried to drown it in drink, but that couldn't touch it. Only made me more thirsty. So I crawled into my basement and turned to my pen. And when I grew tired, I would turn out the light, board up my secrets, and poke my head above the surface. Then Bones found me, patched me up, and I poured myself into my work. Wasn't difficult. Living numb made me better at my job. That's not to say I didn't care about the people I searched for—I did and still do. But not like . . ." I faded off.

"A decade passed. Writer. Rescuer. Twenty-four-seven." I stared at her. Studying the quiver in her eyes. "No matter how many boards I nail across the hole, I can't kill the ache. Something still lives down there. Something unkillable in the darkness. Maybe we're all born with that. Maybe it's part of being this thing we call human. The ache for another. The desire to reach into the night and find someone's hand reaching back. To wake to the sound of someone breathing in your ear. To know the warmth of another. To pour two cups of coffee."

I held her at arm's length, waiting until her watery eyes focused on mine. The uncertainty told me that while I'd published more than a million and a half words, I wasn't connecting. Summer was scared of what I was about to say.

I shook my head, speaking as much to myself as her. "Why is it I can write what I mean but seldom say it?" I tried a second time. "When I was a kid looking out across my future, I didn't see the me I've become. The one I see staring back at me. I didn't see scars and tattoos and memories I can't ever share with you. I saw someone else, and I'm not him. I want you to take a long look at me. Despite the fact that Angel is safe, I wonder if I am. Is being with me unsafe? Something broke me long ago. I walk with a limp. And after all I've seen, I don't believe people are good. There's no gray. I see black and white and often the image is fuzzy, so I make split decisions on partial information and I'm constantly forced to live with the consequences of that. I've seen things I can't . . ." I shook my head.

She held my face in both her hands. "Murph . . ."

I was studying the shoreline.

Her tone of voice changed. She whispered, "David Bishop Murphy."

My name brought me back. I looked down at her. The memory of our meeting returned. She tried to speak but I cut her off. "Remember how when we first met and I took you to that diner—"

"And you told me that water can be dangerous when you don't swim?"

"Actually, I was thinking more about the part where you told me that life can be sucky when you don't know how to dance."

"Oh." She smiled. "That part."

"You told me how you lived with the hope that you weren't condemned to live and die alone on the Island of Misfit Toys."

I was trying to finish my thought when she kissed me, then leaned into me, staring out across the water. "I'm not going anywhere. You're safe with me, and I've never felt safer than when I'm with you. There are no bad men on this beach or in this water. You can say whatever you want to say. Whatever you need to." She tapped the cross and then held me tight, pressing her chest to mine, her breath on my face. "I'm not in this for what I get. I'm here for you. I want the you who is standing right here. All of you. Even the broken, busted pieces." She flipped the cross over. "And if you ever turn this thing on and the screen doesn't show me next to you, then somebody has taken me from you." She smiled. "And I'm not a willing participant."

I thought back to our first real conversation in the all-night diner after I'd picked the oyster shells out of her back. I tried to speak softly. "I would like to bring you coffee in the mornings. Finish your sentences. Protect you from the world that wants to hurt you."

She smiled. "You already do those things."

I lifted the second blue box out of my jacket and raised the lid. "Then dance with me. For the rest of our lives." Summer eyed the ring, covered her mouth, and let go the remaining floodgate. Her knees buckled and she collapsed, the once shin-deep water now cradling her hips. And in that instant, that painful picture of her now washed in the water reminded me that a change in circumstances doesn't render someone whole. Only one thing does that.

I knelt, eye level, and waited while what had been bottled up most of her life poured out. A pouring she could not control. It was a shoulder-shaking, soul-purging cry. Evidence that it had been stuffed down in there a long time.

I'm no expert, but in my limited experience, women aren't born women. They start out as girls. And every girl, from the moment they can dream, imagines the rescue. The knight. The castle. Life in a fairy tale. If you don't believe me, watch boys and girls on a playground. No one teaches us to do this. The kid in us actually believes in things that are too good to be true. Before life convinces us we can't and they're not.

Then life kicks in. Boys become men. Girls become women. For any number of reasons we are wounded and, sadly, wounded people wound people. So many of us grow into doubting, hopeless, callous adults pro-tecting hardened hearts. Medicating the pain. Life isn't what we imagined. Nor are we. And we didn't start out trying to get there. Far from it. But it's who we've become. One day we turn around, and what we once dreamed or hoped is a distant echo. We've forgotten what it sounded like. Once pure and unadulterated, the voice of hope is now muted by all the stuff we've crammed on top of it. And we're okay with that. For some illogical reason, we stand atop the mine shaft of ourselves, shoving stuff into the pipe that is us, telling our very soul, "Shut up. Not another word." Why? Because the cry of our heart hurts when unanswered. And the longer it remains unanswered, the deeper the hurt. In self-protection we inhale resignation and exhale indifference.

Summer's cry had never been answered. If hope deferred makes the heart sick, then Summer's heart had been sick a long time.

But not everything we bury is dead. Some stuff is just buried beneath the rubble. Lying in the dark, muted, waiting in hope for another to peel back the rocks. Some shake their fist and categorically reject the notion of the fairy tale. They're not in need of rescue. Never have been. That would suggest being dependent upon another. Which they are not. And it's sexist to suggest they are.

But I say we are. Designed to do life "with" rather than "without."

Summer had been waiting a long time for another to come along and offer his heart without reservation. And ask for hers without manipulation. Summer was shaking in the water because, all her life, she'd hoped against hope that the voice was true. That she wasn't crazy. That maybe, just maybe, the music would play and some guy would tap her on the shoulder and lead her across the dance floor.

No longer was she relegated to a seat along the wall, excluded from the floor—or worse yet, teaching others how to dance. I was inviting her to center stage.

To dance with me.

And so I waited while she said nothing. I sat in the water that birthed me, wrestling with her silence, rewinding my words in my head. But words are like bullets. Once they exit the barrel, it's impossible to bring them back.

After a minute, I spoke again. "Summer, I'm sorry . . . I saw this happening differently in my mind's eye. I tried to say it right and I know I didn't. I wanted to—"

She shook her head, but no words came. After a few seconds, she held up a finger. The universal sign for "give me a minute."

So I did. Then another. Then one more.

Finally, she sat on her heels, her shoulders relaxed now, a slight smile creasing her lips. "It was perfect."

"It was?"

She nodded and wiped her face and nose. "I thought you were telling me you didn't want me, and you were just trying to break it to me easy."

"Really?"

She nodded.

I sat on my heels. "Everything I just said, and that was your takeaway?"

Another nod.

The difference between what she heard and what I intended, or even what I thought I said, is evidence that the stuff in the pipe is real. That what we breathe in and what we breathe out can actually alter the words that are spoken so they fit a false narrative. But pain, like fear, is a liar. And it has but one lie: *This love is too good to be true, and even if it were true, you don't deserve it.*

Which is a lie from the pit of hell.

I know. We battle it every day on the streets of Freetown.

It is true and we do deserve it.

I shook my head. "I need to work on my communication." I paused, staring at myself from outside myself, and then spoke primarily to myself. "Next time I'll write a letter."

She smiled and shook her head. "There's no next time. There's just this time."

Oddly enough, I was still holding the ring aloft. An offering.

Slowly, her eyes shifted from the water to the ring and then to me. She held both of my hands in both of hers. "I know all this about you."

"You do?"

She nodded matter-of-factly.

"How?"

"I'm a woman."

"Well, why didn't you say something?"

"I've been waiting for you to say it."

"Is that the way this works?"

She nodded again. "I hope so."

There it was. That one word. The singular remedy.

I scratched my head. "My experience in this conversation is like backing up a trailer. If I want to go right, I turn the wheel left. And don't, under any circumstances, try to navigate by looking through the rearview. Turn around."

She laughed, wiped her face on my sleeve, and held up her naked hand. "You have to put it on me."

"Somebody should offer a class on this."

"They do." She smiled. "They're called dance lessons."

I slid the ring on her finger, staring at her as it came to rest where her finger met her hand. "Summer, I—"

She lifted her right index finger, pressed it to my lips, then kissed me and smiled. "Shhh . . . You're perfect."

Given the two-hour difference, the plane landed at Freetown shortly after 8 p.m. where, thanks to the crew who had helped me plan this, a party was waiting. They were beaming. They'd strung lights, chilled champagne, lit seven fire pits, and filled the air with Summer's favorite classical music: Pachelbel. Angel and Ellie were giddy. Clay broke out his best suit and penguin wing tips. Even Bones looked satisfied that after weeks of planning we'd pulled it off and I hadn't messed it up. At least not that they knew.

Bones stood alongside me. Sipping wine. Bumping shoulders. The butt of his Sig imprinted beneath his flowing white robes. Firelight danced across his chiseled face, adding a sheen to his white hair. We were staring at Summer, who was in the process of giving gifts to Angel, Ellie, Casey, and Clay. A mother hen and her chicks.

Bones nodded, smiling smugly. "She said yes."

"You seem surprised."

He looked at me. "Are you?"

I nodded. "Yes."

He wrapped an arm around me and said nothing. Which said everything.

I had no idea what was involved in planning a wedding, but evidently women are born with this thing that kicks into gear when a wedding is to be planned. The following morning my trio of wedding planners woke with the sun and began doing whatever women do that involves a "Yes, I will, and yes, I do."

I stared across and down at them from the mountain. Sweat pouring off my face. I had awakened early, hit it hard, and was met at the trailhead by Bones. Ten years my senior and still taking me to school. Several times I tried to lose the old man, but neither Gunner nor I could shake him. A little more than an hour later, we stood on the porch of the Eagle's Nest and sipped Nicaraguan coffee. Something he'd read about in a book about a drug runner who ends up in love with a girl in Nicaragua who owns a coffee plantation with this storied well. He told me I should read it.

I gestured with my coffee. "I'm going to start calling you Superman. Or the Freak. Something other than Bones."

He nodded. "Not as easy as it used to be."

"Fooled me."

"Residue on the Whaler fragments suggests a rare and expensive explosive. Military grade. Recorded satellite images show three men exiting the water, setting the bombs in less than seven minutes, and disappearing back into the water."

"They knew what they were doing."

"Precision."

"You think they can get to us here?"

He shrugged. "I didn't think they could get to you there."

"That's comforting."

Bones studied me. "Why so tense?"

I held up my phone. "Keep waiting for you to send me a picture of some innocent soul in a bad mess and I've got to flip my switch, exit this fantasy, and get back to the real world where people are living and dying."

He took my new phone, only days old, and sailed it like a Frisbee out across the vast expanse before us. It spun saucer-like through the air and fell to the rocks some thousand feet below where it bounced and shattered. He sipped the last of his coffee. "Race you down."

# CHAPTER 23

My publisher discovered quickly that Casey's story sold itself. Between the quality and transparency of the writing, interview requests poured in. With growing attention, Casey's dread rose in equal measure. The idea of having to jump into and out of her story, day in and day out, made her physically sick. Summer was the first to point out that Casey wasn't eating. I took this as clear evidence she'd never survive a book tour. Knowing what a book release would require and wanting to protect her, I suggested we control the ground. If they want the story, they can come to us. No one liked that idea more than Casey.

We spent a month prepping for the release party. The idea of a dozen media trucks parked along Main Street in Freetown didn't appeal to us. Too much we couldn't control. What happened when some ignorant reporter decided to interview one of the girls who was not Casey and then plastered her face across the six o'clock news where she could be quickly identified by her exploiter? Not good. We chose a town thirty minutes away and then cut the security team loose to control the ground.

Which they did with a vengeance.

My publisher cranked up the marketing engine, word spread, and media outlets brought in giant, antenna-topped trucks en masse in anticipation of Casey's emergence. We also tripled security. While we wanted to give her a chance to tell her story, we did not want Casey exploited for that story. Too many girls like her had been rescued out of slavery only to be further undressed by media talking heads pushing ratings. Which meant we would protect her like hawks. At the first hint of inappropriate questions or too much emphasis on the horror rather than the resurrection and the hope, we'd lift her out. Period. No questions.

What the media did not know was that sixty percent of our security were dressed as news personalities and cameramen. The guys loved the change in decor.

By 7:00 p.m. on a Thursday night, the auditorium was three-quarters full. Several of the top talking heads in the country had traveled from Los Angeles and New York City to interview the girl with the funny last name. Those who had not would regret it soon enough. Casey sat offstage, one knee bouncing nervously, chewing one nail to the quick. When Bones introduced her, Ellie and Angel escorted her, holding her hands and standing alongside her at the podium. Everyone, me included, thought it best if I remained in the shadows. Unknown. Throughout both the writing and the lead-up to tonight, Casey had promised never to mention my name. Only to call me Wilby. Clay stood prominently behind her. His presence alone said both "caretaker" and "bouncer."

Casey had prepared a short summary of her story. Something to break the ice. A beginning. She had spent the last two days rehearsing it before the mirror. Her life in twelve minutes. She grasped the podium, blinked under the spotlights and camera flashes, and swallowed. Then the caterpillar cracked the shell of her cocoon and opened her mouth.

Two minutes later, she had them eating out of her hand.

Trafficked across continents from porch to palace to trailer park, sold multiple times on the black web and across coffee tables and the hoods of cars, subjected to multiple forced abortions, she was used, discarded, then found, only to be used, injected, and sold again. A pattern that repeated more than her mind could remember. Casey had purposefully worn a sleeveless shirt, unwilling to hide the holes the needles had torn and the self-inflicted scars on her wrists. When I asked her if she was sure she wanted to do that, she'd responded, "If I'm going out there, then me is going out there."

Seven minutes in, after she'd detailed her addiction and second suicide attempt, she paused and lowered her face, and I wondered if we'd lost her. If she'd climbed back in her shell. *Did we push her too hard?*

I took a step toward the stage when Bones placed a hand on my arm. "Give her a minute."

After a long, quiet minute in which her right hand traced the scars on her left arm, she lifted her head, smiled, and waved her hand across all of them. "I'd like all of you to know that we brought you here so we could steal your cars." Laughter rippled across the audience. "That's happening as we speak. But don't worry, it's only a twelve-mile walk to town. Most of which is downhill."

When she finished, the room fell awkwardly quiet. Even the cameras were quiet. Casey put a hand on her hip and broke the silence. "I rehearsed that little speech a dozen times in the mirror using my toothbrush as a microphone. Was it that bad?" The laughter was good for all of us. Over the next hour, she fielded one question after another. Never stumbling. Never faltering.

While uneducated beyond sixth grade, she surprised us on several levels. One interviewer asked her, "How many languages do you speak?"

Casey weighed her head back and forth. "I can speak in seven and write five."

Bones turned to me. "Did you know that?"

"No idea."

The interviewer continued his questioning in French. Which Casey answered in French. The interviewer then asked his question again. This time in English. "How is this so, given that you have had no schooling beyond sixth grade?"

Casey laughed. "Oh, I went to school. Just my classroom probably looked a little different from yours." More laughter. "Early on, while I was still"—she made quotation marks with her fingers—"desirable, I was moved around a lot and the people who owned me liked to make customers comfortable, including their surroundings, so they'd put me in places that looked like homes. And given that most homes include books . . . I read." She tilted her head. "In between . . ."

At this point, several reporters were firing questions. "What'd you read?"

"Everything."

"How many books have you read?"

Casey shook her head. "Thousands."

"The title, *The Resurrection of Casey Girl*. Why'd you choose that?"

"My birth certificate is a bit of an anomaly. My first name is listed as 'Casey.' My last name is listed as 'Girl.'"

Casey let the truth of that sink in while whispers rippled through the crowd.

"You just described yourself as 'still desirable.' What do you mean by that?"

Casey considered how to answer. "One of my owners liked to bet on greyhounds. He'd set me up in a room, take the client's money, and walk to the window. This meant I spent a lot of time at the track, but I never watched the races. When I wasn't working, I'd wander out back where they walked the older dogs—the ones who once won them a lot of money but now had lost a step. Rather than rest and feed them, they walked them down this long straightaway followed by a blind right turn. Minutes later, they'd return carrying the leash. One day I wandered back there. On a board above the shed where they stack the bodies, someone had spray-painted, 'Undesirable.'"

A hush fell across the room.

A female reporter in the back of the room spoke up. "Can you explain the scars on your arms?"

Casey lifted her arm, revealing the holes. "Needles tear the skin when you have the shakes. You're just trying to hit your arm, much less a vein. And . . ." She turned her left wrist to the cameras, which clicked rapidly. "Box cutters." Then, exposing her right arm, she said, "A thirty-second-story windowpane."

A voice from the crowd. "Were you thinking about jumping?"

Casey looked at me. Then at the voice. "Yes."

"What stopped you?"

Casey shrugged. "The thought of meeting the concrete."

More laughter. Casey had a beautiful way of making people comfortable with her own story and the pain that accompanied it. A gift unparalleled. I'd never seen anything like it.

The last question was the one we'd all anticipated. While Casey was a story unto herself, she was, in some ways, only half the story. Someone had rescued her. They wanted that person. "Casey, what can you tell us about the one who rescued you?"

Casey shrugged and locked arms with Angel, who featured prominently toward the end of her book. "She's standing next to me."

"What about the man you call Wilby?"

"What about him?"

"Is Wilby his real name?"

"No."

"Why that name?"

"I named him after William Wilberforce. A member of British parliament in the nineteenth century."

"Why him?"

"He spent his life, his fortune, and sacrificed his political career to help eradicate the East India slave trade." She shrugged. "Because of him, the powerbrokers and elite of Britain willingly gave up several hundred million pounds sterling. The name fit."

"What's he like?"

She considered this. "Quiet. More comfortable in shadow than spotlight. And he has no interest in you."

"Will we ever meet him?"

"Not if he doesn't want you to."

"But, Casey, you of all people must understand that his story deserves to be told as well as yours."

She found the voice in the crowd and zeroed in on it, pausing briefly. "And you, of all people, must know that there are tens of thousands of girls just like me. Still flat on their backs. Raped repeatedly for profit. Right this second. Day after week after month after . . ." You could have heard a pin drop. "And if you focus your attention on him, then you're not focused on them." She scanned the crowd. "During the eighteenth and nineteenth century, men whose only aim was profit would retrofit cargo ships with decks and shackles. Stacking people eight and twelve deep, where the urine and the feces and the vomit drained downward. Those on the bottom often drowned. Those who survived the crossing were sold again to equally evil men who put them to work during the day and forced them to lie flat at night." She paused, studying contorted faces. "Do my words offend you? Make your stomachs turn?" She held up her book. "I was one among many stowed below deck. Drowning. If Wilby were here, he'd tell you to spend your resources and talent finding and exposing the masters of the ships. Doing so will free those shackled below."

The ovation lasted ten minutes. And while I knew she meant well, her words would only serve to heighten the search for Wilby.

By the time the antennae trucks had cleared, *Resurrection* had climbed the charts and was flirting with number one on Amazon. In the comm center, Bones and the team were fielding calls for interviews that would keep Casey busy for weeks. Most requested her presence in studios on either coast, but Bones was resolute. "Nope, we hold the high ground. They come to us."

Casey weathered the storm, and we all watched in wonder as her story caught a rocket ship to the moon. She was everywhere. Given the increased attention, scrutiny, and people, we doubled security again and hung HD cameras on every lamppost, telephone pole, and building apex in Freetown. Not to mention the satellite coverage Bones occasionally tapped into. The comm center looked like mission control at NASA.

Watching the frenzy, I pulled Clay aside. "I need a favor."

He raised his eyebrows.

"I can't be everywhere, so I was wondering if you wouldn't mind—"

He held up a hand. "Done."

From that moment, wherever Casey went, she found Clay had already been there. And whenever she stood still, she did so within the boundaries of his shadow. While this was good for Casey, it wasn't so good for Clay, which I would later discover.

With every question, every interview, we watched in wonder as Casey emerged from her broken shell and became the voice of the unheard and the silenced. One night, in a prime-time interview, the lady asked her, "If you could reach back into time and speak to yourself, if you could speak to those like you, what would you say?"

Without blinking, Casey turned, looked into the lens, reached through the camera, and spoke. "You in the darkness with the water rising around your neck. You with the needle hanging out of your arm. With the palm full of pills . . . the blade resting on your wrist . . . you're not alone. And no matter what the voices say, you are worth rescue." She leaned closer. "I know you don't believe me. I didn't either. Until somebody found me. You're not invisible."

Her world would never be the same.

And while that was good for the story, it was not good for us. This, too, we would learn too late.

A few days after the press conference, Casey found Summer and me on the porch watching the sunset. She was staring silently at the ground as she stood in my doorway. Saying nothing.

I prompted her. "You okay?" She didn't look it.

"Was wondering if you could help me?"

"Sure."

"Do you have a favorite girl's name?" She paused. "It'd be better if it wasn't someone you knew. Like if it wasn't already attached to a face."

"I've always liked Adriana."

Casey looked to Summer, who said, "Always wished my mom had named me Rachael."

Casey wrote down both names. She glanced up and then quickly back down at the ground. "How about a boy's name. Or . . . two boys' names?"

I had a feeling there was more going on here than simply fishing for names. "I've always thought Michael and Gabriel were good names."

Summer nodded.

Casey seemed to like those as she scribbled quickly.

"Now just give me two names. Doesn't matter if they're boy or girl."

Summer spoke first. "Bonnie . . . and Peter."

Casey wrote again. Nodding as she did. Turning to go, she said, "Thanks."

My voice stopped her. "That all you need?"

She turned slowly, made eye contact, and shook her head. "I need a priest."

I stood. "Okay."

She returned to the door. A moment passed while her mouth tried to form the words. Shame covered her like a shadow. "I was forced to have three abortions. And . . . maybe two more, but they're kind of foggy. Doctors told me"—she thumbed over her shoulder—"I can't ever have kids. So . . ." Her eyes darted. "I'd like to bury the five I have."

I took a step toward her. "Say when."

She swallowed and her voice trembled when she spoke. "Tomorrow morning?"

Sunup found us standing on the mountain just shy of the Eagle's Nest on a small, flat, grassy area where the first rays of daylight touched the mountain. At Casey's request, I'd dug a hole. A difficult task in the rocky ground. Summer stood with her arms wrapped around Casey. As did Angel and Ellie. Gunner sat staring at all of us. Bones stood alongside me. I climbed out of the hole and motioned to Casey, who stood holding a shoe box in her hands. "Would you like to say a few words?"

She glanced at the sun, then down into the hole, and finally at the box, speaking to faces only she could see. "If I were you, I'd have a lot of questions about me. I mean . . . I don't know what kind of mom I would've made." A forced chuckle followed by wiping her nose on the blanket wrapped around her shoulders. "Probably not very good. A kid raising kids, but . . . I wanted to speak to you so you could hear your mother's voice, and I wanted to tell you that I'm sorry."

Holding the box, her hands began to tremble. "I also wanted, if you'll let me, to tell you your names. At least the names I would have given you if I had been in my right mind. A baby should have a name. Even if . . ." She paused and rubbed her hand along the top of the box. "So, Adriana, Michael, Gabriel, Bonnie, and . . ." She shot a glance at me. "Bishop." A pause. "I think they're good names. I like them. At least this way the other angels will know what to call you." She gritted her teeth and held back the building wave. "I'm looking forward to meeting you one day. To holding you, if you'll let me. And if I could just say one more thing, I hope when that day comes . . . that you won't hate me . . . as much as I hate me. Maybe we can all sit together a little while with the sun on our faces and the breeze in our hair and you could tell me about you and your hopes and your dreams and . . . if that wouldn't be too much trouble."

Casey swallowed and tilted her head sideways. She'd held it off as long as she could, but the wave crashed down over her shoulders, forcing her to her knees and drawing a sound up and out of her stomach. Out of her womb. The sound was long, loud, and less human than more. When finished, she rested her head on the box, touching the lid tenderly. Staring to the borders of this world, Casey whispered, "I wrote you each a letter. And . . ." We sat in silence as the breeze washed over us and the sun warmed our faces. "I'd like to know the color of your eyes . . . and what your hand feels like when I hold it in mine."

I helped her place the box in the hole while Angel and Ellie helped her cover it with dirt—one small handful at a time. With each measure, the box disappeared. When gone completely, she rested on her knees, eyes closed, staring out across Colorado. Slowly, she lifted her arms. Olympus pressing up on the world. Arms extended, she released the spirits of her children to her Father in heaven. "Please take care of them, rock them to sleep, love them, tuck them in at night . . . and . . . when I knock on the door . . ." Casey shook her head, staring back through memory and pain. She placed her hand on her heart, then she made a fist and pounded it several times. "Please don't remember the me I used to be. Remember the me that I am."

Gunner stared at each of us, walking in circles, whining slightly. Bones stood stoic, tears dripping off his chin.

"Father," I said softly. "Please receive these children." I gently placed my hand on Casey's head. "All of them."

Bones disappeared behind a boulder only to return carrying something covered in a sheet. He set it on the ground next to Casey, lifted the sheet, and revealed a cage holding five white doves. Bones nodded, and

Casey slid the latch and opened the door. One by one, they landed on the small platform, cooing, uncertain at the possibility of their own freedom. Eventually they launched themselves out across the expanse. The last leapt from the cage to Casey's shoulder, skimmed in a circle, cooed, and launched airborne.

Below us they circled, then climbed, rising and falling in acrobatic wonder, only to return in a final flyby and disappear above the Eagle's Nest.

# CHAPTER 24

Two months passed.

Casey and her beautiful story lit up the world. Climbed charts. Won awards. Got picked by actors and their reading clubs. Movie rights were optioned. Her picture covered a few of the magazines at checkout counters. And whenever her picture appeared, Clay was never far behind. White hair. Sunglasses. Suit. In a beautiful exchange, Clay was becoming the father she never had. Often the pictures showed them holding hands. Or his arm around her. And not in some creepy way suggesting impropriety, but in a beautiful manner. A manner that said, *I cherish this woman.*

Given sales, the publisher released a royalty payment before it was due. Nearly seven figures. Casey took one look at the check and shook her head. "This would keep me high the rest of my life."

"Yep."

She handed it to me. "Take it."

"Not a chance."

"I'm serious."

"I am too."

"You won't take it?"

"Not in ten lifetimes."

She turned to Bones, but he cut her off. "Don't look at me."

She frowned. "You two know I cannot be trusted with this."

Clay spoke up. "I can. We'll go dancing."

She laughed and sat in Clay's lap. "Thank you." I watched her with no small amount of joy, for it was here, for the first time, that I knew she'd make it. The fact that she'd just sat in a man's lap and wrapped her arms around his neck meant she'd started to forgive men. What's more, she was blooming in front of our eyes.

# CHAPTER 25

The Colorado night was cold as we camped above eleven thousand feet and beneath a blanket of ten trillion stars. We huddled around the campfire wrapped in blankets, puffer jackets, and each other. While Bones sipped wine, some twenty-year-old product of the vine from a valley in France, the rest of us cooked s'mores. It's been said you can tell a lot about a person by the books on their shelves, and I would agree. I also think you can tell a lot about a person by how they cook a s'more.

Ellie stabbed two marshmallows onto the end of her cooker, shoved them into the center of the heat just inches from the coals, set them on fire, waved the stick like a torch, and then when the whole mess was good and sooty, she slapped it on top of half a Hershey's bar sandwiched between two cinnamon graham crackers. And shoved it in her mouth. All at once. When she bit down, marshmallow goo oozed out the corners of her mouth.

She could not have been happier.

Angel worked a bit differently. She slow-cooked hers, baking the marshmallow to a golden, crispy brown, and then gently set it between the crackers with just the right amount of chocolate. She then pressed gently, squeezing out the mallow and licking the edges clean. When she'd mopped up the ooze, she ate the s'more one quarter at a time.

Ellie wore nearly as much as she ate. Her fingers were covered in both marshmallow and chocolate, while Angel's were spotless.

Casey worked at a different pace. Ellie could eat four s'mores in the time it took Casey to cook one. Casey held her marshmallows at a safe distance. Warming them more than cooking them. Every five minutes or so, she'd inch them closer to the fire. Given the temperature, she'd be lucky to cook them by tomorrow. Having never really cooked the mallows, she set them on top of a piece of chocolate and half a cracker, then nibbled on it.

Casey ate as if she were afraid of hurting the marshmallows.

I felt like I was watching three people approach a swimming pool. Ellie dove in the deep end. Angel walked elegantly down the stairs. And Casey circled it, dipping her toe and testing the water.

It was a complex look into both the depth of their pain and the magnitude of their joy.

I added wood, fed Gunner a hot dog off the fire, and then that beautiful thing happened that happens around all campfires. Stories were told. Ellie began by asking Bones about his life. How he got his start. His history with me. At one point, she asked, "You have any siblings?"

He nodded. "I had a brother."

I did not know this. I sat up. "You have a brother?"

"Had."

Ellie, not picking up on his body language, which suggested he didn't want to talk about his brother, asked, "You keep in touch?"

He stared into the fire and sipped his wine. "He died some years back."

Angel asked her mom about Broadway and her favorite shows. Who she'd starred with. To which Summer responded, "I was never really the star." Her favorite role? Longest-running show? Boyfriends? Favorite things about New York City?

Finally, they got to me. They wanted to know about my younger life, growing up, where I met Bones, where I learned to write, how many times I'd been shot and shot at. My favorite food. Favorite place I've ever been.

Casey listened with rapt attention. Hanging on every word. A fact not lost on Summer. It struck me as I watched the firelight dance off her face that all of this was new for her. Conversations with family around a campfire. Normal conversations where people share laughter and authenticity, and don't steal or demand from one another. Where the joy of a moment wasn't simply a disguise to mask the coming deception of the next hour or week or month.

Casey had cut her hair Audrey Hepburn short. The peroxide white of months ago was replaced by a natural sandy blond. The black circles and black eyeliner had given way to no makeup at all. And anorexia had been supplanted by beautiful curves. Casey's external transformation was one of the most complete I'd ever seen. Much of which could be credited to Angel and Ellie.

Finally, Ellie turned her twenty questions on Casey. "What's your first memory?"

The process of writing her book had opened many a locked door in the basement of her mind. To my surprise, the answers were easy in coming. "I was maybe two or three, and I remember something hot being spilled on me. Oatmeal or grits or something. And my pajamas were those awful one-piece, footed, synthetic things they don't sell anymore. The kind that melted near heat. When the heat fell on me, I reacted. I jumped or fell back or something and touched the heat source. Melting the pajamas to me. My foster parents didn't realize it until a few days later. They didn't change me often." She held up the back side of her right forearm. "When they did, they just ripped it off . . . like you would a Band-Aid." She nodded. "I remember that."

"Favorite vacation?"

She looked around her and smiled. "This one."

Ellie waved her off. "No, really."

Casey looked down, up at me, then back at Ellie. She was trying to be careful with her answer. "I've never been on one."

We knew a lot of Casey's story from her book. We'd all read it. But there were gaps. Obvious sequences of time purposefully left out. "What about Taos? That seemed like a good home."

Casey waved her head back and forth, again weighing the answer. "My sixth foster parents were wealthy. Lived in what felt like a castle. Couldn't have kids so they opened their doors to me, and while the wife doted on me and treated me like a doll, the husband . . ." Casey stared off into the Milky Way. "Didn't. At night, after the wife—I think her name was Margaret or Margo or something like that—had gone to sleep, he'd take me to the basement." She fell quiet a few minutes. "I did not like that basement." More silence. "When I was about eleven, I was snooping around his medicine cabinet, looking for something, anything, to take away my pain, and I found this medicine he'd hidden in this little compartment. I used to wonder how his wife stayed asleep through . . . everything, but then I searched the name on the computer and I didn't have to wonder anymore."

Ellie put her arm around Casey, saying nothing. Casey tried to make us feel better. "I don't think about it much. It was a long time ago."

Leaning on my shoulder, tucked with me under a blanket, Summer had her fists clenched and her heart was pounding.

Casey's life was one ginormous bucket of pain. And while we were doing everything we knew to help, I wondered if it was enough. Was her pain deeper than our love?

Ellie tried to shift direction. "You have any memory of any man treating you kindly?"

She never took her eyes off the fire and nodded.

"Who?"

Casey lifted her right hand and pointed with two fingers. Her middle finger at Bones, and her index finger at me.

An hour later, the carb-crash occurred, and the girls piled into their tent. Wasn't long and they were wrapped like cocoons in their down bags, sleeping—or so I thought.

Somewhere after 2 a.m., I sat next to the fire, listening to the noises coming from the girls' tent. The sounds of someone dreaming bad dreams. Muted screams. Some not so muted. Torment and torture housed within the human soul. I pulled aside the tent door and saw both Ellie and Angel lying on either side of Casey. Both were awake. Casey lay drenched in sweat. Eyes racing back and forth beneath their lids.

I whispered, "She do that often?"

Angel brushed the hair out of Casey's face. "Every night."

Ellie added, "This one's not too bad."

"Anything make it better?"

Angel shrugged. "Not sleeping."

"Anything else?"

"Really powerful drugs."

I returned to the fire and found Bones bathed in firelight, his Sig and two spare magazines resting in a chest holster. I didn't need to ask him if he was expecting trouble. He was. Always. And the sounds coming from that tent told us it was never far.

# CHAPTER 26

We scheduled Casey's interviews so that she would feel more comfortable in known surroundings. Summer suggested we control everything from the chair she sat in, to the light coming into the room, to whether she backed up to the door or a window, to the distance between the camera and her face, to the temperature in the room. And without exception, we controlled every question they asked her. If anyone went off script, one of us would remove them. Forcibly. And without delay.

We intended to control everything for her benefit and her comfort. While we wanted good reviews and positive press for the book, we did not want to purchase them at Casey's expense—however that might occur. We were singularly focused on giving Casey a chance to tell her story in the way she could tell it. Given her Broadway and New York City experience, Summer stepped into the role of manager where, behind the scenes, she vehemently defended Casey's interests without Casey being aware. Which was good because had she known, it would have made her nervous.

One evening Casey sat finishing an interview while Bones and I watched offset. I did so with coffee, he with a wrinkle between his brow. Neither of us were comfortable. I voiced it. "Something bugging you?"

He nodded but never took his eyes off Casey.

The interviewer asked her, "What have you learned about yourself?"

Casey never hesitated. "One of the problems with rescuing someone is that their spirit isn't always quick to follow their body. Especially when they've learned to distance or disconnect themselves from the body that houses them. You can take us out of prison, but it may take a while to take the prison out of us. And while the body may heal completely—and it can and does—and we can monitor and measure that healing and that recovery, the spirit is not so easily quantified. What works for the body may not work for the rest of us. All of us who have experienced the trauma of trafficking are bruised, wounded, and scarred not only on the outside but the in. And the amount of time needed to heal is as different as the people themselves. No two of us are the same. One girl's healing will look different from mine."

To our surprise, and despite questions that grew more difficult with each interview, Casey bloomed before our eyes. She had learned how to handle every question and had a unique and beautiful ability to speak "with" both the interviewer and viewer rather than "to." A talent she'd earned and paid for the hard way.

At Freetown, we'd never had a story like Casey's. Yes, we'd rescued girls who'd suffered horrific stories lived out over years, but we'd never had one exit that life only to enter one illuminated by so national a spotlight. So public. Everyone else healed in private. Not Casey. And as I listened to her, I wanted to believe what she shared about that healing.

Problem was, I did not.

# CHAPTER 27

Since arriving at Freetown, Casey had taken to the mountains like a Sherpa, often hiking eight or ten miles with relative ease. I could barely keep up with her. She spent as much time in the mountains as her room.

One of the conditions of living in Freetown is that your private life is not private. You agree when you walk through the doors that everything about you is open to scrutiny and observation. Twenty-four-seven. This does not mean we hang cameras in the bathroom, but the reasons are obvious: your protection. Along with everyone else's. And everyone agrees this is a good idea. Especially those who have been trafficked.

The men who once owned and capitalized off these girls are masters at psychological warfare and deception. Pimps are referred to as "daddies." And given that most girls have massive father wounds, their daddy artificially fills that hole. From gifts to time spent to adoration to promises, they give them what they want, need, and have never had.

While Casey was like the other girls in most every way, she possessed one striking and unavoidable difference: she was making money while at Freetown. Lots of it. Given her success, we'd recommended a wealth management guy with whom she was working, and at her own suggestion, she'd made me a signer on the account for anything over a thousand dollars. This meant she had to acquire my approval for anything greater. Which was never, because Casey never spent money.

We knew it would be unfair to Casey, her readers, and anyone who followed her story to make her totally inaccessible. Doing so would defeat Casey's purpose of allowing them to share their stories, which she knew was vital to their healing. From the "Contact Casey" button on her website to a half dozen social media avenues, the response to both Casey and her story was overwhelming. In return, Casey emptied herself into helping other girls. She often wrote long into the night communicating with any girl who had either escaped or wanted to. Every voice mattered. So she responded to each one.

This meant that no matter where you were in the world, getting to Casey was only one or two clicks away. Casey was no dummy and understood the doors and possibilities this opened. With her permission, we monitored every one of them. Not to mention that the guys in DC had written programming code that allowed us to dissect every word sent to her, sifting for patterns and hunting for a hundred "signal" words. This did not mean we knew everything. But we knew a lot.

About a week after our camping trip, Ellie found me in my basement standing at my piddle table. Her voice betrayed more than her words. She said, "I can't find Casey."

The smell of cleaning solvent filled the air. "Is that normal?"

"Not like this."

I checked the mudroom for her hiking boots and day pack. Both were gone. As was her sleeping bag. An overnight was not unusual for Casey, but she always checked it with us beforehand and took one of the girls with her. Often she included Gunner. She never ventured out on her own. To complicate matters, the necklace I'd given her was hanging on the mirror next to her bed. Meaning I couldn't track her.

Several hours later, Bones called me to the command center. When I walked in, he shook his head and pointed to the screen. "Sneaky. Which is why we missed it."

The screen showed a comment under the review section of her book page on her website. Not something we routinely scoured. The comment, posted the first week the book released, read, "Miss you." Then gave a URL for a Google document. This web address was no longer valid, but after a rather thorough examination of the deleted files on the hard drive of Casey's laptop, the tech team uncovered a new address. One that had not been changed. What they found was an active and running Google document shared by two people. Documents like this were not new and often were shared by lovers who didn't want to be discovered because there was no trail. No bread crumbs. No to or from. This was simply a document, housed in some cloud, accessible only by those who knew the exact address. But if you did know it, you could access it from anywhere in the world—without a trace.

Bones downloaded everything. Which was roughly akin to the size of a novel.

I stared at the ream of paper. "How'd we miss this?"

"She used several computers to access it and then deleted the cookies."

This meant Casey had circumvented the very controls we, with her approval, had enacted to protect her. The Google doc was enlightening. And it proved what I'd feared. While we'd freed her body, he still owned her mind.

"What do we know about him?"

"Not much. He's slick. But he seems to know her a lot better than we do and has for a long time. He knows how to ask the right questions."

"You think he's the reason she's missing?"

Bones nodded.

"Any clue where they might have gone?"

"She spends a lot of time documenting her hikes. Caves she's discovered and explored. Deserted cabins. Favorite trails. She's done a lot of walking. More than we thought. And farther than we thought. And . . ." He tapped the papers. "He's no dummy. He never mentions money, but he's asked several questions about sales and what she might do with the rest of her life now that she doesn't have to work."

Cunning. "What's the last thing they wrote to each other?"

"Like everything else, it's written in a convoluted romantic lover's code. Something Romeo initiates and to which she quickly and willingly responds. He uses words from their past, which he established in earlier communications, suggesting he's a master at calculation."

The mercury was dropping and a dusting snow had begun to fall. Temperatures were below freezing and would remain that way for several days. I returned to Casey's room, grabbed a fleece jacket she often wore, and knelt with Gunner, allowing him to rub his nose in it. "I need you to find Casey." I patted the bed where he often napped alongside her. "Find Casey."

I then walked him downstairs and stood at the trail, which led into the mountains. I let him smell the fleece one more time, pointed to the trail, and said, "Find Casey."

Gunner bounded off, climbed Paraclete Peak, and disappeared into a wall of white. The snow would erase both Casey's tracks and her scent, so our chances were slim at best. I returned to my basement and began packing, which was where Summer found me. When she appeared, she was carrying a pack and wearing boots and a down puffer jacket and beanie. "I'm coming with you."

I'd learned not to argue with her when her voice sounded like that. I stared at her but said nothing.

She continued, "If she's willingly gone with Romeo, then you're not just rescuing her body but her heart and mind. And . . ." She shook her head. "I don't think you're the one to do that."

I had a feeling she was right. "Why do you say that?"

"Because you're a man, and whether you like it or not, she's running from you . . . and everyone like you."

It made sense in a twisted and messed-up way.

While Casey had spent a lot of time in these mountains, no one knew them better than me. That included Bones. Chances were good I knew every cabin and cave for miles and had slept several nights in most all of them. Unless we were totally incorrect in our interpretation of the vague descriptions of their rendezvous, they were headed to a cabin. Someplace with a fireplace and a view. Someplace he could access with a Jeep and then wine and dine her and talk about all the good times they once had. Where he could rewrite their history. Then drug her and drive her out of Colorado and hole up until she gave him the account numbers. Then he'd contact me and use her as leverage. "Transfer the money or never see her again."

Simple.

I could think of half a dozen cabins within fifteen miles that served this purpose.

We stepped into the snow and my phone rang. It was Bones. "His name is Carl Mason."

"What do you know about him?"

"Served several stints for trafficking, drugs, weapons. Owns a tattoo parlor. Presents himself as some sort of an artist with ink."

"Got a picture?"

My phone dinged. I opened the pic. Flame tattoos crawled up his neck and onto the sides of his cheeks. Ink tears dripped from the corners of his eyes, and the fingers of a demon, dripping with blood, appeared on his forehead and temple, sliding out beneath his black hair—suggesting that at one time someone had tattooed his shaved head. His eyes were permanently inked with black eyeliner. And his arms were entirely sleeved. Everything about this guy was dark.

Bones continued, "Don't let him get you in a small room. He was NCAA Wrestler of the Year twice and then spent six years studying jiujitsu in Brazil, where he was undefeated against some of the best fighters in the world. While there he learned to traffic flesh. Currently, he's making his way up the MMA ranks. None of his fights have gone into the second round. His fight videos are . . . not entertaining."

"How's he know Casey?"

"No idea. But if she's run off with him, then he must have gotten to her early in her life and he's using those hooks."

I was about to hang up when Bones's voice stopped me. "Murph?"

"Yeah."

He was quiet. I knew what he wanted to say. I was coming off some difficult injuries and it'd been a while since I'd strapped on my helmet.

"I got it, Bones."

The phone clicked dead.

Summer and I stepped into the night where the moon was high and cast our shadow on the trail. Gunner had been gone an hour. He'd return when he picked up her trail or got hungry. Casey was smart. She knew I'd send Gunner, and if she'd hidden this much from us, then I knew not to trust or bank on my experience with her. His tethers were anchored deeper than mine. Casey was a puppet on a string, and I was not the puppeteer.

Freetown sits high in a valley. Jagged ridgelines stretch north and south over peaks ranging from twelve to fourteen thousand feet, and the trails up here are faint. This area was settled a hundred and fifty years ago by opportunistic miners digging for silver and gold. The digging gave rise to boom towns at ten thousand feet. Complete with schools and bars and churches and whiskey stills. When the ore ran out, folks deserted, giving rise to ghost towns. Frozen in time a century ago. Colorado is full of them. Many are accessible by Jeep. Many are not. I didn't know if Casey had gone north or south, so with a fifty percent chance of being either right or wrong, we headed north.

Three hours and four miles later, the snow began falling harder so we stepped beneath a boulder outcrop and huddled against the stone. It was cold, the wind was blowing, but I chose not to build a fire because I didn't want to give away our presence or location. I knew she was cold, but Summer never complained. The expression on her face told me she was worried.

Time was not our friend. It never was. The more that passed, the more difficult it'd be for Gunner to find any scent, and the deeper tattoo-boy could sink his hooks. Two miles away sat a cabin where we could rest up and get warm. It wasn't accessible by Jeep so I doubted he'd use it, but it brought us closer to those that were. So, despite the worsening weather, we kept moving.

Two hours later, I crept through the pines and sat studying the cabin. Summer shivered behind me. With no sound or movement, I pushed open the door. Nothing but four walls and a cot built along the wall. A wood-burning stove in the corner. Probably built by an itinerant preacher or schoolteacher, the cabin was nothing more than an overnight shelter for anyone moving between towns who needed to escape the elements.

Summer's teeth chattered as she spoke. "I don't suppose you'll build a fire in that thing?"

I shook my head.

"I was afraid you were going to say that."

I sparked my Jetboil to life, boiled water, and handed her a hot cup of instant coffee. She held it between her hands, hovering over the steam. "Best cup of coffee in the history of coffee."

Over the next hour, the snow fell in large flakes, filling our footsteps and covering any tracks. Sipping my third cup of coffee, the satellite phone rang. It was Bones. "I've got a heat signature on satellite about six miles north of you."

"Any bodies?"

"Not yet. Which means he's smart."

"You got a track on Gunner?"

"He's about to walk up to your door." Gunner's collar had been fitted with a GPS tracker similar to what I'd given the girls, although his would last for weeks at a time simply because the physical size of his collar allowed for a larger battery. Bones continued, "Looks like he's been up to the cabin, turned around, and now found you."

I opened the door and Gunner stood staring at me. A grin on his face. He walked around me and snuggled up with Summer under the blanket. "Nice to see you too."

Between the snow and the terrain, it took four hours. Over the last half mile, we could smell the wood-burning fire. Years ago, I'd weathered a night here when a whiteout forced me inside. The cabin sat at the tree line at twelve thousand feet, had been built of huge logs, and had a gas range, hot and cold running water, and battery-powered lights charged by rooftop solar panels. It was self-sufficient and off the grid. We studied it through binoculars for almost an hour before moving to the barn, which sat tucked inside an aspen grove. The snow had quit, which meant we had nothing to cover our tracks, so we approached through the trees beyond the barn, accessing it from the rear. We climbed into the loft, and I cracked the door, allowing us a view of the house where smoke spiraled out of the chimney. A dim golden hue of light revealed shadows walking around.

I turned to Summer. "I need to get a closer look. Keep Gunner here and don't follow me."

She nodded. "How do you know he's not expecting you?"

"I don't."

"I was afraid you were going to say that."

Just then my satellite phone vibrated. The message read, "Five million dollars. Six hours." The text included a picture of Casey. Eyes glazed over. No doubt drugged. He knelt behind her. His intention clear. The message concluded with account numbers.

He was savvy, working fast, and I'd underestimated him. He wasn't going to use her as leverage to get her money. He was going to use her as leverage to get to the deeper pockets of whoever was funding Freetown. Smart. I forwarded it to Bones as I heard the Jeep engine turn over.

We didn't have long.

I made my way around the house as a muscled body carried a female frame out the door and trudged through the snow. I knelt and whispered to Gunner, "Choctaw." In my training of Gunner, I'd chosen unmistakable words with distinct syllables. This one meant, "Get him."

Gunner shot through the snow like a wolf, launched himself through the air, and caught Mr. Clean in the groin. The guy immediately dropped the body and began screaming at the top of his lungs. While Gunner latched a vise lock on his ability to continue his lineage, I made it to Casey, lifted her off the snow, and was thinking about stealing the Jeep when a second man I'd not seen with muscles like a silverback gorilla jumped on my back like a cat. He wrapped me in a knot like a pretzel and was causing no small amount of pain when Gunner let go of gorilla number one and latched on the face of gorilla number two, who quickly let go of me. In the dim light of the house, gorilla number two lifted a pistol from his hip and was about to press it into Gunner's chest when the +P 230-grain hollow point from my Sig 220 caught him in the right shoulder, spun him, and sent him to the ground—where miraculously he focused on me and pressed the trigger.

His round missed me, and in the air I heard myself whisper, "Front sight . . . pressss."

Nobody shoots my dog. Period.

Gorilla number one lay in the snow, moaning, trying to stand yet finding it difficult, so I turned out his lights and returned to Casey, who had yet to wake. I lifted her a second time as Summer appeared. I nodded toward the Jeep, set Casey in the backseat, and was in the process of slamming the gear shift into reverse when I felt the burn in my left shoulder followed by the report of the rifle. I dumped the clutch, spun snow ten feet in the air, turned the Jeep a hundred and eighty degrees, and we shot down the hill under the echo of two more rifle reports. The rounds narrowly missed my head as evidenced by the two small holes in the windshield in front of me. I redlined the engine, and we descended five hundred feet down a treacherous incline before I stopped and turned to Summer, who sat ghostly and white-knuckled in the backseat holding Casey's head.

About the time I clicked on my flashlight I saw we had a problem. A really big one. Casey wasn't Casey. Summer was holding the head of a girl neither of us had ever seen. When they'd carried her from the house, I'd assumed she was Casey.

I was wrong.

We sat speechless. The girl was beautiful, and her carotid proved a strong pulse, but she wasn't Casey any more than I was. I cussed beneath my breath and turned to Summer. "Drive this thing down this mountain." She tried to protest, but I stopped her. "Take it as far as it will let you. Bones can track both you and Gunner. He'll meet you."

Summer started to protest again when my sat phone vibrated. Another message. This one read, "Five hours." It included a picture of Casey wearing less clothing and concluded with a smiley emoji. In the back of my mind I heard Casey asking me to protect her, and me telling her that I'd never let anything happen to her.

Summer grabbed my left shoulder, smearing blood across both of us. "I'm not leaving you."

"You have to. Bones'll pick you up about a mile down where this road meets the county road."

She was not convinced. "Murph."

"It's okay. Just drive."

I'd underestimated this guy twice and didn't plan on doing it again. I hopped out of the Jeep and began trudging back up the hill. Gunner tried to follow, but I stopped him. "Stay." He turned in a complete circle, telling me he didn't like that idea, then jumped back into the Jeep and whined. I climbed quickly through the snow, my lungs burning, while the Jeep's taillights disappeared through the night. I needed to return to the barn to grab my pack, which held my crossbow, so I circled west, climbed hand over fist through the biting cold, and appeared in the trees just behind the barn. I tried to step quietly, but there's no such thing as walking quietly in snow. I reached the barn door, slipped inside, and felt two muscled hands rip me off the ground and toss me through the air, where I slammed into the wall of the barn.

Make that three times.

I tried to stand, but Hercules had wrapped around me like a blanket and was doing a good job of trying to separate my head from my shoulders when I sliced through the back of his right hamstring. He flinched long enough for me to grab a breath of air and turn my head slightly to take the pressure off my carotids, but he never let go. Suggesting he was probably a good bit tougher than me. We rolled around the barn floor and broke through one of the stall doors while I tried every trick in the book, which had zero effect on him. With the walls closing in, I stood and launched myself at the stall door while wearing him like a cape. Just before my forehead contacted the cross bar, I ducked, allowing it to contact him square in the chin. The blow dazed him, and my forward momentum peeled him off my back.

By the time I got to my feet, he was already waiting on me, which presented me with another problem. He was not the guy in the picture Bones had sent me. Given that he was quicker and stronger, he shot low, took me to the ground, and was doing a good job of closing my eyes when a snarling thing latched itself around his head, causing him to shriek like a girl. While Gunner chewed on his face, I wedged his head between the stall door and the post, cinching it tight with the rope that secured the gate.

Within a few seconds, I had his attention and pulled Gunner off him. While he struggled to breathe and Gunner licked the blood off his muzzle, I knelt and asked him a few questions. His voice was thick with accent and he said nothing to answer my questions, so I tugged on the stall door, squeezing off the blood flow to his brain, and put him to sleep. I then bound him hand and foot, rolled him on his stomach, hog-tied his hands to his feet, and shoved a dirty rag in his mouth.

I collapsed on the barn floor while Gunner licked the sweat off my cheeks. Struggling to breathe, I said, "Next time I tell you to stay . . ." He looked at me and rolled his ears forward. "Just do whatever you want."

I found my pack, which was good because my crossbow and rifle were latched to it. It was starting to look like I would need them. I paused long enough to force myself to think clearly, which was not easy. If Gunner had returned to me, then Summer had intersected Bones. Or so I hoped.

He answered after one ring. I managed, "Summer with you?"

"She was."

"What do you mean 'was'?"

"Well, she was here. We talked. Or rather, she talked and I listened. And then she left me with a sleeping girl, turned that Jeep around, and shot back up the hill." Just then Summer appeared at the barn door.

"Never mind."

Bones interrupted me. "You all right?"

"No. I'm not. Every time I turn around I'm wrestling an angry cat or a gorilla or something. These guys are the strongest human beings I've ever laid hands on. What are they eating? It's like they're playing in another gear or something."

"It's that new style of cage fighting."

"Well, whatever it is, I need some lessons. I've got no defense against these guys other than Gunner. Every time I turn around one of them flips me into a pretzel and hands me my tail on a platter."

Bones laughed. "You're not a spring chicken anymore."

"Tell me about it."

"Need help?"

"Not yet. I think we're down to just one."

"Don't take any chances."

I stood and the searing pain in my shoulder reminded me of the bullet that grazed it. "Stay close to the phone."

"Roger."

Summer appeared next to me. Breathing heavy.

I frowned. "How's this going to work if you don't do what I tell you?"

She pointed in the direction of the road. "I did. I drove down the mountain."

"What about the 'stay there' part?"

"You told Gunner to stay. Not me."

She was right, but we were arguing semantics. "I thought that was self-explanatory."

She pointed to the house. "Casey?"

Tattoo-boy already knew we were here, and he'd already unloaded all his goons on us, so I took the subtle approach, marched around to the front door, and kicked it off the hinges.

Searching the house, we found it completely empty. Which meant all of this had been a diversion. A decoy. If he'd been here with Casey, they were long gone now.

Make that four times. It wouldn't happen again.

I returned to the barn and the hog-tied gorilla. I pulled the rag from his mouth and asked him, "Where'd they go?"

He laughed.

I turned to Gunner. "Choctaw."

Within seconds, my gorilla had become a monkey, screaming valuable information.

Summer and I stepped out of the barn as daylight broke the ridgeline. It was cold, but the snow had quit. Summer tugged on me and pointed at my shoulder. "You should let me look at that."

She cleaned and bandaged my arm and then asked, "How do we know he's telling the truth?"

"We don't." I pointed at the tracks half full of snow. "These lead away from the house. They're several hours old. One is smaller than the other, suggesting a female. One is deeper than the other, suggesting he's carrying a load. And the direction and number agree with what he told us. It's a gamble."

Summer frowned.

"What's wrong?"

"No struggle. If this is Casey, she's walking with him. Not fighting him." She knelt and studied the prints, then stared up at me. "She's in front. Leading him."

I nodded.

"This doesn't surprise you?"

"Maybe at one time."

"What do you mean?"

"It gets twisted. Psychological warfare at its most evil. Girls who've been trafficked long enough become attached to those who own them. He still owns a part of her."

Summer flashed red.

The footsteps led to the ridgeline and then turned south, doubling back several times to throw us off. Gunner kept us on course. At 10 a.m., our deadline for the transfer, my phone vibrated again. "Six million or you lose." The picture did not encourage me and I didn't show it to Summer.

By noon, we'd walked six miles southwest. Casey seemed to be heading to a hidden valley that sat at about twelve thousand feet. A rustic miner's cabin and a Jeep trail that descended into a small town. If they reached the town, we'd lose them.

By late afternoon, we'd crested the plateau and could see the valley laid out before us. A land washed in white set beneath a canopy of blue. The cabin sat on the far side, some two miles away, smoke rising from the chimney. I was tired of them being warm and us being cold. We circled the valley, keeping the ridgeline between us and in line of sight of the cabin.

Two hundred yards off, we studied the cabin through binoculars but spotted no movement. I could hear talking inside but couldn't make out what they were saying. Suddenly, I heard raised voices and a loud crash followed by a snapping sound, and finally a scream coming from Casey's mouth.

Gunner and I shot out of the snow and crossed the distance. Reaching the front door, I again decided to skip the subtle approach, running through it, rolling, then coming to my feet. When I did, I found Casey standing over tattoo-boy. She was holding a fire poker in her hand about the length of a baseball bat. Carl lay on the floor with both his shin bones sticking through his pant legs. Casey was leaning over, pointing in his face. She spoke through gritted teeth, saying the same thing over and over. "You don't own me! You don't own me . . ."

I touched her hand and tried to slip the iron rod from it, but she turned quickly, shouting, "You don't own me!"

While she was looking at me, I don't think she was seeing me.

Tattoo-boy lay writhing. He would have to learn to walk again, and I had a feeling his MMA career was over. Not to mention his freedom. It struck me as telling that so powerful a man had been taken down by so diminutive a woman. She had done what no MMA fighter could: render him powerless. Which means you can never underestimate the power of the heart. Summer appeared behind me and stood next to Casey, who was staring at what remained of the monster at her feet. Hefting the poker in her hand. Wanting to finish the job. I didn't blame her.

Summer slipped the metal from her hand, led her outside into the fading sun, and turned to face her. Casey's eyes were glazed over, staring years into the past. She had checked out. Slowly, Summer placed her hand on Casey's chest. On her heart. Then she took Casey's palm and laid it flat across her own heart.

Then she just breathed.

They stood there thirty minutes, pulse to pulse. And with every heart-beat, Summer brought Casey back from the brink. Back from hell. Had I not seen it I would not have believed it, but with each minute that passed, I watched in wonder as Summer proved true what she'd spoken to me. While I could rescue Casey's body, I was not the one to rescue her spirit. That would take someone else. Someone else's touch.

An hour later, Casey's head turned slightly and her eyes focused on Summer, and then on her own hand transmitting the pulse of Summer's heart to her own. Finally, she crumpled in Summer's arms. Crying.

Wailing.

Releasing all the pain inflicted by others. The memory of that which was stolen. The sound was guttural. She kept screaming one phrase over and over: "You don't own me . . ."

There is a thing that happens when someone comes back from hell. Their eyes show it best. While they're gone, their eyes are absent. Blank. Dark. Hollow, even. We say, "They're not behind their eyes." When they return, the curtain pulls back, and when they look at you, they're standing behind their eyes.

Summer held her, rocking back and forth. Speaking softly. Words not meant for me. When Carl started to laugh, I shut his mouth and turned out his lights. In approval, Gunner rolled onto his back and stuck his paws in the air.

A federal marshal airlifted Carl to a prison hospital near Gunnison where he would await trial. Given Casey's testimony, chances were good he'd never breathe free air again. Bones and I watched him leave. "What happened to his legs?"

I pointed to Casey.

"She did that?"

"All by herself."

Bones smiled. "What happened to his teeth?"

I pointed to Gunner.

Bones laughed but said nothing.

That night we rode the lift to the Eagle's Nest where Clay entertained us with stories, some of which were true, and Summer used me as a guinea pig and taught us to dance, and Bones opened expensive wine, and Casey and Angel sat before the fire with their knees tucked to their chests and made the sound of the free, and Gunner lay with his paws in the air. And somewhere a few minutes shy of midnight, moon high, night clear, and air cold, while dancing with my daughter, who was standing on my toes and telling me to loosen up and that my hips were too tight, I stared at my life. At what had become of it. At the mystery, the majesty, and the memory.

And for the first time in a long time, I liked it.

When Casey tapped me on the shoulder and asked to butt in, I caught a glimpse of her. And there she was. Standing behind her eyes.

I tried to lead, but I'm not much of a dancer. Given that Casey wasn't either, we danced well together. Halfway through the song, she stood on her toes and whispered in my ear, "I'm sorry." Then her eyes darted to the floor.

I waited until she lifted them.

She continued, "I know my leaving betrayed you." She glanced around the room. "Everyone. But . . ." She stopped dancing and looked up at me. "This world I'm living in here is so different from the world I lived in for so long, I don't always believe it's real. Most of the time I feel like this is all a dream and one day soon some guy is going to snatch me back to hell. So I figured I'd find out for myself. Kind of like ripping off a Band-Aid. If this is a dream, I'd rather it come to an end, because it's too good to be true and staying here any longer just hurts too much 'cause it's all I've ever wanted. So I did the very things you told me not to, and . . ." A tear trailed down her cheek.

I waited.

"Despite all you have done, Carl was still walking around inside me. And as much as I didn't want to admit it, he still owned a part of me. I needed to know for myself if the part he owned was the real part and all this was make-believe, or if he was the counterfeit and all this is real. So . . . I let him find me. And . . ."

I waited while her lip trembled.

"And I'm really sorry I did that to you. To all of you. After all you've—"

I shook my head. "There's nothing to forgive."

She placed her hand on her heart. "I know you say that, but I know better. I know what I've cost you. I know what you've given. I've seen the scars . . ." She trailed off. "I'm not defending me. I'm just saying that every day I woke up in a no-man's-land. Not really here. Not really there. Just wandering somewhere in the middle. And I couldn't live that way anymore. I had to either give him all my heart or cut him out of it."

"Did you?"

Her eyes were the clearest I'd ever seen them. She tapped her heart. "He doesn't own me anymore. Not any of me."

# CHAPTER 28

Bones said he wanted to drive, so Summer and I climbed into the Jeep and he eased off the clutch, idling through the high alpine roads accessible only through the back side of Freetown. Bones was fit, trim, had grown a beard that was solid white, and while he was never without his Sig, he was also seldom without his camera—recording life as he lived and saw it. Most evenings he'd disappear into his darkroom with a bottle of wine in tow and develop slides long into the night.

If Freetown had a recordkeeper, it was Bones.

An hour later, we crested a plateau. A dilapidated miner's shack sat nestled in the rocks on the far side. Bones scratched his chin and pointed. "Freetown needs a backup plan."

The shack had no roof. "That's your plan?"

He laughed. "I can see potential." This was one of Bones's great qualities. He spoke that which was not as though it was.

That included me.

He wound a serpentine path around the boulders toward the sheer rock face a half mile away. Turning in front of the shack, Bones navigated between two boulders, each the size of a small house. Doing so brought us to the base of the rock face and a steel door that sat hidden in shadow until you were on top of it. I'd been in this valley a dozen times and never seen it. The door was large enough to drive a Jeep through—maybe twelve feet high and fifteen feet wide.

He pointed through the windshield. "It's a Cold-War bunker. Deserted in the seventies."

Summer looked intrigued. "How'd you find it?"

He weighed his head side to side. "That's between me and God." A pause while he idled closer. "Structurally, she's solid, so I brought in some engineers and other really smart people and made a few changes. Updated generators, solar panels, reverse osmosis filtration, food stores. We could last . . . a while. If something were to happen to Freetown"—he glanced over his shoulder at me—"like what happened to your island, and we had to evacuate, we could get here. And we could probably do it with very little notice." A knowing nod, almost as if he were talking to himself. "If something happens, we could cover our retreat. Hold the high ground." A longer pause. "At least long enough to figure out who's trying to hurt us and get the girls out safely one at a time. To better circumstances."

Summer looked confused. "Why not just call in the cavalry?"

He nodded. "We could, but sometimes the psychological damage is worsened."

He was right. Everyone in our care has entrusted us with their safety. Not anyone else. If we shuffle them around, passing them between hands, their subconscious can tell them they're being trafficked again. It's touchy. It would never be our intention, but we're dealing with the effects of emotional warfare. As long as they see us as caring for them, they continue to heal. But the nanosecond they think we're offloading them to someone else, even if our intentions are good, the damage is real.

I studied the massive door. "You've been busy."

He nodded and his tone changed. "I thought I was good at this rescue thing until I spent time with you. Then I watched you and realized I'm not. You're one in a million. Personally responsible for cutting into hundreds of millions of profit. Because of that, you have enemies, and we're a target. We can only stay hidden so long. Sometimes it's best to hide in plain sight. Right under someone's nose. Other times it's best to disappear. This is the disappearing play." He shot a glance toward Freetown. "They trust us. And . . . we owe it to them. I'm betting that whoever blew up your island is still looking for you. And would love nothing more than to bring their explosive talents to Freetown."

"Speaking of my island, you got any thoughts?"

"Yes. But nothing certain." He pointed at my phone. "You can access it with any phone. Just dial the number."

"Which is?"

"Something you won't forget."

"Which is?"

"Written across the top of your back."

Summer laughed.

I punched in A-P-O-L-L-U-M-I on the keypad, and the giant doors unlocked and began swinging open as overhead lights clicked on. Bones drove the Jeep inside and parked, revealing a fortress that traveled a half mile down and into the mountain. A nuclear blast couldn't dislodge us from here.

I marveled at what he'd accomplished. "You've been really busy."

He admired his work.

I pressed him. "How'd you find this place? Really?"

"Long story."

During our walking tour, Bones told us the history as much as he knew it. Built in the '50s when the Cubans were parking missiles ninety miles off the Florida coast and the Russians were threatening to annihilate the world with the press of a button, "the Bunker," as it was affectionately known, was an underground city built to protect members of government in the event of a meltdown—and to do so for a long period of time. A year or two even. To increase their prolonged comfort, they'd built an indoor pool, a bowling alley, volleyball and basketball courts, a sauna, and a two-hundred-seat theater. It had all the amenities of home and was designed to allow life to be as normal as possible when lived five hundred to a thousand feet underground. Many of the rooms were suites, designed for family living. Others were singles and doubles. When needed, communal bunk rooms could be opened to accommodate overflow. The Bunker contained multiple kitchens, large freezer and refrigeration rooms, and given the constant fifty-some-degree temperature, an extensive wine cellar. It also contained one centrally important aspect when considering people's safety: a single way in and out. No back door.

It was the perfect solution to a possible problem. Even more, it showed the extent to which Bones thought constantly about the safety of those in our care—and how to maintain it.

Not long into the return trip, Summer tugged on my arm. "You mind if we walk?" The expression on her face told me she wanted to talk. Which meant I'd missed all the signals leading up to this one. Which was not good.

Bones let us out and Summer grabbed my hand. Walking alongside and with. She leaned into me when she asked, "You okay?"

"What do you mean?"

"You seem tense."

I nodded. "I live tense."

"No, I mean with me."

"I am?"

"You're not talking to me."

"Summer . . ." I waved my hand across the landscape.

She shook her head and raised her left hand. Which was the signal for "Hush, I'm talking." Her facial expression suggested she'd been thinking about this several days and gotten herself worked into a lather. "Everything comes out of your head and nothing with us is connected to your heart. Is there something wrong with me?"

I wasn't following her. My facial expression betrayed this thought. I checked my watch. Our current elevation was almost thirteen thousand feet. Must be the altitude.

She continued, "You don't look at me. Don't touch me tenderly. Don't . . ."

Gunner bounced by us. Unfazed by the altitude. "Summer, what are you saying?"

"What are we doing?" she asked.

"I'm confused."

She cut me off. "What's the barrier between you and me? Why the distance? I'm standing two feet from you, but my heart . . ." She pointed at a mountain peak some sixty or seventy miles distant. "Might as well be over there."

Summer's female intuition ran laps around my male disguises. The mask I unconsciously wore. And she had just put words to what I felt but could not voice.

She lifted her hand, displaying the ring. "You gave me this." With the same hand, she tapped me in the chest. "I'm just not sure you've given me this." A short pause. "If you've changed your mind, just tell me. I can handle it." A tear swelled in the corner of her eye and her lip trembled. "But just tell me."

The question of her heart. So beautifully spoken.

Since I had watched Summer head south down the Intracoastal in a boat she couldn't steer and in water in which she could not swim, I'd come to love her magnificent and courageous heart. The fact that she faced every confrontation head-on. Afraid of nothing. And these words coming out of her mouth were driven by and bathed in that same love.

I stopped walking and turned to face her. "For a long time I've trained my words to leave my mind and my heart and travel down my arms to my fingers, where they speak onto a page. I did this because the person I was trying to speak to couldn't hear me. Or I thought she couldn't. After years of training, that pathway is now hardwired. Sometimes words just don't make it to my mouth."

She blinked and the tear cut loose, spilling down to her chin. "Last week I stood in a room surrounded by my daughter and her friends, and we drank champagne while I got fitted for a beautiful white dress. We're making plans to spend the rest of forever together, but you seem indifferent. As if 'it'll get here when it gets here.'"

I knew enough to know she had yet to ask me the question that got us out of the Jeep. "Why don't you tell me what's really on your mind?"

She thumbed away a tear. "Why don't you love me the way I want you to love me? And if you don't do it now, how are you going to do it then?"

I stared into her eyes and smiled. "Are you afraid of anything?"

She nodded. "Yes."

"What?"

She looked away and wiped her nose on her sleeve. "Discovering that you don't."

"What?"

"Love me. That . . ."

"Go ahead."

Another ring display. "You gave me this because you just feel sorry for me."

I brushed snow off a boulder and cleared a place for us to sit. With the world stretched out before us, I fumbled with my hands. "Where to begin."

Summer sat uncomfortably.

"Can I be gut-level honest?"

She spun the ring on her finger. Bracing herself against the cold.

"I've spent the last decade of my life trying to erase my pain by writing about it. And instead of erasing it, I've etched it into this stony thing I call a heart. Whenever I look inside, I see Marie. Whenever I look at you with hope or longing or love, Marie walks by the window of my soul. I can't help that. And as much as I try, I can't stop it. She alone owns the slideshow in my mind. I love you with all that I am. With all that remains of me. But I'd be lying if I said I was over her. I don't know how to get over her. And to be honest, I don't want to. How do I push her aside? How do I erase the memory of her to give you room to make your own memories?" I shook my head. "I don't know how to honor her and love you. I'm stuck between two women. Unable to let go of the one in order to grab hold of the other. Even now, looking at you, Marie is standing just offstage. One half of my heart is looking at you with longing and all I want to do is dive in, and the other half is asking the memory of her if it's okay to love you. Because—"

"What?"

"Loving you scares me."

"Am I that horrible?"

"You're perfect."

"What then?"

"I have scars. Holes. My heart is a colander. Leaking. I plug one hole only to turn and find one bigger. It's a full-time job not bleeding out. I don't want to . . . promise you me when I'm not able to give you me."

She placed her palm on my cheek with a laugh of release. "Is that all?"

"Isn't that enough?"

"So . . . you really do want to marry me?"

"Of course."

"No second thoughts?"

"None."

"Bishop . . ." She let the name sink in. "You may be Superman without a cape, but . . ." A sly smile. "I'm a woman."

"I'm well aware of that."

"Marie isn't the only woman on the planet who can imprint your impressionable little mind with images." She tapped my temple. "There's room in there for both of us."

Gunner looked at me and tilted his head sideways.

She placed her arms around my neck. "I'm serious. That's all that's bothering you?"

"Isn't that enough?"

"Well, it's a thing, but we can overcome it." She stood and twirled in that beautiful dancer's way. "You just have to give me a chance." Another twirl. "All is not lost."

"I just want to be honest about me and want you to know who you're getting in the deal."

"Am I?"

"What?"

"Getting you . . . in the deal."

I laughed. "Well . . ."

She pulled me to my feet, kissed the corner of my mouth, and slid her hand up my shirt, placing her palm flat across my heart. "I'm all in. You're getting all of me. Stretch marks. Bunions. And I want all of you. Nothing held back. Scars. Holes. Limp. I want it all. Not half. Not ninety-nine percent. I want you. Broken or unbroken doesn't matter. Just trust me with all the pieces."

How I love this woman. "Your hand is freezing."

She was swaying now. Dancing slightly. "Yes, but I am not. You're unlike any man I've ever met. You pour yourself out without ever considering the cost. Who does that?" She studied me. "I am willing to share you with the . . ." Her fingers slipped inside my collar and traced the letters of the single word tattooed at the top of my back. She kissed my cheek and pressed her forehead to mine. "Just come in out of the cold and let me throw my blanket over you."

I turned, she sank her arm inside mine, and we began following Gunner through the snow. With Freetown in view, I whispered to myself, "I need a manual."

Summer laughed. "For?"

"The female race."

# CHAPTER 29

Summer said she wanted a short engagement and she got one. Given that I'm not a public person, Bones got on the phone and alerted the people he knew would want to know about my engagement. Meaning those who'd graduated from Freetown. The final two weeks were spent attending party after party—one scarcely ending before another had started. Everybody wanted to celebrate us. People and their families I'd not seen in years came out of the woodwork to meet Summer, wish us well, and thank me for Freetown and what it had meant in their life.

I didn't know what to do with it all. Had no place in my mind to process all of that. Literally, when they heard what was happening, the names etched in ink across my back came out of history, walked back into Freetown, and placed young babies in my arms or introduced me to their adolescent kids for whom, years before, they'd dared not hope. But here they were. Hope breathing. Hope walking. Hope talking. Hope running down Main Street.

Summer and I had a lot of questions yet to be answered—starting with how to be us in the life I'd carved—but Bones told us not to worry. We had time. We could figure it out. Besides, his experience hanging out with Ellie convinced him he wanted more grandkids.

I told him, "You're getting soft."

He gritted out between his teeth, "Race you to the top."

In the days leading up to our wedding, I spent a lot of time at the

Eagle's Nest. Trying to make sense of a life that didn't make sense. I'd stand at the railing, Gunner lying alongside, and I'd hold Bones's unopened letter.

One afternoon Bones found me turning it over in my hands. "Read it?"

I shook my head.

He leaned on the railing. "You should."

Problem was, I could not. I was afraid of what he might say. If the letter said what I thought it said, then more than just my friendship with Bones was over.

On the day of our wedding, daylight cracked over the peaks of the Collegiates as I stood on the balcony of the Eagle's Nest. The three of us— Bones, Gunner, and I—had climbed up in the dark. I'd found my strength. Bounding up. I was me again.

Bones turned to me. "You read my letter?"

"No."

He wiped the sweat off his face with a towel.

I leaned against the railing, watching the steam rise off my coffee. "A lot there?"

He nodded. "Understatement of the decade."

"I will."

He spoke knowingly. "If you won't do it for yourself, do it for Summer."

A few hours later, Clay found me in the back of the church fumbling with my hands. He reached into his jacket pocket and pulled out a folded and ironed handkerchief on which he'd written the date and then both my and Summer's names. "At some point, probably tomorrow, your wife will need this."

I smiled. "You think of everything."

"It's the little things."

"It's thoughtful."

"Actually, it's a memento. It marks the moment. And Summer will mark moments in the next couple days that you miss entirely, but the fact that you have this in your pocket and can offer it to her during one of those moments when she might need it will tell her that you're at least aware of that fact and trying." He laughed at himself. "A good first step."

"Thank you."

"No." He placed both hands on my shoulders. "Thank you."

Standing at the altar, I felt an inexplicable wave wash over me. I stared at the huge logs, the stained glass, the hand-hewn pews, the stone, the views of western Colorado some seventy miles out the windows, and then the memories of the dozens of women and their men who had preceded me in this place. To be standing here among so many dreams realized was overwhelming.

Following construction of the Eagle's Nest higher up, the chapel was the first building we started in the town itself. Bones's orders. "We can help their bodies, but it's their spirits that will need piecing back together." He nodded. "And love, the real kind, the kind that walks into hell and says me-for-you, is the only thing in this universe or any other that does that."

Gunner stood alongside me, tail wagging. Ellie had dressed him with a bow tie, making him look regal. Bones stood to my right. My heart was about to jump out of my chest. Just outside the door, standing among the aspens, waited Summer. Dressed in white, she was resplendent. Above her, given the breeze, the leaves were clapping. One of my favorite sounds. Because both her parents were gone, Clay had agreed to walk her in and give her away. Although, he argued, she might pick someone more respectable. Angel, Ellie, and Casey stood giggling opposite Gunner and me. It was a perfectly normal and totally dysfunctional wedding, and we wouldn't have had it any other way.

With increased vulnerability, all being in one place at one time, we had increased the rolling patrols through Freetown, but not in such a way as to scare the girls. Our guys were pretty good at being invisible. Most only let you see them when they wanted you to see them. We also doubled video security, and I'm pretty sure there wasn't a square inch of the city we couldn't or didn't capture on live feed—day or night.

I'm told Summer processed to Canon in D, but I couldn't hear anything over the pounding of my own heart and the voice inside my head. I don't remember those in attendance, though it was standing room only. All of Freetown had far exceeded the occupancy. I only remember Summer and the contrast of her white dress and the snowcapped peaks against Clay's dark skin.

When they reached the altar, Bones asked, "Who gives this woman?"

Clay cleared his throat. "I do." Then he turned toward her, lifted her veil, kissed her forehead, and placed her hand inside mine. As he did, he said, "Albeit reluctantly."

The audience laughed. It was one of the more beautiful things I'd ever seen. And it broke the ice, which I needed. We turned to Bones.

He whispered, "You ready?"

Her hand was shaking. I don't remember the words Bones spoke. I wanted to. Even tried to. But I couldn't take my eyes off Summer. At one point he tapped my shoulder. "Murph?"

"Yeah?"

More laughter.

"You with us?"

I stammered, "I am."

Loud laughter. Bones set a reassuring hand on my shoulder. "The correct response is 'I will.'"

I never took my eyes off Summer. "Always."

I stood there unable to get beyond the surreal fact that my life had brought me here. To this moment. I stood somewhere between the reality of the moment I was in and the impossibilities of my past. I thought of all the foreign lands into which I'd ventured where the possibility of not returning was greater than returning. Of the horrors I'd seen, endured, and—truth be told—inflicted on those responsible. The act of standing where I stood surprised me. Not that I felt guilty. I did not. You cannot walk through hell and avoid smelling like smoke when you exit. It permeates your clothes, even your skin, and doesn't wash out easily.

I stood there wondering if the smell would come out. If it was as strong to everyone around me. A week ago, when I'd mentioned this to Summer, she flipped my hand over and sniffed it, then placed my hand behind her on the small of her back—one dancer with another. "That's why they make soap." She twirled away, then spun back, making it appear as though I knew what I was doing, and then she wrapped herself tighter in my arm, her face inches from mine. "And water."

In Summer's world, life was a dance. And every time she did that little twirl thing, I felt my heart flutter and follow.

For the second time in my life, Bones declared, "Man and wife." Then smiled. "You may now kiss your bride."

Stripped bare, the human soul has one real desire: to know and be known. And in that moment, I was.

I will admit that given the experience of my last wedding reception, followed by a subsequent lifetime of training to prepare for and expect the worst, I was a little gun shy about what might come next. This was not a conscious response on my part. It was more reflexive. And whatever I was feeling did not come out of some distrust of Summer. I trusted her completely. Yet I'd spent most of my life trusting few people, and the choice to do so had often kept me alive.

If my life experience had taught me anything, it's this: the wounds of the past carry a lot of weight when it comes to walking into one's future, and if anything can rob you of now, it's yesterday. We are really good at taking the pain of our past and projecting it into our future because it's what we know, and yet our past has almost nothing to do with our future other than being connected by seconds. That's it. So we face a choice. Either shine a light on yesterday and expose it, or forfeit the joy of now and the hope of tomorrow. I realize this is easier said than done, but left untreated, experiential pain becomes a fortress in our gut that houses a lie spoken by fear. And behind that fear is an idol of our own making. One we carve by hand when we, as self-made people, worship our own creator: us. As if we can do anything to protect ourselves. Maybe it's articulated in the statement, "I'll let you in, but only so far. And under no circumstances will I let you down there. That's the basement. That's off limits. We don't go there." We raise a finger. "Touch that doorknob and I'm gone."

This whole thing is a cyclical downward spiral. We can't protect us. Fear would suggest we can, but fear is a liar. Always has been.

While I'd written my way through and out of my pain, stories that had resonated with millions, I'd never invited anyone to walk down into my basement with me. Which was what I needed. I'd simply adorned it. Made it pretty. But as in Pharaoh's tomb, the body was still dead. My life's work, everything I'd done with pen and paper, had brought attention to the fact that I, unlike many men, could talk about my pain. This alone had brought great accolades and praise to the mysterious and still unknown writer of my books, but here's the unwritten truth: If a man has a telephone pole stuck through his chest, just pointing it out does nothing to remove it. He doesn't need you to sit alongside and empathize. "I know that must hurt. I'm here with you . . ." That's total horse crap. The man needs surgery. And quickly. Otherwise he'll bleed out, if he hasn't already.

Summer knew this, as she intuitively knew most everything about me. So as we walked down a candlelit path en route to a seated dinner, she turned left, held up a finger, said, "Wait right here," and disappeared. A moment later, Angel appeared through the same door, kissed me on the cheek, and said, "She'll see you now, Padre."

I pushed open the door and found Summer standing in front of a mirror. Fussing with her hair. A second dress hanging beside her. The intoxicating residue of her perfume hanging in the air. I stood looking nervously over my shoulder, not quite sure what to do with my hands. She read me and pointed toward the room full of people. "They can wait. It's our reception." She handed me a slender box about the size of a sheet of paper, covered in gift wrap and tied with a ribbon. "Open it."

"I thought we agreed not to exchange gifts."

She nodded. "We did."

"Can't believe I fell for that."

While I fumbled with the ribbon, she lifted her hair off her shoulders and said, "Unzip me." Then pointed at her wedding dress. "Can't dance in this thing."

I did as instructed and then returned to the gift. Inside the box, I found an 8.5" x 11" ebony picture frame. No picture. No glass. It was simply a smooth, see-through wooden frame. I studied it like a monkey staring at a Rubik's Cube.

Laughing, she said, "Hold it up."

When I did, my eyes focused on the image through the frame.

She smiled. "Stop moving it around."

Centered in the frame stood Summer. Her dancer's body laid bare. On stage yet shared with a singular audience—me. The only thing she wore was the cross I'd bought her. Both my jaw and my arms dropped, which brought another giggle out of her. She shook her head, saying, "Nope," and reached forward and lifted my arms. "Keep 'em up."

I tried.

She walked closer. Then she just stood. Unashamed. Unafraid. Unfiltered. She whispered, "You're blushing."

I nodded and swallowed. "Yes, I am."

She placed her thumbs on both of my temples. "Before we go any further . . . in that room . . . with those people . . . in our life . . . I want to replace the pictures"—she tapped both sides of my head and tilted hers just slightly—"rolling around in here. I want to give myself to you, before I give myself to you."

Her skin was warm and soft. Another swallow. I managed, "Mission accomplished."

She lifted the ebony frame, focusing my eyes once again through it, and then stepped back and twirled. Once. Then twice. She half turned. "You good?"

I shook my head. "Not really."

Sweat misted on her temple and across the top of her breast. I handed her my folded handkerchief, which she used to dab the sides of her face and top lip. She eyed the unwrinkled and spotless white cloth, reading the date and our names. "You do this all by yourself?"

I shook my head. "Clay."

She laughed. "Love that man." Another twirl as she clutched my handkerchief. "You starting to get the picture?"

Music and laughter from the reception spilled through the walls. "You don't actually expect me to eat dinner with these people now, do you?"

"And dance."

She turned, pressed her body to mine, and kissed me, her hands hanging behind my head. "I can't compete with your past. No woman can. It's been there too long, and to make matters worse, you immortalized it in books that are now in every civilized country in the world. In maybe the most beautiful way imaginable—of which I'm your biggest fan—you idealized a painful reality. And because of your magnificent words, and a heart that is bigger than this body, we all love Marie, and I love you all the more for it. But"—she laid her hand flat across my heart—"we cannot start the rest of our lives staring through the rearview mirror of that life. So, rightly or wrongly, I brought you here to push pause for just a moment and give you a glimpse of me with"—a laugh—"all my cellulite and wrinkles, and my dancer's body, which lacks some things men find attractive, before we walk in there." She held my face in her hands. "I brought you here to give you an unedited image into our future that, I hope, drowns out the written, rewritten, and edited echo of the past."

"There's that word again."

She closed her eyes. "Which one?"

"Hope."

She nodded. Waiting.

I stood in wonder. "I don't see any cellulite."

She pointed above us. "It's the lighting."

"Or wrinkles."

She pressed her forehead to mine. Exposing the risk she was taking in this moment. When Summer had stolen the boat and set off down the Intracoastal, full throttle, in search of her runaway daughter, she did so while unable to swim. Driven by love, she risked the consequences. Even death. Here and now, she was risking her heart to rescue another.

Me.

Summer had rescued me.

Her heart was pounding and a single vein throbbed on the flush of her neck. When the sweat dried across her chest and chill bumps rose on her arms, I realized what this moment had truly cost her—and I loved her all the more for it. She whispered, "Good answer."

I was wrong about one thing. While a deep need in each of us is to know and be known, there is one deeper. One that undergirds everything else. It's the stuff of us. Out of it, we breathe, or not. We wander the earth like shipwrecked castaways, intersecting other island dwellers, and when we meet them, we hold ourselves out in offering and grant them a chance to accept or reject us. With our souls held together with twine and tape and glue, we bounce from rejection to rejection until we find the one who accepts us.

This is the thirst of the human soul, and only one thing satisfies it: to be accepted in the knowing.

Prior to that night, I'd not laughed that much in all my entire life put together. We danced until my feet blistered. Toward the end of the night, as I sat soaked in my own sweat staring at Clay dance with a dozen Broadway dancers at once, I realized what Summer had done. What she'd pulled off. Single-handedly. She'd created a reception at which I—a man who can easily get wrapped up in his own mind—never thought about my first marriage. Not once. I never equated this with that. And it wasn't as if she buried it or shied away from it. She did no such thing. She just celebrated us in this moment, and in so doing didn't compete with my past.

It was like being married for the first time. A priceless gift. One I could not repay.

At midnight, just moments before Clay drove us in the golf cart to the plane that would take us on our honeymoon, Bones gave me the sign. My turn to toast my wife. I tapped my glass with a fork and waited while the audience quieted. Behind me, the band played softly. Not one for long speeches, I did not plan one here: "It's winter outside. Supposed to drop to single digits tonight." I turned to Summer, who stood glowing. A glass in one hand. My handkerchief in the other dabbing the corner of her eye. "Thank you for throwing your blanket over me, for without it, I would have grown cold."

I lifted my glass aloft and said, "To Summer."

Only then did I smell the smoke.

# CHAPTER 30

Bones and I were the first out the door. Below us, a quarter mile away, flames climbed out of the Planetarium and one corner of the hospital. The children's ward.

Gunner and I hit Main Street at a dead run. A minute later, I screamed at Gunner, "Stay! Do not go in that building!"

He did not obey me.

I ran through the hospital door and up the stairs, where five or six members of our security team were lugging coughing, smoke-charred children via fireman's carry. Most men carried two children. Kids connected to IV medications either carried their clear bags or their lines had been cut and hastily tied like umbilical cords.

I reached the third floor, where the heat was intense and smoke burned my eyes and lungs as I followed the screams and sounds of breaking glass from room to room. I lifted two crying kids off their beds and carried them out and into the snow before I realized that the emergency and redundant sprinkler systems had not put out the fire. *What's taking so long? Where is the sound of sirens?* Nothing made sense.

Returning inside, I passed Clay carrying three kids. One in each arm and one on his back. "Clay! Stay out of this building!"

He laughed as he passed me, his grizzly paws tenderly cradling a toddler in each hand. "Not likely." Something had torn his tux and his shoes would never recover.

I helped the security team clear the fourth and fifth floors before Bones found me. I screamed, "Bones! What is going on? Where's the—"

He caught his breath. "This is planned, choreographed, and it's occurring in—" He was in the process of getting the word *stages* out of his mouth when the first explosion occurred. Followed quickly by a second. Then a third higher up. He pulled me by my jacket, nearly yanking my feet out of my dress shoes. "We've got to get you out of here!"

"But—"

"Now!"

I tried to grab Clay's arm as we passed on the balcony of the second floor, but he turned and said, "One more room. Be right out."

Bones and I landed on the ground floor and had cleared the front door when, for the second time in less than a year, I do not remember the blast that rocketed me from the earth. The last image to pass across the lens of my eyes before someone turned out the lights was that of Bones.

His robes were on fire.

And this time, Clay would not pull me from the wreckage.

Debris was still falling from the sky when I came to. I climbed to one knee, then my feet. While I could see people's mouths moving, I couldn't hear them. The world had gone quiet. Whether temporarily or permanently, I did not know.

Bones had made it to his knees. He was bleeding from a gash in his head and his robes were still on fire. I launched myself at him and rolled him in the snow. "Where's Clay?"

Bones pointed at what remained of the building.

I ran back in.

Clay lay crumpled in a pile when I got to him. Folded up like a bag of sticks. I lifted his smoking and broken body and carried him back down the stairs and out the door, setting him gently in the snow. His eyes were staring above me, but the light was fading and his breathing was shallow.

I held him until the paramedics arrived. When they did, they quickly assessed him as a LifeFlight priority and moved him to the helipad, leaving me standing in the street watching the lights of the ambulance fade and feeling something strange inside the palm of my hand. When I uncurled my fingers, I found Clay's pocket watch, which was no longer ticking.

The town stood in a fiery chaos. People were running everywhere. To my left, Bones stood with members of our security team. I'd never seen his face so pained. So contorted. He turned to me. "I need to show you something."

# CHAPTER 31

Security and surveillance of Freetown occurred in one of three dens, as we called them. Triangulated in strategic points around town, they served as both lookout and bunker with enough computers and screens to run Microsoft or Google. They were placed in such a way that the guys working in them could come and go without anyone knowing it. Sort of like how they run Disney World. You know there's a person in that suit; you just don't know how they got in there or where they came from. Bones led me to the nearest den, where a bunch of smoke-charred men were busily studying video feeds from our close-captioned cameras.

Eddie, our lead IT tech, brought up a series of videos showing a progression from the reception, to Main Street, to the hospital. Each video was accompanied by a time-lapse depicted across the bottom, which allowed him to arrange them in a grid to show what was going on in the reception at the same time people were walking Main Street.

The montage began inside the reception hall with my toast of Summer. You could see the bubbles rising in my glass and the sweat on Summer's face. Every few seconds she'd dab the corners of her eyes with the handkerchief. The second set had been captured by cameras mounted on light poles along Main Street, which had recorded our full-speed run toward the hospital. The third camera had been above the hospital door and captured our running in and out of the hospital. My eyes quickly focused on Clay. At last count, he'd made five trips in and either carried or led twenty-one people to safety. In the last video, he disappeared through the front door where he passed me and said something while laughing. The next video, shot from inside the stairwell, recorded his shadow followed by the explosion.

Finally, Eddie clicked a series of keys and exchanged the videos for a series of heat-signature shots showing the mountains and trails around Freetown. Our perimeter. In the previous three days, the cameras had recorded some mule deer, a few elk, several black bears, and our team patrolling. This meant no one had slipped under the wire.

Whoever had done this had come through the front door.

I asked Eddie to rewind to the reception and focus on the girls. Ellie, Angel, and Casey stood together a few feet from us. Summer next to me. He slowed the video as I ran out into the street, the girls following close behind me. Then Main Street. Still they were behind me, each of their dresses flowing as they ran. A block from the hospital, I exited one frame and then entered another and finally into the hospital. The next video recorded something I had not known—the girls never hesitated. They followed me into the burning building, a contrast of dress, glitter, and flame. When I hit the stairwell, I'd climbed to the second floor. They had turned right and run toward the nursery where, unbeknownst to us, fire had already disabled the cameras.

Minutes elapsed as Clay and I and others ran in and out. More and more smoke poured from the building. And no matter how many times I watched that video, Ellie, Angel, Casey, and Summer never reappeared.

They never exited the hospital.

Which meant they were still inside.

I walked out of the den and down to the hospital, which was being showered in spray from three trucks and two teams of men on their knees bracing hoses fed by red street hydrants. Above us, black smoke spiraled upward and mixed with the lighter water droplets, some of which would freeze and fall, melting into black water on my skin.

After a minute, I sensed Bones standing next to me. Tears running down his face.

I'd never felt more pain in my entire life.

# CHAPTER 32

Despite the pain, Bones and I had to wrestle with one question immediately: What should we do with everyone else in Freetown? Their safety was now priority number one. What if they were next? We couldn't guarantee they were not. Bones scanned the girls huddled in groups. Crying. Shaking. Holding each other. He asked without looking at me, "Do we move them?"

"The Bunker?"

He nodded. "I don't know what's worse, the threat of abduction or the psychological damage that will occur if we move them through the night into a granite black hole in the middle of nowhere."

Ideally, we needed time to acclimate them to the Bunker. Take them up on weekends, treat it like a retreat center, let them personalize their rooms, bowl in the underground alley, swim in the pool, pile into the theater and watch sappy romance movies. The more we could familiarize them with it, the less shock it would be to their systems and the easier it would be to evacuate if needed. Obviously, we had not done any of that.

"I say no. It's too much too soon. We have to hunker down here. If we drag them up there in the cold of night, dressed in their pajamas, only to parade them single file into a sterile hole in the side of a mountain with no windows and only one way out, I'm pretty sure we'll trigger some dormant PTSD. The damage could be a long time cleaning up."

Bones nodded. "Agreed, but we've still got the problem of protecting them. I say we circle the wagons. Gather them all in one place. A giant slumber party where they can gain emotional strength in numbers and not fear the bad man they can't see."

Over the next few hours, we moved mattresses and pillows and blankets and turned the floor of the gymnasium into one giant bed. And then we surrounded it with armed men. Some you could see. Most you could not.

When finished, the POTUS was not so heavily guarded.

By midmorning, the firemen had contained and turned the fire, which had burned too intensely throughout the night to allow any kind of search. When the sun broke the snowcapped peaks, I stood staring at the charred steel beams of the hospital—a cup of coffee in my hands and a blanket wrapped around my shoulders. Bones's face mirrored concrete. He spoke over me. "Clay is . . ." He swallowed and his voice cracked. "On a ventilator. They don't think he'll . . ."

It would be late afternoon before our guys could bring in dogs and a forensics team to safely sift both the rubble and the fumes without danger of a secondary explosion. I sat on the hillside and watched the dogs as my mind replayed the evening's events. I could not make sense of my emotions, so my mind began trying to solve a problem—the underlying fact that none of our systems had registered an alarm. Despite one programmed redundancy after another, we had no warning, no detection, and no sprinkler response. Hundreds of thousands of dollars spent on the best system known to man and yet it detected nothing.

Bones was right. This was no accident. The system had been overridden. Shut down.

Though I hadn't slept in more than forty hours, nightfall found me wandering the skeleton of the hospital like a man on Mars while Gunner tiptoed next to me, letting his nose lead him. His step-step-freeze, step-step-freeze looked more coyote than dog. He knew, maybe in the same way he knew there was a bomb on my boat, that he shouldn't disturb anything. So he didn't.

At 3:00 a.m., I sat down in what was once the kitchen. The combination of stress, emotions, and exhaustion had come crashing down. I could neither sleep nor think straight. I wanted to run to my computer, tap a few keys, click on Summer's GPS tracker, and watch it flash in rhythm with her heart. If she was alive, it would flash with every beat. If she was not, it would show constant red until the battery died some seventy-two hours later.

But there was no cross. No chip. And given the heat of the fire, there were no bodies.

There would be no pulse. No flash. No "X marks the spot."

When I sat against a concrete wall and sank my head in my hands, Gunner lay his head and one paw across my lap. I wasn't sure if he was half hugging me or wanting to prevent me from hurting myself. Next to us, a ventilation grate washed us in fresh air from the loading dock, which had been used to receive all deliveries to and from the hospital. Trucks supplying the hospital came in through a tunnel cut through one side of the mountain large enough for several side-by-side eighteen-wheelers. Access to the tunnel was granted through a service entrance manned twenty-four-seven by one of the dens, and given the frequency and volume of traffic, it was one of our most secure points of entry. Our guys guarded this breach in the wall with a fanatic zeal.

While the current and constant flow of fresh air washed out the toxic smell of burnt rubber and chemicals, its designed purpose had been to purge the tunnel of diesel fumes from the trucks. It served like a fireplace chimney. By design, huge fans, now incinerated, once pulled air out of the loading dock and kitchen area and flushed that air out the other side of the tunnel. Up until twenty-four hours ago, it had worked flawlessly. Sitting there feeling the reversed airflow across my skin, I realized the explosion had altered that, creating a fireplace of sorts at the top of the chimney that was larger than the other side. The change was simple physics. The explosion had reversed the flow.

Every few minutes Gunner's ears would flicker and he'd stick his nose into the flow of fresh air. Then his body tensed and he sat up.

This time I did not tell him to go away and leave me alone.

# CHAPTER 33

G unner ran to the grate, sniffed the air, and began digging at the steel with his paws. He did this five or six times, but it wasn't until he barked that I stood up. When he barked again, I led him around the wall, down a hallway where the roof had been blown off, and into the circular roundabout where the delivery trucks turned around. Gunner's nose hit the airspace, something registered, and he took off at a dead run down the tunnel.

Barking.

Gunner and I ran through the yellow hue of the emergency lighting, winding through curves and cut granite. Four hundred meters later, we topped a small rise and reached the exit where a massive security door now rested in the nonsecure and open position—a security feature programmed to open automatically to allow first responders access. Strange how that had worked and yet the sprinklers and halon system had not.

While much of the hospital ran off solar energy and a small percentage from our own power grid, no hospital is complete without backup and redundant generators, of which we had several. Those were fueled by propane, which was topped off once a month and held in underground tanks outside the massive door—for obvious reasons.

Fuel trucks were checked at security and, once cleared, allowed through the gate, where they then drove a hundred meters into a cul-de-sac. Once they turned 180 degrees and were facing the opposite direction, they would stop, transfer fuel to the tanks, and then exit the same way they came in. All of this happened under the watchful eye of our team and several cameras.

Gunner disappeared out the exit and through the area where the trucks filled the propane tanks. When I got to him, the hair on his back was raised and he was growling at the darkness.

So I walked into the darkness.

The fill receptacle for the underground tank lay beneath a hinged steel lid in an area of space about the size of a loaf of bread. Gunner inched alongside me but never took his eyes off the lid.

I whispered, "What do you see, boy?"

More growling.

"Easy," I said, allowing my eyes time to adjust. When they did, I slowly lifted the lid. I'll give you one guess as to what lay tucked inside.

# CHAPTER 34

I 'll never know how Gunner smelled the handkerchief from more than
a winding quarter mile away, but somehow, with the reversal of the
airflow, he had. Was it Summer's sweat? Her perfume? Or was it the fresh
blood? I don't know. I just know that he did. As I stood there staring in
disbelief, I tried to force my mind to click into gear.

*Think, Murph. Think.*

The blast had not blown it in there. The blast would have incinerated
it. That could only mean the handkerchief had been placed inside that
lid—by hand and probably in haste. Its location was purposeful. No accident. Summer must be trying to tell me something, but what?

Was she alive? Was Ellie? Angel? Casey? If she wasn't, then who put
the handkerchief in that location? Why? I tried to block the questions as
I ran back through the tunnel. I found Bones in Den 2, which had been
converted to Command Central. He was hovering over a cup of coffee,
his Sig hanging in a chest holster, and he was staring at video replays of
Main Street looking for clues. He, too, was dead on his feet. I threw open
the door and spoke to Eddie while pointing at the screen. "Bring up all of
yesterday's video of the delivery gate."

Eddie's fingers sounded like horses' hooves pounding the keys.

At 10x speed, starting with the morning of the wedding, which was
now nearly forty-eight hours ago, Eddie began playing the video. Several
trucks rolled in, then through the tunnel where our cameras captured them

along every inch of the route. Each one circled the roundabout, then backed up to the loading dock and offloaded their delivery. Then our folks checked the contents and signed the papers, and the trucks returned down the tunnel and out the gate. Everything worked as it should.

Then a large propane truck appeared around 10:45 p.m. I spoke out loud to Bones. "Does that strike you as strange?"

He nodded at the driver of the truck. "Those guys are local. Nine to five. They're not long haul."

Bones was tracking with me. Long-haul drivers make deliveries when they reach a destination. No matter the time. So almost 11 p.m. wouldn't have been too unusual. But guys who punch a clock deliver on a more regular schedule because they're part of a route. More like a mailman. I spoke to the team of guys who had gathered just over my shoulder. "What time is that normally?"

More keys clicking. "Over the last six months, between 9:45 and 10 a.m."

"Like clockwork," I said.

"And how long do they normally stay?"

"Forty-five minutes max."

Bones looked up at me. "What are you getting at?"

"Eddie, bring up my toast at the reception." Eddie complied and the video began playing. "Can you slow it down?"

Eddie slowed the video. Summer appeared. Glass in one hand, handkerchief in the other. "Stop." I pointed at the screen, then unfurled my fingers, allowing Summer's handkerchief to hang from my hand. "I found this tucked inside the lid where the trucks fill the tank."

Bones eyed it. Then me. "That means . . ."

I spoke for both of us. "They may not be dead."

Bones was now firing on all cylinders. Problem solving. "But why there?"

"Unless it blew in there mysteriously, which I doubt, it was placed there purposefully. Which suggests intention. Which could also mean she's trying to tell me something."

He nodded in agreement. "But what?"

I pointed at the truck on the screen. "When did that thing leave?"

We watched as the truck exited the gate at 12:02 p.m.

"And when was the explosion?"

Bones spoke from memory. "12:04."

"Does it strike anyone as strange that our unscheduled propane delivery enters and then exits what is normally Fort Knox just two minutes before an explosion blows half the mountain away?"

Silence enveloped Command Central.

Bones looked at me with both anger and tears in his eyes. I glanced at Eddie, who rewound the video of the truck leaving the gate. Four cameras had captured it coming and going. Everything looked perfectly normal. Nothing out of the ordinary. "Bones, how many people do you think could fit in the tank of that truck?"

He weighed his head side to side. "Properly outfitted? Maybe a dozen. Packed like sardines?" He shrugged. "Twenty-some." He turned to me, the picture clearing in his mind. "That thing would make an excellent Trojan horse."

I nodded. "Which is the only reason I can imagine Summer would tuck that handkerchief inside the lid. She knew, sooner or later, that Gunner—who runs around this place at will—would find it." I shook my head. "How else would she tell us?"

Bones stood and pointed at Eddie, whose fingers immediately produced a map of Colorado. Bones looked at me. "If he clicks that button, it's T-minus seven days. Track them too soon and we can lose them in transit because we haven't given them time to get to a destination."

I finished his sentence. "And track them too late and they're gone forever."

Bones crossed his arms and started at the screen. "It's delicate."

"Currently, whoever has them doesn't know what we know. He thinks we think they're all dead. And given that's what he wants us to think, he's probably not in a great big hurry, and he's probably not looking behind him. But sooner or later, and probably sooner rather than later, he'll strip the girls of everything and might even find our trackers."

"Which means we're on the clock."

Bones nodded.

Eddie spoke. "If they're in that tank, or in anything enclosed in metal or concrete or whatever, the signal won't initiate the tracker until she's outside."

"Unless she's sitting by a window. And Summer would be."

Bones turned to me. "What about Angel, Ellie, and Casey?"

"We never told them about the GPS. No need to worry them."

Bones spoke again. "But if they're alive, I'd bet most everything I have that Summer has told them by now."

I spoke almost to myself. "Why take only them?"

"What do you mean?"

"It seems targeted. Why take only Angel, Ellie, Casey, and Summer when sixty-three other women sat defenseless during the moments following the fire and leading up to the explosion? Our attention wasn't focused on them. We were trying to put out the fire. Get kids out of the hospital. They had us by the jugular. If they really wanted to hurt Freetown, or they were in it for the money, why not back up a tractor trailer while our attention was elsewhere and load it up with as many as they could? It just doesn't make sense."

Bones stared beyond me. "Unless it's personal."

"Correct."

Bones continued, "The only reason to single them out and walk away with those four rather than two dozen is because somebody is trying to make a statement."

"You mean like the statement they made with my boat?"

A nod. "Maybe."

"You think it's Mr. Montana?"

Bones shook his head once. "It could be anybody, but I wouldn't exclude him. I might even put him at the top of the list."

"So let's assume for a minute that it's personal. If it is, then he's not in it for the money. In fact, he may not sell them at all."

Bones scratched his beard. "I'd rather he auction them. Post their faces on the black web. That would buy us some time."

"If he doesn't, we can be pretty certain this isn't a business proposition. This is personal. And if it's personal, and if he's as wealthy as he'd have to be to pull off an explosion like that"—I pointed to the hospital—"both here and on my island, I can see two possible outcomes. First, he'll unload them in Canada or Mexico. Wash his hands and either dump them or give them away."

"Which means their life expectancy isn't long."

"I agree."

Bones raised a hand. Playing devil's advocate. "Why would he do that?"

"To hurt us." A pause. "Revenge . . . plain and simple."

"But would a guy who just went through all this trouble get rid of them that quickly? Whatever happened here took planning. A guy who can plan like this wouldn't score the winning touchdown only to hand the ball to the ref and jog to the sideline. He'd dance a little."

"If I was my enemy, I'd do backflips."

Bones nodded. "Which brings us to option two."

"He wouldn't be in a hurry. He'd savor the moment and sit in his smug retreat while the dust settled. Once he felt enough time had elapsed, and we'd accepted their deaths, he'd begin trickling videos to my inbox, which he'd string out over time, depicting the hell in which they lived. Then, just before we lost our minds to grief, he'd dump their bodies where we'd find them or sell them overseas."

He interrupted me. "Which is the same thing."

I continued, "If this guy is hell bent on inflicting as much pain as possible on me, then he would want as much time to pass as possible to cause us as much pain as possible. Time for him means pain for us. Death by a thousand cuts. Somewhere we took something from him. Caused him pain. He's not in this for the money. He probably has enough of that. He's in it for wrath. Revenge. Somewhere in my past I took the one thing he values more than money."

Bones spoke without prompting. "Power."

"Exactly. Which explains all this. What happened here is not some haphazard thing some guy did in his spare time. This took planning, time, and patience. Which means his motivation is power. It's the only explanation for the deception. For the timing. For taking the four of them rather than a boatload from the reception."

Bones considered this. "So what's the play?"

"Make him comfortable. Convince him we have no idea."

"While we search like crazy."

Eddie sat at the keyboard, waiting. When I nodded, he punched a few keys and the satellite initiated tracking and began its search. The countdown started. T-minus seven days and counting. A minute passed. Six days, twenty-three hours, and fifty-nine minutes. Then another. Six days, twenty-three hours, fifty-eight minutes. Halfway through the third minute, a single solid red light appeared. When it did, my heart jumped into my throat.

"Where is that?" Bones asked.

Eddie stared at the screen and clicked the mouse twice. "In a plane. Thirty-nine thousand feet. Final approach to Miami International."

"That's not good."

Bones agreed. "He gets them on an international flight, we may never see them again."

Neither of us took our eyes off the solid light. Eddie read our concern. "It takes it a minute to read pulse."

Ninety seconds later, it held solid. No flash. Eddie tapped the screen with a pencil. "These things have been known to malfunction."

My tone changed. "Whose is that?"

Keystrokes sounded. Eddie looked up at me. "Ellie."

"So either she's dead or it's not registering."

Eddie nodded and said nothing.

"What would happen if it weren't next to her? If it was, say, hanging on something?"

"The satellite would pick up the track but not the pulse."

"So it would do exactly what it's doing."

Another nod.

I turned to Bones. "If you were locked in a solid metal tube flying close to the speed of sound and you knew the satellite couldn't read your tracker, what would you do?"

"Hang it near a window."

I leaned against the wall and pleaded with the solid light to flash. It did not. I stared at the ceiling and spoke as much to myself as him. "All we have is supposition and assumption. For all we know, those girls are in Tahiti or Kosovo."

Bones agreed. "All we know is that the tracker is"—he tapped the screen—"right there." He stepped closer. "What do your instincts tell you?"

"Not sure. But something doesn't feel right."

In these high-altitude parts of Colorado, Freetown was known as a private rehab and addiction facility. That's all. People who worked here were screened relentlessly and most had either military or government backgrounds. Many of them had worked in intelligence. Our reason was simple— they knew the value of keeping a secret. We weren't naïve enough to think all our secrets were safe, but it helped. You can't rescue people from bad people and then expect to keep them safe if you're constantly airing your laundry. This was why we'd never told anyone's story, which made Casey so different.

To ensure a cone of silence, Bones insisted on conducting all final interviews. So he could sniff out a fake. This bubble of self-protection meant we were very careful when the press started knocking on the gate and poking their nose in our business. Most often we responded with "No comment," but tomorrow needed to be different.

I stared at the solid red light. "I need to get to that light. And if they're anywhere near it, get them out of wherever he's taking them before he knows they're gone. And I need his guard to be down more than it is." I turned to Bones. "Which means I need you to buy some time. That smoke cloud won't go unnoticed. It would help us if you put on your collar and fed the press what we want them to know."

"You want me to lie?"

"I want you to lie your face off and tell them that a talented and gifted off-Broadway dancer gave up a career in sold-out shows to care for her daughter, who was recovering from an opioid addiction, plus two adopted daughters, both recovering from multiple issues, not the least of which was ritual sexual abuse."

Bones saw the ripple effects play out in his mind. "Which means I need to conduct a funeral this week."

"We need to publicly bury four memories." I considered this. "Actually, make it five. Tell them Gunner died in the fire. All we found was his scorched collar." I slipped Gunner's collar off and handed it to Eddie. "Make this look burned."

Bones smiled. "You should write fiction in your spare time."

I continued, "Further, this selfless mother and her three daughters volunteered in the neonatal ICU taking care of and feeding premature babies born to other recovering mothers."

Bones sat down and crossed his legs. "You have real skill."

"You need to leak the video of them running into the building followed by the explosion. And, Eddie, you need to edit it in such a way as to leave no doubt that all four are buried beneath the rubble. More importantly"—I pointed to the dot moving westward across the screen—"we need whoever that is to believe that we believe they're gone. End the video with Gunner racing into the flames followed by a fireball and the video goes to black."

Bones raised a finger. "All four ran into the hospital looking like they just came from a wedding. That may raise a few questions."

I shook my head. "All four had changed into their dancing dresses. Spin it that they were at a going-home party for one of the girls when they smelled smoke."

Bones nodded. "That'll print."

I turned but Bones stopped me, pointing at one of the screens, a live feed from the gymnasium where mattresses had been brought in. All of Freetown was huddled in groups while armed men stood outside guarding the perimeter. "They need to hear from you before you disappear."

I nodded.

"Do we tell them?"

I shook my head. "No."

"But we said we'd never lie to them."

"You're right. I said that."

"And you're going to anyway."

"Yes. I am."

"We may never recover from that. They may leave Freetown in mass exodus when they learn the truth."

I pointed at the solid red light. "Is she worth it?" A pause while the satellite searched for the other three. "Are they?" Bones and I stared at the screen. "Right now they're probably sitting in the dark. Scared beyond hope. No telling what's been done or is being done to them. So is there anything you or I wouldn't say or do to get them back?"

Bones shook his head.

I turned to Eddie. "You got a video camera?"

He held up an iPhone.

"Turn it on. I want you to record something. We may need it later."

Eddie stepped back and began videoing with burning Freetown as the background. With Bones standing next to me, I stared into the video. "It's late. Freetown is burning, Clay is on life support, and Angel, Ellie, Casey, and"—I stuttered—"and Summer are gone. Initially, we thought we lost them in the blast." I held up the handkerchief. "Now we're not so sure. We think this was a coordinated attack to kidnap them for the purpose of revenge. I can't go into all the details, but I need you all to understand what Bones and I are dealing with in this moment. We're about to create a false narrative, which all of you are going to live out. You will suffer by the lies we're going to tell. We're going to sell it to the media that they're all dead, including Gunner." I waved to Gunner, and Eddie moved the camera, showing the dog with his tongue hanging out.

"This week all of you are going to mourn and go to a funeral with five caskets, and you'll put stuff in each because we're going to talk about how their bodies were incinerated, and all of you will hurt and cry tears and your hearts will break. All the while, we in this room will know it is a fabrication." I pointed to the screen. "We think they're alive. But we don't know for how much longer, so we're trying to buy some time. Unfortunately, all of you are puppets in that play. I wish I could tell you I'm sorry, but . . ." I shook my head. "I can't be. I've got to—" My voice cracked. "Try to find . . ." My voice trailed off.

"When you came here, we told you we'd never lie to you. Until now I haven't. But I'm about to. It's a big lie. And when it's over and you learn all of this, I'm asking that you forgive me. Why? Not because I deserve it but because I'd do the same for every one of you."

Eddie clicked off the video and I wiped the tears trailing down my face. I spoke to Eddie. "Make sure you save that someplace safe. If he blew us up, he can hack into most anything. And we don't need him seeing that."

Eddie slid his phone in his pocket. "Check."

I walked into the gymnasium to muffled sobs and groups huddled and hugging one another. They'd spread out sleeping bags. A giant slumber party. Pajamas all around. Minus the smiles.

They were scared. A few were shaking. I knew each one: Beth, Tilly, Ray, Tracy, Sally, Cindy, Billy, Amanda, Margaret, Jennifer, Ashley, Kristen, Simone, Lisa . . . Sixty-three girls were staring back at me. Along with several of their mothers and more than a few sisters. I knew their stories. Their horrors. And I'd seen them laugh. Seen joy return. Each one of these women had suffered the feeling of drowning, of some giant unseen hand holding their head beneath the water. They'd been domi-nated, manipulated, intimidated, and controlled—and in most cases, by a man who looked like me. They huddled in a circle. Or rather, lay across one another like pick-up sticks. Interwoven. Three strands are stronger than one. Their faces were puffy. Eyes red. Makeup smeared. The dresses of dance and celebration had been replaced by the comfort of sweats and pajamas. Something soft to counter a granite world.

Bones read my hesitation. He put his hand on my shoulder. "If you were hiding Jews in your basement and the SS knocked on the door, what would you tell them?"

I turned a chair around backward and sat leaning my chin on the top and studied their faces. Each was looking at me to rescue them again. To make the bad man stop. To drive a stake in the world and declare to the evil, "You will come no farther."

To tell them the truth.

The faint smell of smoke wafted on the air. A reminder of what had been lost. Flashing red lights reflected off the foyer glass while men on extended ladders shot giant rainbows of water across the wreckage. Bones stood off to one corner.

I hated myself for what I was about to do.

When I studied each face, each story returned. I rubbed my hands together, willing my soul to spit out the lies. "We have yet to find Angel, Ellie, Casey, Summer, and Gunner." A single shake of my head. "The video shows them running in, followed by the explosion. The heat melted metal and glass. So . . . it might be a day or two before . . ." The implication was clear: we might never find their bodies.

The sobs were no longer muffled. The collective cry was excruciating. Each of these children of God had been exploited. Abused. And lied to ten thousand times over. For many, the idea that there is actually a truth that they can bank their lives on is a fantasy. It's one of their deepest wounds—those they thought they could trust turned out not to be trustworthy. I scanned the sea of faces, all of whom trusted me. With their lives. It's why they were sitting here. Until now, I'd never taken that for granted. But in this moment, Bones and I were using their emotions to prove to whoever did this that four people and one dog were dead.

*How will they respond to me when they discover otherwise?*

I knew that in order to pull this off, to sell it to whoever did this, we needed the girls' unfiltered reactions. Or rather, that's what I told myself.

"Clay's on life support." I paused. "He's a tough old man, but nobody knows." Their faces spoke their stories. Stories of evil run rampant. And here I sat, inflicting more. "I've got a window where I maybe can find who did this. So . . . Bones will be here. I hope to make it back for the funeral . . ."

At the word *funeral*, the floodgates broke loose.

I waited for the wave to pass. "I know you're scared. You're wondering how'd they get in? How'd they find us? What will happen to us?" I shook my head. "I can't answer any of those questions. But . . ." I turned to Beth: "I had no idea how we'd make it out of that trailer park." And to Tilly: "Or that meth lab disguised as a motel." And to Ray: "Or that hotel in Vegas."

To Sally: "That beach bungalow in Maui." To Cindy: "A tractor trailer at a truck stop." To Amanda: "A houseboat in the Gulf."

I shrugged. "I didn't know then how we'd ever get here. But I hoped we would . . ." Tears slid down my cheeks. "Hope is what we have. It's the fuel that feeds us." I rubbed my hands together. "In ancient times, when kingdoms were attacked and once-impenetrable walls fell, people inside the city would emerge from the rubble, stare at the wreckage, and then ask the only question that remains: Do I stand in the breach, or do I run? Those who ran lived in fear, forever looking over their shoulder. Those who stood climbed up on the remains and spoke to the darkness. And when they did, the darkness rolled back like a scroll. It has to. Darkness can't stand light."

I glanced at Bones and then stood. "I know your walls are pretty thin and cracking, and disconnected pieces lay scattered. I know you're hurting. And I know that you of all people deserve to not be in pain. To know joy and not sadness. Beauty and not ashes." I waved my hands across the carnage spread across the streets below us. "Don't despair. Any seed that is planted first must die and fall to the earth. Only then do we bury it and trust that what comes up is not the same as what we put in the ground. Nor could we ever have imagined it."

Tilly spoke for the group. The question on the tip of each one's tongue. "Murph, are you going to rebuild Freetown?"

I shook my head. "No . . ." The effect of my answer rippled through them. I studied each of their faces. And when I spoke, the ripple died. "You are."

Bones met me at the door. "I don't need to tell you to be careful, but . . ."

"I have no intention of being careful."

He knew that too. "What will you do when you find them?"

"Haven't gotten that far."

He prodded me. "What would you do to guarantee that any of these four women wouldn't make a run for it?"

"Tie up the youngest."

Bones finished my thought. "Exactly. They'd know what would happen to the youngest one if they bolt."

I studied the embers of Freetown. "Find this man. I want him."

Bones's facial expression was one of deep pain. Torment even. He nodded. Then raised his hand and extended all five fingers, followed by four. Then one finger. One finger. And one finger. 9–1–1–1. Or 91:11.

*He will command His angels concerning you.*

I shut the door, bounded down the stairs, and began sprinting the trail to my house. Main Street lay to my right, lit up like a runway. Beyond that the hospital smoldered. Three firemen stood atop long extension boom ladders holding water cannons shooting high-pressured streams through the air like rainbows. The smell of burning rubber and chemicals stung my nostrils and eyes. I tried not to think about what was swirling beyond my control.

Running through the night, Gunner matching me stride for stride, my breath exiting my lungs like smoke in the freezing temperature, I had one singular thought. Nothing else mattered. If I didn't bring them home, then what was the point of all this? Not Freetown, not happiness, not living a long healthy life, not coffee on the porch, not wine at the Eagle's Nest.

I reached the door and the same echo sounded that I'd heard a thousand times since Bones plucked me from the academy:

*We always leave the ninety-nine to find the one.*

*Why?*

*Because the needs of the one outweigh those of the many.*

I flew down the stairs, ripped off my tux shirt, and punched the code into the keypad: "LOVESHOWSUP."

# CHAPTER 35

Three hours later, the plane touched down at Miami International. I felt certain the bad guys wouldn't be looking over their shoulder. There was no way they could know we were on to them this quickly. If they had moved that far that fast, they were making a move to get the girls out of the country. While I was in the air, Eddie connected my phone with his portal, allowing me to watch the tracker in real time.

By the time I landed, the signal from the tracker had exited a private plane and then walked into the private airport where it disappeared. That wasn't uncommon since the GPS tracker required a line of sight to the satellite, and that line was broken as people walked into or out of buildings, cars, buses, etc.

"Be patient," Bones said.

I bought a cup of coffee and rented a car just in case. Then I sat in an office cubicle near the lounge, where I alternated between watching the three exit doors leading to all private planes and staring at my screen.

Six hours passed.

When the red light next appeared, it was sixty miles from my location moving west down Alligator Alley at sixty-seven miles an hour. I exited the airport, started the rental car, and was turning onto the off-ramp when my phone rang. It was Bones. "Looks like they turned off the Alley and into the Glades."

"I see that."

"You following?"

"Got to make a stop first."

"Get ready to navigate rough terrain."

I stopped at my storage unit and swapped out the rental for my BMW 1250 GS motorcycle, along with some gear. Four minutes later, I was back on the road. The thought did not escape me that the last time I'd ridden this bike, Summer was behind me, her arms wrapped around my chest as we traced Angel to a house in the Everglades.

I rolled west on 98 to the southern tip of Lake Okeechobee. Just south of the lake, I turned due south on 27 to the Miccosukee Casino and then west on 41. The road was bordered on either side by canals, which were part of the intricate network of the more than eight hundred square miles called the Everglades.

I was once again looking for a needle in a haystack.

I passed the Everglades Safari Park and the ValuJet Flight 592 Memorial, followed by the Miccosukee Indian Village, until I turned north on a limestone road paralleling the L-28 Canal Eden Station. This all felt eerily familiar, and I did not like where it was going.

I traveled this same limestone-dusted road for thirty minutes until both the road and canal abruptly ended at a thin trail marked by fresh four-wheel-drive tracks. I followed the trail, which eventually ended on a dirt road that did not appear on my GPS map. A mile away I saw a house and the shine of a vehicle. Looking at my phone, the red light appeared to exit the vehicle and enter the building, where it disappeared once again.

To advance during daylight would be a mistake. So I parked the bike and stared through binoculars throughout the afternoon and into the evening. Just before dark, a man exited the house, smoked several cigarettes, then returned inside. I highly doubted one man had been sent to guard the girls, but I needed to make certain. Barging into a house I think is guarded by a single man only to find five would not be good.

Under cover of darkness, I crept within two hundred yards of the house. At 10 p.m., a man walked out of the house backward, dragging a limp body. As he did this, the tracker returned on my screen. Solid. No flash. The man dragged Ellie across the yard and tied her to a tree. Then he quickly loaded into the vehicle and drove out the dirt road away from the house and away from me.

The light remained unflashing, and there was no movement at the house.

I crawled through the grass within sixty yards. Ellie had been tied to the back side of a tree and left sitting with her back to me, slumped over.

I circled counterclockwise, putting the tree between me and the house, where every light had been left on. Seeing no movement, I sprinted for the tree.

But I did not find Ellie.

I found a mannequin wearing a wig, Ellie's reception dress, and her necklace. The sight of the mannequin's blank stare caught me off guard and it took a minute for the absurdity to register. When it did, I ran to the house, pushed through the front door, and sprinted into and out of each room—but there were no bodies. No people. Just me.

When I returned to the tree, the mannequin appeared to be smiling. That's when I glanced into the tree above the mannequin and saw the phone. Filming me.

I'd been worked. The screen of the phone projected my image back to me, proving someone was on the other end watching the same picture of me. As I stared, the phone received a text picture. I touched the screen and the picture expanded. It was Ellie. And it was not a good picture. My anger flared and I felt the first wave of hopelessness.

I knew if I was going to be any good to the girls, I had to control both emotions. If I raged, I'd lose the ability to think clearly, and they needed me to think . . . clearly. If I despaired, I'd never find them.

I ended the call on the phone taped to the tree and dialed Bones. He answered mid-ring. "Find her?"

"We've been played."

A pause. "Talk to me."

"Ellie's not here. None of them are. The tracker was hanging around the neck of a mannequin with a live phone taped in the tree above."

"Seems we've played this game before."

"Or some variation of it. Any sign of the other trackers?"

"Not yet. Grab the phone and let's see if Eddie can pull anything off it. You'd better get back to Miami. There's no telling where the trail will lead next."

"Chances are good he will do this with each tracker while he flies the girls to Siberia. And we can quit trying to sell the story to the media. He knows we're on to him."

"What choice do we have?"

"My gut tells me this guy wants to bleed me slowly. This is just the first cut. Nobody goes through all this simply for a good giggle. Somehow we've got to get in front of him."

I could hear Bones scratching his beard. "If he knows we're on to him, then why sell the funeral? He knows. So why keep up the charade? But if I walk in there and tell all of them it was a ruse, we lose all credibility."

"Which is exactly what this guy wants."

Bones muttered in agreement. "He's trying to cause those who've placed their faith in us to lose their faith in us."

"Delay it. We don't need to put them through the emotional torture of a funeral if we can prevent it. Tell them I got called away and we need to tend to Clay. Buy a week."

"Agreed."

Three days had now passed since the explosion, and I'd only slept in fits. Moments here and there. So I returned to my storage shed, pulled the door down, collapsed on my cot, and caught a few hours' sleep, knowing Bones would call me if anything showed.

Twenty-four quiet hours passed. I tried to sleep, but every time I dozed off, helplessness woke me. On the morning of the fourth day, my phone rang. "You're not going to believe this."

"Try me."

"Remember the party house in Palm Beach that was destroyed?"

"The one where I found Casey?"

"Yep."

"Let me guess . . . Casey's tracker just came online. At that house."

"And this time with a pulse."

*Gone Fiction* had been blown to pieces, so a water approach wasn't feasible unless I rented or stole a boat, which I didn't have time to do. So I threw a leg over the bike and began riding east. Twenty-seven minutes later, I was staring at the house.

Last time I'd been here, the house had been destroyed by the party of all parties. There were motorcycles in the pool, giant lizards and monkeys running around the backyard, two feet of water in the living room, and a human bowling alley upstairs. Since then, the house had been bought by someone else and placed under renovation. If $2 million had been inflicted in damage, they were improving it by $4 million.

Bones spoke in my ear as I parked the bike. "The tracker is still reading a pulse."

I glanced at my phone. "I see that."

Given the enormity of the project, twenty-four-hour security had been stationed at a guard gate. The guard was reading a comic book and eating potato chips. I skirted the guard house, hopped the fence, and made my way inside. The improvements made the house unrecognizable, but I crept upstairs, through the second and third floors, and into the loft apartment where I first found Casey.

The water was not running and there was no steam. But I did find a body lying in the shower. A live person. A beautiful girl. Maybe fourteen. But she wasn't Casey any more than the mannequin was Ellie.

I knelt and gently shook her. She rubbed her eyes, sat up, and stared at me. A little bit shocked. Slightly afraid. But also looking like a fish out of water. The necklace was hanging around her neck. I pointed. "You mind telling me where you got that?"

She protected it with her right hand. "Guy gave it to me."

"How'd you end up here?"

"Same guy."

"What happened?"

"He paid me to sit here. Said somebody would be along in about thirty minutes. I was tired so I laid down. Am I in trouble?"

"No. Did you know the guy?"

She shook her head.

"Ever seen him?"

Another shake.

"You live far from here?"

"Forty-five minutes."

"Can you get a ride home?"

"Don't need one. That's my brother in the security shack. He lets me sit by the pool on Sundays when no one's working. This guy came up and gave me this and offered us both money to keep quiet." She proffered the necklace. "Is this yours?"

I stared at it. Then her. "It was."

She took it off and handed it to me.

I closed her fingers around it. "You keep it. I don't think the previous owner is going to want it anymore."

I stepped outside. Bones had heard all of that, so I didn't need to fill him in. "What now?" I asked.

Bones was silent. When he did speak, his frustration was evident. "I got nothing."

"We're chasing our tails here."

Bones agreed. "Wild-goose chase."

I glanced at my phone but the screen was blank. No signals. No trackers. "Bones? There are three scared girls and one scared woman out there right now. We need a break. Or I'm afraid I'm too late."

"If you were doing to us what is currently being done to us, what would you do next? Where would you fake the tracker?"

"One of two places: either my rock off Key West or my island."

"One is about a nine-hour drive from the other."

I agreed. "We've got a fifty-fifty shot at being right."

"You're three hours from Key West."

I could make it by sundown if I hurried.

I drove south down U.S. 1 over the Card Sound Bridge and then through the Keys. If I couldn't make the trip by boat, then motorcycle would be my second choice. Although I'd rather have Summer sitting behind me.

I drove quickly. Paying little attention to speed limits. I drove through Islamorada, where the traffic had cleared for some reason, so I gave it more throttle. The last time I looked down I was traveling 127 mph.

I reached Key West at noon and rented a hotel room overlooking my rock jutting up and out of the water like a submerged Volkswagen on the southern end of the key. From my perch on the second story, I could see anyone coming or going, so I spent the afternoon staring at the rock where I'd spent hours purging my soul.

Toward evening, Bones called. "Anything?"

"Tourists."

"You sure you'd pick that rock if you were him?"

"Only other thing I could think of would be Sisters of Mercy, but what does Marie have to do with either Angel or Summer?"

"No idea. But it's worth a look. How far away are you?"

"I can be there in a few minutes."

I drove east along the island to what was once the driveway of Sisters of Mercy Convent. The driveway had been gated and every cabin boarded up. Evidently with the death of their last sister, the state took it over and had done nothing with it since. I hopped the fence and took the coquina drive to the main house and cabins. Grossly overgrown, this place was one hurricane from erased. I wound through to the beach and walked to what had been Marie's cabin. The doors were boarded up and someone had thrown rocks through the windows. I didn't like looking at it.

Behind me I heard footsteps. When I turned, Sister June stood staring at me. Smiling. Hands behind her back, she was barefoot and looked as if she'd been gardening. "Looks like you healed up," she said.

"Yes, ma'am." I waved my hand across the landscape. "Thought you'd left."

"Lord brought me here. He can take me away at the time of His choosing."

I prompted her. "You seen anybody other than me nosing around here?"

She placed a small metal box in my hand. "They said to give this to you if you showed."

My heart sank. We'd been outflanked again. "Did you know them?"

She shook her head. "Couple of guys."

"When?"

"Earlier today."

"They say anything?"

"Only that you'd be showing up and to give this to you."

I opened the box, and Summer's Jerusalem cross glistened in my palm. Three seconds later, the tracker lit on my phone screen and began registering a pulse. Two seconds later, my phone rang. Bones. "Call you right back."

Sister June looked up at me. "You look tired."

I nodded. "Probably am." I lifted the necklace and gently hung it on her neck. She stared down at it, then at me, resting her fingers on the diamond. "I haven't worn jewelry in over eighty years."

I kissed her on the cheek, took a last look around, and returned to my bike.

Bones answered on the first ring. I said, "Nothing here. It's like this guy is reading our mail."

"Agreed." Bones was silent a minute.

I paused. "Bones, if the tables were turned, what would we be doing to this guy?"

"We'd be inside his communication."

"Exactly."

"Ours is near impenetrable."

"Maybe, but I think he's in it. I think he's listening right now."

Bones paused, sucked through his teeth, and hung up. Which told me everything I needed to know. I pulled onto U.S. 1 with Jacksonville through my windshield. I had eight hours of seat time ahead of me, but I had one stop to make first. At the first roadside cellular store, I bought two burner phones. Single-use cell phones. If used rightly, they could eliminate the problem we might be having. The challenge came in telling Bones the new number without using the old.

During my training at the academy, Bones had prepped me for this. We'd used it a couple times since and the remedy was simple: I'd buy a new phone and use the old to text him the number—with one difference. The number I texted him was the actual number + 1 + 2 + 3 + 4 and so on. So a 904 area code was actually 027. Bones, meanwhile, would dig up his own burner and call me back immediately on my new number with his new phone before anyone had a chance to trace it. I'd then give him the number of the second burner verbally and throw away the first. Seems paranoid but it works.

I texted him the number. He called one second later and I gave him the new number, then I disassembled the first phone and tore the SIM card in two as my second phone was ringing.

I answered, "We good?"

"Yep."

He didn't waste time. "Where're you headed?"

"My island."

"You think that's next?"

"I have no idea, but I can't sit here twiddling my thumbs. I'm about to lose my mind. A hamster on a wheel."

"Stay in touch."

I circled Jacksonville on 295 and exited at Heckscher Drive. Thirty minutes later, I walked through the woods and crossed over to my island in knee-deep water.

Quiet met me. As did footprints that were not mine. Voices soon followed.

I climbed into the arms of a live oak tree that spread out over the trail and leaned against the trunk, the afternoon sun hanging behind me. Two men walked nonchalantly toward me. When they were below me, I dropped on the first one and turned out his lights, then turned my attention to the second, who looked shocked to see me. I needed him to be able to talk and think, so I flipped him, dislocated his shoulder, stuck my finger into one eye, and dragged him to the water where I held his head below the surface.

After a minute, I pulled him up and asked him if he was ready to tell me what I wanted to know. When he cussed my mother, I returned him to the water for another ninety seconds.

This time when I lifted him out of the water, he coughed and choked and continued berating my lineage. This continued a few minutes. In the water, out of the water. Finally, I dislocated his other shoulder, rendering him helpless, at which point he read the writing on the wall.

As expected, he didn't know much. Hired goons. They worked in teams of two, had no idea who was giving orders or where they were. They got paid cash weekly in a drop box with new phones. These teams functioned like independent terror cells—no two cells knew what the other was doing. And only one man knew the number of teams. This duo had been hired to drop the necklace at what remained of the chapel and take off.

I left them tied to each other and made my way to the chapel where the necklace hung on a rusty nail sticking out of the charred coquina walls. I laid it in my palm, and three seconds later Bones called. "Any sign of Angel?"

"No. Just the two guys who left it."

"They know anything?"

"Only what they were told."

I stared at my island and sank my head in my hands. Five days had passed and we were out of trackers. While we were speaking, my regular cell phone began pulsing in my pocket. I read the caller ID but didn't recognize the number. Ordinarily, I'd send it to voicemail. This time I pressed Accept. When I did, I heard voices speaking in what sounded like a hollow room. I put my phone on speaker and immediately held it next to my burner so Bones could hear. The voices were muffled and unintelligible—as if the phone had been dialed but shoved in a pocket. Echoing in the background, I heard a harsh woman's voice I did not recognize saying something like, "Hurry up."

Then I heard what could only be Summer's voice saying, "What's your hurry? You headed to a midnight ballet?"

The woman responded with laughter and then something verbal that sounded like, "Oh yeah, I forgot you were once a dancer," to which Summer responded, "You wouldn't know a midnight ballet if it started in three days beneath the stars."

I smiled. *That's my girl!* Summer had found a way to tell me what I needed without letting her captor know she was telling me. Evidently she'd stolen a phone and dialed me. Everything I needed was in her statement.

Summer didn't have to reinvent the wheel because we'd dry-rehearsed this during our last time together in the Keys. When Summer offered to go on a date with the mysterious man on the Daemon boat in an attempt to locate Angel, we'd created a system of text phrases to pass me info without informing whoever might be looking at her phone.

Our story and code had been simple. Summer was a designer from Los Angeles. On a long-needed break. A workaholic dealing with a painful breakup. Amber, my new name in her contact file, was her assistant, holding down the fort while they readied some line of clothing for next month's release. So Summer would text me instructions about seemingly nothing but use color words to let me know she was okay. Any color was a good sign. But the moment she used either the word *black* or *white*, then things had gone badly and she needed immediate evac. Bring the cavalry. If at any time she sensed Angel's presence, or had any information about Angel, she would tell me the stars were beautiful last night. If he brought her somewhere and there were other armed men, she would tell me not to worry, that she'd be home in that many days and we'd talk about it then. So three men meant she'd be home in three days. Four men meant four days and so on. Lastly, if he brought her to a place where there were other women, and Summer believed those girls or women to be there against their own will, she would tell me their number as it related to the number of days before the clothing release.

So "Use the red silk and turquoise belt" meant all was well. "You should have seen the stars last night" meant Angel was in play. "I leave in three days and we'll have five days to get ready for the show" meant three bad guys and five girls. And any mention of black or white meant things were not good. Come running. Lastly, the nuclear option was one word: *ballet*. No particular reason other than it is so different from anything else. *Ballet* meant things are bad and he knows about me.

When we finished with our code debriefing, Ellie had shaken her head and asked, "Is all that NCIS stuff really necessary?"

I remember saying, "I hope not."

Ellie had scratched her head and asked, "So what's the worst thing she could say to you? Like the world has come to an end . . ."

I had responded quickly. "Midnight ballet."

Summer had just pressed the nuclear option while adding to it the fact that they had three captors and the girls were with her. Now if she could just leave the call connected long enough for us to track it.

I whispered the number to Bones, who no doubt spoke it to Eddie, who then began a trace. Thirty seconds passed while I listened to both calls. From Summer I heard more muffled voices, shuffling, and then what sounded like large truck engines starting. Finally, Bones whispered, "Got it!" I dared not speak into Summer's phone, but I let the call remain active.

Eddie read the location. "Murph, they're about seven hundred miles north of us. Highway 90. Just out of Sheridan, Wyoming. About to cross into Montana." He paused, reading something off the screen. "Traveling forty-eight miles per hour."

"They're still in the truck?"

"They're in a vehicle. I'm not sure what kind."

"Bones?"

"Get to the airfield. Plane'll be waiting."

I exited the island on foot, jumping over the two goons who had turned on each other. I promised them I'd call somebody in a couple of days—after the mosquitoes and ticks ate them for breakfast, lunch, and dinner. At the road, I cranked the bike and put the island in my rearview. Forty minutes later, I ran across the tarmac, climbed into a G5, and the pilot closed the door behind me.

Three and a half hours later, we landed outside of Billings, where Bones met me with a rented Suburban and Gunner. Who was almost as glad to see me as I was him. Eddie was there, too, and he fed me the latest GPS coordinates from Summer's phone. I charted an intersect course, which would take less than an hour, and Eddie connected my phone with his server so I could follow her phone in real time.

It was a long hour. Even Gunner was quiet.

We drove past Last Stand Hill, where Custer made his final miscalculation, costing his life and the lives of his men. I tried not to make the connection.

Given that we now knew there were three bad guys, their need to stop and sleep was significantly less than mine. With too many unknowns I kept driving and tried not to solve problems with too little information. To occupy myself, I studied every truck and vehicle that passed me headed northbound. Just after daylight, Summer's phone stopped on Highway 90 and sat dormant for several minutes.

Bones texted me. They're at a truck stop. Seven minutes away.

I pulled into a parking lot where close to seventy tractor trailers sat parked in uniform rows behind a well-lit gas station buzzing with people and cars. The tracker was accurate to three feet, so I followed the light on my phone, which brought me to a tour bus that looked like it was owned by rock stars. Million-dollar plus. Easy.

This made sense. If I was transporting women I'd kidnapped and I didn't want to raise suspicion, I wouldn't load them into something that looked like I was driving them across the border to dump them in Mexico. The tour bus was bronze with black trim. Shiny silver wheels. Immaculate.

Smart. Very smart.

I knew Summer would try to communicate. I just didn't know how. She couldn't know I was this close, but she had to hope I was, so I had a feeling she'd be looking over her shoulder.

I also had to assume the driver knew what I looked like. He'd be crazy not to. So I couldn't just start walking around showing my face. Especially with Gunner in tow. That meant I had to wait. I thought about casually walking by and snapping a picture of the VIN on the windshield. Bones could search databanks to determine if it was linked to a satellite, which would allow us to punch a few keys and unlock it remotely. But while it was no doubt linked to some satellite, the lock on the door indicated it had been manually locked by the driver. Obviously a safety precaution installed for this very purpose—to keep people in who would otherwise want out.

I parked, and the signal on my phone showed Summer's phone was ninety-seven feet in front of me. The bus's windows were mirrored, and while I couldn't see in, my thermal imager could detect body heat, which would tell me if anyone was in the bus.

One person materialized on the image in the back of the bus. A smaller frame. Horizontal. Head propped up. Feet crossed. She wasn't moving, which meant she was either asleep or had been prevented from moving. Chances were good this was Ellie, but in reality it could be anybody and I needed to remind my mind of this. Then, just as I was looking away, I saw two feet move from behind the steering wheel. Given that the bus was parked, I'd simply not thought to look there. But there he was. Staring right at me. Or I thought he was. The binoculars showed him asleep, which eliminated a casual walk-by. Too much risk of being spotted. His being left in the bus meant the other two were inside the truck stop.

I studied the diner through binoculars and found several groups sitting at tables, but Summer, Angel, and Casey were nowhere to be found. In the event I did spot one of them, I needed some way to get their attention without their captors knowing. And I had to do it in a way that only made sense to them.

I couldn't sit still any longer. I had to make an attempt. I also knew I couldn't walk in there looking like me. The temperature outside hovered close to twenty. Well below freezing. Which meant heavy coats and head coverings would be normal. I put on a beanie and my sunglasses, wrapped a scarf around my neck, and shrugged into a puffy down jacket. Glancing in the mirror, I doubted anyone could make me out. Including Summer.

I walked across the parking lot and into a side door. Making myself look busy at the antifreeze section, I studied my surroundings. Still no sign of them. I reminded myself, given that the girls had more than one captor, they probably would have split up when they walked in. Acting like they'd never met. So even if I spotted the girls walking with someone I didn't know, that did not mean there wasn't someone of whom I was unaware standing overwatch. Probably behind me.

Other than the bathroom and the diner, what could be taking so long? Then the sign for the showers caught my eye. Obviously I couldn't go waltzing into the showers. Not only would that get me arrested but it would alert the bad guys to my presence, and I couldn't risk that with one of the girls lying in the back of the bus.

After a minute, I noticed a man standing at the drink machines taking a little too long to make up his mind for a soda. But from where he stood, he could watch everyone coming from or going into the female showers. He was fit, adequately muscled but not a gorilla, and dressed nicely. Not a gangster. He did not have the look of a man transporting women. They seldom do. But he fit the mold. As did the bulge in his jacket when he leaned over.

If he was that focused on the showers, that could mean they were all crowded in there and guarded by the third person. Obviously, a woman. Probably the one I'd heard on the phone. I listened for voices I recognized but heard none. Just outside the showers stood a group sink. A designated place for men and women to wash their hands outside the bathroom. I moved down the aisle of motor oil and windshield wiper fluid in an effort to conceal myself from the man at the soda machine but make me visible to whomever would exit the showers. If they looked my way. Which was a big if.

Thirty seconds later, Angel walked out of the shower. Wet hair. Correction. Wet, bleached hair. She did not look happy. She was also wearing new clothes that didn't look like she had picked them out. Casey followed wearing a hat I did not recognize, and her hair, too, had been bleached. Casey walked to the shelves, waiting on someone still in the shower. A display of screwdrivers hung behind her. She reached behind her with her left hand, plucked one of the screwdrivers, and quickly slid it up her sleeve. Finally, Summer walked out. The left side of her face was swollen, her lip was busted, and one eye was turning black. She was limping and her hair, too, was bleached. Unlike Angel and Casey, Summer didn't look afraid. She was angry. Summer was followed by a tall, Amazon-like woman who herded the girls with head motions. When Summer stopped at the sink to wash her hands, the Amazon motioned her silently toward the bus.

Summer took her time, slowly washing her hands, and I saw my window. Summer was standing with her back to me, but I could see her face in the mirror. I needed to get her attention without getting everyone else's. Tricky.

I busied myself with cans of carburetor cleaner, making an attempt to read labels through reading glasses I'd stolen off the display next to me. When I clanked two cans together, the man at the soda machine immediately looked at me. So did the woman. Angel, Casey, and Summer did not.

Maybe that was too obvious.

Risking bringing too much attention to myself, I moved on to a display of more than a hundred coffee mugs printed with some of the most common first names. I began fumbling with the mugs. Doing so brought a glance from Casey, but she immediately looked the other way. Summer stood lathering while the Amazon woman grew irritated. Summer said something about the hair chemicals burning her hands, which must have meant they'd made her do the bleaching. The Amazon woman laughed and then walked a few feet away to the soda machine. They knew none of the girls would make a scene as long as the driver in the bus held Ellie.

I cradled a couple of the mugs in my arms, which made noise but not too much. Drawn by the sound, Summer looked right at me in the mirror. Not recognizing me, she looked away. I risked one final clang, drawing the attention of both the man and the woman, but they were off to one side and my scarf concealed my face.

But not from Summer.

This time she looked and her eyes grew wide and she began blinking furiously. Just then the Amazon woman returned and stood guard over her, unintentionally blocking Summer's view of me. Summer said, "I'm coming," dried her hands, and began walking out. As she passed by the tall woman, she said over her shoulder, but loud enough for me to hear, "You wouldn't know a ballet if it shot you in the face." The woman laughed but didn't know what had just transpired. That a message had been sent. They were heavily armed.

The five of them walked across the parking lot and stood outside the bus until the driver unlocked and opened the door. As they did, Summer took one glance around and paused slightly at the Suburban. Then she climbed aboard.

As Casey was boarding the bus, soda man stopped her, reached inside her left sleeve, removed the screwdriver, and tossed it on the ground. Then he motioned for her to get on the bus. She spit in his face and stepped up.

I could storm the bus right now and attempt to shoot the three captors before they shot me, but chances were good they'd shoot one of the girls before the smoke cleared. I couldn't risk that. I had to be patient. Which meant following the bus.

I also had to assume Summer would tell the other girls about me when she had a chance. It might not be immediately, but soon they'd know and all be on the lookout for me. Which was good.

# CHAPTER 36

I called Bones, filled him in, and gave him the license tag of the bus, and he began tracking it via satellite. Visually. This meant if Summer's cell phone failed or lost coverage or the battery died, we had a backup. I followed two miles back. Never in a direct line of sight. But also never outside of two minutes.

I asked Bones if he could determine whether the bus had internal cameras. Often they did. It allowed the driver to know what was going on. If the bus had been used for trafficking in the past, then chances were good it had a lot of cameras.

Evidently, it had been used a lot.

Bones hacked in and had a direct feed within minutes. Soda man reclined on a bunk behind the driver. Watching TV. He was armed but not overly concerned. He looked like he could handle pretty much anything anyone threw at him—and had. Amazon woman sat in the back of the bus with Ellie, who was cuffed and chained to a steel eyelet secured to the wall. She wasn't going anywhere without the keys to those locks.

For the next two hundred miles, Casey, Summer, and Angel lay next to one another in the middle bedroom. Which would have given Summer ample time to tell them about me. With his camera connection, Bones could also hear what was being said. Which wasn't much. Neither between the captors nor between the girls. An hour after leaving, Summer walked out of the bedroom to the rear of the bus. Amazon woman stood and met her at the door, intent on not letting her see Ellie. Unlike Summer, Ellie's face was riddled with fear.

Summer appealed, saying, "There's no reason why I can't sit with her." Summer raised her hands. "What am I going to do?"

Amazon woman shook her head, but Summer didn't back down. She stood toe to toe. Neither said anything. Finally, soda man said, "Let her."

Amazon woman returned to her post, allowing Summer to climb up next to Ellie and wrap an arm around her. When she did, Ellie buried her face in Summer's chest. Amazon woman told her to shut up, but Summer just rocked her, telling her, "Shhh. It's all right."

We drove through Crow reservation lands, around Bozeman, and into the Flathead National Forest. Late in the afternoon, the driver switched off with soda man, which meant they didn't stop all day. I stopped twice for gas, never letting my tank get lower than half full in the event I needed it, followed by long stretches at a hundred miles an hour trying to catch up. Bones kept me apprised of my progress. By midnight we'd circled our way to the sparsely populated hills southwest of Fort Smith and the Bighorn Canyon National Recreation Area. Through the windshield, my headlights shone on a prairie landscape that looked like something out of *Dances with Wolves*.

At 1:00 a.m. the bus exited the two-lane state highway and began winding several miles up a narrow road that eventually topped out on a grassy plateau and traveled the river for several miles before finally arriving at a narrow drive three quarters of a mile long that descended slightly toward the river. The road changed from asphalt to gravel at a large metal gate, which, when signaled by the driver, swung open electronically, granting access to the half-mile drive that terminated in a log cabin backing up to the canyon and the Bighorn River below. Satellite showed no other dwellings within a mile in every direction, which meant the only real access, other than helicopter or parachute, occurred via this driveway. You'd have to be part mountain goat to come up the back side. The Bighorn Canyon is Montana's version of the Grand Canyon. Not nearly as expansive but every bit as steep and treacherous. It was no-man's-land. The definitive badlands. Especially in winter.

The bus parked in front of the cabin, but only the larger driver exited, walking into a smaller cabin located south of the larger one. Inside the bus, thermal imaging showed the girls asleep, or pretending to look like it. Ellie tossed and turned the most, but a larger figure, probably Summer, never left her side, wrapping around her like a cocoon.

I parked the Suburban two miles out atop the plateau behind a cluster of short, stubby trees and huge granite boulders probably left by the last Ice Age. Then Gunner and I began trekking through the snow en route to the cabin. The wind up here was constant and biting, which meant the ground was frozen and snow hadn't accumulated save in drifts farther behind us. Loaded heavily, I moved slowly carrying my AR, my crossbow, and my Sig. If it was cold, I didn't feel it.

The plateau gave way to a slight descent and then fell off more to a smaller shelf upon which the house sat. A half mile from the house I began looking for sensors. Anything that would alert those in the cabin that somebody was approaching. At four hundred yards, I spotted my first camera through the thermal imager. The heat signature suggested it was active and connected by an electronic or Bluetooth daisy chain of other cameras strung out through the distance behind it, creating an unbroken perimeter. Smart.

The camera was pointed away from me, which probably meant another camera was currently aimed at my back. I turned slowly and quickly found the heat signature just ten feet away. Motion detectors would do them little good up here as mule deer, elk, bear, wolf, and the occasional moose would constantly set them off, so live-feed cameras were essential. Which meant someone had to monitor them visually to determine the difference between man and beast. But Bones had said none of the cabin or bus lights were on, and according to the thermal imagery of the satellite, the body of the driver in the smaller cabin was horizontal and unmoving.

Which meant no one was watching me.

Yet.

I moved quickly but knew I had to make it appear as if nature had disabled it and not man. I lifted a downed tree about the diameter of my thigh and leaned it against the camera, turning the lens down toward my feet but not killing it. Now whoever looked at the feed from that camera on a display monitor would be looking at the ground and a fallen limb, giving me plenty of room to navigate undetected between cameras.

When the cabin came into view, it did so against a midnight backdrop. While the front and sides were snow-covered, the canyon dropped off behind it on three sides. The house sat on an island of sorts jutting into the river, and the only vehicle access occurred over a spit of canyon that served as a road. From the air it looked like an island green on a golf course. Whoever had chosen this place knew what he was doing. This was no retreat. It was a compound. I knew cameras had to be monitoring the bridge, but the topography gave me no choice. Expert rock climbers would have a difficult time scaling up here in daylight, much less dark. Gunner and I climbed to the road and began walking across the bridge, convincing me that if I was in that bus, I'd be monitoring one camera. This one.

We crossed the bridge, but thermal imaging told both me and Bones that nobody was moving. Gunner and I circled the cabin and approached from the rear, allowing the cabin to block our view both of and from the bus. With the canyon falling off only a few feet behind us, we stopped a hundred yards from the house, allowing the multiple cameras pointed in our direction to see us. The cabin was probably seven or eight thousand square feet and three stories. From my vantage point, I could see two cameras covering our approach. I couldn't reach them, so I wouldn't be able to dismantle them, meaning I'd have to move quickly and hope no one was monitoring the feed.

It's one thing to get into a house populated with bad people. It's another to get out. So, planning my retreat, I stashed the crossbow in a spot I could find later. With two hours to daylight, Gunner and I crept across the backyard to the back door because I doubted a security system was installed there, and even if one was installed, I doubted it was active. Houses like this were protected when people were in them. Not when they weren't.

Checking the knob proved me right. Unlocked and no alarm set.

The house was sparsely decorated with little furniture. No wall decorations and nothing of a personal nature. It was more hotel than home. The refrigerator was cold but empty save some ketchup that expired six months ago. And while the heat had been turned on, it had been set at fifty, suggesting no one had been here in a while.

Daylight would offer my best chance at making an offensive play for the girls, which brought my attention to the sleeping driver in the smaller cabin some seventy yards away. I needed to lessen the odds in their favor. I spoke into the mic on my comms set. "Bones?"

"Check."

"Is the driver in the cabin still horizontal?"

Bones paused. "Yes, but tossing and turning."

"Which means he's partly awake."

We crept out of the house and through the gnarled trees to the smaller cabin. The driver had not bothered with the curtains, which allowed me to see him on his bed. Still dressed and facing me. He hadn't even bothered with his shoes, and by the sound of things, he was snoring slightly. But he was also moving. Which didn't comfort me since I was hoping for the element of surprise.

I turned the knob and pushed the door slightly, revealing the fact the hinge had never been oiled. If I pushed any farther, I'd wake not only the driver but everyone in the cabin. I stopped and whispered something that sounded like "George" but mumbled it enough so as to make it unintelligible. Especially to someone who was half asleep. When he didn't move, I pushed the door again and whispered, "Hank," just loud enough to be heard behind the squeak. The man raised his head, listened, then set his head back down. He was working on falling back asleep when I did it a third time. At that, he rose to his feet, rubbed his eyes, and was about to step into the cold night air.

Movies make a big deal of hitting someone in the face, as if that guarantees a knockout. Truth is, hitting someone in the face is stupid. None of us are Mike Tyson, and hands break easier than facial bones, which is why a brachial stun or reverse choke works pretty well on most everyone. Especially the unsuspecting.

I stunned the driver with a fast and violent blow to the side of the neck and then wrapped him in what looked like a headlock but was actually a well-placed choke. Kneeling behind him, I squeezed my forearm and bicep against both of his carotid arteries and then pushed his head forward into the *V* of my elbow with my other hand. Seven seconds later, the big man went to sleep. I dragged him into his bed, bound his hands and feet, gagged him, and covered him with sheets and blankets. Then I pulled the curtain, allowing just enough room for someone to see him "sleeping." I also removed his phone, used his thumb to open it, and then reset the passcode to one of my choosing.

I didn't know how much time that would buy me, but every second counted, so I returned to the house where Gunner and I watched the bus as the sun came up.

Just after daylight, the bus door cracked open and Amazon woman walked to the smaller cabin, where she peeked through the window and the cracked curtain. Seeing the driver "asleep," she turned toward the bigger cabin. Thinking she was headed for either the bathroom or kitchen, I stood in the shadows, able to meet her going either direction. Gunner alongside me. I couldn't risk the sound of a gunshot, so I grabbed a solid wood cutting board. Not ideal but it would work.

She stepped onto the porch, pushed open the door, and didn't immediately turn on the light. She turned right, away from me and toward the only locked door in the house. She unlocked it with a key hanging around her neck and pulled open the door, which showered us in blue light emitting from multiple screens. She had been sent to monitor the feed. She sat in a chair and began clicking files, bringing up the last several hours of recording. Quickly, she used software to scan sixteen camera feeds, many of which I never saw. The software stopped anytime movement was detected and gave her the chance to continue or zoom in. Showing experience and dexterity, she continued rapidly through several animals until she got to me.

At least nine cameras had recorded my and Gunner's advance on the cabin. Not to mention infrared. When my face first hit the screen, she reached for her phone but never finished dialing because I brought the cutting board down across her head, resulting in what I could only imagine was a rather nasty concussion. Hard to tell, but as I was swinging all I could see in my mind's eye was Summer sitting with Ellie. The effect of that image on me was not good on the Amazon. I dragged her bound to one of the bedrooms and shoved her in a closet.

I knew when she didn't return in a reasonable time that soda man would exit the bus. And as much as I wanted to simply shoot him in the face and be done with it, we needed him to be able to talk. We needed to know who was paying them.

A few minutes later, soda man did as expected and entered the house, where he immediately turned on the lights and called out, "Jody?"

When Jody didn't answer, he unholstered and then suppressed a CZ 75 and began walking toward the media room. I own several CZs, and one thing I know for certain is that I don't want to get shot by any of them. A 9mm exiting any barrel is still a 9mm. Suppressed or not.

He cracked open the door. When he saw Jody wasn't where she should be, he turned and was met by me and the cutting board. I broke his nose and he dropped the CZ, but the rest of his reactions were catlike. He rolled and, within a millisecond, had me rolling on the ground with him. Somewhere in there I saw a flash, and when I reached for it, my hand told me it was a knife.

I hate knives.

He'd obviously been a butcher in a former life because he handled it with dexterity. Sixty seconds later, I was bleeding out of five holes and he had managed to get me in a choke hold. My walls were closing in so I brought in the reserves.

"Choctaw!"

Gunner leapt at him, latched hold of the muscle just below his groin, and began tearing at the man, who started squealing and immediately let go of me. Tiring of this circus act, I drew the Sig and blew out his right knee. But driven by either rage or reaction, he continued slicing at me unfazed, so I blew out the other as well. That second bullet distracted him long enough for me to get untangled and pull Gunner off him before he went to work on my dog with his knife. Thus far, I'd worked to keep him alive—but if he hurt my dog, that would change quickly.

I dodged the knife one last time, sidestepped, and kicked him in the head, finally putting him to sleep. While he was unconscious, I cut two curtain cords and made two tourniquets, because as much as I didn't like him, I didn't want him to bleed out before we had a chance to talk to him. What he did after that would be up to him.

"Bones?"

"Check."

"See any movement around me?"

"Nothing."

"You need to hurry. I've got these three mopped up, but I got a funny feeling." I studied my surroundings, especially the media room. Something just was not right. "This was too easy. Someone else had to be monitoring these cameras remotely. There are enough electronics in that room to supply NASA. We need to get everyone out of here before somebody sends reinforcements."

"Twenty minutes out."

I had a feeling he was close. He was never one to let me have all the fun.

I crossed the driveway and pulled open the bus door. When I did, Summer—followed by Casey and Angel—jumped on me like spider monkeys and commenced beating the life out of me. They got in six or eight lip-busting blows and somebody kicked me in the groin before I said, "Hey! It's me. It's me!"

In their minds, they were all fighting for their lives, so my words didn't immediately register. What did get their attention was a really friendly dog trying to lick their faces off.

Summer finally came to, stopped trying to gouge out my eyes, and grabbed my face in her hands. "Murph!?"

Evidently, soda pop boy had gotten the better of me and I wasn't looking too fresh, because she said, "What happened to your face?"

At this point, I was lying on my back while the three of them sat on me. I pointed inside the house. All three were staring at me in shock. Summer asked, "Are we okay?"

I tried to sit up. "I was about to ask you that."

From there all three of them started talking a thousand miles an hour, and I couldn't make out or get in a word. Finally, I held up my hands. "Where's Ellie?"

I had held it together pretty well until then, but when I walked into the room and Ellie started sobbing uncontrollably, I lost it a little. With Ellie literally chained to the wall, I returned to soda pop boy, who smiled and started laughing when I began searching for the keys. So I lifted the cutting board and relieved him of all the teeth in the front of his mouth.

When I unlocked her cuffs and ankle fetters, Ellie threw her arms around me and wouldn't let me go, so I carried her out of the bus and we collapsed in the snow, where she pressed her face to my chest and screamed. All I could feel was her heart beating 180 beats a minute, so I carried her into the house and set her on the couch in the living room where Angel was busy making a fire.

When finished, she latched her arms around my neck and kissed my cheek, saying, "Padre, if you weren't married to my mom, I'd make out with you right now." She then put her hand on her hip. "And I don't know much about much, but if there's tequila in this house, I'm about to add it to my hot chocolate."

Returning to the smaller cabin, I found the driver awake and staring at me but unmoving and unable to do so. I poked my head in the door. "You good?" He nodded and tried to mutter something, but the gag prevented any real noise from leaving his mouth. He wasn't going anywhere.

When I returned outside, Casey met me. Waiting on me. Behind her, standing on the porch, Summer stood with her arms crossed, watching from the house with concern on her face.

Casey was shaking. Hands, face, lips. The dam she'd held back was starting to crack right in front of me. I tried to make eye contact but she was not behind her eyes. At some point since being taken, whether voluntarily or involuntarily, she'd checked out. The pain had been too much. She couldn't go back there.

Her voice broke when she spoke. "You said you'd come for me."

"I did."

"But you really did it."

"Casey, I'm sorry. We should have done a better job of—"

"But you . . . you really came for us."

"Told you I would."

She shook her head. "Those were just words. This . . ." She touched the blood trailing down my arm. The puncture in my bicep. Another in my shoulder. The gashes on my neck and face. "These are not words." The look on her face expressed total disbelief. "Why would you do this? Don't you know?"

"Know what?"

"Who I am."

I held both of her hands in mine and then lifted them to my face. With her palms on my cheeks, I reached out and placed mine on hers. We stood there nearly a minute while I said, "Casey . . ." Still no eye contact. "Casey . . ."

After nearly two minutes, she blinked, her pupils darted to the side, and then the light returned. She blinked again, focused, and I was looking at Casey. When she came back and stood behind her eyes, she saw me. And her. And all of us. And she smiled and fell into my arms.

Which I thought was a good sign.

While I held her, she just kept saying over and over, "You came for us. You came for us . . ."

A few minutes later, Bones drove the Suburban into the drive and found us sitting in front of a roaring fire. The girls were alternating between crying on the couch, making hot chocolate, snuggling with Gunner, and staring at the closed door of the room currently echoing with obscenities. While Bones debriefed with Angel and Casey, and then sat with his arm around Ellie, Summer tended to my wounds—which were many. I was more swiss cheese than man. Soda-pop boy had skill, and my adrenaline had been pumping so fast I didn't take notice of it. That's the problem with a knife. You never know until it's too late.

She turned to Bones. "He'd better get some stitches on a few of these."

"I'm fine. Really."

Summer stuck a stiletto finger in my face and shook her head. "Not another word out of you."

I loved the way she fought for me.

Bones nodded and began making arrangements to get me checked into the nearest ER, which was an hour away. When he suggested that everyone climb into the bus, they revolted, saying they were never climbing in that thing again.

I didn't blame them.

Bones put in a call, and both federal and local authorities would be here within the hour, but we didn't plan to wait around. We also knew that while the girls didn't want anything to do with that bus, we needed to disassemble it because it might help us determine where it came from or who had programmed it.

We decided Bones would drive the girls in the Suburban. Summer and I would follow in the bus. I'd never driven one, but how difficult could it be? Having finished her hot chocolate, Angel stood, walked to the closed door, and pushed it open. Below her, spread across the floor, lay two of her captors. Seeing her, she was met by the rather arrogant voice of soda man saying, "What do you think you're doing, bi—"

He got the *b* and *i* out his mouth about the time I heard bone snapping and soda man screaming, followed quickly by another snapping sound and Amazon screaming at the top of her lungs. I jumped to the door to find Angel hovering over both like Cassius Clay standing over Sonny Liston.

"Angel?"

She turned and glanced at me, but her eyes were lit up like rubies so I left her alone. Kneeling, she whispered something to the both of them, then exited the room and climbed into the Suburban, followed by Ellie and Casey.

Bones watched all of this with mild amusement.

With the sun just breaking the skyline, Bones drove the girls out the drive. We were headed down into Fort Smith to find someone to sew me back together. I cranked the bus engine, put her in drive, and began circling the drive when I remembered my crossbow. I shifted to park, told Gunner to stay, and jogged around the house and out across the backyard. Weaving through the trees, I returned to my hiding spot, but there was a problem.

My crossbow was gone.

I studied the ground around me, making sure I was in the right place. Judging from the footprints left in the dusting of snow, I was. Having stashed the weapon in the dark and now searching for it in the light, I knew shapes and angles could play tricks on me, so I retraced my steps and tried to reenact what I'd done when I left it. All my double-checking brought me to the same spot. There was no mistake. I was certain.

I studied the ground below me. That was about the time I noticed the footprint that was not mine.

# CHAPTER 37

A crossbow makes a distinct *click* followed by a *phhhtt* as the trigger is depressed, releasing the string and sending the arrow toward its target. Incidentally, the speed of sound is 1,125 feet per second, while the speed of the bolt leaving my Mission crossbow is 410 feet per second. That means the sound of the *click* and *phhhtt* touched my eardrum and sent a signal to my brain only a millisecond before the bolt entered my back and exited my stomach. My eyes picked up the flight of the bolt after it passed through me and sailed out across the canyon, allowing me to register the color of the bolt, which was now red.

*That's not good.*

I knew that to stand here was not smart. Even a novice shooter can cock and reload in just a few seconds. I attempted to take a step but quickly learned that while the bolt had not passed through my spine or spinal column, it had gone through me a few inches to the left, which meant it cut the muscles in my back and stomach required to lift my legs. With the first attempt unsuccessful, I tried again to move but fared no better. In fact, I made things worse. The second frantic attempt threw my body weight forward while unsupported by my legs, which meant I began falling.

Which was bad given that I stood only feet from the edge of the canyon wall.

My forward fall landed me on the edge while my body weight pushed me over the icy precipice. Unable to find purchase, I began tumbling. The thought cycling through my mind struck me as strange: *I can't believe someone just shot me with my own crossbow.*

The canyon wall was not a straight drop. Vertical, yes, but more seventy-five degrees than ninety. The snow-covered descent hindered my plummet and began spinning me like a snowball. By the time I reached the bottom, I was flying. While most of the canyon wall flared outward toward the water, the final thirty-plus feet did not. The wall launched me out into the air where I began freefalling.

A half second later I met the water, and what air had not been knocked out of me by the sheer rock face of the canyon was sucked out of me by the surface of the water. Not to mention the cold.

Because the river flowed, it had not frozen, but the temperature was still freezing. My body registered the cold, shock set in, and I knew I had very few seconds to make it to the edge. Pulling with my right arm, I dog-paddled to a rock wall. For several seconds I fought to keep my head above water and stop my flow downriver but was hindered from doing so. To complicate matters, I had landed in a collection of driftwood, which simply spun on top of the water every time I tried to grab it. Losing air and strength, I looped one arm around a cut timber bigger than me. And for whatever reason, it didn't spin. I threw my right leg over, pulled myself up, and lay across the log. A perfect target for someone from above. As the water pulled me downriver and around the first bend, I looked up and saw how the last forty or so feet of the rock wall fell straight down and then curved inward, where the river had cut farther into the rock face over thousands of years of flow. This feature alone might have saved my life, because whoever had shot me with my own crossbow was probably standing up there searching the water below, yet was prevented from seeing me by the physical nature of the rock.

I don't know how long I floated, but the cold overtook me. The only warmth I felt was below me where the blood seeped out of the hole in my stomach. Somewhere in there I passed out.

When I woke, I found myself wedged against another canyon wall that looked like all the rest in a collection of similarly sized timbers. I tried to move, but I'd nearly frozen and a stiffness akin to rigor mortis had set in. I knew if I didn't get off that log I'd be dead in minutes, so I scratched and clawed my way off and into the shallow water. Mustering my strength, I crawled up the bank and dragged my waterlogged body along the frozen ground. I tried to stand. Couldn't. Tried again. Made it to my knees, but this only pushed more warm fluid out of my torso. I pressed my left hand against the hole and began clawing and climbing my way up the small embankment. I didn't know how far I'd floated or who was above me and whether they were coming down to find me, but I wasn't going to hang around to find out. The only good thing I could report was daylight—I wasn't attempting this in the dark.

Now generating body heat, I managed to get my muscles moving and climbed fifty or sixty feet up the canyon, which, fortunately for me, was now more forty-five degrees than ninety. Knowing I couldn't press it much farther, I began looking for a hole. Someplace to get out of the wind and make a fire. If I didn't get warm quickly, I'd die before the hole in my stomach killed me.

A few more feet and I climbed into a shadow. Which struck me as strange because the sun was climbing and the sky above was cloudless. Looking up, I discovered I'd climbed into the mouth of a cave. A cylinder carved by the water when the river level flowed here. The cavity was large enough to stand in and maybe fifteen feet deep.

I collapsed at the mouth, caught my breath, and dragged my body under and into the opening. I lay there trying to catch my breath, knowing I needed to do something to stop the flow of blood but also knowing I needed fire first.

That's when I noticed I was not the first person to visit this cave. Not by a long shot.

To my left sat a pile of driftwood. Dry driftwood. Collected in days past by some angel of mercy. Judging by the sight of the serpentine footpath that climbed up from the river's edge, this must have been a popular spot in summer. Folks would travel several miles upriver from Okabeh Marina, tie up to a stake or boulder, and then backpack provisions up the last fifty feet for the weekend.

I carved some wood shavings, collected them into a pile, and had to be careful not to cut off my own hand given that I was shivering so badly. Having created a pile, I then snapped and stacked the smallest driftwood and dug my Zippo out of my pocket. The wood was too cold and I didn't have enough tinder to think I could just light some of the shavings and start a fire. I knew better. I needed fuel. I could disassemble several of the .45 ACP cartridges from my Sig, pouring the gunpowder on the shavings, but I had one other option I thought I'd try before I rid myself of the only way to defend myself.

I disassembled my Zippo and pulled out the cotton stuffing inside that held the lighter fluid. I spread it apart, allowing air to the fibers, then sparked my Zippo above it. On the third strike, it lit. I fed the shavings gently alongside and after several long seconds, a few lit. Before long, I was feeding twigs into the flames and, within a few more minutes, driftwood. Ten minutes later, I was peeling off clothes both to get to the warmth and to the wound.

While the fire lit and warmed the cave, I stripped to my underwear and wished I had not told Gunner to stay when I went looking for my crossbow. Having peeled away the clothing, I became more aware of my condition.

And my condition was bad.

The bolt from the crossbow had entered my back left of my spine and just below my rib cage, although it may have nicked a rib. It then exited a little more toward the center of me, suggesting that the shooter had not been standing at six o'clock behind me but more like four. I didn't know if the broadhead had nicked any of my organs, nor do I really know where my organs sit inside me. But judging from the green, yellow, and brown mixed in with my leaking blood, the bolt had nicked my stomach.

I knew what I needed to do. I just didn't want to do it.

I imagined Bones was looking for me by now, but if he was tangled up with the same person who shot me, it could be a while. If at all. I also didn't know how far I'd drifted from where I'd fallen in. I could be a quarter mile. I could be two. It was anybody's guess.

All of this told me I had no guarantee of rescue and certainly not anytime soon. And given my predicament, I couldn't rescue myself. Any movement would only make matters worse and accelerate my departure from planet earth.

While I'd been shot in the back before, I had little experience being shot through the stomach. If I wasn't dead already, then chances were good the arrow had not nicked vital organs. That left two options. I could die from bleeding out, called exsanguination, or I could die from infection caused by internal bleeding. Commonly known as sepsis. Theoretically, the latter would take longer, although neither would be fun. Realistically, bleeding out would be easier. Blood would leak out, my pressure would drop, and I'd just go to sleep before infection set in. But if I wished to hang around a while longer, which I did, I had to seal up the entry and exit holes. Which gave me more time. How much time? Maybe two days. Three max.

But a few days was a few days.

I placed my knife in the coals developing at the base of the fire and then fed in more wood. I knew as soon as I closed both wounds I would need to limit movement, so I forced myself to scour the bank and glean any driftwood I could. Fire was keeping me alive, and I didn't know how long I could feed it with my present supply.

I also knew I didn't need to put anything new in my stomach.

The blade turned red, and I grabbed the handle with my wet shirt. Then I held my arm behind me, judged the location of the hole, and pressed the red blade to my skin. When I woke up, the sun had climbed higher. My left hand told me I'd closed the wound, which was good news. I didn't think I had the stuff needed to do that again.

My stomach was still oozing, so I placed the blade back in the heat and repeated the process—although this time I managed not to pass out but rather lapse out of and into consciousness the rest of the afternoon.

With darkness falling, the fire died and cold woke me. I quickly fed wood into the coals and tried to blow the flames into life, but blowing was excruciating. So I just waited for them to light. When they did, I fed the fire again and waited for the heat to push back the cold.

With the leaks in my hull plugged, the clock was now ticking. All I had to do was lie on my back and wait—in a cave, in a canyon fifty feet above the water line, miles from my fall, where nobody would think to look. The only hope I had was the smoke trailing out the mouth of the cave, but given the dryness of the driftwood, the smoke was negligible. Of course, while the smoke would attract my rescue, it could also signal my enemy, who might this minute be staring down on me.

I unholstered the Sig, press-checked the chamber, and counted one spare magazine with eight rounds. Including the round in the chamber, I had a total of seventeen rounds. Enough to defend myself for a few seconds or make a lot of noise if needed.

I slept fitfully throughout the night and fought off thirst like I'd seldom known. I wanted badly to take a drink of water, but that presented two problems: I doubted I could make it to the water, and I was certain I couldn't make it back. Second, I could not risk putting anything in my stomach.

I was stuck being thirsty.

On the second day, the pain in my torso had worsened. As had the swelling. I looked like I'd spent the last year drinking beer and not running to the Eagle's Nest. I was also starting to lose my clarity. I fought hard to clear my mind, but fatigue pressed in on me and I passed in and out of consciousness.

The next time I woke it was dark, suggesting I'd slept through day two and into night two. The fire had again died, and while I was running low on wood, I needed the warmth while I could create it. So I fed the coals and waited. The pain and swelling told me infection had officially set in and I'd need more than antibiotics to clear this. I was probably nearing the point of no return. I tried not to move, but no matter how I lay I could not get comfortable. Sitting up was almost impossible.

The morning of day three brought a coyote sniffing the mouth of the cave. In truth, he smelled me. I raised the Sig and leveled the sights on him, but I had no desire to kill a curious coyote just doing what coyotes did, unless of course he started gnawing on my foot. I whistled. He saw me, froze, and then bolted, never to be seen again.

Somewhere in there I quit sweating and grew so dizzy I couldn't sit up. While that was bad, the good news was that I was no longer thirsty. Toward late afternoon, my mind started playing tricks on me. I suppose some might call it delirium. I'm not sure.

Fading in and out, the slideshow of my life began playing across the backs of my eyelids like Bones's show in the Planetarium. I saw pictures of me as a kid, fishing with Marie on our island, jumping on that boat and finding the girls trapped below, meeting Bones, running track, finding Marie seven miles past the jetties in the ocean and bringing her to safety, my time at the academy, training with Bones, my first wedding, chasing Marie, the years that passed and finding her, twice, then staying drunk a year in the Keys, and Bones lifting me out of the water and putting a pad in front of me, and then that lady editor asking me, "What're you writing?" I remembered each book and where I was when I finished them. The characters, their names, and why they did what they did. I remembered visiting bookstores after a book release wearing a hat and sunglasses and watching people stand in line waiting on my books, only to then sit on park benches and read and laugh and cry as they furiously flipped pages. I remembered the girls whose names populated my back. I remembered Angel. Gunner. Clay. Casey. Ellie. And Summer.

When I got to Summer, the tears broke. Twice now I had been married, and neither time had I spent any of my life with my wife. I wanted to sleep breathing the air she'd breathed, bring her coffee before she woke, and watch her laugh at me and tell me that the color of my T-shirt didn't fit in my color wheel. I wanted all that and more.

Looking back across my memories, one constant remained. Bones. He'd lifted me when I was down and celebrated with me when I was up. Which brought me back to the sting of Marie and why he'd never told me. I wished we'd talked it through.

Then I remembered it. Bones's letter.

I'd zipped it in my jacket pocket. The jacket I'd been wearing when I took my Peter Pan off the canyon rim. The same jacket spread beneath me.

I unzipped the pocket and slid the letter from its home. I opened the envelope and unfolded the letter, and, while wet, it was legible. It took a minute or more for my eyes to focus.

Murph.

I know you have questions. Were I you, I would too. I owe you much in this life and an explanation may be first on the list. I am giving you the enclosed to allow you what you need to either hate me or understand me. If understanding is possible. I've been wrestling with my silence a long time, and even I realize there might be no justification. If I've asked myself once, I've asked ten thousand times, how far does the protection of the confessional go? Not telling you about Marie may well be the most evil thing I've ever done. Then again, maybe not.

You told me not long ago that I might wake one day to find your hands wrapped around my throat. I wouldn't blame you. Might even thank you for putting me out of my misery. I hope it's some consolation to you that I've suffered hell since the day she came back into my life. If you want to part ways and want nothing more to do with me after you've read this, I totally understand. Before you go, please know I've admired many men in my life. None more than you.

—Bones

I opened the second letter, and while my vision was blurry, Marie's handwriting caught me off guard. I tried to sit up but could not.

Dearest Bishop,

If you're reading this then you know Bones knew about me during the years of my stay at Sisters of Mercy. As a result, there's probably some friction, bad blood even. You can't understand how he never told you I was alive.

There's a simple reason . . .

I asked him not to.

When I arrived at Sisters of Mercy, I began walking the

beaches. Waiting to die. If I didn't, I'd lose my ever-loving mind first. I hated me and all I wanted to do was hold you. But after having behaved so badly on two occasions and been given a death sentence with a virus attacking my heart, I knew I couldn't. Or at least I felt I couldn't. I was sure you'd take me back. But that wasn't fair to you. I'd already betrayed you. Beyond forgiveness. Appearing once again seemed only further betrayal.

But then I spotted you. I was walking the beach. You were sitting on a rock. Writing. You did this every day. Purging your soul. Writing the love you wished you'd lived. Then you'd tend bar, sleep, and start over the next day. I used to stare through your window at night and watch you sleep. One night I even crept in your room and sat next to your bed. Breathing air you'd breathed. And when the nightmare came and you screamed my name, I kissed your lips. And you held my hand.

You held my hand.

I expected to die any week. Any minute. So watching you those first few days was such a sweet gift. I bought binoculars, and that's when I saw it. Your back.

That's when I knew.

That's when I knew I could not waltz back into your life because the moment I did, two things would quit happening. You'd quit writing because you'd start to live out your love rather than write it, and you'd quit leaving the ninety-nine to find the one, because you'd found her.

I knew if you took me back, that while I would gain and live the love I'd always wished, the world would lose. So, in the most difficult thing I've ever done, I gave you back to the ninety-nine.

The offering for my sin.

Why?

Because their needs outweigh mine.

You taught me that.

I'm gone now. But you're not. You're still here. And I'd like to think that I have some small part in every one you find.

After I discovered you on the beach, I tracked down Bones and asked him to hear my confession. He was so excited to see me, he lit up. He couldn't wait to call you. So I knelt in the confessional and dumped a lifetime of stuff on him of which I'm not proud. And just before I stood up, I confessed a sin I was about to commit. I was about to ask him not to tell you about me. That he could never tell you I was alive. I told him if he really was a priest, then he'd honor my request. For the rest of his life. He shook his head, cried, and begged me not to ask that. And despite the torment I knew it caused him, I did. I demanded his silence because I needed to give you back to the world.

David, you have a gift. You are relentless and can find anybody. Anywhere. And you never count the cost. Especially the cost to yourself. You're the most selfless person I've ever known. It's the reason you found me that night seven miles out in the ocean. You're the one.

I've known it all our lives: you have a gift and the world needs it. And as difficult as it is to say, they need you more than I do.

I wish that wasn't true.

As I watched you pour your heart out on the page, I could not envision a life where I kept you to myself and ignored those whose lives depended on your finding them. I just couldn't live that way. Knowing I'd kept you from one single person was one too many. The thought that they'd died a slow death, alone, was more than I could bear.

So blame me.

But before the taste turns bitter, I want you to realize something. Something you may not have considered. Every name inked across your back was etched by me. I simply used the tattooist's hand. And every name is just one more way for me to tell you I love you. And one more reason I was right. The names etched into your skin are the record of you and me.

263

*Staring through my binoculars, watching you scribble those magnificent stories in your notebook, I began to ask myself, what is one name worth? Eventually the question became, is it worth you and me?*

*As painful as it is, there is only one answer.*

*Yes.*

*How do I know? Simple. I asked myself if you would sacrifice any one of those girls for us.*

*The answer didn't take long.*

*Not in ten lifetimes.*

*Life is a crazy thing, and I didn't see it turning out this way. You should know that Bones took good care of me. He treated me like a daughter, came to see me, and begged me every time not to keep my silence and not to ask it of him. Next to you, Bones is the finest man I've ever met. I'll miss him. And remember, while you're angry, he's hurting too. Don't be too hard on him. He's just a man. Who kept his word. And did what I asked of him.*

*I gave you back to the ninety-nine for a reason. And no matter what pain or mess you might find yourself in, or what doubt has crept in, what tiredness of soul has wrecked you, there is still one who needs you. She's out there. Right now.*

*Find her.*

> *I love you.*
> *I'm with you always,*
> *Marie*

I tried to start over but couldn't. I couldn't read through tears.

Throughout the afternoon, I read and reread the letter. Maybe a dozen times. I understood her reasons. But hearing them didn't make it easier.

I couldn't argue with what she said. She loved me and that love drove her decisions. And even if I wanted to, she was gone. Who would hear my complaining? I couldn't be mad at Bones. He did what she'd asked him even when I knew it caused him great pain. He was just as stuck in the middle as me.

None of this made me feel any better. The truth of me was this: I was dying alone in a cave racked with pain in both my body and my heart and, despite my skill, my experience, and my desire, there was nothing I could do about it.

Marie was right about Bones. She'd put him in an impossible situation. One for which he'd not asked. My anger at him was just misdirected blame. In her absence, I had wanted to blame someone. To vent my anger. Yet he was only guilty of keeping his word. Of honoring her wish, even if he disagreed. If anything, he was a pawn. Like me.

My resting heart rate had jumped to nearly twice normal, followed by a fever. I'd quit sweating yesterday. I'm no doctor, but I knew my chances of getting out of this cave were slim. Sepsis had set in, and the infection in my blood was multiplying exponentially, minute by minute. Knowing he needed to hear it and I might not get the chance to tell him, I pulled a piece of charcoal from the fire and wrote on the back of the letter, "Bones, there's nothing to forgive."

I fed the fire the last of the driftwood and faded in and out of a restless sleep while holding the Sig close to my chest. If whoever shot me found me, I wanted to look like I'd put up a fight, but truth be told, I'd grown too weak to lift my hand. Much less aim and shoot.

I had been chewing on two questions I could not answer. The first was simple: *Who did this?* Honestly, I had no idea. The second was equally as simple: *Why?*

In my work around the world, I'd encountered some sick people, but whoever had done this was different. He might even top the list. I was also pretty sure that taking the girls was a setup. They were bait, and he was fishing for me.

A man who will stage an explosion at a fully functional hospital, during a wedding, and then bring the building down on top of the rescuers, values only one life. His own. This man was on the level with the tailor who makes the suicide vest, recruits the bomber, and sends him into a school. You can't reason with such a man. Evil is not reasonable. If it were, it would, by definition, not be evil. Any conversation is a head fake while he cuts off your legs at the knees. A man like this is driven by one thing—domination. His power at your expense. He wants your head on a platter. There is no land for peace. No quarter. No cute "Coexist" bumper sticker.

I was unable to answer either question, and a third surfaced: *When do you leave the sheep to hunt the wolf?*

For that I had no answer.

Somewhere after midnight, when the fire died and the twenty-degree outside air crept in, my fever spiked high enough to keep me warm while the pain kept my mind occupied. As I slipped further out of consciousness, the sun rose and another day passed, followed by a colder afternoon and falling snow. Night brought high winds that blew heavier falling snow inside the cave, dusting me in white. Soon I was shivering so hard I thought my teeth would crack. Fortunately, the shakes didn't last long. I had grown too weak and too ravaged by infection.

Delirium became my friend.

Years ago, I tracked a kid to Stuttgart. Found him in a warehouse awaiting transfer. It was early. Before dawn. His exploiters were still jacked up from the night before. Extraction was cut-and-dry. I walked in, lifted his emaciated body off the floor, and asked him, "What's your name?"

"E-E-Eddie."

"How old are you?" I knew these answers but I was trying to get his mind off the hell he'd endured.

"Tw-tw-twelve."

"How long have you had a stutter?"

"S-s-s-since I was a k-k-k . . ." He swallowed, closed his eyes, and started over. "Kid."

From his file, I knew his birth father had abused him and left him, leaving a hole. Into that void, the stutter stepped. The mom remarried, a good man who adopted the boy, but the stutter remained. No amount of love could root it out. Six months ago, playing video games at a movie arcade, he was lifted, sold, and shipped overseas—all in less than a day. When the exploiters discovered they'd lifted the son of the CEO of a solar company worth a couple hundred million, the first ransom note came in. Five million dollars. Which the parents quickly paid. That was followed by a second note asking for more, which they also paid. "Transaction complete." But still no boy.

When the third demand came in, Bones got a call, and I got on a plane. "Don't pay it."

As I walked out of the warehouse, he put his head on my shoulder and I listened to his labored breathing. But he wasn't crying. His shock wouldn't allow it. Not a single tear. We flew overnight, landed in DC, and I returned him to his mom and stepdad, who were inconsolable. It was weeks before he started to cry. Once he did, they couldn't get him to stop. He didn't eat, didn't sleep, didn't speak, didn't hug them back. He had been muted, save the tears.

So I went to see him.

He sat up when he saw me. Tears streaming down. I sat down, took off my coat, and unbuttoned my shirt, which made him flinch. Then I turned slightly. I said, "Can you read?"

He nodded.

"Can you read the last one?"

He studied the names on my back, finally reading the last installment. "E-E-Eddie F-Fisher."

He read it without any inflection. "Can you read it again?"

"E-Eddie Fisher." The second time he read it, his eyes opened slightly, and he whispered, "Eddie Fisher." It was his name.

I faced him, buttoning my shirt. "Wherever I go, I carry you with me." At the sound of this, he almost smiled. "F-f-forever?" The side of his mouth turned up.

"Can you count to a hundred?"

"Y-yes."

"Two hundred?"

He nodded.

"If you were to count all the names before yours, you'd find 173. That means there are 173 kids like you. Many of whom now live at a place called Freetown."

"Wh-where's th-that?"

"The mountains of Colorado. Would you like to go there?"

He looked at his parents, who nodded, smiling. He said, "Are you there?"

I weighed my head side to side. "Sometimes."

"Wh-wh-where do you g-go?"

"To find kids like you."

"Do you c-c-come back?"

I laughed out loud. "Yes."

"Always?"

"Until now, yes."

"Can-can I h-h-help you?"

"What do you mean?"

"F-f-find k-k-kids like m-m-me."

It was the first time the rescued had ever asked to rescue. I glanced at his folks, who quickly said, "Anything you need."

Which explains why much of Freetown runs on solar power and why Eddie, now nineteen and soon to enter college at MIT, works in our communications department. This was the very same Eddie who turned on the girls' trackers when I asked and was probably at this very moment scouring satellite images looking for any evidence of me—or my satellite phone. Which he'd programmed.

After a few years with us, Eddie's stutter lessened. Then, just shy of his seventeenth birthday, it disappeared altogether. I can't explain that. I just know it's gone.

I thought of Eddie as I lay there shivering uncontrollably, unable to speak. For the first time since we'd met, I had some sense of how helpless he must have felt.

The thought of Eddie yielded to others, and soon I had trouble connecting real with unreal. I can't tell you that I knew one from the other, but somewhere in there a man dressed in dark clothing walked in, followed by a second man who was carrying my crossbow. The first man reminded me of the guy I saw in Montana strolling nonchalantly through the flames toward his plane. He knelt, took my Sig, and poked at my stomach with the barrel, studying me much like a man watching water boil. Then the two of them rolled me on my side and casually discussed the names on my back. Their tone of voice reminded me of a man ordering breakfast at a diner.

Having finished their conversation, the first man pressed the muzzle to my forehead and stared at me. I was too tired to fight him so I just lay there, staring back. I saw nothing in his expression save amber pupils. I'd never seen their equal. His face was void of emotion, but for the second time I had the feeling we'd met before.

Oddly, the second man poked at my swollen stomach and told the first, "Do him a favor and pull that trigger." My eyes wouldn't focus, but I could see well enough to know his features had been altered by plastic surgery. And while his face was unfamiliar, his tone of voice held an odd echo of familiarity I couldn't place. He continued, "He's done. Only the waiting remains." To which the first man smiled. He hefted the Sig, dropped the magazine, left one round in the chamber, and placed the Sig flat across my chest. Then they walked out.

They hadn't been gone long—in fact, they must have passed each other on the ledge outside—when Marie walked in, leading Summer by the hand. Marie looked so young and vibrant. She kissed me on the cheek, then set Summer's hand in mine, and both women sat alongside me while Marie entertained Summer with stories from our youth. Hours later, Marie asked Summer if she could have one last dance. So they stood me up, and Marie both steadied and swayed with me. I knew this was real because I remember feeling her warmth on my chest. The smell of her hair. The sound of the tune she hummed in my ear. And I remember apologizing for not being able to move my feet but the holes in me had yet to heal. Somewhere in the dark, when our dance finished and the tune stopped, she kissed me, slipped Summer's hand in mine again, and walked outside where she stood until the snow covered her like a blanket and I could see her no more.

Summer gathered wood, stacked it, and breathed life into a bonfire. She then set Gunner alongside me and wrapped me in a blanket, which was nice because it was the first time I'd been warm since I crawled into this cave. Oddly, my thirst returned, as did my ability to feel hot and cold, because I began shivering though not sweating. Having dressed my wounds, Summer stuck a needle in my arm and forced cold IV fluids into my veins by pressing on the bag while speaking to someone behind her. Having emptied the bag, she lay alongside me and placed her head on my chest, listening to my heartbeat and breathing the air I'd breathed. Minutes later, I told her we should move because the cave was dripping onto my chest—and oh, how I wished I'd known that spring was there before. I might not have been so thirsty.

Every few minutes, Gunner would stand, spin in a circle, lick my face and stomach, then lie back down, whining and resting his head on my hand. Finally, as sleep was pulling heavy on my eyelids, Bones appeared inches in front of my face, sank his arms beneath me, and lifted me off the floor of the cave, only to carry me out into the snow and down to the water's edge, where I felt snow on my face and heard something that sounded like a distant drum. And while the world had gone black and I couldn't see any light anywhere, my ears worked perfectly. I could hear everything.

I remember being lifted and floating, followed by what felt like a nap in a hammock turned roller coaster abruptly interrupted by bright lights, frantic voices, the unpleasant shock of electricity coursing through my veins, and then inexplicable calm. Like the sea after a storm.

Lastly, I heard Bones whisper over me, "This is the cup . . . Do this in remembrance of . . ."

When Bones faded out, the slideshow returned and flashed before my eyes. Starting with Summer twirling and saying, "Dance with me," and the risk she took as we walked to our wedding reception and she pulled me aside and gave me the picture frame and then filled it with herself. How her heart pounded and the sweat beaded on her brow and above her lips. The next few slides were from the reception. How we all danced for hours. The blisters on my feet. Clay in his wing tips and all the girls fighting over him. Ellie standing on my toes. Casey and Angel singing karaoke and something about having friends in low places. We laughed so hard our stomachs hurt. The last few slides belonged to Bones. I saw him everywhere. Freetown.

The sanctuary. My island. Key West. Planes headed to parts around the world. My boat. Our mountainside perch above the academy. And finally, the boat where he first plucked me from the greasy guy who'd kidnapped the four girls. *Tell me what you know about sheep.*

I'd miss him.

I had held the sleep at bay through long days and longer nights, but I could hold it back no longer. There was so much left unsaid. Undone. But I had not the strength. The weight of the earth pushed down on my eyelids, so I stepped aside, let my eyes close, and drifted into that place where only the questions follow.

# CHAPTER 38

I don't know how long I was there, but when my thoughts returned, I remember feeling warm. And I remember two familiar smells. They swirled around my mind, finally settling on a memory. The first was Gunner. Which would explain the furry rug to my left. The second was Summer. Which would explain the feeling of skin on my skin and a leg wrapped around mine like a vine.

I was in a predicament. Either I had died and gone to heaven, which would also explain the bright light boring a hole in my eyelids. Or I was dreaming. And this was the really good part right before the part where I woke up.

I didn't want the second option to end, so I lay there trying not to wake. But I had one problem.

Singing.

Which sent me back into my predicament. Either the angels had come to escort me home, or someone was piping it in. But why? Why were so many female voices singing that beautifully?

Then the hand on my chest moved. It had been lying flat across my heart, and now it was wrapped around my rib cage. To my left, I heard a door open, then footsteps and a familiar voice. It was Bones. He was whispering. "How's the patient?"

Angel's voice responded from the foot of the bed. "No change. But his vitals are all good and the doc says he can't find the infection."

This conversation suggested I was more in the second predicament than the first.

Bones again. "Any movement?"

Angel offered no verbal response, which meant she must have shaken her head.

"Mom work the night shift?"

"Won't leave his side."

This, too, suggested Summer was the body keeping me warm. And if this was a dream, I definitely did not want to wake up.

*Don't wake up. Don't wake up.*

Bones paused, then I heard pages shuffling. "Book five. You two are making real progress."

Angel's tone softened. "We just keep thinking if we read his words back to him, he'll remember us and . . . come back."

Somebody patted my toes but said nothing.

The next time my thoughts returned to me it was dark, and a cool breeze washed across my face. Like a window had been left open. The rug on my left was gone and the body to my right was moving. Wrapping tighter. Possibly leg stubble. Then I felt a kiss on my cheek. Followed by a hand stretched flat across my chest and a longer kiss on my lips, accompanied by a whisper. "Come back to me." Then breath on my face. Followed by another breath on my face. And another.

Somewhere in here I must have returned to the cave, because water dripped on my cheek.

The third and final time my thoughts returned, both the rug and the body were gone but the singing had returned along with what can only be described as flickering flames in dim light accompanied by people crying all around me.

Above their voices, I heard Bones say, "Lord . . ." His voice cracked so he started over. "Lord . . . receive this one . . ." His voice stoked the crying, making it worse and bringing the rug next to my face.

This next part is a little fuzzy, so bear with me. I'm trying to put words to something for which I have no words. While Bones spoke and people cried and flames flickered and Gunner licked my face, a muscled hand grabbed mine, lifted me up, and led me outside. Which was nice because I was feeling a little cooped up. He then took me on the chairlift up to the Eagle's Nest, although the furniture was different. He led me to the railing, where we looked down on two towns nestled in a snow-swept canvas. For a long time we stood studying each.

On the surface, they were similar. Exact copies. Save one thing. The city on the right had one thing the city on the left did not.

He waved his hand across them. "Pick one."

So I did.

And that's about when I opened my eyes.

# CHAPTER 39

The opening of my eyes brought what can only be described as total chaos for several minutes. People who up until now had been stationary and church-mouse quiet started running, opening doors, pulling carts, carrying machines, and talking way too loud. I wanted to tell them to calm down, but I had a tube down my throat so I just figured I'd keep quiet until they removed it. People dressed in white were hovering over me, poking me with needles, shining lights in my eyes, staring at screens, and talking quickly on phones and to each other.

The room filled quickly. Angel. Casey. Ellie. Everybody was out of breath and smiling and staring at me like I'd become a circus performer on the trapeze or high wire. After a few minutes, Clay appeared in a wheelchair and scooted himself through the crowd and next to the bed, where he sat nodding and saying, "Uh-huh, I told you so. I said that man ain't finished. He coming back. I said that."

Bones appeared next. Wearing robes. Looked like he was headed somewhere important. He stood at the foot of my bed, patting my toes. Nodding. He must be getting soft because tears cascaded down both sides of his face and dripped off his chin.

Then Summer appeared.

Her eyes were sunk back in her head, surrounded by dark circles, and she'd lost weight. She walked around my bed, steadying herself with the hands of others, then held my face in her hands and kissed me, pressing her forehead to mine, dripping tears. Which caused me to wonder if the cave ever rained on me at all.

Bones was the first to speak. Or at least the first to try. He opened his mouth, but no words came. So, amid chuckles and the corporate laughter of release and the exhale of breath held a long time, he tried again. This time with marginal success. "Hey."

I tried to smile but the tube made that difficult.

More laughter.

"You . . . good?"

I raised my hand. Forcing my fingers to move. They felt stiff and unresponsive. Finally, I managed, "1–1–8 . . . 1–7."

Bones blinked, pushing out the largest of the tears, and nodded. Then he spoke to the room. "He's good."

Once the fog cleared, they told me their side of the story.

After Bones and the girls drove the Suburban out of the driveway at the cabin, they waited on me and Summer to appear with the bus. When we didn't, they returned and started looking. Gunner found the blood. Summer said Bones exhausted himself searching the canyon and didn't sleep for four days, walking every inch and searching every crack and crevice. The thought that I might have drowned haunted him. Back at Freetown, Eddie relentlessly read satellite images and saw what looked like smoke spiraling up, but he couldn't narrow it to less than a mile. When he gave the coordinates to Bones, Bones sat with Gunner and said, "Murph. Find Murph." Gunner bounded down the wall of the canyon and was gone a night, a day, and a night. Returning on the afternoon of the second full day. Barking.

My cave was twice as far downriver as anyone had imagined. Some seven miles. As they approached from the rim above, they watched two men exit the cave, slide down to a waiting boat, and disappear. Bones assumed that whoever shot me had also been looking and found me just moments prior. When they did, they decided to let infection take me slowly rather than a bullet take me quickly.

What they intended for torture actually saved my life.

Gunner was the first to find me. Bones carried me down to the water and then downriver to a helicopter that lifted me to a hospital, where I spent a month in a coma while infection ravaged me from the inside out.

The bolt from the crossbow had in fact nicked my stomach lining, allowing a slow leak—a perfect shot if you wanted someone to die slowly and with much pain. Closing the entry and exit holes had bought me time but allowed the infection to fester and take root. Those are not medical terms, but they work. By the time Bones carried me out of the cave, my ship had sailed. At the hospital, I coded and the doctors pronounced me dead.

When they told Summer, she ran into the room and pounded my chest, telling me I was not allowed to leave her. "Please don't leave!" Finally, she had kissed my face and whispered, "I'll never dance again."

Then, for reasons no one can explain, my heart beat. Once. Twice. Then steadily.

My doctors cannot account for this.

For a month they fed me the strongest antibiotics known to man and tried to wake me from a coma. When the doctors ran out of options, Bones and Summer brought me home to die.

During this time, Bones brought all of Freetown into the Planetarium and came clean on our premeditated lie. Initially, everyone was angry and hurt. Felt betrayed even. Then Bones played my pre-recorded video and told them what I did following. Ever since, they'd been standing in candlelight vigil outside my window.

Often singing.

While my body ate itself and my organs threatened to shut down, Angel, Ellie, and Casey read my stories out loud, cover to cover. This week they'd started number seven. Gunner lay by my shoulders and growled at anyone who attempted to pull him from my side. Even Clay sat quietly, standing watch. Often, Ellie would curl into a ball and nap alongside me. And in the forty-five days I'd been home, Summer had not left my side.

Yesterday Bones had served me Communion and Freetown had dressed in black.

Then, for reasons no one can explain, I blinked.

Seeing I was able to breathe on my own and wishing to talk, they pulled the tube from my throat, allowing my lungs to do what they were meant to do. Breathe. Which felt really good. I spent the afternoon napping and trying to swim out of the fog in which I'd been living. When they brought my dinner, I realized there was little room on the bed for me. To my left lay Gunner and Ellie. Angel and Casey sat at my feet. Summer was on my right. And Clay and Bones sat sipping wine with their feet propped up.

Two days later, I woke to my publisher sitting next to my bed, her hand in mine. I whispered, "I thought tough New York girls like you didn't cry."

She had nodded. "This one does."

A few nights later, Gunner growled and woke both me and Summer. A figure stood at the end of my bed. I clicked on a light to find Casey. She looked tired. Like she'd not slept. Gunner walked to the end of the bed and let her rub his ears. I worked myself onto one elbow. "You okay?"

"I'm afraid."

"Of what?"

"Going outside."

Summer rubbed her eyes. "Why?"

Casey glanced out the window into the darkness. "'Cause he's still out there."

She was right, and I had no answer for that. My anger flashed. It was one thing to shoot someone. Kick them while they're down. And while painful, physical wounds will heal. What takes longer are the wounds we cannot see. The most evil trauma one man can inflict upon another is that committed against the human soul. And for those who inflict it, there is a special place in hell.

I nodded.

She rubbed her hands together and her bottom lip trembled once. Casey had something else on her mind but seemed afraid to say it. Summer walked to the end of the bed and put an arm around her. "What is it?"

She waved her hand across the two of us. "I was wondering if . . ."

I can be pretty thick. Get caught up in my own stuff. But every now and then I see something coming right before it hits me. And this was a freight train that I should have seen coming. Actually, I'm an idiot for not. Casey had one wound left to heal, and maybe I alone had the power to do so. I put one leg on the ground and tried to stand. When I could not, they helped me. Casey on my left. Summer on my right. Once on my feet, I said, "Can we go for a walk?"

Casey nodded.

Summer wrapped me in a blanket, and the three of us shuffled downstairs and out into the cold. We walked through the Planetarium, across Main Street, up a winding lane, and into the chapel. When we pushed through the door, I was winded and looking for a seat. The moon was high and full and shining bright enough to cast shadows on the floor. Casey looked confused as we walked her toward the front.

Toward the altar.

I turned to Casey. "I want to ask you a favor."

She nodded above a trembling lip.

"One of these days, some young man is going to fall head over heels for you, setting in motion two things that will need to happen. He's going to have to ask someone for permission to marry you." I swallowed. Casey's head tilted sideways, spilling the tears out her eyes. "And then someone is going to have to give you away." At this, Casey sobbed and buried her face in her hands.

I waited.

I lifted her chin, knowing there is no deeper pain than that caused by the rejection or abandonment of a father and mother. Why? Because unlike anything else on earth, it pierces to the starting place of us. And in this moment, I was killing it. "Will you let us call you Daughter?"

Casey crumpled, hitting her knees, and fell into Summer, who sat and just held her.

I knelt alongside her, wrapped my arms around her, and whispered in her ear, "Will you let us adopt you? Right here. Will you be ours? Forever?"

The sound coming out of Casey's stomach had been there a long time, and I had a feeling it was the deepest of the layers. The final wall. The last line of defense. And while it was difficult to hear, I relished listening to it leave. A beautiful cry. The sound of pain leaving and joy entering.

Despite medication still detoxing out of my body, I knew in that moment we were taking back ground that had been stolen. The battleground of Casey's heart. And while evil can inflict wounds and lay claim to the territory of the human soul, it is a squatter. A trespasser. It has no legal deed. And it has no defense against love. It can't touch it. Not now. Not ever. No weapon ever fashioned by man can defeat it, but what we pour from our hearts shatters it on the rocks of its own making.

As Casey melted into the floor at my feet, I began to whisper the one word she needed to hear more than any other. And the more I said it, the louder the cry and the farther she slid.

"Daughter . . . Daughter . . . Daughter . . ."

When I finished, Casey lay in a fetal ball clinging to us.

Behind us, the door opened and Bones walked in. Behind him trailed Angel and Ellie. Clad in pajamas and wrapped in blankets. The three sat around us.

When she'd emptied herself, I sat her up. "Casey?"

Her eyes found mine.

"Casey Bishop?"

She nodded.

"From this moment, we take you as our own. Blood of our blood. Flesh of our flesh." A pause. "Forever."

Somewhere over my shoulder, Bones's hand appeared and landed on Casey's shoulder. The other rested on mine. He whispered, "And let it be so."

When I was younger, I used to wonder what my family would look like. Eye color. Face shape. The sound of their laughter. Sitting on the floor of the chapel, staring at my wife and three daughters, I knew.

And I liked it.

# CHAPTER 40

My rehab took time.

I had no strength. No endurance. Sitting up required all I had. In all my life I'd never known fatigue like I was experiencing. Many days I thought I'd never get back to half the man I used to be. But there's only one Summer.

And Summer was having none of that.

Sitting up led to standing. Which led to three steps. Which led across the room. To down the hall. To outside. To tying my own shoes. To showering myself. To cutting my own steak. Pouring my own coffee. She was the perfect mixture of compassion and tough love. And she never quit.

Every night, whether I felt like it or not, Summer put a record on, set the needle in the groove, lifted me out of bed, and we danced.

Gunner seldom left my side. One day I looked down and realized I'd done a rather crummy job of thanking him. He'd found Summer's handkerchief. Then he found me. Without him, there was no us.

I asked Summer to buy the biggest and most expensive rib eye she could find. Seventy-four dollars and thirty-six ounces later, she returned. "What do you want with it?" she asked.

"Nothing."

I cranked the grill and rubbed Gunner's tummy while the smell caused him to drool like a spigot. Somewhere between medium-rare and medium, I pulled the steak off and cut it into bite-size pieces.

"Gunner."

He sat up, tilted his head, and stared at me. I held out the first bite of steak and inched it toward his nose, where he smelled it and stayed, waiting. Licking his muzzle continuously.

After a second, I said, "Okay," and he gently took the steak from my hand, chewing once and swallowing.

A second piece followed.

As did a second bite and swallow.

And a third.

We continued this way for thirty-six ounces.

When finished, I lay on the floor with him, pulled his muzzle to my face, and kissed him. "Thank you, old friend."

Gunner licked my cheek, rolled over on his back, stuck his paws in the air, and snored like a drunk sailor.

A few months in, I woke in the middle of the night and knew there was no way I was going back to sleep. My body was attempting to detox all the meds they'd pumped into me to keep me alive, and it often did this at night. Of course, they'd prescribed a sleeping pill, but I'd had enough medication. Summer lay next to me, her hand across my chest. My tether. Not wanting to wake her, I slipped out, leaned on my cane, walked downstairs, and punched the code to get into my basement. I wasn't sure I could get back up, but at least I made it down. I'm not sure why I walked down there other than I needed some reminder of the me I used to be. The place was immaculate. Everything had been cleaned and put in its place. Even my Sig was hanging on the wall with the others. I wandered through each room with no particular aim, thanking the organization fairy who'd straightened up my mess.

Leaving my piddle room, I noticed Bones's light was on. I shuffled down the hall where I found his door cracked. He was sitting in his chair, sipping wine, staring at a slideshow on the wall. One I'd never seen.

I pushed the door open with my cane and watched Bones watch his show. I stood there a moment, propped between the doorframe and my cane, before he spoke without looking at me. "Couldn't sleep?"

I shook my head.

"We can get you a pill for that."

Another shake. "I've had enough pills."

"Don't blame you."

The slides changed. "What you watching?"

He sipped and stared at the multiple images spinning around the room as if placed there by a disco ball. All of the images were of me.

"When you were laid up in the hospital, I spent the days with you and the nights in here. Put this together to remind me."

"Of?"

This time he looked at me. "How much I love you."

I sat alongside him, catching my breath. He offered me his glass, which I took. One sip. Then another. We sat there nearly an hour watching the narrative of my life. Twenty years in pictures. From the academy, training, to seminary, my first few assignments, my first time in the hospital, then Key West, writing on my rock, tending bar, and looking for Marie.

"I read the letter."

He nodded and pulled the letter out of his breast pocket. It was dirty, smeared with blood, and inscribed with my charcoal writing. He flattened it with his hand, careful not to smudge the lettering. "We've traveled some miles, you and I."

I chuckled. "Some easier than others."

"But all good."

"Yes. All good."

We sat in silence several minutes. When he spoke, his words were accompanied with tears. "For a long time, I hated her for asking me what she did. To keep her a secret." A pause. "But one day the enormity of it hit me, and I knew not only what it cost me but what it cost her. And hatred grew to admiration and returned to love. Marie saw what I could not." He studied the walls and the thousands of slides.

The faces of the found.

He continued, "She's the reason we're here." He waved his hand across the room. "She's the reason they're here."

I sat up. "You need to know something."

Bones turned to me.

"The man who did this, blew up Freetown, kidnapped the girls, almost killed me—he's still out there. And if he did it once, he can do it again. I won't live looking over my shoulder. I won't sit up at night biting my nails to the quick every time Ellie goes out with friends or Summer goes to the store."

Bones lifted the remote to his slide machine and pushed a single button. The slideshow changed. Black-and-white photos of two boys. Same size. One sandy blond. The other dirty brown. Both handsome. Strong. Shoulder to shoulder. Arm in arm. Cutoff jeans. No shirts. Summertime tans. Fishing poles. Skateboards. Motorcycles. Paddling a canoe. Their smiles were magnetic. And similar. Eventually, the pictures changed. Color. Sepia. High school. And the images changed. One boy always stood in the light. The other in shadow. One a buzz cut. The other hair hanging down over his eyes. Dark circles. One smiling. One not.

I did not make the connection.

I spoke to Bones. "I'm going to get healthy. And when I do, I'm going after him."

He raised an eyebrow and spoke as he brought his glass to his lips. "I thought you were a priest."

I took his glass, sipped, sipped again, and handed it back. "I also priest."

Bones nodded without looking at me. Around us, the slideshow continued. High school led to college. Whereas they once stood together, posing for the camera, now they stood apart. Not even in the same frame. Finally, the show shifted and the pics were only of the light-haired boy who had become a dark-hearted man. Even the pictures showed that.

Bones turned toward me. "You should know something."

"Okay."

His countenance changed. Pain rising to the surface. "He's more evil than we are good."

"I know that."

Bones turned to face me. "I'm going with you."

"I know that too."

"But there's one thing you don't know."

"What's that?"

Bones stood, pressed the remote a single time, and the show stopped. The picture on the wall was the last picture in the chronology where the two were together in the same frame. They were in a small boat. Cast net. Fishing poles. Fish littered the bottom of the boat. One sat with his hand on the outboard tiller. The other stood with the net. One part tossed over his shoulder, one part held in his teeth, and one part spread through his hand. Muscles taut. Eyes trained on the water. Just before the cast.

Something about the lighting brought my attention to the boy seated at the motor. His features. I'd seen him before. Walking through fire in Montana. Looking at me. And in that moment, Bones spoke. "He's my brother."

"I thought he was dead."

Bones shook his head. A tear trickling down. His gaze focused on a memory. And when he spoke I couldn't tell if he was feeling anger or sorrow. "Not hardly."

# THE
# MURPHY SHEPHERD
# SERIES
# CONTINUES . . .

Book Three
coming
June 2022!

# DISCUSSION QUESTIONS

1. Chapter 6 says laughter is the universal sound of freedom. Why? What does it mean to laugh? To not be capable of laughing?

2. In chapter 10 Murph says, "it's the father who tells [girls] who they are. Until he does, they're just floating in the earth . . . Buried in some trash mound. Waiting to be discovered by somebody with a shovel who won't crack it or crush it." What do you think of this statement? Do you agree or disagree? Explain.

3. The visual and performing arts play a role in the story: Bones's photography, Summer's dancing, Murphy's and Casey's writing. Why do the arts help us process life and pain? How? Do you partake in anything like that to process your life and pain?

4. What did you think of Murph's backstory and introductions to Marie and Bones, via the stories he told to Ellie?

5. What do you think Bones intends by using *priest* as a verb? What does *priest* as a verb mean to you or look like to you?

6. What does "Because the needs of the one outweigh those of the many" mean to you? Do you agree?

7. In chapter 20 we read, "There's a thing that happens when we start to believe the lies about ourselves, and when we think other people believe them too. Those lies become our prison." Are there any lies you believe about yourself that have you in prison? What truth can you speak to yourself to drown out the lies?

8. What did you think of Marie's letter to Murph? Do you agree with her decision and the reason behind it? Are Bones's actions forgivable to you with this new information? Why?

9. Which character's story impacted you the most? Why?

10. What did you make of Murph's near-death experience at the end of chapter 38, where he "looked down on two towns nestled in a snow-swept canvas" and was told to pick one? What do you think the one town had that the other did not?

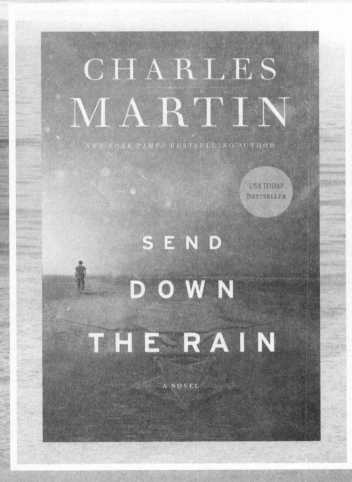

An Excerpt from *Send Down the Rain* by Charles Martin

# PROLOGUE

---

Blessed is the man whose *strength is in You,*
*whose heart is set on pilgrimage.*

—PSALM 84:5

## NOVEMBER 1964

The breeze tugged at my hair and cooled my skin. The waves rolled up and rinsed my heels and calves. Seashells crunched beneath my bathing suit. The air tasted salty. Shirtless and tanned, I lay on my back, propped on my elbows, a pencil in one hand, a small piece of paper in the other. The paper was thick. Almost card stock. I'd torn it out of the back of a book. An amber sun was setting between my big toe and my second toe, turning from flame orange to blood red and slowly sliding down behind the ball of my foot and the edge of the Gulf of Mexico. I busied the pencil to capture the image, my hands giving my mind the space it needed.

I heard someone coming, and then Bobby sat down beside me. Cross-legged. He wiped his forearm across his nose, smearing snot across a tear-stained face. In his arms he cradled a jug of milk and a package of Oreos. Our favorite comfort food. He set them gingerly between us.

I was nine. Bobby was two years older.

We could hear Momma crying in the house behind us. The sun disappeared, and the breeze turned cooler.

Bobby's lip was trembling. "Daddy . . . He . . . he left."

"Where'd he go?"

Bobby dug his hand into the package, shoved a cookie into his mouth, and shook his head.

The sound of a plate shattering echoed out of the kitchen.

"When's he coming back?"

Another cookie. Another crash from the kitchen. Another shake of the head.

"What's Momma doing?"

He squinted one eye and stared over his shoulder. "Sounds like the dishes."

When they got married, Daddy gave Momma a set of china. MADE IN BAVARIA was stamped on the back of each piece. She displayed them in the cabinet. Locked behind the glass. We weren't allowed to touch them. Ever. Evidently she was smashing them piece by piece against the kitchen sink.

"Did Daddy say anything?"

Bobby dug his hand back into the package and began skimming Oreos out across the waves. They flew through the air like tiny Frisbees. A final shake of the head. He unscrewed the milk jug top and held it to his mouth. Two more plates hit the sink.

Bobby was trembling. His voice cracked. "He packed a bunch of stuff. Most everything."

Waves rolled up and over our feet. "What about that . . . other woman?"

He passed me the carton. His words were hard in coming and separated by pain. "Brother, I don't . . ."

I took a drink, and the milk dripped off my chin. He flicked another Frisbee. I sank my hand in the package, stuck a cookie in my mouth, and then threw several like Bobby. The little chocolate discs intersected each other like hummingbirds.

Behind us Momma wailed. Another plate hit the kitchen sink. Followed by another. Then another. The change in sound suggested she'd made her way through all the plates and moved on to the cups and saucers. The cacophony echoing from the kitchen kept rhythm with the irregular drumbeat of our own shattering fragility. I glanced over my shoulder but could find no safe purchase.

Tears puddled in the corners of Bobby's eyes. His lip was quivering. When Momma screamed and had a tough time catching her breath, the tears broke loose.

I tucked the pencil behind my ear and held my sunset sketch at eye level, where the wind caught it like a kite. Imprisoned between my fingers, the paper flapped. When I unlocked the prison door, the crude drawing butterfly-danced down the beach and landed in the waves. I glanced behind me. "We better go check on her."

Bobby pushed his forearm across his lips and nose, smearing his face and arm. His hair had fallen down over his eyes. Like mine, it was bleached blond from saltwater and sunlight. I stood and offered him my hand. He accepted it and I pulled him up. The sun had nearly disappeared now, and cast long shadows on the house. Where our world lay in pieces around us like the ten billion shells at our feet.

Bobby stared at the road down which Dad had disappeared. A thin trail of whitish-blue exhaust was all that remained of his wake. "He said some . . ." He sucked in, shuddered, and tried to shake off the sob he'd been holding back. "Real hard things."

I put my arm around his shoulder, and his sob broke loose. We stood on the beach, alone. Fatherless. Empty and angry.

I made a fist, crushing a cookie. Grinding it to powder. When the pieces spilled out between my fingers onto the beach, a physical and very real pain pierced my chest.

Fifty-three years later, it would stop.

# CHAPTER 1

---

Witnesses say the phone call occurred around seven p.m. and the exchange was heated. While the man seated at the truck stop diner was calm and his voice low, the woman's voice on the other end was not. Though unseen, she was screaming loudly, and stuff could be heard breaking in the background. Seven of the nine people in the diner, including the waitress, say Jake Gibson made several attempts to reason with her, but she cut him off at every turn. He would listen, nod, adjust his oiled ball cap, and try to get a word in edgewise.

"Allie . . . Baby, I know, but . . . If you'll just let me . . . I'm sorry, but . . . I've been driving for forty-two hours . . . I'm . . ." He rubbed his face and eyes. "Dead on my feet." A minute or two passed while he hunkered over the phone, trying to muffle the sound of her incoherent babbling. "I know it's a big deal and you've put a lot of work into . . ." Another pause. More nodding. Another rub of his eyes. "Invitations . . . decorations . . . lights. Yes, I remember how much you paid for the band. But . . ." At this point, he took off his hat and rubbed his bald head. "I got rerouted at Flagstaff and it just plain took the starch out of me." He closed his eyes. "Baby, I just can't get there. Not tonight. I'll cook you some eggs in the morn—"

It was more of the same. Nothing had changed.

Allie Gibson wasn't listening anyway. She was screaming. At the top of her lungs. With their marriage on the rocks, they'd taken a "break." Six months. He moved out, living in the cab of his truck. Crisscrossing the country. But the time and distance had been good for them. She'd softened. Lost weight. Pilates. Bought new lingerie. To remind him. This was to be both his birthday and welcome home party. Along with a little let's-start-over thrown in.

The diner was small, and Jake grew more embarrassed. He held the phone away from his ear, waiting for her to finish. Allie was his first marriage. Ten years in and counting. He was her second. Her neighbors had tried to warn him. They spoke in hushed tones. "The other guy left for a reason." The inflection of their voice emphasized the word *reason*.

Jake didn't get to tell her good-bye. She spewed one last volley of venom and slammed the phone into the cradle. When the phone fell quiet, he sat awkwardly waiting. Wondering if she would pick back up. She did not. The waitress appeared with a pot of coffee and a hungry eye. He wasn't bad looking. Not really a tall drink of water, but she'd seen worse. Far worse. The kindness in his face was inviting, and judging by the appearance of his boots and hands, he didn't mind hard work. She'd take Allie's place in a heartbeat.

"More coffee, baby?" She said coffee like *caw-fee*. Before he could speak, the obnoxious beeping sounded from the phone's earpiece, telling him Allie had hung up a while ago. Furthering his embarrassment. He whispered to anyone who would listen, "I'm sorry," then stood, reached over the counter, hung up the phone, and quietly thanked the waitress.

Leaving his steak uneaten, he refilled his coffee thermos, left a twenty on the table to pay his seven-dollar bill, and slipped out quietly, tipping his hat to an older couple who'd just walked in. He walked out accompanied by the signature tap of his walking cane on concrete—a shrapnel wound that had never healed.

He gassed up his truck and paid for his diesel at the register, along with four packs of NoDoz, then went into the restroom and splashed cold water on his face. The police, watching the diner video surveillance some forty-eight hours later, would watch in silence as Jake did twenty jumping jacks and just as many push-ups before he climbed up into his cab. In the last two and a half days, he had driven from Arizona to Texas and finally to Mississippi, where he'd picked up a tanker of fuel en route to Miami. He had tried to make it home for his sixtieth birthday party, but his body just gave out. Each eyelid weighed a thousand pounds. With little more than a hundred miles to go, he'd called to tell Allie that he'd already fallen asleep twice and he was sorry he couldn't push through.

She had not taken the news well.

He eyed the motel but her echo was still ringing. He knew his absence would sting her.

So amiable Jake Gibson climbed up and put the hammer down. It would be his last time.

Jake made his way south to Highway 98. Hugged the coastline, eventually passing through Mexico Beach en route to Apalachicola.

At Highway 30E he turned west. Seven miles to the cradle of Allie's arms. He wound up the eighteen-wheeler and shifted through each of the ten gears. Though he'd driven the road hundreds of times, no one really knows why he was going so fast or why he ignored the flashing yellow lights and seven sets of speed ripples across the narrow road. Anyone with his experience knew that a rig going that fast with that much mass and inertia could never make the turn. State highway patrol estimated the tanker was traveling in excess of a hundred and ten when 30E made its hard right heading north. It is here, at the narrowest point of the peninsula, where the road comes closest to the ocean. To separate the two, highway crews had amassed mounds of Volkswagen-sized granite rocks just to the left of the highway. Hundreds of boulders, each weighing several tons, stacked at jagged angles, one on top of another, stood thirty feet wide and some twenty feet high. An impenetrable wall to prevent the Gulf from encroaching on the road and those on the road from venturing into the ocean. "The rocks" was a favorite locale for lovers sipping wine. Hand in hand they'd scale the boulders and perch with the pelicans while the sun dropped off the side of the earth and bled crimson into the Gulf.

The Great Wall of Cape San Blas had survived many a hurricane and hundreds of thousands of tourists walking its beach.

No one really knows when Jake Gibson fell asleep. Only that he did. Just before ten p.m. the Peterbilt T-boned the wall, pile-driving the nose of the rig into the rocks with all the steam and energy of the *Titanic*. When the rocks ripped open the tanker just a few feet behind Jake, the explosion was heard and felt thirty miles away in Apalachicola, and the flash was seen as far away as Tallahassee—a hundred miles distant. Alarms sounded and fire crews and law enforcement personnel were dispatched, but given the heat they were relegated to shutting down the highway from eight football fields away. No one in or out. All they could do was watch it burn.

Allie was sitting on the floor of a bathroom stall hunkered over a fifth of Jack. Tearstained and tear-strained. From three miles away she saw the flash off the white subway tile wall. When she saw the fireball, she knew.

The several-thousand-degree heat was so intense that Allie—along with all the partygoers—were forced to stand outside the half-mile barrier and helplessly inhale the smell of burning rubber. They did this throughout the night. By early morning the fire had spent its fury, allowing the water trucks to move in. By then not much was left. A few steel beams. One wheel had been blown off and rolled a quarter mile into the marsh. The back end of the tank looked like a soda can ripped in two. At the blast site, the only thing that remained was a scorched spot on the highway.

Closed-circuit television cameras positioned on the flashing light poles a mile before the curve recorded Jake at the wheel. Facial recognition software, as well as Allie's own viewing of the recording, proved that faithful Jake Gibson with his characteristic oiled ball cap was driving the truck and shifting gears as it ventured north on 30E.

No part of Jake Gibson was ever found.

Not a belt buckle. Not a heel of his boot. Not his titanium watch. Not his platinum wedding ring. Not his teeth. Not the bronzed head of his walking cane. Like much of the truck, Jake had been vaporized. The horrific nature of his death led to a lot of speculating. Theories abounded. The most commonly believed was that Jake fell asleep long before the turn, slumping forward, thereby pressing his bad leg and portly weight forward. This is their only justification for the unjustifiable speed. Second is the suggestion that four days of caffeine overdosing exploded Jake's heart and he was dead long before the turn—also causing him to slump forward. The least whispered but still quite possible was the notion that Jake had an aneurysm, thereby producing the same result. No one really knows. All they knew with certainty was that he went out with a bang so violent that it registered on military satellites, bringing in the Department of Defense and Homeland Security, who both raised eyebrows at the enormity of the blast area. "Shame."

With the site surrounded in yellow tape and flashing lights, it was still too hot to approach. Firemen said it'd take a week to cool off the core and allow anyone near the blast site. Onlookers shook their heads, thought of Allie, and muttered in their best backstabbing whisper, "That woman is cursed. Everything she touches dies."

Rescue and coast guard crews searched the ocean and the shoreline throughout the night. They thought maybe if Jake had been thrown through the windshield at that speed, his body would have shot out across the rocks and into the ocean on the other side, where there's a known rip tide. If so, he'd have been sucked out to sea.

Like everything else, the search turned up nothing. And like everything else, each failed search reinforced the excruciating notion that Jake died a horrible, painful death.

The weight of this on Allie was crushing. Jake, the affable husband who simply worked hard enough to put food on the table and laughter in his wife's heart, was not coming back. Ever. The last year or two or even three had not been easy. He had worked more than he'd been at home, staying gone weeks at a time, months even. Allie knew what people thought . . . that she was just tough to live with.

She was left to plan the funeral and decide what to put in the box. But every time she tried to tell his memory that she was sorry, she was met with the haunting and deafening echo that the final three words she spoke to Jake were not "I love you." Instead, her last words to him had been spoken in a spit-filled tirade of anger.

And for those words, there was no remedy.

The story continues in *Send Down the Rain* by Charles Martin.

*USA TODAY* bestseller *Long Way Gone* tells the heartwarming story of a prodigal son and his long journey toward redemption.

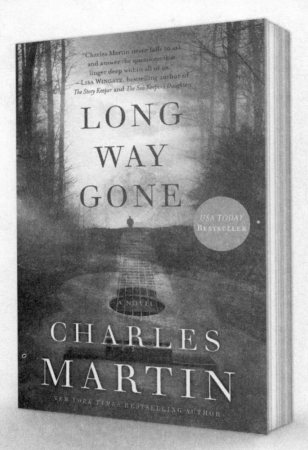

"Charles Martin never fails to ask and answer the questions that linger deep within all of us. In this beautifully told story of a prodigal coming home, readers will find the broken and mended pieces of their own hearts."

—LISA WINGATE, national bestselling author of *Before We Were Yours*

AVAILABLE IN PRINT, E-BOOK, AND AUDIO!

THOMAS NELSON
*Since 1798*

# ALSO FROM CHARLES MARTIN

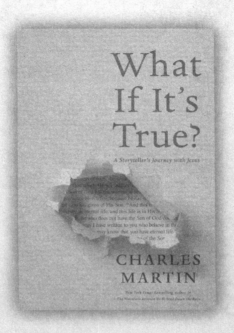

Years ago, novelist Charles Martin opened his Bible and began to wrestle with a few profound questions: What if every single word of this story is absolutely true and I can trust it? What if the King of the universe is speaking directly to me through the words of His book? And if I believe His Word is true, how should I respond?

Now you can read the results of that exploration. Using the same depth, sensitivity, and emotion that has made his novels beloved to millions, Martin helps us engage the fundamental principles of the Christian faith in new and inspiring ways.

# ABOUT THE AUTHOR

© Amy S. Martin

Charles Martin is the *New York Times* bestselling author of fifteen novels. He and his wife, Christy, live in Jacksonville, Florida. Learn more at charlesmartinbooks.com.

Instagram: @storiedcareer

Twitter: @storiedcareer

Facebook: @Author.Charles.Martin